PRAISE FOR *UNSPOKEN*

'Absorbing . . . fuses the everyday with the historical . . . Stembridge has been able to capture the powerful shifts in the cultural and political atmosphere of a historic decade.'

SUNDAY TIMES

'A masterly account of Ireland in the 1960s . . . Stembridge juggles characters and themes seemingly effortlessly, his stories are bedrocked by great humanity, and this huge book is, sadly, over almost before you know it. Wonderful.'

DAILY MAIL

'Unforgettable . . . Reading *Unspoken* is like being mesmerised by a story-telling Janus – all human warmth and compassion from one mouth, cold accuracy and knowingness from the other. A wonderful achievement.'

EUGENE MCCABE

'I really loved this . . . *Unspoken* struck me as what great literature (or one kind of it) should be, a marriage of the personal with the political and social . . . One of my books of the year – if not *the* book of the year.'

JOHN HARDING

ALSO BY GERARD STEMBRIDGE

Counting Down

According to Luke

UNSPOKEN

First published in the United Kingdom and Ireland in 2011 by
Old Street Publishing Ltd

This paperback edition published 2012 by Old Street Publishing
Trebinshun House, Brecon, LD3 7PX
www.oldstreetpublishing.co.uk

ISBN 978-1-906964-98-6

10 9 8 7 6 5 4 3 2 1

A CIP catalogue record for this title is available from the British Library.

Typeset by Old Street Publishing Ltd.

Printed and bound in Great Britain.

For my brother, David

UNSPOKEN

GERARD
STEMBRIDGE

OLD STREET PUBLISHING

'Only connect! That was the whole of her sermon. Only connect the prose and the passion and both will be exalted, and human love will be seen at its height.'

E.M. FORSTER

1959

One: June 17th–18th

Ann Strong did not vote in the presidential election because, on that June evening, her waters broke. She was in the downstairs flat with Martin, her youngest, when it happened. The other children were out playing. Ann was standing over the gas cooker waiting for the milk to boil. She could hardly bear to look at it. Martin was sitting at the table tearing at a slice of bread and dropping the pieces into his special mug.

'Mam, can I put the sugar in?'

'No, you'll put in too much. I'll do that in a minute. Have patience.'

Martin had pestered her to make Goody for him. He loved it when she plopped, on top of the mixture of hot milk, bread and sugar, a big lump of butter that melted and spread into a golden lake. He was getting to be an awful size for five, but, on the other hand, wasn't that better than being skin-and-bone and looking like he'd never had a decent dinner put into him? Ann would later be able to recall the exact time it all started to happen because she had just looked at the clock wondering when Fonsie would get home from work. In the long summer evenings he sold less and had to travel further out of town; it was ridiculous. Sometimes he'd be out until nearly ten but the polling stations were due to close at nine so, tonight at least, he'd surely be home in good time to eat his tea first and clean himself. Ann was not going voting with him if he was black with coal, that was sure and certain.

It was just coming up to quarter to seven. She felt a heave, a shift, deep inside her. The pressure was sudden and made her step back. This was early by a few days at least, but, after four children, Ann knew for certain what was coming next. She grabbed the sweeping brush straight away and banged the ceiling three times.

Poor little Martin got a fright at this and didn't know if he should cry. Ann tried to move quickly to the bedroom so, at the very least, she could close the door against him in case it happened before Mary Storan came down from upstairs, but then she had to stop and stand completely still right in the middle of the front room. One more step and something would burst.

Despite the panic her anxious brain began sorting out arrangements. Ritchie and Gussie would have to wait here to tell their father that she had to go out. What would she tell them to tell Fonsie? Could she trust them to get his tea ready for him? He'd have to eat before he went to vote. She was sure that Mary Storan – was that her coming downstairs now? – wouldn't mind looking after Marian and Martin and maybe she might... At that very second Ann realised she hadn't turned off the gas on the stove. The milk would boil over. Martin was standing in the door between the kitchen and the front room, his face twisting into a big puss. Ann didn't dare to try and move a step, let alone go past him back into the kitchen. Through the wall behind her she definitely now heard Mary Storan's footsteps thumping down from the upstairs flat. The pressure was really painful now; it was the luck of God Mary could let herself in. It was obvious that Martin was going to let out a big wail any second if his mam didn't say something to comfort him. Ann heard the click of the key in the door and thought, Oh thanks be to Jesus!

Mary Storan stuck her head into the front room. 'It's started?'

Ann nodded and waved towards the kitchen. 'The milk... quick.'

'What, you want a cup of milk?'

As long as Ann had known her, which was since they'd met in babies class more than thirty years ago, whenever Mary Storan, or Mary Halpin as was, was requested or instructed to do anything, she automatically asked a question back. Ann's oldest pal was totally incapable of just doing what she was told. It was not some rebellious spirit in her, just a peculiar habit she could not seem to break, even though she'd suffered regular punishments as a child for stubbornness and cheek. Only a year ago, out walking with her husband Mikey, Mary had stepped out onto the road and even though she heard him behind her shouting 'Get back, Mary!' instead of doing the simple thing and stepping back, she'd just kept walking cool as you like and when Mikey kept roaring at her, 'For Jesus' sake!' she turned her head then all right and saw him waving his arms like mad. But still she had to ask a question. 'What's the big panic about?'

Of course the words were hardly out of her mouth when she felt the blow on her shoulder and went flat out on the ground. Mary broke her wrist that day but the accident changed none of her old habits. Right now, Ann, who usually had a good laugh at her pal's little ways, just wanted to scream at her. This was no time for asking questions. Already she could hear hissing and smell burning from the kitchen. Mary, still talking, didn't seem to notice: 'Maybe a drop of water would be better for you than milk. Milk can very heavy on… you know –'

Suddenly, Martin opened his mouth and wailed as if they were all going to be killed. Ann could tell from the way he was facing that he could see the milk pumping over the top of the saucepan and streaming down onto the gas flame. At least his roaring made Mary Storan stop talking and go to calm him. Which meant that, finally, she smelled and saw the foaming, burning milk.

'Martin, love, your mam doesn't want to be listening to – ah!'

Now at last, she jumped to switch off the gas, grab the saucepan and throw it into the sink.

'Jesus, Ann! You're after leaving the gas on. Well, isn't it lucky I came down straight away, God only knows what might have happened. Now! Listen, there's no point in me cleaning that up. Don't worry, I'll sort it out later. God help us, are you all right?'

When Mary Storan came back into the front room, she looked kindly at Ann, because she could tell, from the rigid way she was holding herself, how muddled and panicky she must be feeling, and Mary knew well that was all on account of the miscarriage. Between sitting next to her in school and palling around during their working days in Roches Stores and living above her in Rowan Place since 1950 when her Shamie and Ann's Ritchie and Gussie were only babies, Mary Storan knew Ann Strong, Ann Casey as was, better than anyone. She remembered well how Ann just took it in her stride when she had Marian and Martin, even though Marian, God bless her, was huge, over ten pounds. But once Ann lost her next, six months in, poor thing, that changed her completely. Mary remembered it so well because she was nearly five months gone herself at that time. Indeed she often wondered if maybe it made it worse in a way that she had no bother at all with her Martha. From then on, Ann got it into her head that she'd never have another healthy baby. She had whispered as much to Mary one day when they were walking up to the convent to collect Marian and her Catríona, who were both in senior infants at the time. Mary tried to make light of it.

'Go 'way outta that, Ann, sure there's barely a year between us, and I'm certainly not finished yet, not if Mikey Storan has anything to do with it.'

Ann didn't even laugh along with her. 'I just don't think it's meant to be.'

So, when Ann told her late last year that she was expecting again, Mary could see how nervous and cagey she was. Then, six months in, Ann seemed to relax a tiny bit, but it didn't take much to bring back all the fear. Now, here she was, still as a statue, whispering to Mary like there was hardly any breath in her body.

'Take Martin upstairs out of the way.'

'Are you that close?'

Ann made a terrible face like something was already happening. 'Yes! Straight away Mary. Oh Jesus, Mary and Joseph!'

Something in her voice, or something anyway, made Mary yank Martin's hand and pull him into the little hall. Sure enough, as she closed the door, there was poor Ann, bent over, pulling at her nylons, liquid running down her legs. Mary slammed the door just in time and let out a smoke-cracked roar up the stairs.

'Shamie! Shamie! Martin, you go on upstairs there now, my Shamie has something nice for you. I'll be up in a minute.'

Martin blubbed and wouldn't budge. No sign of Shamie. Mary had left him up there doing his sums only two minutes ago. Oh if he was after sneaking out…

'Shamie! Look after Martin Strong for a few minutes, will you. Shamie, do you hear me? Go on, Martin. Ah, stop crying love, sure Shamie has something nice for you… Shamie!'

Finally, a lazy voice drifted down. 'What?'

'Come down here and take this child up, will you?'

'I'm doing my ecker.'

'I'm warning you, Shamie Storan! If I have to come up t'ya.'

Her eldest appeared on the landing, which was lucky for him because one more second and Mary would have been up the stairs to give him a clatter. She prodded Martin up.

'And give him some bread and jam!'

Mary opened the door of the downstairs flat just enough for her to squeeze in. Poor Ann was on her knees in the wet, her knickers down, her hand over her mouth, trying not to make a noise.

'What'll I do? I don't know when Fonsie will be home to bring me to St Gerard's. The baby's going to die, I know it.'

Her breathing was hysterical now. The only way to calm her down was for Mary to act pure casual.

'It'll be grand. I'll take you now straight away. I'll get your Ritchie to run down and see is Jimmy Mac at home.'

She went to the hot press for towels.

'A taxi. I can't afford a taxi.'

'Ann, Jimmy won't charge much.'

When Mary felt the towels and realised that nearly everything in the hot press was wet or damp, she was wise enough to say nothing. There must be a leak in the tank. That was the last thing Ann needed to know right now.

'No, no, sure Fonsie will bring me in the lorry.'

'Fonsie mightn't come home for hours yet.'

Mary chose what felt like the driest towel. Hopefully, in her distress Ann wouldn't notice. She'd go off the deep end entirely if she knew that all her lovely washing was destroyed.

'No, he said definitely he was going to vote tonight, so he'll have to –'

'Ah Jesus! Ann, you're getting the taxi and that's that. Now here, dry yourself and –'

'I'd better clean the floor.'

'Never mind the floor! Just get changed quick as you can.'

Mary went to the front door wishing she'd brought her fags down with her. She was dying for a smoke. On the green outside, Ann's two eldest, Ritchie and Gussie, were playing football with a load of other boys. Mary knew which of the brothers she could trust to do exactly what he was told.

'Ritchie Strong!'

No child, not even boys lost in the intensity of a football match, could ignore Mary Storan's hoarse man's roar. It carried its authority a very long way. Ritchie, his hand up, calling for a pass, turned immediately and saw Mrs Storan waving at him. 'Come here, I wancha!' What had he done? It sounded like trouble. If Shamie Storan said he'd done something, he was a liar. He ran over immediately. His brother Gussie wondered what was going on, but only for a second because the ball came his way. He trapped it, dribbled past Noel Geary, who was useless, and shot way wide of the two big old trees that were the goalposts. When he looked again there was no sign of either Mrs Storan or his elder brother.

Ritchie Strong was relieved to find out that he wasn't in trouble, but why did Mrs Storan pull him into the hall, close the front door and talk to him in a whisper? He was to run to Mr Mac's as fast as he could and say that Mrs Storan sent him but the taxi was for his mam. Ritchie didn't know what was going on. Mr and Mrs Storan were always out all hours and were often driven home by Mr Mac, but he couldn't ever remember his mother taking a taxi, even once, in his whole life, so there must be something very serious going on. And where was his mam? Why was the door to their flat shut?

'Tell Mr Mac that I said, listen to me now, Ritchie –'

Mrs Storan seemed to think for a second. Then she spoke very carefully.

'Tell him your mam is started already. All right? Now, hurry.'

Started what? Ritchie was dying to ask but he could tell that it was more important to get Mr Mac straight away. He'd never called to his house before, although he'd often seen him coming and going in his black Zephyr. Mr Mac had put concrete down where the front garden used to be so he could park it off the road. Ritchie ran fast and could see the Zephyr from far off, so that meant Mr Mac was home. He knocked and waited, feeling a bit afraid. Was there something the matter with his mam? What if Mr Mac refused to go? If he was having his tea? Mrs Mac opened the door.

'Mrs Storan says can Mr Mac come straight away.'

'Jimmy! It's the boy of the Strong's. Mary Storan is looking for you. Straight away she says.'

'It's for my mam.'

Mr Mac appeared. He loomed over Ritchie, huge everywhere with a baldy head. He sounded a bit annoyed.

'What's Mary in such a hurry for at this hour?'

'He says it's for his mother.'

Ritchie remembered what Mrs Storan had told him to say.

'Mrs Storan said my mam is started already.'

The words were like magic. Ritchie saw the look on their faces change completely. Mr Mac stopped being annoyed and Mrs Mac suddenly smiled kindly and spoke to Mr Mac in a low, careful voice.

'That's right, sure I was talking to her in Curtin's a few days ago and she was telling me that… you know… soon, like.'

Mr Mac grabbed a jacket and walked to the Zephyr. Ritchie was delighted. Mrs Storan would be pleased with him for doing the job right. As Mr Mac reversed out fast, he shouted, 'Close them gates after me.'

Though he didn't want to get his hopes up, Ritchie noticed as he closed the gate that Mr Mac hadn't driven off. Then he heard him say, 'Hurry up, your mam is waiting. Do you want a lift or not?'

Yes! A dream come true. He was going to get a ride in a taxi. Ritchie pulled open the passenger door and dived in. The front seat was like a huge couch. Ritchie knew the ride was only going to last a couple of minutes, so he had to make the most of it. He tried to watch Mr Mac changing gears at the same time as looking out the side window at the houses flying by. He leaned back to feel how soft the big seat was compared to his dad's lorry, and noticed how low down and close to the road he was, which made it seem like they were going even faster.

'So you're Fonsie Strong's youngfellah?'

Ritchie nodded.

'What age are you?'

'Eleven.'

'What are you going to be when you grow up?'

'I dunno.'

'Don't be a taxi driver anyway. Your life isn't your own.'

Ritchie thought that was a mad thing to say. He wished Mr Mac would stop talking so he could concentrate on the journey and remember every second of it. Sure enough, like the donkey rides in Ballybunion, it hardly started and it was over.

'Tell your mam I'm here.'

As Ritchie jumped out he could see that Gussie and the others had stopped playing football and were staring over at him, eyes hanging out of their heads. Ha-ha! Gussie, nosey as usual, came galloping over. Mrs Storan was suddenly at his shoulder, puffing like mad on a fag.

'You're great to come so fast, Jimmy. Listen, she's very near, she's going to St Gerard's. You'll do it for two bob, won't you? I told her you wouldn't charge more than two bob.'

'She's going to St Gerard's and she's arguing about the price of the cab?'

'Ah, Brendan, she's been saving every penny for that place ever since she found out.'

Mrs Storan leaned in and dropped her voice. Ritchie couldn't hear more than a whispering sound. Mr Mac nodded.

'Ah, God help us. Go on so, tell her we'll have her there in no time.'

Mary pulled Ritchie and Gussie closer.

'Now, I'm going with your mam –'

'Is she sick?'

Mary looked at Ritchie, worried, and Gussie, curious. Eleven and ten.

'Sick? Not at all, she's grand, she just has to – to go to the church. She's going to the Redemptorists for an all-night vigil. I'm going as well, but I'll be back in about half an hour. Now you wait upstairs with our Shamie. Martin is with him. Oh, Jesus Mary and Joseph, where's Marian?'

'She's over playing dolls in Pauline Cosgrave's flat.'

'Gussie, be a good boy and go and get her. Bring her upstairs when you come back.'

The last thing Gussie Strong wanted to do was leave all this excitement to go looking for his little sister, but Mrs Storan had that look about her that told him it was no time for arguing. Still, as he trotted across the green to the Cosgraves' flat, he kept looking back in case he missed something.

Now Mary could hear moans from inside the downstairs flat so she raised her voice more as she spoke to Ritchie, hoping to drown them out.

'Tell Shamie I said you can have bread and jam. If Fonsie – your dad – comes back before I do, tell him… tell him… your Mam was ready and she had to go straight away. What'll you say, Ritchie?'

'Mam was ready and she had to go straight away. To the vigil?'

'Don't mind too much about the vigil. Just say your mam was

ready and she had to go straight away. Will you do that?'

'Yeah. Is Dad late again? Is that why you have to get a taxi?'

Mary had to stop herself from laughing. Poor old Fonsie getting the blame as usual.

'No, sure you know your dad is never home this early. He works too hard. Anyway, when he gets home, tell him I'll be back soon. Go on up now.'

Ritchie was sure he could hear his mother through the door making queer noises.

'Can't I go in to my mam?'

'Will you go up! Do what you're told!'

Even though he was worried and a bit afraid, Ritchie Strong was an obedient boy. Mary watched him all the way to the top of the stairs before opening the door to Ann, who had managed to change her clothes and was leaning against the wall, holding a bag. She moaned and caught her breath.

'How often now?'

'It's not too bad. Every few minutes.'

'Here, let me carry that for you. Jimmy is waiting.'

'The place is in an awful state, Mary.'

'Will you go on outta that. I'll clean that up in a few minutes when I get back.'

'I've washed all their clothes. And towels and sheets. You saw them there, airing in the hot press. That should do them for the week, I don't want you putting yourself to any more trouble.'

'Don't worry about any of that.'

'How much is he charging?'

'Jesus, Ann, will you come on!'

'I've left a list of the groceries for Fonsie. He'll do all the shopping, you don't need to worry about that. And he'll make their breakfast before he –'

Mary Storan pushed Ann into the back of the taxi. She sat in next to her and slammed the door. Ann sagged and moaned quietly. She was going to lose it. She knew in her heart she was going to lose her baby. Oh, St Gerard how can you let me lose it at this stage? Where would she be without Mary, who was poking Jimmy Mac on the shoulder?

'Jesus, come on, move, will you?'

*

Peg Ryan's farm was another five miles beyond Mulvey's, just outside Bruff. Fonsie Strong wasn't sure if he should chance going out there so late in the day. It would take him that much longer to get home afterwards and there would be war if he got back too late to vote, but poor old Peg was a good customer and Fonsie didn't want to leave her stuck for another fortnight, which was when he'd be out this way again. He could just manage it. A quarter past seven. If he got to Peg's by half past, say, unload whatever she wanted in a couple of minutes, do his best to stop her telling him every bit of news since his previous visit and get away as quick as he could, he'd surely be home by eight. Or not long after, at any rate. That way he could have a wash, eat his tea, and get to the polling station before it closed. If he didn't, his mother wouldn't ever let him hear the end of it. 'No wonder that fellah keeps getting elected if people like you won't even bother to get out and vote.' Kathleen Strong could rarely even bring herself to say de Valera's name. Sometimes she would twist her mouth and spit out the word 'Dev' in a strangled voice, as if to mock the very idea that such a blackguard should have such a friendly nickname. 'The day you were born that long string of misery was starting the civil war that ruined this country.' Fonsie had heard this repeated all through his growing up. It made him feel a bit like the state of the country was his fault.

Normally, his mother wouldn't have given the presidential election the time of day. What does the President do, only go round in his Rolls-Royce waving at people? she'd say. But this was different because Dev was finally resigning as Taoiseach and putting himself up for President so this was the first time she ever had a chance to vote against him personally instead of against his Party. She was looking forward to seeing the name de Valera on the ballot paper and then putting her mark down for the other fellah, General Mac Eoin, although, as far as she was concerned, if the other candidate had been his father's old horse, Nell, that would have been just as good. Better even. Seventy-eight or not, his mother would have been up first thing this morning, marching herself and his father the mile and a half to the polling station. Fonsie had promised her that he'd definitely be home from work well in time for Ann and himself to cast their vote against 'that fellah'. Luckily, Ann was no lover of Dev either, because there would have been no chance of her voting against him just to please his mother. Anything but.

Fonsie was a tiny bit worried by the time he turned up the long dirt road to Peg Ryan's. Twenty to eight already. He began to wonder how, without being rude, he might put a stop to Peg's gallop once she kicked off. Usually her order was two hundredweight of Polish and he could unload that quick enough if he didn't have to listen to her at the same time. The old woman appeared from the side door, big in her apron and rubber boots, rushing at the lorry like she was preventing a terrible accident, holding up huge leathery hands and crying out with a voice well used to summoning the dogs from the far end of the field.

'Well now, Mr Strong, aren't you very good to call. I hope you didn't put yourself out to come back my way.'

Fonsie reassured her. 'No, Mrs Ryan, sure I'm out this way every second Wednesday.'

'You are indeed, sure, you are, to be sure, don't I know it. Well, Sacred Heart, is it two weeks already and you last here? I suppose it must be 'cause wasn't I saying to you then that it was coming for eight months since poor Seamus and here we are now a week since the eight months…'

Fonsie had the feeling she'd never get over her husband's death. Her whole life had been spent looking after his every comfort.

'… because wait 'til I tell you now. With the weather as balmy as it has been this past while, to be honest with you, I don't be lighting the fire that much. And of course since poor Seamus I do take myself off to bed that little bit earlier with the paper, instead of sitting up on my own.'

Her hand rested on the driver's door as she looked up at him, so Fonsie felt a bit trapped in the cab. Her broad veiny face seemed older and sadder every time he called. Fonsie could think of no way to stop the flow.

'I was down by the coalshed earlier this morning and didn't I think of you, because I was saying to myself, there now, I've hardly used up much of the last load. I wasn't sure was it today you were coming out or not, do you see, but thinking maybe it might be and then of course, when I turned on the wireless a few minutes ago and Joe Linnane had started already I thought, that's grand, he'll never come at this hour so I haven't put the man out, meaning you. And then, next thing what do I hear, only a vehicle coming up the road and of course I'd know the sound of your lorry anywhere.'

It was not the first time today Fonsie had heard a similar story. He still had more than half a load on board after being out for eleven hours. It was hard to sell coal in fine weather.

'I'm awful sorry to put you out, Mr Strong, and you so good to come, but honest to God, if you were to have a look in the shed now you'd see the load of coal still in there and sure, at the rate I'm going, what I have now will nearly do me for the rest of the summer.'

Fonsie tried not to think of the time wasted nor the loss of the few shillings. Poor old Peg, what was she to do? She couldn't be lighting fires just to please him. It was probably loneliness was sending her to bed early.

'Will you come in for a cup of tea at least now you're here? Maybe I could take a bag of slack. Sure, there'd be no harm in getting one in anyway, just to be sure, and 'twould last me. If you have one to spare.'

Fonsie thought of the time. If the tea was made already he could down it fast enough. Make the poor woman feel better about not buying any coal.

'Only if it's made already. Don't go to any trouble.'

'Ah sure, what trouble, after all the trouble you took to come out here.'

The tea had not been made, but by the time it was, it was fine and strong, and the griddle cake was still moist, the tang of sour milk putting an agreeable taste in Fonsie's mouth. Poor Peg talked and talked like she might never get to say another word to a living soul after he left her. By the time he got back into the lorry he was afraid even to look at his watch knowing that, at this stage, the chances of getting home in time for even a quick wash before running out to vote were small. Worse again, what if Ann had the tea on the table waiting for him? The trouble she'd gone to in her condition, the time wasted. To try and make up Fonsie would have to eat it cold when he got back from the polling station, no matter what it was. Peg was still talking up at him as he started the engine.

'Definitely now, in a month or so I'll need an order. Don't worry yourself one little bit until then, but definitely now in a month. Six weeks, say.'

The road from Bruff back into town was twisting and full of potholes, but at least there was hardly any traffic and Fonsie could chance making the lorry rattle along a bit faster. By the time he drove into town past the cemetery and the mental hospital, he finally got up enough nerve to check his watch. Just after half eight. Fonsie Strong never usually thought, let alone spoke, bad words. Even now, tense and agitated, the most violent expression that came into his head was, 'Oh heck.' He knew already that Ann would trail after him into the bathroom, telling him he was always the same, always late, and it was she had to put up with it, her tone as pungent as the industrial smell from the big tin of Swarfega on the bathroom mantelpiece, as aggressive as the way every evening Fonsie had to attack his coaldust-ingrained hands with the powerful green jelly.

As often before, in situations like this, when time was against him and the damage was already done, Fonsie now slowed down.

Things would be as they would be. It had been a long, back-breaking day, so warm and dry it made him think kindly of the chill rain that frequently washed his face in winter as he humped saturated sacks from lorry to coalshed. At least rain sold more coal. Today he had driven about fifty miles around the east of the county and was still coming home with more than half a lorry-load, which meant less than two pounds for himself for his day's work. Not enough. Definitely not enough with another baby on the way. But what could he do but try?

Fonsie noticed when he got into the hall that the voices of his children seemed to be coming from Mary Storan's flat upstairs. Was Ann up there? If so, he couldn't hear her, nor, much more surprisingly, Mary Storan. He opened his own door quietly. Not a sound from inside. He looked into the front room. Though it was not quite dark, Ann would usually have the lights on by now. There was no one in the front room or anywhere else in the flat by the sound of it. The voice he heard now, shouting over the general noise, was definitely Gussie's. And another boy's voice. Still no sound of adults. Fonsie decided he'd better go up and find out what was going on but first he would have a quick gander in the kitchen just in case Ann had left a note on the table. Walking across the room he called out, more for something to say than any expectation of an answer, but skidded and fell before he finished a sentence, 'Ann, are you –?' It was only when his hands touched the lino that he realised how wet the floor was. Sliding a little, he stood up carefully. What the heck was going on? The shouting upstairs was getting louder. There was a thump on the ceiling as bodies hit the floor above. Still no adult voices. He'd better get up there now. When Fonsie arrived at the top of the stairs and pushed open the door of Mary Storan's kitchen, seven roaring children got the shock of their lives. The sight of this black-faced man coming home from work late in the evenings was not unusual. All the local children were well used to Mr Strong the coalman and his jalopy, but this time, lost in their screaming match, the Storans and the Strongs had heard nothing until, suddenly, the kitchen door swung open and a blackened face loomed. It was poor little Catríona Storan who saw it first and let out a huge scream which made everyone jump. It took even Fonsie's own children a couple of seconds to realise who it was.

Shamie Storan was the first to cop on that there was going to be trouble, and he wanted to make sure that Mr Strong knew it was all Gussie Strong's fault. It wasn't his flat in the first place and all Shamie had done was try to stop him cutting up their loaf of bread. It was annoying enough to be told he had to give Martin Strong bread and jam, but then Ritchie Strong came in, who he hated anyway, and after him, Gussie Strong, acting like he owned the place, along with his sister Marian, who started asking his baby sister Catríona why this and why that when she should have been asking Shamie who had been put in charge. That's what he told Gussie Strong when he picked up the loaf of bread and started walking around with it asking where the bread knife was. Shamie told him put it down, this isn't your flat. It's not your flat either, it's the corporation's, said Gussie, who always thought he was so smart. Shamie said to Ritchie, tell your thick brother to put that bread back, it's not his, and Marian stuck her nose in where it wasn't wanted and said your mam said we could have tea and bread and jam and Shamie said how do you know what my mam said when you didn't even see her. That was when Gussie found the knife in the drawer and started giving out orders, telling Shamie, you make the tea and I'll make the bread and jam, so Shamie took a jump at him. Next thing the black face appeared out of nowhere. Shamie opened his mouth to explain this but Mr Strong shut them all up.

'That's enough now, that's enough of that now. Ritchie, Gussie, that's enough now! What's going on? Where's Mam? What are you doing up here?' Ritchie saw his father's eyes turn on him. Now he'd probably get the blame, when it was Gussie's fault. Like when Gussie painted Reidy's dog and Ritchie was told he should have stopped him.

'She's gone on a vigil. Mrs Storan took her in the taxi.'

A vigil? It took Fonsie a few seconds then, suddenly, he understood everything. Even the wet floor began to make sense. Now he felt a little panic. Poor Ann. Was she all right? He'd better go to St Gerard's straight away. What about the children? Leave them here? More fighting? He couldn't bring his gang back down to their flat until it was cleaned up. What about Mikey Storan?

'Is your dad working tonight?'

Shamie nodded. Once the last screening at the Carlton was over, Mikey still had to unspool the reels and get everything ready for the next day. He wouldn't be back until half eleven at least. Was Mary going to stay with Ann? She could be there all night. Seven children stared up at him, expecting the worst. Fonsie had to take charge.

'Right… ah… sit at the table.'

'There's only four chairs.'

'Shut up, Gussie! Right so. Marian, share with Gussie. Catriona, share with Martin. Shamie, put Martha on your lap there. Ritchie, sit there. Now, Gussie, what are you doing with that knife?'

'Mrs Storan said we could have bread and jam. Ritchie said it.'

Gussie was no fool. He knew that Ritchie would be believed before him.

'Ritchie?'

'That's what Mrs Storan said to me, and she said –'

'My mam only told me I was to give Martin bread and jam.'

'All right, all right! Shamie, take the knife and the loaf of bread. Now, you're in charge of cutting the bread. I want you to cut seven slices, all right? Catríona, will you put butter on each slice? And Marian, put jam on.'

Gussie tried to speak.

'I'd be much better at cutting –'

'Gussie, I'm warning you!'

Gussie had never heard his dad's voice like that, so for once he shut up, though he knew for sure he'd be much better at cutting bread than that fool Shamie Storan, who was doing it all crooked.

'Now. I'm going downstairs for a wash. Take one slice of bread and jam each and don't let me hear a peep out of you for the next five minutes.'

His heart thumping, Fonsie walked downstairs scarcely believing the obedient silence behind him. Where had he suddenly discovered the voice to take control like that? It was only when he passed the mirror in their hall that he realised how terrifying he must have looked even to his own children. His green eyes dancing out from a coaldust face made him look demented. Instead of going straight to the bathroom for a wash, he turned on the light in the front room to look at the pool of grey liquid. Poor Ann. She must have been up the walls. He picked up last week's *Chronicle* and got on his hands and knees. She had herself convinced that this child was going to die and of course he had never been able to think of anything to say that might reassure her or persuade her of a happier outcome. He pulled the pages of the newspaper apart and spread them out on the lino to soak up the liquid. As it seeped across, darkening each page, he prayed that Ann was all right. Would the baby be OK? As best he could he covered most of the wet. A familiar husky voice took him by surprise.

'Jesus, Mary and Joseph! Fonsie Strong, I wish I had you for a husband.'

Mary Storan lit a Craven 'A' and sat down. What was it about her? She was cool out. Never got herself in a tizzy about anything. Between puffs her chatty tone had a calming effect on Fonsie as she told him that Ann was grand, flying it, in a lovely comfy bed, and that Mrs Lynch had said it could be three hours or it could be twelve, so it was up to himself if he wanted to go down now and wait around or leave it until the morning. A couple of voices from upstairs rose loud enough to be heard. Mary casually bellowed at the ceiling.

'I'm down here now and I swear if I have to come up t'ya!'

An arctic silence followed. Mary grinned and took a puff.

'Take your time, Fonsie, have a wash and something to eat and then go down. I'll clean this up. And don't worry about those balubas above. Go on.'

Later, crossing town to St Gerard's, a scrubbed Fonsie rattled by the Our Lady of Consolation convent school that was the local polling station. The election workers were just locking the doors. Well, even his mother might accept that he had a reasonable excuse for not voting tonight. Might.

*

Once daylight began to fade and the lamps were lit in the parlour, Éamon liked the golden scrim that filled his old eyes like mist on a summer dawn. He heard tip-tap steps coming from the kitchen up the tiled hall, and then he saw the little round shape of her carrying what he knew was a tray of tea and coconut creams. Éamon stepped in the direction of the rattling porcelain as she placed the tray next to his favourite chair. When he sat down she took his hand gently and guided it to his cup, then his little plate, then the larger plate with the coconut creams. There would be five. He knew this of old. Two for him and two for her and then the last, which she would offer and he would decline, leaving her free to take it. The sound of tea pouring. If he could focus his gaze directly enough he would surely see her smile in his direction. Then a generous sup of milk was added. The gentle hand guided his to the saucer. He took it in his grasp, in control of it now. Once he had it, he could place it down and pick it up at will. He could reach out his free hand on the other side and find, precisely, the telephone, where it was placed by the reading lamp to the left of the armchair. He saw her form ease down into the chair directly opposite. He saw the motion of an arm and heard her sipping tea. Very soon, she would speak.

'*Síochán ag deireadh'n lae.*'

Éamon could not have agreed more. It was indeed peaceful at this day's end and her soft Irish was, to him, part of that, like birdsong in the country air. Such tranquillity after a hectic election day. All that going about, speaking and thinking in English. It was peaceful now to hear her melodious *blas*. He reached forward with precision and planted two long fingers on a coconut cream, which he plucked and placed in his saucer. A pleasure deferred, a pleasure increased. The polls had been closed for half an hour now. Seán would ring before ten.

'I suppose Seán will be calling very soon?'

Éamon smiled at the synchronicity of their thoughts. Parallel lines that had long ago reached their infinity. Again he saw the motion of her arm and heard a soft crunch of biscuit as she bit into her coconut cream. It made him crave the elastic sweetness of mallow in his mouth. He pondered the dangerous urgencies of a sweet tooth. Most of his cabinet, his former cabinet now, wouldn't thank you for a biscuit, if whiskey was the alternative. Often, during a meeting, it would come upon him, even as he leaned forward to snatch at another fig roll, that he had already eaten twice as many, and more, as anyone else there.

'Soon. Before ten.'

He bit and chewed softly. Will victory be with me? After forty years of elections Éamon accepted that, during these hours, this long night and day between the closing of the polls and the declaration of a result, it was virtually impossible for the mind to accommodate grand policies, long-term ideals, or anything very lofty at all. Like the dog who sits staring at the cat in the tree. Like the cat who waits with perfect patience for the opportune moment to leap free, for these few hours at least it all came down to the one question above all else: will victory be with me? On the face of it, it seemed certain. He would know a little more when Seán phoned and he would know without doubt this time tomorrow. Why then sit with tea and a sweet biscuit, conjecturing on a future reality which had been, in fact, already determined? It was an illogical activity, entirely at odds with the rigour of his training and his ideals.

'Have you any wish on you to listen to Radio Éireann?'

'Please yourself.'

He watched the little round form move across the parlour in a halo of golden light. If he won they would have to leave Herberton for the next seven years. He would miss this calm graceful avenue where they had been content for so long. Though they'd had three different homes on the one road, this comfy parlour was his favourite place of all. Was it because the children were more or less grown up and gone by the time they moved here that the house felt like it belonged more to themselves only? A solo concertina played a foot-tapping tune. The music seemed of a piece with the warm light that filled his eyes. Her face came close, almost in clear focus.

'You won't refuse another drop?'

'I won't.'

He lifted the cup and she poured the tea. La-tata, la-tata, la-tatatatata. Ta-ta-ta-tee-ta-ta-ta-ta-ta, taaa. Where could there be more contentment than this, in its simplicity and joy? Was it not this vision of such moments that he had tried to articulate to the people all his political life. Had they listened? Had they learned? Was it now too late for him to do anything more? He knew better than anyone the nature of the office he might be about to accept. After all, he had created and defined it. And limited it. When Éamon wrote the Constitution he had designed the Presidency as a position of great privilege and honour, indeed, the highest honour the State could bestow on a citizen of distinction. He had also made absolutely sure that no real power resided in the office he now sought and seemed likely to win. Éamon had no *meas* on irony.

Some months ago Seán had sat in the armchair where, just now, the little round form was easing herself back down. The late afternoon sun through the bay window had struck his old lieutenant directly from behind, making of him a sinister black form. It was only a few days before last Christmas. The talk had seemed to turn in quite a natural way to what lay ahead in the coming year but as soon as Seán had said, 'Now Taoiseach, the presidential election,' Éamon understood his larger intent.

'We'll have to find a good replacement for Seán T. Fine Gael will definitely want to fight an election this time.'

In the silence that followed this observation Éamon wondered how many of the more cowardly colleagues had nudged Seán forward to come and speak to him at this time? How many of the young ambitious impatient ones had exhorted him? There must have been a lot of pressure if poor Seán had called round so close to Christmas, talking of nothing and everything.

Éamon weighed the choice that was delicately, but determinedly being laid before him. If he did not offer himself as President on this occasion, then the opportunity would be lost for seven years. Could he continue to run the country as Taoiseach for another seven years and then, at eighty-four, take on the Presidency as a dignified retirement gift? Seven more years' daily political cut and thrust? In these times? He would have to win at least one more general election during that time or else he'd be out on his ear entirely. He recognised that Seán was gently nudging him to consider these things; what might be considered the logic of his situation. It was Éamon's greatest pride that, as well as being a man of vision, he was a man of logic. He had often noted in the past, however, how so few had any proper understanding of the true nature of logic.

The phone rang. Éamon reached and placed his hand directly on the receiver. He picked up and greeted the caller in his own tongue. After a '*Dia dhuit a Thaoiseach*' and an enquiry as to how he was after such a long busy day, Seán, as Éamon expected, reverted to English.

'I've been ringing all round, and the general assessment is that we're home and hosed. Mac Eoin might do all right in Dublin, but even there he won't be ahead of you. Oh, by the way, Dr Pat said to tell you that County Clare came out in force as you'd expect. An eighty-twenty margin he thinks.'

'That's a great relief, Seán. And overall?'

'Well, obviously don't hold me to it now, Éamon, but my lads think it'll be around sixty-forty. Comfortable enough. I think we can safely say that by this time tomorrow night you'll be our new President.'

And it will be over, Éamon thought. He couldn't help but notice that regret was his instant and prevailing emotion on hearing Seán's words, but he covered it well by immediately asking other practical questions.

'Was the turnout good overall?'

'Oh yes, so I'm told. Excellent considering… ah…'

Seán's voice trailed off. Considering what? Éamon knew what the unspoken caveat was. Emigration. So many young men of voting age, women too, no longer living in the country to cast their vote. Gone to England and the States and wherever else. Éamon never believed the figure constantly thrown at him; not four hundred thousand nor anything like it. Never. That would be twenty-five per cent of the adult population. It couldn't be as bad as that. Anyway, what had the other crowd done about it when they were in? Hadn't it gone from bad to worse? Why did these lads and girls go off like that in their prime? Éamon, deep in his heart, felt that there was more than a hint of selfishness and disloyalty in their departure. Of course he was well aware that it was not acceptable politically for him to voice such an opinion, but nothing could convince him that there wasn't decent work to be found here at home for many of them. Privately he wondered what cravings, what dissatisfactions sent these young people from their own land and families? How much money did anyone really need to be happy? It was a tragedy out and out. Still, at least most of those who stayed supported him. But was their vote today, in reality, a vote to move him along, nudge him on to the long acre? Was that what they really wanted?

Seán broke the silence. He spoke cheerfully, looking forward to tomorrow evening's victory celebration. Though there was no awkwardness between them – they had soldiered together too long for that – something had changed nonetheless, and Éamon understood that it was irrevocable. As he put down the phone he noted that Seán did not end formally with Taoiseach, or even tribally with Chief.

'Good night so, Éamon. Sleep well.'

His tea was now but lukewarm. A *seannós* lament quivered from the radio. He closed his eyes and tried to control and master his fear of what was to come. After so many years in charge, could he come to terms with no longer having the levers of power in his hands? When Seán and Kenneth had presented their new economic plan to him last year, his instinct had been to say no out of hand. He understood exactly what this plan meant and the very heart of him cried out against it. To open the economy, encourage businesses from the States and England and Europe to come here and give such people incentives to build factories, could only mean dilution of the National ideal, there was no two ways about it. And for what? Seán's reply had been typically pithy.

'Jobs. It's all about jobs, Chief.'

But it wasn't, of course it wasn't. Surely Seán knew that there was so much else? Yet, somehow, on that day, Éamon discovered he no longer had the wherewithal to argue his case with the subtlety and certainty of old. Kenneth had, in his diffident, formal manner, posited the theory that this new strategy might allow many young people to come home and bring communities alive again. If he hoped this would convince his boss of the value of their plan, he misunderstood his man. Éamon had doubts about the attitudes and values these emigrants would carry home in their bags from years on the streets of London and New York. It might well be that these souls were lost already, culturally, morally; no longer Irish in any sense that he would care to define, and might never be again. They might even infect those who had stayed and so destroy the careful work of many years. What was it prevented him from voicing these thoughts aloud, even in private conference with his most trusted lieutenant and Kenneth, the most discreet of civil servants? Although that day he didn't fully appreciate what was happening to him, Éamon understood now that it could only have been some unspoken realisation that power was seeping away from him. Was it age and nothing more? He had agreed to their plan but perhaps Seán, no fool, saw the elemental doubt behind his dim, downcast eyes.

Why was Seán Lemass, as true an Irish patriot as ever there was, less concerned about what forces would be unleashed once the world was invited in? Éamon was aware that all over Dublin these days, even here on elegant Cross Avenue, people were renting television sets and strapping ungainly aerials that stretched high above their chimneys, wavering uncertainly, desperate to catch the signals from BBC and the commercial channel. Thankfully most of the country beyond Dublin could not yet receive these signals. Éamon's old eyes no longer allowed him to experience the full visual impact of these aerials, but the image in his mind's eye was dreadful enough; to look up and, instead of the natural wonder of a Dublin sky, view a demented configuration of twisted metal bending in the wind was shocking to him. What were people in Dublin, at this very moment, watching? What images of the world were they receiving into their homes? What attitudes and pseudo-philosophies? He wouldn't ever know precisely because he had no television, but he understood very clearly that whatever they were looking at was mediated through the language and values of Great Britain. Some of his younger ministers, Charles, Jack, even quiet Dr Pat, thought why not create our own television service, as was done with radio. Bring an Irish message to the people. If only it was as simple as that. Éamon could see, even if the younger generation of politicians could not, that television was a far more terrifying power. Were they just innocent about what this medium could do, or too confident of their power to control it?

Her hand caressed his shoulder, her voice soft now as a pillow. 'Are you in your sleep, pet?'

He opened his eyes to show he was not asleep. How could he sleep tonight?

*

The contractions were much more frequent and painful but Ann didn't mind that. This was pain she remembered from before and knew how it would end. Anyway, now she was safe in her narrow spotless white cubicle. Mr Carr, the gynaecologist, had been phoned as Ann requested and Mrs Lynch told her that he sent his best wishes and was standing by at a moment's notice, if needed.

Mrs Lynch smiled and told Ann she didn't think there would be any need for Mr Carr to be bothering himself. Everything was going to be fine. Ann knew that now. The panic of a couple of hours ago and the terrors of the last few months had disappeared. It had been worth every penny she saved to have this peace of mind. Her baby would be fine. Everyone said Mrs Lynch was the best.

'A woman as hearty and healthy as you will have no bother at all.'

Mrs Lynch leaned in a little closer and dropped her voice as if to make sure that no one else heard. It pleased Ann that the most revered midwife in the city seemed to be confiding in her.

'I wish I could say the same for some of the rest of them here tonight. But sure we'll manage them all anyway with the help of God. You'll be the least of my worries, Mrs Strong.'

Ann was thrilled to hear such praise. She hated being a bother to anyone. Judging by moans from the other cubicles, it seemed that Mrs Lynch had quite a few other women needing care and attention, yet here she was, her hand on Ann's stomach, pressing confidently, taking time to make sure that everything was as it should be. Mrs Lynch, her head turned a little, listening closely, as if hearing things that the normal run of humanity could not, waited in stillness and utter silence until the next contraction came. Ann's breath quickened but she tried to be as brave and calm as possible. Mrs Lynch smiled.

'Good for you. It'll be a few hours yet. We'll look in again in a while – is that all right?'

'Oh that's fine Mrs Lynch.'

*

The smell of cleaning fluids was so overpowering in the tiny scrubbed waiting room that Fonsie knew he didn't need to worry about any of the other fathers-to-be catching a whiff of Swarfega from him. The others, sitting close together on the wooden benches, nodded and muttered greetings, then returned to silence as Fonsie sat and clasped his hands on his lap. After a few moments he shifted them to his side. Then he folded his arms making the hands virtually invisible. Though it was clear that no one was even looking in his direction, he couldn't help feeling a bit awkward. It was obvious to him that none of the other men worked with their hands. Soft faces, too. Fonsie didn't recognise any of them even to see and, from the lack of any conversation, it seemed that no one else knew each other either.

A different kind of man might have considered the curious coincidence of time, place and event that brought five strangers together like this and how soon, in one way or another, each of their lives would be changed, but Fonsie Strong did not have such thoughts. His only passing reflection was mild surprise that they were all strangers but he guessed that, if they started talking, some connection would be established very quickly, as was always the way in a provincial city that wasn't much more than a town. He, however, would never be the one to begin such a conversation. Arms folded, he stared at the door, hoping someone would come soon and let him know how Ann was doing.

The young man directly opposite Fonsie, Brendan Barry, sat quite still apart from occasionally flicking his blond fringe back from his eyes. He didn't recognise himself in any of these other men. They were all much older, of course, but it wasn't just that. It still felt like a bit of a shock to be here at all. Brendan had grown used to being the kind of young man that girls looked at in a certain way although he never really analysed why, preferring just to enjoy the attention and steal the kisses. His new wife Elizabeth Flanagan could have told him exactly what had enticed her that first night barely nine months ago. The combination of delicate good looks, genuine politeness and a strangely alluring passitivity of manner had been somehow irresistible. She'd walked into Cruise's Hotel expecting nothing other than a boring night celebrating her parents silver jubilee with their boring friends. Then she noticed the young trainee manager. Brendan had immediately clocked her clocking him. Leslie Caron; that's who she was like with her short-cropped hair, slim frame and dancing eyes. Later, when he wheeled a trolley with cake and champagne into the party, he felt those eyes on him all the way, so it was no surprise when, later, she wandered out to the lobby, sniffing round. Of course he enjoyed flirting with her, of course he could have just laughed off, as a joke, her suggestion that he steal a key to an unoccupied room and of course, even after he got a kiss off her and a shift in the darkness of room 35, he could have resisted going all the way, but the pleasure of the adventure, the thrill of the secret encounter, made it hard for Brendan to stop himself. Young Elizabeth Flanagan definitely didn't want him to stop. Anyway, it had been a brilliant laugh.

As a particular favour the marriage service was arranged in great haste by a close friend of the Flanagan family, Father Connolly, parish priest at the Mother of Good Hope church on the North Road. Circumstance alone had made Brendan Barry from Claughaun Terrace an acceptable Flanagan son-in-law, the birth of a healthy child in wedlock being the first priority for everybody involved in this awkward situation. His father-in-law bought the couple a brand new semi-detached house in College Park and opened a generous current account to take care of household bills. Both the house and the account were in Elizabeth's name only. Brendan wasn't that bothered by the insult. The Flanagan family could not organise all things, however. They had prayed that Elizabeth might be sufficiently overdue to allow them to create the impression in their circle that the birth was respectably premature, but nature thwarted them. Now that the moment had arrived, several days early as it happened, and quite definitely less than seven months since the wedding, Brendan still did not know exactly what his true feelings were. The force of Elizabeth's passion for him could still be exciting. He regretted none of the rampant pleasure of their escapade nor its consequences, and he was quite giddy at the notion of becoming a father. But what lay beyond now seemed more complicated and difficult. Duller too, maybe? His knee briefly touched the man on his left. They both shifted position immediately, silently.

This man, Cormac Kiely, sat waiting in placid contentment, perhaps because it was his seventh such vigil, or perhaps because he was, broadly speaking, a contented man. He had been content to become an architect as his father had been and content to continue the business practices that had proved fruitful in earlier difficult times. A carefully maintained relationship with the Bishop meant he was always first to be called on by the diocese for their many building projects, while he and his wife Louise, insofar as so many joyful pregnancies allowed, also involved themselves enthusiastically in local society: the Lion's Club, the Junior Chamber of Commerce, Castletroy golf club and the Cecilian musical society. That pleasure and profit should flow equally from such pleasant social interactions was something Cormac continually gave thanks for, as he gave thanks for each of the six previous vigils he had undergone in this same waiting room, itself part of an extension to St Gerard's that he had designed. His wife swore by Mrs Lynch, and there had been no mishaps yet. Of course a new baby meant that Louise would not now play any part in the Cecilian's autumn production of *The Merry Widow*. Cormac didn't at all mind the idea of attending rehearsals solo. He even had a notion that, this time, he might put himself forward for one of the lead roles. He was an untutored but decent baritone, certainly good enough to take on Baron Zeta. Why not? Silently, his head nodding in time, he began to hum 'Women! Women! Women!'

In curious contrast, the man next to him, George Collopy, was silently praying, his prematurely balding head bowed low. A deeply religious man, and a traveller for Mattersons Meats, he sold their pork and bacon products to retailers all over Munster. Having been graced with three girls, he hoped that God would understand why he had been praying for a boy-child since arriving at St Gerard's several hours before.

'Oh Jesus, Lord of mercy, though I am but a poor sinner

and have no right to ask favours of You, yet I know that in Your compassion and love You will listen to my plea and grant my humble petition. I pray for the safe birth of my child and I implore that, on this occasion, You will grant me the miracle of a healthy boy. Oh blessed Mary, mother of God, intercede for me and beg the indulgence of your most wise, merciful and loving Son, to allow me the opportunity to raise a strong and upright Catholic boy, who I will teach to be your humble servant all the days of his life.'

George Collopy's lips didn't move as, on and on, the words tumbled through his head. Sometimes he drifted on to decades of the rosary, keeping count of the Hail Marys by moving his right thumb from finger to finger and, after five joyful mysteries and a Hail Holy Queen, reverting again to another variation of his specific heartfelt personal plea for his one abiding wish.

The man sitting, slumped forward, between George Collopy and Fonsie, the last of this coincidence of fathers-to-be, desired neither son nor daughter. Michael Liston's black bowed head seemed to assert his reluctance even to be here. He had last become a father twelve years ago and didn't want to be one again. He didn't even want to be married any more. Not to her, anyway. Right now he just wanted a drink. To have been caught, snared like this left him brooding and resentful. The one and only time in more than two years, for Jesus' sake! Drink, he had to concede, had played its wretched part, although it in no way prevented Michael from blaming that cow for luring him into some kind of trap. This suspicion had befuddled him for months since. Had she somehow heard about his opportunity of a move to Dublin? How could that be? He hadn't told her anything. The phonecall was strictly on the QT from a high-up in the Department of Industry and Commerce, a special word in his ear because Michael's expertise and loyal support were much appreciated. Things were about to change at last, he was told. Dev was being moved on, economic regeneration could begin, everything was going to loosen up, especially in the whole area of re-zoning and urban planning. Dublin was about to be transformed. That was the exact word the high-up used. Transformed. Planning experts like Michael would be in demand. Was he interested in a move? Michael was more than interested especially if, at the same time, it allowed him to engineer a gradual withdrawal and ultimate escape from married life, even though he could never end the marriage itself.

Then the fiendish bitch told him she was pregnant. For the first time in twelve years. It was a miracle, she declared.

It was hard to tell if the smile on her face was true maternal joy, a sign that all was for the best and their love had been renewed and borne fruit, despite all their little trials and tribulations – or triumphant malice. Michael had never hated her so much. With a child on the way he couldn't leave her and if they all moved to Dublin together he'd never ever escape. Ever. The only reason he was sitting here at all, staring at the floor, savagely smoking, was because his sister had called to the house earlier, looked him in the eye and said she was sure he must be up the walls wondering how poor Eva was getting on and she'd be more than happy to mind the twins while he went to St Gerard's. How closely women stuck together in these situations. Michael Liston was sure of one thing. Whether this creature turned out to be a boy or girl, it would not be wanted or loved. Not by him. And no one could make him, not she, nor his sister. Not anyone.

Fonsie's thoughts, less fixed and certainly less livid than the man seething quietly next to him, were like the invigorating Atlantic tide that, every August, he loved watching as it rolled and crashed on Ballybunion strand. No matter how much flotsam washed about in his worried head, the high-tide mark was always Ann, and each time his thoughts returned to her she seemed to roll in that little bit closer. First, he allowed himself a vague reassurance that she must be all right because if there was any problem surely someone would come and tell him? Should he go home then? Was Mary Storan managing all right looking after his four as well as her own? At nearly twelve, Ritchie was probably old enough and sensible enough to be of some help. He tried so hard to get things right. Always does his best, they said in his school reports. Ritchie would always be Ann's favourite, though she'd never admit it.

Ann. The wave rolled up the strand again and his uncertain imagination now saw her in a big iron bed in a spotless ward, surrounded by large comforting women with basins of hot water and towels and scissors. But the moment he closed in on her face, twisted in pain, he shifted his thoughts quickly. Would the bags of coal left on the lorry outside be all right? Barrington Street wasn't the safest at this hour. Maybe he should go out and have a look. Whatever about stealing the coal, messers could easily jump on the back and start throwing lumps at each other. He tried to recall how it had been the last time, not the last terrible time when the baby was lost but the time before, with Martin. That was at the flat. Fonsie had been able to go to bed and sleep. Someone had woken him up with the good news. With Marian, before that, it happened in the middle of the afternoon while he was at work. Maybe things went much faster in a nursing home with everything laid on? He wondered how long these other lads had been sitting here. Had anyone told them what was going on? Ann had taken on sewing work and saved and saved so she could afford to come here. It was all paid for already. She was amazing that way, once her mind was made up. All on account of the last time, of course.

When he'd mentioned to his mother how upset Ann was, his mother had said he should tell her just to get on with it. Everyone lost babies; she herself had lost three. It was God's will. Say a Magnificat and pray for intercession on behalf of the poor little soul in Limbo. Fonsie did all those things himself and they helped him, but he never mentioned any of it to Ann, who would have gone through the roof, especially as the advice came from his mother. Of course, if it had been his father saying exactly the same thing, Ann would have said how kind Robert was to be thinking of her. Lovely old Robert. A true gentleman. Fonsie knew that, as far as his father was concerned, the best decision his son ever made was to marry Ann Casey, a sensible smiling girl with a lovely gentle singing voice.

'Is Mr Barry here?'

It was just two o'clock when a young girl of no more than twenty came in to the waiting room, looking around as she spoke. There was a couple of seconds delay, then, as if suddenly remembering his own name, the youngest of the five men leapt up.

'Oh sorry, yeah. Me, yeah, that's me.'

'Your wife Elizabeth had a lovely baby boy a little while ago.'

'Yeah? Yeah? Oh Jesus, really? Really, yeah?'

Flicking back his fringe, his pink face flushed even more in embarrassment at his own excitement.

'Do you want to come up and see them?'

As the youngfellah hurried out ahead of the girl, Fonsie caught the eye of the man he did not know was Cormac Kiely, who was smiling the smile of an old hand.

'One down. His first, I'd say.'

'Oh yes, yes.'

Fonsie gestured politely as he smiled and spoke but quickly noticed how visible on his palm were lines of ingrained black that even Swarfega couldn't shift. He folded his arms again. Fonsie wondered how many children did these other men have already. Two seemed near his own age, in their thirties, and the one who had spoken to him was definitely older, maybe forty-five or so. Would Fonsie be still having children at that age? Not for him to decide. It was going to be hard enough now taking care of five. At least it meant moving up the council list for a three-bedroom house, but that would mean higher rent. Ritchie was finishing national school next year so there would be fees if he went on into secondary. There would be no week's holiday in Ballybunion this August for the Strongs and maybe not next year either. He'd better pray for a freezing wet fire-lighting winter.

Dozing off, he woke to hear the girl telling the older man, who she called Mr Kiely, that he had a beautiful new daughter born just after three o'clock. He took the news in his cheerful stride as if this happened every other week.

'That's four daughters to comfort my old age, and three sons to spoil it. Good night gentlemen and God bless you and keep you.'

After he left, the one who was going bald seemed to get more nervous. Fonsie didn't like to look but he could sense him shifting about on the bench and even heard him whispering to himself. The next time the girl put her head round the door he jumped up like he was electrocuted as soon as she said his name.

'Mr Collopy.'

'Yes, yes, that's me.'

'Congratulations. You have a new baby boy born at ten to four.'

Mr Collopy couldn't speak. He put his hands to his mouth and breathed in and out. Then he blessed himself, raised his head, and prayed aloud.

'Oh most loving and most tender Jesus, You have heard the prayer of an undeserving sinner. I am Yours unto eternity.'

He blessed himself again and made a little genuflection in front of the open-mouthed girl.

'Can I go see him?'

The man who smoked stared after the man named Collopy. As soon as the door was pulled shut he shook his head.

'Sweet suffering divine Jesus!'

A few moments later he stood up and left. Fonsie waited alone. He released his hands from hiding to stretch his arms and his spine. Surely it wouldn't be much longer.

*

The relief came suddenly as Ann knew it would. Then she realised she wasn't screaming any more, just panic-breathing. Mrs Lynch gestured to tell her to lift her head and see. There it was, held up by the little smiley girl. Ann couldn't, in that moment, put a name on her. Smeared and wriggling, its teensy newborn face looked ready to cry out but it hadn't uttered a sound yet. Another girl was snipping the cord. Only now did Ann realise she had had a boy. Then he opened his mouth…

'WAAAAH! AAAAAAAAAGH!! WAAAAAAAAAA-AAA-AAAGGGHHH!!!'

He was whisked away. Ann lay back and closed her eyes, waiting for that last part she hated. The poor little thing seemed fine. Loud enough, anyway. Everything was going to be fine. Her heartbeat finally began to slow a little but she still felt sweaty. Someone touched her shoulder. She opened her eyes. Mrs Lynch was holding him, all clean and wrapped in a white blanket.

'Seven pounds, four ounces. Sit up, so you can hold him.'

Ann pushed herself up, despite the pain, and held out her arms. Wrapped so completely he didn't move much now, but he howled as she took him into her and touched her chin gently against his temple so as to feel some part of him, skin on skin. 'There, there, there, there.' Then a brisk nod from Mrs Lynch and the little smiley one took possession again and carried him off.

'Let's see how he'll take to his bottle. We'll bring him back soon. Your husband is downstairs, waiting patiently. Take your own time now, but let me know when you're ready for him to come and see the two of you.'

Mrs Lynch was so good, everyone was so good. Rita. That was the little smiley one's name.

*

The man who smoked had come back, looking more sour if anything. Fonsie closed his eyes to avoid any contact in case it antagonised him more. There was something about him now. Was he drunk? Time was passing very slowly.

Barry… Kiely… Collopy… Liston… Strong. Five children would bear those names and grow up sharing an important detail of their lives. Would their paths ever cross?

Fonsie's eyes jerked open as a hand gently squeezed his shoulder. The room seemed different. Whiter. The man who smoked was not there now. The young girl was smiling down at him.

'Mr Strong?'

Fonsie realised that the early-morning sun was shining in the window.

He smiled hopefully at the girl.

'Have you news for me?'

Two: June 21st

Mary Storan wore the ivory two-piece she had got married in when Fonsie drove her in the lorry to St Gerard's on the following Sunday. Father Mullally had agreed that the child could be christened in Our Lady of Consolation parish church after last Mass. Mary and Mikey were delighted to be godparents. Ann still had to decide on a name. On the evening of the birth she and Fonsie had talked about it. As the nursing home was called St Gerard's and she had lit candles at the altar to St Gerard in the Redemptorists throughout the pregnancy, it seemed to be the favourite choice, although John, in honour of the new Pope, was also mentioned. Fonsie was easy either way and left it up to Ann. He said as long as she didn't call him after her favourite film star he didn't mind. She said now that he mentioned it, Rock Strong had a bit of a ring to it. She was joking of course, and Fonsie was glad to see her smiling again so soon after the birth. When he and Mary Storan arrived in the convalescent ward, Ann was sitting up with the child asleep in her arms.

'Francis.'

Fonsie had no idea where that came from. It hadn't been mentioned before. Still, he liked the sound of Francis. Or Frankie even. Frank Strong. Yes that would do fine. Francie. Not so good. Try and avoid that. He smiled.

'Very nice. You're sure now?'

'Yes. Francis John. What do you think, Mary?'

'Gorgeous, Ann.'

She put down her cigarette and cradled the boy.

'And you're a dote, aren't you Francis? He's beautiful, Ann.'

Mary fell in love with her godchild that instant. On the

journey to the church she held him close and, when he woke, she goo-gooed at him non-stop. When he started wailing she rocked him and hummed until he calmed. Outside Our Lady of Consolation the family and relations waited: the other children, Ritchie, Gussie, Marian and Martin, Fonsie's parents, Robert and Kathleen Strong, Marg his sister with her husband Peadar Crowley, and their children John, Mary, George and Theresa, Ann's mother Bernadette, her brother Dan and her sisters Una, Mona and Bernadette with their husbands Seán Durack, Seán Enright and Seán O'Donnell, and all their children, Seán junior, Cathal, Brendan, Connie, Joe, Anthony, Gerard, Alphonsus, Mary, Mary, Eva, Louise, and Monica. Godfather Mikey Storan waited in his best suit, hands in pockets, fag in mouth.

Fonsie pulled up outside the church and said to Mary, 'Stay as you are, that door-handle is a bit awkward.'

As he walked round to the passenger side and fiddled with the door there were friendly jeers and heckles started by the three Seáns. The older boys took their cue and joined in. Ann's sisters smiled; that Fonsie and his old jalopy! The door jolted on its hinges as Fonsie finally got it open. Mary stepped out, laughing, and turned to give everyone a good look at the latest addition. There were aaahs from the women and girls and whoops from the men and boys. While Fonsie got backslaps and slagging, Mary brought the baby to Mikey.

'They're calling him Francis.'

'Grand. After Sinatra yeah?'

'I haven't a clue.'

Mikey, realising that the baby was being offered for him to hold, flicked the cigarette away and took him in his arms. He couldn't have been more shocked when, as he looked down at little Francis, out of nowhere, he felt tears come popping. This hadn't ever happened to him, even with his own children. He kept his head down so Mary wouldn't notice as he blinked the stupid things back. Suddenly everyone was in on top of him for a closer look. Mary reached out.

'Here, let me. Before you drop him.'

His head lowered, Mikey passed the baby over and backed out of the family scrum. Once clear, he turned away and rubbed his eyes as if to get at a bit of dirt. Jesus! Was it because it was his first time being godfather, was that it? It must be. He lit up again and went to sit on the low wall.

Father Mullally appeared in the church doorway, unnoticed at first. Looking at the large group, he wondered how many different families were represented. Were they all from his parish? So many children, none older than fourteen at a guess, but he could tell that every effort had been made to turn them out respectably. That was something. It showed that these were people of dignity despite their circumstances. As their new parish priest he felt both a duty and an inclination to help such deserving families get on. He could certainly influence potential employers. A timely word in an appropriate ear might make all the difference to the future of any one of these children.

Because of what seemed to have been a miraculous interweaving of his personal circumstances and extraordinary recent developments in the Church itself, Fr Mullally had become fascinated by the quicksilver nature of change, the potential for radical alteration within a relatively short time frame. Relative, that is, to the history of mankind as a whole. In his specific case, to move from serving God's purpose as a willing but, he would accept, deeply intellectual and rather ascetic curate in the respectable calm of St Michael's parish in Cork, during the resolute and, some would say, stern papacy of Pius XII, to being, coincidently with the coronation of that joyful and humble man John XXIII, elevated to parish priest and shepherd of a rather poorer flock in a very different city, was surely remarkable? Fr Mullally could not but be convinced, in the face of such sudden convergent events, that his own ultimate purpose was bound in some mystical way to the new papacy, and that he must allow himself to be led wherever it brought him. Who knew how long it would take for the tangle of threads that was the future to unravel and weave itself into a sacred new garment? Step by tiny but confident step was the only way to proceed for now. Today, for example, he would meet a new family and initiate its latest soul into the faith. Another part of the mosaic; perhaps insignificant, perhaps not. The father was a local coalman, apparently. The young curate, Father Tierney, had an idea that he delivered to the parish house. One of the men from the family group now acknowledged the priest with a respectful smile and began to approach. The child's father at a guess; the face weather-worn and lined, probably beyond his years. The man's eyes, however, were honest and clear, as he reached out his hand and introduced himself. Fr Mullally was delighted at how the cracked roughness of the hand he grasped contrasted with the softness, gentility even, of the man's voice. It was exactly the kind of arresting juxtaposition that the parish priest enjoyed. And his name was Strong. A coalman called Strong. How perfect. He realised that, lost in his own engaging thoughts, he had not registered the man's first name, and now instructed himself to concentrate so as not to miss the godparents' names and of course that of the newborn infant. He repeated these names carefully in his head as he heard them. Michael and Mary Storan. Also residing in the parish. Good. The child would be Francis John. Excellent. As they walked together to the font, he congratulated Mr Strong sincerely on the choice of names, noting favourably the acknowledgment of the new Pope, albeit, as he wittily phrased it, in a supporting role to the gentle Saint of Assisi. John XXIII himself would consider that entirely apt. Father Mullaly said he looked forward to meeting the mother… what was her first name? Ann… Yes, he looked forward to meeting her soon when she came to be churched. Indicating where Michael Storan and his wife were to stand with the child, he turned at the font and waited as the family group settled themselves into the nearest pews. He was pleased to note some interested women parishoners hovering in the entrance. Everyone at last was silent, anxiously awaiting his first words.

Then the child screamed.

It was a high clean unstudied shattering sound.

*

Seán T was struck by how silent Dev was on the subject of his election victory. During the meal he spoke of recent events in the Congo, offering his thesis, long familiar to Seán T, on the chaos, division and distress that colonial powers inevitably leave behind when they are finally forced to withdraw and the horrendous task that now lay ahead for the various parties remaining. As ever, his knowledge of the issues and personalities was detailed. He was just as commanding on the new regime in Cuba. There was, in his view, no doubting the intellectual capacity of a number of the leaders. Castro, Martinez, Guevara and, especially, Cienfuegos, who he considered to have a very fine mind. He accepted their idealism was sincere and they clearly had the support of the people. There were even some things about them that reminded him of themselves in the old days of struggle for independence. He agreed with Seán T that there were clear signs however, that their populist agenda was hardening into Communist ideology. Dev suspected that Guevara had the makings of a demagogue. Seán T was concerned that persecution of the Church would inevitably follow.

Dev was kind enough to inquire if Seán T had, during his recent official visit to America, heard any rumours about likely presidential candidates? Seán T was more than happy to pass on what gossip he had gathered. Nixon, of course, was a foregone conclusion for the Republicans, but there was strong word that Adlai Stevenson would not get his Party's nomination without a fight. Irish-American Democrats were putting it about that young Senator Kennedy might toss his hat in the ring. Dev thought it unlikely this time round. 1964 perhaps. Unless of course he was as devious and self-serving as his father, that walking paradox, an Irish-American Anglophile. Seán T laughed and then said cautiously, imagine though, a Catholic in the White House. Dev shook his head. Even when the chat shifted with ease from world affairs to the problem of damp in the master bedroom when winter came round and a faulty chain in the toilet, which Seán T pointed out as he led the de Valeras around the Áras living quarters, it didn't coax the old Chief into saying anything about his newly changed circumstances. This avoidance of what anyone would reasonably have thought might be the main subject of the day made Seán T feel a little sad for Dev, perhaps because he understood the cause and knew that, in the long run, there was no cure. After fourteen years in the job no one knew better than he how little it meant to be President of Ireland. He could well imagine that was how Dev saw it also.

As soon as the election result had been confirmed, President Seán T Ó'Ceallaigh had telephoned to congratulate the President-elect formally and, less formally, as was his way, to invite Éamon and Sinéad for lunch at the Áras after mass on Sunday. Before he made the call he and Mary had discussed how the invitation should be framed. Seán T's Irish was nowhere near as fluent and subtle as Dev's and, in this circumstance, it was important to get the tone and the vocabulary absolutely right. His old comrade didn't want his invitation to sound patronising. After all, the man was not exactly a stranger to the Áras over the years, not least having called on six occasions to receive his seal of office as Taoiseach. It was Mary who reminded Seán that there was another reason to choose words carefully; the business of the old Chief's eyesight. They, no more than anyone else, apart from his physician presumably, knew precisely how badly his vision was impaired. The word was that, while not yet totally blind, he could no longer read his own speeches and so had to learn them by heart or extemporise which, of course, Dev being Dev, he did remarkably well. Mary was very firm with Seán on this matter.

'On your life don't be saying things like "take a look at" or "would you like to see?"'

'Oh yes, of course, yes.'

'Even "we'll show you around" mightn't sound right.'

Seán T took the point absolutely as he usually did with

Mary, who was a rock of sense. Between them they composed a very careful yet friendly and casual invite. A final exercise in Presidential diplomacy.

'We thought it might be a nice way for you and Sinéad to acquaint yourselves with the inner workings of the house, the domestic side of things.'

With Mary standing over him, Seán T had, for once, been word perfect. It was a brief but warm exchange. Dev had thanked him and accepted the invitation.

By the time the visit was ending, as they said their goodbyes, little Seán T could not help but feel that the Long Fellow seemed diminished, even physically, no longer towering over him as he had always done. Later again, alone, before their nightly rosary, Seán T and Mary sat by the fire, each with a whiskey, and conducted a relaxed post-mortem on the visit. All in all they deemed it successful. Sinéad had enjoyed meeting the domestic staff, and both of them seemed to appreciate the little tour. Mary thought the conversation over lunch very stimulating. In her view the occasion had been not only an excellent way to ease the de Valeras into their new home but a lovely friendly way of bringing down the curtain on their own time in Áras an Uachtarán. Her interpretation of Dev's reticence about his election victory was that it was nothing more than the quiet modesty of the man. Seán T did not argue the point because by the time Mary concluded her observations his mind had drifted back to an uneasy moment earlier in the afternoon. While viewing the master bedroom, Dev had paused at the east window and stood staring out, for all the world as if he was surveying the park beyond, observing even the tiniest figures far off, little Dublin folk out for a Sunday stroll. But how much could he see at all? Seán T had wondered. And what was going on in his head as he gazed? Who ever knew with Dev? Seán T was looking forward to a retirement he considered already overdue, but here was the old Chief about to start another seven years of service. Was this house going to be little better than a prison for him? The silence had become uncomfortably long but Seán T could not think of any words to break it. Then, without turning, Dev spoke.

'Do you know, I'm hungry. Is lunch ready do you think?'

The Ó'Ceallaighs, in contented silence now, sipped their whiskey; perhaps their final tipple in the old house.

Gazing past his wife to the great sash window beyond, Seán T marvelled at the light in the cloudless sky at such a late hour. Midsummer 1959.

Poor old Dev, he thought.

1960

Three: August 7th

Sometimes, though not often, Dom got sick of the sound of his own voice. This time it happened quite unexpectedly, inconveniently, over a meal in the famous Grill Room at Shannon Airport after what was, by any standards, a hugely successful day. The first visit of Seán Lemass to the region, since becoming Taoiseach, could not be other than a singular opportunity for Dom. For starters, it meant being at the leader's side all day as press photographers snapped every move and gesture. Sure enough, not a camera was aimed in the direction of the Taoiseach that did not catch at least an eye and ear of Dom nudging into shot. In the famous duty-free shop he examined a bowl, while pretending to discuss with the Taoiseach the exquisite craftsmanship of Waterford crystal and was happy to hold an Aran sweater up to his chest and grin for the cameras. In Lemass's earshot he asked O'Regan intelligent-sounding questions about footfall and forward projections. He cleaved to his elbow when they toured the new Aer Lingus transatlantic jet, the Boeing 720, and observed the crew in training. He strolled shoulder to shoulder with the Taoiseach around the new industrial estate, introducing him to workers as if to old friends. Now, here they were at dinner, discussing O'Regan's latest big idea, a Shannon Airport development company. The beat of Dom's heart was still uncomfortably fast, but he was happy as a pig in the proverbial, and the wine chosen for the main course, a Chateau Larmande 1957, capped it all. What a morning. Political gold. Days like this made all the difference.

Across the table Dr Pat was smiling at him and encouraging him to tell that brilliant story of his. The one about the rat. Modest Pat with his soft flat country-doctor voice, always deferring, always agreeing, the smart fucker. He was never the funny man, never seemed interested in being the centre of attention. But he was in the cabinet already; Dom was not. Dr Pat gestured towards him as if making the Noble Call at a singsong. 'Go on Dom. Taoiseach, you'll love this one.' O'Regan held a forkful of beef stroganoff in midair as he added his voice. 'Oh yes do. Don't tell me you never heard this one, Taoiseach.' Dr Pat, nodding and smiling like an eager fan, mounted some minted garden peas precariously onto a chunk of Quilty lobster. 'It's brilliant now, absolutely only brilliant.' How could Dom resist? An Taoiseach's wrinkled, deceptively lazy eyes turned to him, his charming old smile already at the starting gate. This was what the whole day was about anyway, wasn't it? The chance to razzle-dazzle the boss? Since taking over, Lemass hadn't been clearing out the deadwood as fast as Dom would have liked, but he was getting round to it. In the long run he would need to find the coming men to fill the vacancies, and if ever there was a coming man then surely Dom was it. Coming man? He was thirty-eight already, for the love and honour of Jesus! Fair enough if he had to wait until the other side of the next general election, that was only a year away, but if a ministry wasn't offered at that stage, he might as well roll up his tent and fuck off out of it. There was old slyballs Dr Pat already well set up and, technically, Shannon, which was such a big deal in Lemass' plans for the future, was his bailiwick. But most of the workers and their families and relations lived in Dom's backyard. Thousands of votes that he could deliver for the Party. That might be his trump card. After a couple of coquettish demurs, and a few preparatory sips, Dom began the rat story, the bare bones of which was not very interesting and, in essence, not even true but, in Dom's hands, always had the Party faithful in stitches.

'This was during the '57 campaign, I was banging on doors in Ballynanty when this mad-looking oul' wan poked her head out the door. The kind who'd ate you without salt, as we say around here.'

Dom started to demonstrate his humorous command of the

city's working-class accent, a skill that had never been encouraged by his Jesuit teachers, but always got him laughs.

'"Come here to me now youngf'llah, what crowd are you from?" says she, still nothing but the head sticking round the door. I was actually beginning to wonder had she a stitch of clothes on her, heaven forbid. "Fianna Fail," sez I, "looking for your number one." "Are you in the govamint?" says she and by the tone of voice I make a reasonable guess that had I been in the "govamint"' – the others were chuckling already – 'I would not have been popular with the lady in question. "Most certainly not," I said. "I'm looking to kick them out, and I'm hoping you'll help me with your vote." "Oh yeah, and what'll you do for the likes of me?" says she, oh cute as you like. I knew there was some aul moan coming but I didn't know what, a leak in the roof, or a hinge off the door, or whatever you're having yourself. "I'll be aiming to make your life better in every way I can, Missus." "Oh will you now, come in here so, 'til I show you what you can do for me. Come on now so. In here. Come in here after me."'

Egged on by An Taoiseach's obvious enjoyment of the story, after a quick gulp Dom now added physical details to his wicked vocal creation. He squinted and sunk his neck into his shoulders, which he then rocked from side to side as he walked his audience through the imaginary little house into the imaginary scullery. The accent became flatter and impossibly nasal. He added sniffs and nose-rubs.

'"I'm sick and tired of goan down dere to de depot giving out. I might as well be talking to de wall as dose fellahs, dey do be only blackguarding me. One o' dem, Skelly I tink his name was, treated me like dirt. Made me out to be a liart. Well, I want you to show him I'm no liart. Look dere now and you tell me if I'm a liart." And she stuck out her finger. I looked to where she was pointing under the table in the scullery. At first all I saw was an old iron pot lying there. Then I spotted it; a tail sticking out. "Now," sez she, "now am I a liart? I'm only just after lammin' dat fellah before you came. I was over at de sink minding my own business and next ting didn't I spot him out of de corner of me eye. Well, Jesus, Mary and holy St Joseph, he put the heart 'cross me, and I don't know how I did it but next ting I had de pot in me hand and I sent it flying after'm and it stuck him to dat wall dere. He was twitching dere for a while after. And I'm telling you now, he's not de only wan, so dere you are now, if you want my number one you'll bring dat ting down to de depot and land it in on top of Skelly and tell dat bastard I'm no liart."'

All eating had now stopped. Dr Pat's Quilty lobster, O'Regan's stroganoff, and Lemass' sole bonne femme, the finest cuisine that Shannon airport's famed Grill Room could offer, perhaps the best in the whole West of Ireland, had to play second fiddle to Dom's vaudevillian recreation of a crazed oul' wan in a corporation flat. He filled his glass again as he continued.

'So what choice had I? If I chickened out I'd be no better than the blackguard Skelly, a decent conscientious God-fearing official, by the way, and she'd have the whole road turned agin' me, or, alternatively, with one hmmm… small gesture I could guarantee the votes of herself, her whole family, and probably all the neighbours for life.'

Dom paused, unable to resist basking for a second or two longer in the balmy warmth of An Taoiseach's admiring attention. Now was the time to get his message across, humorously, with a light touch, but loud and clear all the same.

'Well, rest assured, there is nothing I will not do for the Party. I said to the good lady, "You're a brave woman. I wish there were more like you and I will certainly see to it that your rodent problem is dealt with immediately." I turned to one of my lads and told him to get me a bag, quick. Then I went down on my hunkers, took a hanky out of my pocket and… I picked up the rat.'

He draped his white linen napkin over a hand and held it high above the dining table, the better to allow his audience to imagine the rat, held by the tail between finger and thumb. The men groaned and laughed and An Taoiseach even applauded as he threw himself back in his chair.

'Well, that's the best yet. Did you deliver it to Skelly?'

'I did not. That bag was flung over the nearest hedge as soon as we escaped. But the next day two corporation lads were around with rat poison to sort her out.'

An Taoiseach gave him a slow approving nodding wink. 'Good man.'

Dom glowed, lifted his glass, and drank deep. That look from Lemass made the whole day worthwhile.

'I love that story no matter how often I hear it. You're a gas man.'

Something in the way Dr Pat chuckled on, long after was necessary, nettled Dom. What did he mean by that? A gas man? Good for a laugh, but with no substance, was that what he was saying? Dom poured one more time.

'Go on, tell us another one. He has no end of stories, Seán.'

What did that bollocks think he was, a performing monkey? And this 'Seán' business, touching Lemass' sleeve like he had special access. Suddenly Dom preferred to drink than speak.

That was the moment he felt sick of the sound of his own voice. Instead, he heard a different one, Father Coveney's, in Clongowes, his words snapping in time with the crack of the ferula on either hand: 'Always has to be the funny fellah. Silence is never golden where our Dom is concerned is it?' Would this pathetic desire to entertain wreck his chances? Lemass might enjoy these stories but would he trust him with significant responsibility? Dom emptied his glass in one long gulp, shook his head, gestured at the food, and deliberately made his tone measured: 'No, no. No more stories, the dinner will be cold. And there are more important things for us to hear about.'

He turned his eyes to O'Regan. Now shut up, he pleaded to himself. Just shut up, and listen.

*

Until the screaming began, Ann had had such a relaxing day. The Men's Strand at Ballybunion was just gorgeous. It seemed to stretch for miles and felt so soft and luxurious under her feet.

It was worth any amount of scrimping and saving to enjoy this one week in the year. Having missed out last year, after she had Francis, it was especially welcome. This morning Ann and her sister Mona were on the strand by eleven o'clock, with Marian, Eva and little Francis. Fonsie had taken the older boys off for the day to give Ann a bit of a break. She and her sister spread out two old Foxford blankets, wedding presents that Mona didn't use much any more. They placed their bags at the corners to hold them down. The girls were dying to go in the water right away so Ann threw them their towels and togs. Mona barked at her Eva. 'Cover yourself properly now, do you hear me?'

'Yes, Mammy.'

Ann, who thought Eva was a lovely laughing well-behaved little girl, couldn't understand why Mona never let her be. If the wind lifted her towel for as much as a second the poor thing would get a slap. Honest to God, who'd be looking at a four-year-old in the few seconds it took for her to undress and put her togs on? Did her sister want to go back to the days when the Men's Strand really was for men only and women had to go to the Nun's Strand, which wasn't half as nice? It was too small and hemmed in by the cliffs. That whole idea of separating men and women was like something out of the Ark as far as Ann was concerned. They weren't really two different beaches anyway, just divided by a bit of headland sticking out, Castle Green, but when the tide was out anyone could stroll along the beach from one side to the other so what was the point? Mrs Brosnahan, up at the boarding-house, had told her how, when she was a young girl, the parish priest of the time, Monsignor O'Súileabheán, used to plant himself up on Castle Green near the old ruined watchtower with a pair of binoculars.

'I mean, had the man nothing else to be doing with himself? He'd know, to the minute, the exact time the tide would be out, do you understand me now Mrs Strong, and there he'd be, up above where everyone could see him and he could see them. Observing. I tell you, there was little enough in the way of comings and goings as long as he was on guard.'

Ridiculous, that's what it was. Eva had managed to wriggle into her togs without scandalising her mother. Ann volunteered to take her and Marian down to the water. Warning the girls not to splash her, she trod in to slightly above her ankles. As usual in Bally B, it was freezing. Marian, already in up to her waist, held Eva's hand and urged her mam in further. Ann stepped forward slowly, grimacing as her knees were splashed, then her thighs and, finally, as always happened, a surprise big wave wet her bathing-suit. Then she gave in, crouched down and splashed her face and upper arms. To cheers from the girls she finally lurched forward, lifted her legs and swam a few nervous yards, holding her face high away from the water until, again, one of those nasty sneaky waves crashed over her and she staggered up, spluttering. She trotted back to Mona and Francis.

'Oh, that was gorgeous! It's freezing first but once you get used to it, it's lovely.'

'Will I bring Francis down for a dip?'

Mona was a strong swimmer but Ann wasn't sure she could trust her with the child in the sea. It would be just like her to get distracted and start gossiping with other swimmers and completely forget that he was there. But, not able to think of any good excuse not to, Ann let them go. She sat up and watched like a hawk to make sure that nothing went wrong. Mona swung his tiny toes into the water, then she trickled a little on his head, then, hugging him to her chest, she began walking in, deeper and deeper, until the waves were splashing around both their necks. Then Mona lifted him high and plunged him down and lifted him high again. Jesus, Mary and Holy St Joseph! Ann's heart was in her mouth and it was all she could do not to run down screaming to rescue her baby, but she stopped herself because, even at that distance, she could tell, from the way Mona was behaving and the way the girls and some other children were dancing around them, and from what she could see of his little face, that Francis was enjoying it. He seemed to be laughing. The girls came haring up to Ann, calling did she see Francis swimming? Mona carried him out of the water and popped him down to let him crawl the rest of the way himself. He arrived covered in sand and making happy sounds.

At about one o'clock the picnic was laid out; a flask of tea, a small lemonade bottle with a cork in it full of milk, salad sandwiches and some plain scones. Mona had bought the ingredients and Ann had prepared everything. This arrangement suited both of them. Mona never had money troubles on account of her Seán's grand secure job in the gas company, and anyway she had no patience for cooking, even making a few sandwiches was beyond her. God knows what they would have ended up with if it had been left to her. Ann, of course, would try to pay Mona for her half of the ingredients. Mona would refuse. Ann would say she wouldn't eat any of it if Mona didn't take the money and Mona would tell her she didn't care, she wasn't taking a penny. And back and forth the sisters would argue until Ann finally gave in but had the last word. 'All right so, but I'll make it up to you some other way.'

The children loved the wet tangy sandwiches, with the salad cream and the juice from the tomatoes already soaked into the bread, and even ate most of the crusts. Mona only nibbled at a corner of one sandwich while resting on her elbow sipping tea and criticising other women on the beach. Ann spent almost all her time collecting Francis' bottle when he threw it away, wiping sand from the teat and persuading him to take it again. The sun stayed out, the Men's Strand was packed, and everyone seemed to be having a fine old time. It was days like this were the reason why Ann always made such a big thing about going away on some kind of a holiday every year, no matter how hard they had to save to get here. Between missing out last year on account of Francis and then moving into the new corporation house, which she didn't like as much as the old flat even though it was bigger and only around the corner, Ann was convinced that if they hadn't got away this year she would have just gone mad. She had to have this little break. As soon as they got back Ritchie would be starting in secondary school and they'd have to save for his school fees. Luckily the Christian Brothers were willing to take it in small instalments. The coal business was pure useless, with no money in it until October or November and then Fonsie would be out until all hours in the cold and wet. The state of him most nights when he got home. And what was the work doing to his back?

Watching Mona on her Grand Tour of the beach distracted Ann from worrying thoughts. She started laughing when her sister stopped to gossip happily with two young single girls, the same pair she had read from a height earlier about their hairdos, their taste in swimwear, the cheapness of their lipstick and the vulgarity of their nail varnish. By the time Mona returned to tell Ann that they seemed to be a right couple of loose ones looking to trap some man, it was time to go. Marian put on her saddest face and Eva copied her, but the breeze was wilder and colder now and clouds were getting the better of the sun, so there was no arguing really. Francis was popped into his pram and the girls trotted ahead as the long walk up the cliff path began.

Then the screaming started.

At first Ann was not that bothered. She had noticed recently that Francis seemed less and less at ease in the pram. It wasn't that he was too big for it, more like any kind of confinement at all seemed to upset him. She gave the pram a soothing jiggle as they pushed upwards. It didn't do a bit of good. Ann began to feel a little embarrassed as other holidaymakers, passing by, started looking at her. The screaming was very loud now and constant. The little devil didn't seem to need to take a breath. Ann stopped the pram and leaned forward, going, 'Shh… shh… shh, love,' as Mona touched her shoulder and repeated, 'He'll be grand, he'll be grand.' Francis' cries reached such a pitch he started to cough. Then he began again with a howl of anguish that brought Marian and Eva running back.

'Is Francis all right?'

Now Ann began to panic. She pushed the pram faster up the cliff path.

Suddenly people seemed to be deliberately blocking her way and staring at her. Where was Fonsie when she needed him? Mona called after her but Ann kept going faster and faster. She had to get him to the top, where she could lift him out and sit down somewhere and soothe him. Something! The screaming now sounded evil in her head, as if he was deliberately trying to get at her. What did he want? A hand landed on hers and stopped the pram. Mona had caught up. 'Take him out. He'll stop then.'

Maybe she was right. Ann unstrapped Francis and lifted him. She held him close and whispered. 'What is it, what is it love, shh now, shh!'

But it was no use. Absolutely no use. The screams speared her ear and the pain vibrated in her head. She didn't know if she was going mad or what but it actually sounded like his screaming was getting louder and louder. Was that possible? How could his lungs keep going? Why did he not burst? They weren't far from the top now. Maybe Fonsie would appear. She started running, moaning in Francis' ear.

'Oh stop it, Francis, will you please stop it!'

All she wanted now was to get that noise away from her. If only Fonsie would come and take him, then he could scream all he liked as far as she was concerned. At the top of the cliff the paths were crowded with families buying duileasc and periwinkles from two carts. Everyone turned to stare at Ann. She knew they were all wondering what was happening to that poor child. It was suddenly clear that there was only one thing to do. She would throw him over the cliff. Ann started to run towards the old ruined watchtower. If he didn't stop screaming by the time they got to the edge she would fling him over.

'Ann, Ann, what are you doing?'

Ann didn't look back, she kept on moving.

'Ann, Ann, Ann, give him to me. Here, give him here.'

Could she trust him with her sister? The sliver of common sense left to her recognised what a stupid thought that was. Ann slowed to let Mona catch up. The girls were further behind, pushing the pram. The screaming was indescribable. She pushed the demon into her sister's hands.

'Take him away. I can't cope. Get him away from me or I'll throw him over that cliff. I swear I will!'

Mona walked away quickly, the screams fading as she went further and further. Ann thought, oh thank God, thank God, feeling the comfort and freedom of her own arms clutched about her. She could still hear his cries, but far away now and mixed in with other cheerful holiday voices. Even the crashing of the waves below sounded soothing. What was she to do with the child, what was she supposed to do?

Suddenly, the screaming stopped entirely. Where had her sister taken him? Had they gone off somewhere? But when Ann looked around, there was Mona in full sight no more than fifty yards away, standing with the girls next to the periwinkle cart. Francis, smiling, was balancing on his own two feet and Mona was holding his hands up high. It looked for all the world like he was dancing.

pushing the plant. The screaming was louder than ever. She pushed the demon into her sister's hands.

1961

Four. December 31st

It wasn't night yet but it might as well have been. The unbroken grey of the sky made the countryside all round soggy, flat, dark and dead. The rain drizzled on and on. Nothing seemed to be moving on the landscape except for Fonsie's old lorry. He was doing great business today. Everyone wanted even more coal than usual after such a miserable wet Christmas. Already he'd had to go back to Tedcastles for a second load. If only he could get around faster, then he might get rid of the whole lot before the end of the day. He worked his way through his town customers at a great rate but out in the county the cottages were far apart, up long mucky lanes. He got stuck once or twice and had to ask the owners to come and help out with a push. His shoulders felt damp and his back ached, but his pockets were stuffed with notes and heavy with change. Everyone was glad to see Mr Strong with his lorry-load of fuel. In weather like this people liked nothing better than to cosy up to a blazing fire. Tonight, with everyone calling to each others' houses to say Happy New Year, it would help make the welcome special. At home around this time, Ann would be telling Ritchie to light the fire, so the back room would be lovely and warm for the party. Their first big do since moving to number 66. A few drinks, sandwiches, a bit of cake and a sing-song. Fonsie's thoughts couldn't be cheerier.

*

The sense that history was being made was palpable, evident in the expressions on faces, in the way people moved and gestured, perhaps most of all in the restraint and seriousness of everyone's speech; proper grammar studiously observed, sentence structure more complex and formal. Not so much as a mild obscenity had been heard all day. Even the floor managers were disconcertingly hushed and polite. Instead of the familiar booming pot-pourri of barked instructions and camp asides, there was a serenity of tone between production control and studio floor; all very businesslike. No one was dawdling. In the makeshift canteen set up in the Gresham Hotel's Tara Suite, crew members wolfed their tea and Club Milks and got straight back to work. Some even used the break for little informal meetings, sorting out last-minute glitches and anticipating potential problems. On this special day no one was a passenger, there were no slackers in the system, everyone seemed utterly committed to the cause, from the director-general down to… but such a phrase did not apply. There was no high or low, up or down, in Teilifís Éireann. Such notions belonged to the past. The convention established among the entire staff of the new television service was first names only and casual attire. Status was of no account, only the product mattered: the images revealed, the words spoken, the stories the nation would tell itself. There was a feeling that, at 7 p.m. on this New Year's Eve, the sixties would begin in Ireland. Only two years late – not bad by Irish standards, one producer had waggishly observed.

In the Gresham Hotel a production team was in rehearsal for Teilifís Éireann's first ever live programme, an outside broadcast to ring in the New Year.. Inevitably, the huge importance of the occasion was creating some tension. At this moment, in the production van, the director and the vision mixer were locked in heated whispered consultation; should they cut to presenter Éamon Andrews in mid-shot or close-up? Down on set, waiting calmly for a resolution, cameraman and crew leader Baz Malloy had loftier matters on his mind: 'We accept that a great painting or poem can bring about change, alter things irrevoceably, but we don't seem to believe that television can.'

His young camera team had grown used to musings of this sort from Baz during their training period. As usual, no one knew exactly how to respond. Young Joe on camera three made an effort.

'Wasn't there something, Baz, about Nixon losing the election last year on account of how he looked on television?'

Even though Baz smiled and nodded he somehow managed to convey that Joe was missing his point by a country mile.

'I believe so, but I was thinking more of the kind of relationship between Art and Life that Picasso had in mind when he replied to the Nazi officer who looked at his painting, *Guernica,* and asked, "Did you do this?" And Picasso fixed those fierce fierce eyes on the Nazi and replied, "No, you did." … Now, what did Picasso mean? That the Nazis had inspired the work of art or that the work of art had transcended their violence?' Baz paused for an answer. His camera crew knew the safest option was to nod knowingly. 'And when you think about television and society –'

'OK, camera two, get me a mid-shot on Éamon.'

The voice of the director, Ed Loebwitz, intruding on their headphones, denied Baz's crew the opportunity of hearing more of his thesis. Immediately they turned their attention back to live television.

'Camera three, coming to you next, stand by with the group shot.'

More than anything else, it was the remarkable voice of Ed Loebwitz, heard constantly 'down the cans', as the crew had learned to say, that reassured everyone involved that they really were making proper professional broadcast television. It was commanding, crisp, precise, assured, ironic, inspiring, decisive, badgering, bantering – with a timbre redolent of cigar smoke, hard liquor and layer upon layer of experience. Most significantly, amidst the cautious sing-song of Irish voices, he sounded American in that sidewalk-savvy, hard-boiled sense that inspired belief. Didn't Americans know all about making television? A Yank voice giving orders was, somehow, acceptable in a way an English voice could never have been. 'That would be too reminiscent of the yoke of oppression all over again' had been Baz Malloy's comment and for once his colleagues knew exactly what he meant. His trenchant view was that this new television service should be, above all, a joyous and confident expression of the independent Irish spirit.

It was precisely this prospect that had lured him, at twenty-five, back from exile. Training as a studio cameraman in Granada Television, he had listened long enough to English directorial voices down his cans, ex-army chaps who marshalled their crews as if on manoeuvres; all that briskness, clippedness and, to his Irish ears, sheer sneeriness. It wore Baz down in the end. Sincerely grateful though he was for the undoubted technical precision of the training he had received at the Manchester studios in the craft of television camera operation, Baz's spirit was languishing. The idea of returning home to witness, and perhaps even contribute to, what might be a transformative moment, brought tears to his eyes. Literally. Which, when it happened, had been vaguely embarrassing, though also, he told himself, quite beautiful in its small sudden way. He had shown Jarlath, the Galway barman in his Manchester local, the letter he was about to post enquiring about work in this new television service. Jarlath remarked that such a thing in Ireland, supposing it ever got going at all, would never pay as well as Granada, surely? It was while replying to this question that Baz had felt the uncontainable emotional surge. 'Do you know, I've no idea, Jarlath. I hadn't thought about that. It's more this instinct I have that something, possibly something extraordinary, might be about to happen. And it might make a difference. Imagine, you know, if –'

Baz had to stop speaking. He was overcome. Whether Jarlath noticed this, or not, was not evident from his next comment: 'If you ask me nothing'll ever change over in that fucken place.'

But Baz believed otherwise. He believed that in Life, as in Art, the tiniest adjustment sometimes made the decisive difference. He saw in his own craft how even a subtle crabbing movement could change the emphasis in a frame and, with it, the emotional resonance of the scene. In the choice between a high or low angle lay the expression of quite different world views. Why should sudden unlikely change not be possible, at least? And wouldn't those present to experience such moments become the fortunate few? So now, as Baz practised an intricate little tracking move on the slightly uncertain Gresham Hotel floor, he thought of poor old depressed Jarlath, and was glad that he hadn't allowed emigrant cynicism to deflect him. Despite the dodgy surface, Baz's camera flowed like honey and came to land perfectly on its mark.

'That was a doozie, Bazman. Can you repeat that when we go live?'

'Well, I'll make a good stab at it, Ed. It'll be a reasonable facsimile.'

'Jesus, can't you guys ever just say yes or no?'

'Did I ever tell you Ed, there's no word in Gaelic for either? We're wary of certainties.'

'OK, maestro, are we all happy bunnies?'

Gavin Bloom's voice intruded. It had the quality, very useful for a floor manager, of being able to impose itself effortlessly on any babble. Having timed his interruption precisely, he took control.

'Because, if we're thrilled to bits with item nine, we should crack on. Time and tide and so on, Ed, dearheart.'

There were some, including Gavin Bloom himself, who wondered by what miracle he had been chosen to floor-manage the first live broadcast ever in Ireland. Yet here he was, cool as all get out, cheekily hinting to Ed Loebwitz, his mentor, teacher, the God of his training course, the man who introduced him to the phrase, 'I don't want it good, I want it now,' that they just might need to get the fuck on with it, as Ed himself would say. Six months ago Gavin Bloom had been a trainee stage manager at the Gate Theatre. It was, as he often said in sly reference to the Gate's loudly proclaimed dedication to the spirit of Oscar Wilde, a position of no importance. Hilton Edwards himself had encouraged him to apply for this job in the new television service, promising to put a word in for him. 'My dear darling boy, you were created for this kind of work.' As so often with Hilton it was impossible to know whether his remark was intended as a compliment or an insult. He may have detected in Gavin talents which, he divined, only the singular challenges of television production could reveal, or it may have been just an easy way of getting rid of him from the Gate without appearing cruel.

'Of course I'm happy with item nine, Gavin. The question is, are you ready to rehearse item ten?'

From the moment he first put on a pair of headphones and heard Ed Loebwitz's masterful growl, something in Gavin Bloom's confused failed world began to make sense. As a badly paid, sometimes not paid at all, theatre dogsbody he had shocked himself, and many others, with the discovery that, at twenty-four, he was about to become a father, but had surprised nobody by his inability to offer much to mother and child beyond good intentions and perpetual apologies. But as he progressed through this training course in TV floor-management, everything seemed to change. When it ended he was offered a secure, responsible, permanent, well-paid, pensionable and much sought-after job in the new national television service. Of course the Gavin Bloom everyone knew would have very quickly found a way to destroy such good fortune but, luckily, he had already discovered something extraordinary. Whatever it was made the perfect floor manager, he had it. Friends wondered was it because he was a stickler for time-keeping and enjoyed acting the cissy. Although both these qualities were useful for the job, it was actually the aspect of his personality with which he was most uncomfortable that became his greatest asset in this new profession. Gavin Bloom always put himself forward; he loved being out in front, leading the charge, rousing others to action. As his mother always said, he was 'flamboyant'. But at the same time he was incapable of making decisions. He envied people like Hilton and Ed their insouciance, their outspoken self-belief. He could never run the whole operation as they did and yet he was too brash to lurk in the shadows. But in floor-management this defect, as he had always considered it, was actually a prize attribute. When a tetchy director bellowed down the cans, 'Tell him do it again and this time shove a grenade up his ass,' Gavin would relay the director's message in his own special way: 'He loved it, absolutely loved it. But it would make him even more ecstatic if he saw more of those gorgeous teeth of yours. More of the smile and more smile in the voice as well, dearheart.' Presenters and performers loved having him around. Directors trusted him. Gavin Bloom, young waster, fish out of water, hopeless parent, had found a home of sorts on the studio floor.

Perhaps if he were to pause, at this moment, on this particular day and look around at the large crew and the distinguished presenter and all those tables dressed for important guests and all the forbidding hardware that was part and parcel of a big television production and the terrifyingly long running order in his hand, a chunk of it as yet unrehearsed and then think of the viewing audience, all over the country, excited beyond logic, waiting to turn on their little box for the first time and experience what was, after all, the most dramatic event in Irish life since... Gavin searched for parallels: Ronnie Delaney won the gold in Melbourne, Michael Collins signed the Treaty, Pearse read out the Proclamation in 1916 – he was on a roll now – Brian Boru won the Battle of Clontarf! If Gavin were to pause and consider the extent of his role and responsibility in making all this come together, it might well be that the dizzy old queen act, which was such a part of his performance and his charm, would take over and send him scampering, screaming, from the set. That indeed might have been Gavin Bloom in the past. But, for whatever reason, it was no longer so. Right now, with the clock ticking relentlessly towards the 7 p.m. transmission time, and everyone on set awaiting the result of his little exchange with the director, Gavin just nodded calmly, ticked item nine on his running order, said, 'Check,' sashayed over to the podium area, the better to command attention, and waved a languid hand towards nothing in particular. 'Maestro Ed is happy. We're moving on. Rehearsing item ten, my darlings, positions please.'

And everyone set to work.

*

Mr Humphries had delivered six extra pan loaves. Ritchie was cutting and Marian was buttering. Ann had to keep telling her not to put too much on. By the looks of it there was going to be enough sandwiches to feed an army. She had bought four pounds of Galtee, two pounds of sliced corned beef and, for the men, a pound of sliced ham. Earlier on Bernadette arrived with a big tray piled high with sandwiches, and Una sent her eldest over with two bags of sandwiches done up in greaseproof paper. On top of all this, Fonsie's sister Marg Crowley had promised Ann that she'd make a few griddle cakes and bring them with her when she was coming. Gussie had been sent to Curtin's for salad cream. She hated buying anything from those robbers but what could she do at the last minute on a New Year's Eve? In the middle of it all Mona sailed in from town with a bought cake from Keane's and sat down with no notion of offering to help, but every intention of gossiping.

'The house is very quiet. Where's Francis?'

Ann deliberately kept on the move as she answered, 'He's over at Mary Storan's. She said she'd take him so I'd have a bit of peace to get everything ready for the party.'

The hint went right over Mona's head.

'Isn't she very good? Can she keep him quiet?'

'Oh sure, he's like an angel with her. Sorry, I haven't even time to make you a cup of tea Mona, I'm up to my eyes.'

'You're grand. Ritchie! Put the kettle on for your mother and me, would you?'

It was all Ann could do not to tell Mona that Ritchie was too busy to be making tea, but she would never speak like that to her sister in front of the children, so she bit her lip and continued pulling furniture around to try and create more space in the back room. One of the things about the new house that drove her mad was that the corporation had built them with three pokey rooms downstairs when they'd have been much better off with two decent-sized ones. None of them was big enough for a party crowd. As Ann dragged the big table into a corner, Mona relayed every detail of who she met on her procession around the town, what they were wearing and what was said. When Ritchie brought the tea, Ann said she was grand, tea was the last thing on her mind at that moment. Mona sat, enjoying hers. She complimented Ritchie and Marian on helping their mother and asked had Gussie dodged off as usual. Speak of the devil. They all heard Gussie before they saw him. 'Mam, Mam!' He ran in and slammed the salad cream on the table, breathless, but that didn't shut him up. 'You said no one around here had a television.' Gussie had been on and on at his mother about getting a television since he heard about the new Irish station starting up.

'Gussie, I've no time for you now.'

It seemed Gussie and his Aunt Mona had one thing in common at least – neither could take a hint. He talked on as if Ann had not spoken.

'Dwans have one, I just saw it.'

'How could you see it? They live in an upstairs flat.'

'Come here, look.'

'Gussie, I told you, I'm up to my eyes. I've no time for your antics.'

Gussie was already at the front door, looking out and pointing.

'No, look, just for a sec.'

Ritchie and Marian couldn't resist going to see whatever it was had Gussie so excited. Ann looked at Mona, who threw her eyes to heaven. She hadn't the slightest intention of budging from her chair.

'Ignore him, Ann. That's the only way.'

'He's right, Mam, c'mere, look.'

Now Ritchie seemed to be caught up in Gussie's excitement, Ann decided she'd better take a look. 'Get in out of the rain for God's sake.' They all crowded around the doorway and stretched their heads out. Ritchie and Gussie were gone so tall she had to push them out of her way to see what all the hysteria was about. She had no intention of getting wet herself so she only barely stuck her head out the door. Gussie pointed. Ann squinted.

'What am I supposed to be looking at?'

'Look at the Dwans' roof. See what's tied to the chimney?'

How could she have missed it, the size of it, rising high against the mucky sky? A big grey metal H.

'See. It's an aerial.'

'So?'

'So that means they have a television.'

'Just because they have an aerial doesn't mean they have a television.'

With that Ann walked away. She wasn't going to let Gussie get the better of her on this one.

'But that's stupid.'

'Don't be so cheeky to your mother.'

Ann knew Gussie would pay no attention to his aunt.

'Why would you have a television aerial if you didn't have a television?'

'To show off. Maybe they're just pretending they have a television.'

She had the rare satisfaction of shutting Gussie up. For about three seconds.

'I bet they rented one.'

Ann fixed him with one of her stares, the one that was supposed to warn him that she was very near the end of her patience.

'Gussie, I couldn't care less what the Dwans do or don't do. It's their own business.'

'Yeah, but you can get a Sobel T279 seventeen inch for only two and six a week.'

Where did the child get all this from? He was obsessed. The only way to put a stop to this nonsense was to give him something else to do, something that would get him out from under her feet.

'I've told you before Gussie, there'll be nothing ever rented in this house. Do you hear now? For the last time we're not renting any television. I don't care if the whole road has one. Don't take your coat off yet. I need more chairs. Mary Halpin said I could have a loan of some of hers.'

'Who's Mary Halpin?'

'Mary Storan, don't be smart, you know well who I'm talking about. Go and get them.'

To Ann's shock Gussie just said OK, and trotted off. No moaning.

'I don't know how you put up with him, Ann.'

Putting up with Mona was even harder, Ann thought. She wished she could get rid of her as fast.

Instead of going round the corner to Storan's, Gussie went to the green and stood outside the Dwans' flat looking up. His mam, without knowing it, had given him an idea how he might get to see their television. Was anyone home? It was nearly dark but there was still no light on in the Dwans' front room. Gussie was disappointed and unsure whether to give up or hang on a bit longer when, suddenly, out of the gloom, a strange glow lit up Mr Dwan's face at the window. He was leaning over something in the corner of the room. It wasn't like a lamp, it was a different kind of light, blue not yellow. Gussie knew that had to be from the television. It just had to be. He was sure he was right. He made up his mind, walked up the path and knocked on the Dwans' front door.

*

There was nothing Dom liked better than a bit of afternoon delight in a luxury hotel room. There was something stolen, dirty, about it that really got him going, even if it was within the bounds of marriage. Now, here he was, scarcely an hour afterwards, gratified, unwound, done up to the nines, in the lift gliding down to the Gresham Hotel foyer, his Beauty on his arm, she looking her incandescent best on what promised to be a night of nights. To look at them now, no one would ever guess what bould sweaty antics they had just been essaying. Dom would also happily lay out a hundred quid that none of the other distinguished assemblage here this evening had been getting their oats in the last few hours – the last few years for some of them. Certainly, none of his political colleagues, Government or Opposition, was married to anyone worth riding, as far as he was concerned. Of course a few of his Party associates were partial to a bit of whoring round, but only in the wee small hours when a load of drink gave them courage as well as the horn. Their efforts were never exactly *l'Affaire Française*; no waiter tapping discreetly at the hotel door, no shimmer of champagne in crystal flutes, no rustle of silk negligée draped on a chaise longue. More like a crotch rub in the kitchenette of a two-room flat in Phibsboro, beer spilt down a blouse, then pawed at in pretend apology. Occasionally Dom still envied his wayward pals the thrill of the chase, no matter how grubby and futile. Stepping out of the lift, he intercepted a passing waiter with a full tray and relieved him of a Power's Gold Label. First of the day. Bit of catching up to do. He opened his mouth and threw it in; gone. His Beauty was already smiling and waving at Charlie's wife. A plainer creature altogether but the boss's daughter, which seemed to have worked out well for Charlie. He was sitting pretty, four years younger than Dom and a Minister already, whereas he – too late Dom spotted where the bitter runaway train of his thoughts was headed but couldn't apply the brakes. Why could no day go by, no matter how richly filled with good things, without thinking about that meeting? Inevitably, bitterly, somewhere along the way, he would suffer a flashback. On bleaker days he spent hours brooding on it. Of course he knew the heart of the problem was rooted in his own expectations on that day, but knowing this didn't help in the slightest. He had swanned in to the meeting on such a high, having topped the poll in his own constituency. They were back in government; by the skin of their teeth, but who cared, as long as they made it. The call to come and speak to the Taoiseach surely meant only one thing. A cabinet post at last. It had to be. So naturally, having built himself up, as soon as he heard the words 'Parliamentary Secretary', he went cold inside. Not a ministry. He would not sit at weekly cabinet meetings. He could not be introduced as Minister on public occasions or be called Minister by all and sundry. It made it worse that, judging by the warmth in the Taoiseach's smile and voice, Dom could tell Lemass thought he was giving him a great leg up. Parliamentary Secretary was a very significant advance it seemed. He'd be number two in the Department of Finance. But I'm not in the fucking Jaysus cabinet! he wanted to scream at him.

Dom caught his Beauty's eye and her smile helped him slow the aggressive drumbeat of his heart. Enough dark thoughts. This was a great and important national occasion. Television would change everything. Not only was he convinced of that but, if truth be told, he had a strong notion that television would be good for him. Unlike most of the cabinet, he wouldn't look like a moron or sound like a gobshite in front of the cameras. Dom fancied he could charm the entire Nation just as he always charmed the local voters, or the cheering faithful at Party occasions. Imagine some of the older ministers, the likes of poor old MacEntee, sweating under the studio lights, or O'Moráin dribbling on in an accent that no one outside his home town could make head nor tail of. It would not take Lemass long to see the value of having men in cabinet who understood this television thing.

'What are you smirking at?' His Beauty pinched his arm.

'I'm not smirking, I'm smiling.'

'I'm looking at it, and I can assure you, it's a smirk.'

'I was just thinking that we are the most elegant, handsome and intriguing couple in the room. By a fair stretch.'

'Was that really what you were thinking?'

'More or less. Maybe not in those exact words. How are you fixed?'

He summoned a nearby waiter.

'I'm grand.'

Placing a friendly hand on the young lad's shoulder to prevent him dashing off, Dom took a Gold Label, knocked it back, popped the empty glass on the tray, and took another. He released his grip. 'You're a lifesaver.' Now he sipped. He was beginning to feel full of the joys. 'I was actually thinking, I'm looking forward to being interviewed on television.'

'And why not? You'll be in your element.'

Hands clapping and a high-pitched bossy voice silenced the crowd.

'Attention please, ladies and gentlemen. Attention please. Thank you. An Taoiseach, Mrs Lemass, Lord Mayor, Director-General, distinguished guests, welcome. My name is Gavin Bloom, and I am the floor manager for this evening's outside broadcast, and I'm afraid I'm going to have to be a bit of a bossy-boots and ask you all to take your seats immediately if not sooner because, as we all know, tonight's show, the first broadcast of our new national television service, Teilifís Éireann... yes, lovely, *bula bos,* thank you... is a live transmission. Oh, and just to warn you, don't be surprised if while we're on the air you see me flapping about giving all sorts of hand signals...'

Dom made a limp-wrist gesture, murmuring in his Beauty's ear, 'Mostly this one.' She slapped him softly and whispered out of the corner of her mouth.

'Stop it, you brat.'

'So don't worry about what I'm up to, or any of the rest of the crew. How and ever, I will occasionally need your full attention and co-operation. For example, when a guest is introduced, or when an item has concluded, our director might want an enthusiastic burst of applause, so you will see me mime like this and that means I want you all to give me a big hand.'

Dom smirked but his Beauty shushed him before he had a chance to make a comment.

'When you go into the function room please, *please* sit in your allocated place. It's most important that the director knows where to find you if he wants to get a shot of you, and I'm sure no one here tonight is camera-shy. Have a wonderful evening everyone.'

*

Mrs Dwan opened her door. She always had a nice smile.

'Hello Gussie.'

'Hello Mrs Dwan.'

Now that it came to it, Gussie was nervous. If his mam found out –

He tried to sound casual.

'My mam said to ask if you'd do us a favour. We're having a

party in the house tonight and she was wondering if she could borrow some chairs off you.'

The smile stayed on Mrs Dwan's face but she said nothing for a couple of seconds. 'Chairs? Ahm, hold on there a minute so.' She left the door open and went back up to the flat. That was no good to Gussie. He needed to get upstairs too. He didn't have the nerve to follow her up without being invited. Maybe he should just go away. But then Mr Dwan might come round to the house to find out what was going on. He heard whispering up on the landing. He couldn't hear any television sounds. Then Mr Dwan's head appeared.

'Come up, kid.'

Gussie nearly tripped himself in his anxiety to get up the stairs. Mrs Dwan wasn't to be seen. Mr Dwan smiled at him and turned towards the kitchen. 'So, you're looking for chairs.'

Gussie didn't follow. His eyes were glued to the front-room door which was only open a tiny bit. He couldn't see in the corner, and he still couldn't hear anything that sounded like television.

'There's these kitchen chairs if they're any use to you, we can let you have a lend of them all right, but you'll have to call back after tea because …'

Gussie pushed at the door with his foot and it creaked open enough for him to see a bit of Mrs Dwan sitting on a couch with their little boy whose name he couldn't remember. If he pushed it a small bit more. The door squeeked and then he realised that Mr Dwan had stopped talking. Gussie slowly turned his head. Mr Dwan was not smiling. 'What are you up to?' Gussie felt himself go red. He couldn't think of anything to say. Mr Dwan stepped nearer. Gussie backed away to the top of the stairs. Mr Dwan was now at the front-room door. As he looked in, Gussie thought, run, that's the only thing to do now. Then he saw Mr Dwan's face change. He was smiling again and it was a much bigger smile than before. He pushed the door open fully. 'Breda, I think Gussie here would like to have a look at the television set, is that all right?' He nodded to Gussie. 'Well, do you want to?' Still not sure if it was all a trick and Mr Dwan would give him a fong up the backside as soon as he got close, Gussie came forward. He went past Mr Dwan safely and stepped into the front room. There in the corner near the window was a Bush 21TG100. Wow! A twenty-one inch! But there was no programme on, just the same test picture he had seen in the shop. Mr Dwan read his mind. 'Nothing to see yet. It's not starting 'til seven o'clock tonight. Sorry about that. We have it on just to make sure the signal is all right.' Gussie was torn between disappointment and awe. A television, not in a shop but right there in a room. On their road. A twenty-one inch. Even if there was nothing on it yet, there would be later on tonight and every night from now on.

'So, the chairs. Do you want to go ask your mother if she still wants them? Don't worry if she's changed her mind.'

Sometimes Gussie was no fool. He got the message and he thought fair dues to Mr Dwan for letting him off. After he left the flat he took one last longing look at the blue glow in the corner of the Dwans' front room, before walking on through the rain to Mrs Storan's.

*

Seven p.m. Nationwide transmission had begun. The live broadcast would start later but first, the audience in the Gresham Hotel responded to Gavin's mimed invitation and looked at the monitors to see President Éamon de Valera deliver a pre-recorded welcome message. He sat in the library room of Áras an Úachtarán, his face angled slightly away from the camera lens. Behind the glasses his eyes blinked and shifted about. His voice was as precise as ever, but slower.

'I am privileged in being the first to address you on our new service, Teilifís Éireann. I hope the service will provide for you all sources of recreation and pleasure, but also information, instruction and knowledge...'

He stumbled a little and paused. It occurred to Dom that the whole country would be thinking how, on screen, in black and white, the old Chief looked ancient, from another time.

'I must admit that sometimes when I think of television and its immense power I feel somewhat afraid. Like atomic energy, it can be used for incalculable good but it can also do irreparable harm…'

Jesus Christ, Dom thought. Comparing television to the atomic bomb? That's the ticket Dev. Talk it up.

'… in the hands of man an instrument so powerful to influence the thoughts and actions of the multitude. It can build up the character of a whole people, inducing sturdiness and vigour and confidence. On the other hand, it can lead through demoralisation to decadence and dissolution…'

Dom looked around at all the silent attentive tables. Were others as impatient as he was with this tripe? For Christ's sake, was this a wedding or a wake? What fucking century did Dev think they were in, let alone what decade? He finished his drink but could see no one available to bring him another.

'Sometimes one hears, when one urges higher standards in information and recreation services, that we must give the people what they want… and competition unfortunately leads in the wrong direction and so standards become lower and lower.'

'Just like our mood, listening to this, ha?' Dom muttered, leaning in to his Beauty, who shushed him. She was right, he'd better behave himself. But honest to the sweet living Christ! could the old Chief not at least try and pretend he thought this television thing might be a good development for the Nation, some joy and entertainment for misfortunate people at least? Dom began to notice how poorly Dev related to the camera. As if he was avoiding its gaze. It made the old man look shifty.

'You, the people who will ultimately determine what the programmes on Teilifís Éireann are to be. If you insist on having presented to you the good and the true and the beautiful, you will get these. I find it hard to believe, for example, that the person who views the grandeurs of the heavens or the wonders of this marvellous mysterious world in which the good God has placed us will not find more pleasure in that than in viewing, for example, some squalid domest– ah domestic brawl or a street fight.'

Dev faltered. Dom wondered was the poor old goat forgetting his lines? Who wanted to hear about street brawls tonight? He knew no one could tell the Chief what to say but why hadn't the Party sent out someone to keep an eye on him while he recorded this? Drop a hint or two to keep it light and try and look as if he was enjoying himself, for the love and honour of Christ. This was a disaster. People tuning in all over the country, all excited and they get old Tiresias squinting out at them, prophesying doom? How much longer was he going to ramble on? Dom noticed that the shot suddenly changed to a new angle. He knew that meant they had stopped filming, moved the camera and started again.

'I have great hopes in this new service. I am confident that those who are in charge will do everything in their power to make it useful for the nation…'

Dom smiled. Ah, maybe someone did have a word in his ear. End on a high note please, Mr President, before the whole country switches off.

'… and they will bear in mind that we are an old nation and we have our own distinctive characterisics, and it is desirable that these will be preserved. I am sure that they will do their part and, as I have said, it is for the public now to do theirs. I wish all those who are in charge God speed. And I wish all of you a happy New Year. *Beannacht Dé againn.*'

As the old man faded to black, Gavin Bloom raised his hands high and mimed applause.

*

'Girls were made to love and kiss,

And who am I to interfere with this?'

His mam said he was only seven, of course he couldn't stay up for the party, so Martin Strong sat at the top of the stairs peeking down, trying not to be seen. The hall below him was packed, mostly with men smoking and drinking out of bottles. He recognised one of his uncle Seáns, and Mr Reidy from next door and Mr Storan, Mikey. His aunt Marg came out of the kitchen with a plate of sandwiches. Hands grabbed at them and the plate was empty in seconds.

'Am I ashamed to follow nature's way?

Shall I be blamed if God has made me gay?'

Someone in the back room was singing one of those stupid old songs. Martin couldn't see him from the top of the stairs. Through the smoke he spotted his Auntie Mona and his Auntie Una, and Mrs Storan, another of his Uncle Seáns and Mr Tuite, from three doors away and Uncle Peader Crowley and there was his mam with a big smile on her face, nodding her head and humming. Everyone was waving a glass or a bottle along with the song. Martin knew that Ritchie and Gussie had been let stay up for the party because they were old enough now but he couldn't see them. Nor his dad. The whole crowd in the back room joined in with the singer.

'I'm a man and kiss them when I can!'

Then everybody clapped and said, Good man, Josie. Beautiful Josie, beautiful. Your Noble Call. Martin still hadn't a clue who Josie was until he heard him talking.

'I call on – the woman of the house herself. Come on now Ann, we haven't heard from you yet tonight.'

It was Mr Benson from up the road. Martin wondered why he put on such a funny voice when he was singing.

'No, no, I'm grand here just joining in.'

'Go 'way ourra that now, you know the world of songs.'

Martin was worried about Mr Benson trying to make his mam sing when she didn't want to. Whenever she sang along with the radio it was only humming or la-la-la. What if she tried to sing a whole song now and couldn't remember the words? Would everyone laugh at her? Mrs Storan blew out a puff of smoke and poked his mam's arm.

'Do your Nelson Eddy and Jeanette MacDonald one.'

'From *Maytime*? God, can I remember it?'

'Go on Ann, sure we'll help you.'

'All right so. What's the first line again Fonsie?'

Martin heard his dad's small voice from somewhere inside the room.

'Ah... love is so sweet in the springtime.'

'That's it. You'll all have to help me now if I forget.'

And she began. Martin was really nervous now. He didn't want his mam to make a fool of herself.

'Ah love is so sweet in the springtime
When blossoms are fragrant in May
No years that are coming can bring time
To make me forget dear, this day.'

It was all right. His mam knew all the words. Every single one. She lifted her chin high and smiled and swayed her head along with the song. Martin never knew his mam could sound so soft or look so happy.

'I'll love you in life's gray December
The same as I love you today
My heart ever young will remember
The thrill it knew, that day in May.'

'Isn't your mother a lovely singer? She broke a few hearts with that voice when she was a young one.'

The man spoke in a whisper, but Martin got a big scare, because he was so lost in his mam's singing. He looked down. Standing below him in the hall, Mr Storan winked up. Mikey. He always had a big smile when he was drunk.

'Sweetheart, sweetheart, sweetheart.
Will you love me ever?'

'What are you doing up at this hour? Here cowboy, are you hungry?'

Mr Storan held up what was left of a sandwich he'd been eating. Martin reached down through the banisters and grabbed. Corned beef. Brilliant.

'Will you remember this day?
When we were happy in May.'

Mr Storan pointed towards the back room and put his fingers

to his lips. When his mam got to the last line of the song she lifted her hand and nodded to everyone to join in.

'Springtime. Lovetime. May.'

Someone went aahh and then there was a big cheer with Mrs Storan loudest of all. Martin would have cheered too but he didn't want to get caught.

'Your Noble Call, Ann.'

'Oh, let me see now.'

Ann looked around and saw her sister Bernadette's husband. Perfect.

'Seán Enright. Come on Seán.'

Ann picked Seán Enright because he knew every Percy French song there was and Percy French was always just the thing to liven up the party. She didn't want another slow song after hers, so she hoped her brother-in-law would do 'Phil the Fluther' or 'Eileen Óg' and get the whole crowd clapping along. Seán Enright lifted a finger, crouched and beamed around the room. He had beautiful teeth. He started quietly.

'You may talk of Columbus's sailing
Across the Atlantical sea…'

Ann was delighted. 'Are you right there, Michael?' was a great laugh. This would get everyone going.

'But he never tried to go railing
From Ennis as far as—'

Seán paused before the next word and everyone sang or shouted it.

'Kilkee!'

'You run for the train in the morning,
The excursion is starting at eight.
You're there when the guard gives the warning,
And there for an hour you'll wait.'

Ann looked around to make sure everyone had something to drink. She knew people would be raising their bottles as they joined in the chorus. Even Mikey Storan and Seán Durack, who were usually too busy drinking and smoking in some corner to take part in a sing-song, had stuck their heads in to listen. Fair dues to Seán Enright. Ann loved the way he had a kind of a twinkle in his eye that made everyone see the humour in the song. Now all the bottles and glasses were swaying in the air as the whole crowd sang.

'Are ye right there, Michael, are ye right?'

Mikey Storan went 'Whoo whoo' like a train whistle.

'Do you think that we'll be home before the night?
Ye've been so long in startin',
That ye couldn't say for certain
Still we might now, Michael,
So we might!'

Now Seán stopped and sighed and shook his head like there was some terrible thing about to happen. Before he even started again, people were already laughing.

'Kiiil-kee! Oh, ye'll never get near it,
You're in luck if the train brings you back.'

He was just brilliant, there was no one better to put over a song. The way he did the actions when he sang about the passengers pushing the train up the hill was so funny. And then he made his voice very deep. Going. Down. Slowly.

'For All The Way Home Is Dooowwwnnn-hill.
And as you're wobbling through the dark,
You'll hear someone make this remark.'

Ann saw Fonsie swaying, his whiskey glass in the air, with a big smile on his face. He looked so fresh and young when she made him dress up and he was properly washed. That coal dust drove her mad, it was so hard to get rid of entirely.

'Are ye right there, Michael? Are ye right?'

Now all the gang looking in from the hall roared, 'Whoo whoo!'

'Do you think that we'll be there before it's light?
Oh, it's all depending whether,
The oul' engine holds together,
But it might now, Michael,
So it might!'

Ann's 'Lovely, Seán' was nearly drowned out by the roars of approval and before the cheers died down another voice from the corner of the room burst into song without even waiting for the Noble Call.

'The flowers that bloom in the spring, tra-la,
Have nothing to do with the case.'

Ann couldn't see who the singer was through the crowd of bodies, but what matter. Everyone was joining in loudly on the tra-las. The party was really flying now.

'I've got to take under my wing, tra-la!
A most unattractive old thing, tra-la!'

Out in the hall Mikey Storan looked to see if Martin was still enjoying his sneaky peek from the top of the stairs. The little body was curled up, his cheek pressed against the banisters. Fast asleep. Mikey grinned. He stuck his head into the back room, caught the wife's eye, and gave her the nod to come out. Mary mouthed back, 'What? What?' Mikey gave her the nod again, bigger this time. She slipped out. No one noticed 'cause they were all going full belt.

'Tra-la lala la-ah. Tra-la lala la-ah, The flowers that bloom in the spring!'

Mikey pointed up the stairs. Mary looked.

'Ah sure, God help us. Better get him back to bed before Ann sees him.'

While Mikey lifted Martin gently so as not to wake him, Mary went ahead and opened the door of the boys' bedroom. She rolled back the blankets and once Mikey laid him down, she tucked him up. On the way out of the room. Mary stopped to look at Francis in his cot. 'And look at our little angel godchild. Can you believe he's sleeping through all this?'

'For once. Let's keep it that way, come on.'

They tiptoed out but in the dark of the landing Mikey suddenly pulled his wife close to him. Mary didn't protest and it was a few more minutes before they came downstairs. As she returned to her seat next to Ann, Úna Durack with the banshee voice was coming to the end of her party piece. Very slowly.

'For one… is my mother… God bless her… and love her,
And the other… is my-y… sweeeeet… heaaart.'

Ann, applauding politely, whispered to Mary, 'It's a pity, because she sings lovely when she's sober.' Úna Durack now spoke in her most official voice.

'My Noble Call is for my nephew Ritchie Strong, where is he? I have a special request for that beautiful song I heard you sing before. The one you learned in the scouts.'

'Oh, the little coon? That's gorgeous. Go on Ritchie.'

Ritchie had always liked singing although since his voice broke he wasn't so confident. He felt his face go a bit red with all the attention.

'Tell him to sing, Ann.' 'Ah, he's shy!' 'You've a lovely voice Ritchie.'

He looked to his mother, who was passing round a plate of corned beef and cheese sandwiches. Ann smiled and nodded. Ritchie decided to give it a go.

'Lilac trees a-blooming in the corner by the gate,
Mammy at the little cabin door,
Curly-headed pickaninny comin' home so late,
Cryin' 'cause his little heart is sore.
All the children playin' round
Have skin so white and fair,
None of them with him will ever play…'

The tune had a gentle lilt, and Ritchie sang it very sincerely. The thing he liked most about it was the way it always made people cry.

'Now honey, you stay in your own backyard,
Don't mind what dem white childs do…'

Already he could see tears starting to fill up in eyes all round the room. His mam was smiling at him, encouraging him. His voice sounded innocent and gentle.

'Every day the children as they passed old mammy's place,
Peeped inside the fence at night or noon,
Then one day they looked around but everything was still.

God had called away that little coon…'

In the scullery Marg Crowley listened to her nephew sing. She always liked helping out at parties, rinsing and drying plates and filling them with more sandwiches. She preferred to stay in the background and enjoy the sing-song without having to join in, because she hadn't a note in her head. Now she stopped to wipe tears from her eyes and went near the door to listen to the song more closely.

'What do you supposin' they's gonna give,
A black little coon like you?
Stay on this side of the highboard fence,
And honey don't cry so hard.
You can go out and play, as much as you may,
But stay in your own backyard.'

Marg Crowley was thinking what a sweet, kind, boy Ritchie was to learn a nice sad song like that when, to her horror, she heard her husband's name called.

'Peadar Crowley. Ritchie, call on your Uncle Peadar there.'

Oh God no, thought Marg. He's going to make a show of himself again, going on about coming from Cork. If he sang 'The Boys of Kilmichael' she'd die of embarrassment. Then she heard the fussy sing-song tones.

'As you know friends, I am a Corkman which, of course, is my good fortune.'

Marg resumed washing plates noisily but it was hard to drown out a voice as insistent as her Peadar's.

'But having been enchanted by an angel from your fair island city, I ended up living and working amongst you, so I suppose tonight I should commemorate one of your local heroes in song.'

He cleared his throat. The voice, precise and tedious in speech, was, in song, a ponderous bass.

''Twas on a dreary New Year's Eve.
As the shades of night came down.
A lorry-load of volunteers approached a border town…'

Immediately everyone joined in, apart from Fonsie Strong, who dropped his head so no one would see that, even though his hand was politely beating time on his knee, he wasn't singing the words.

'And the leader was a local man,
Seán South from Garryowen.'

Fonsie's sister Marg had never heard her husband perform this particular Republican rabble-rouser before. This was even worse than 'The Boys of Kilmichael' as far as she was concerned. Thank God her old mother hadn't felt up to coming tonight. She'd have been raging. Peadar Crowley paused and held up a warning hand to let everyone know there would not be a happy ending to this heroic tale. He slowed the tempo and his voice grew sad as the daring plan was foiled, Sten-guns roared and two men died. One was Seán South.

'They have gone to join that gallant band
Of Plunkett, Pearse, and Tone.
Another martyr for old Ireland.'

He gestured once more to invite the crowd to join in for the last line. They did so respectfully.

'Seán South from Garryowen.'

'*Maith an fear,* Peadar.' 'Up the republic!' 'Ya boy ya.'

Peadar waved for silence. He was by no means finished yet.

'Now I suppose yours truly can make a modest fist of a song when called upon. But, my friends, as regards true singing talent, I'd never place myself remotely in the same category as the man I'm about to call on now, because he is in a class of his own. A stalwart of the Cecilian Musical and Choral Society for many years, we are fortunate indeed to have him here tonight.'

Mary Storan nudged Ann. 'Oh Jesus, not Paddy Dundon.'

'I sincerely hope he will honour us with something from his repertoire. Perhaps a certain charming old Neapolitan love song that he has made his own. My Noble Call is to our great friend and compatriot, Paddy Dundon.'

There was no protestation, no false modesty. Paddy Dundon did not stand but simply acknowledged Peadar's call by raising a hand to quell the cheers of encouragement. Once silence had fallen, he sat forward on the edge of his chair, placing the palms of his hands on his knees. Eyes closed, head lowered, Paddy Dundon breathed in deeply. Most of the crowd were already familiar with his thin and nasal tenor.

'Catariiii, a-Catariiii,'

He jerked his head up, and it shook from side to side a little.

'How I adore you Catarì, my da-a-arling,
Although your heart is cold…'

He lifted both hands, making imploring fists.

'My Catarì, I love you so.'

The hands fell to his knees again as he sat back.

'Catariiì, Catariiì, my love you can't deride.
Life was sweet when you were by my side…'

The voice gradually softened, almost to the point of inaudibility, then returned at startling volume.

'Calling! I'm calling for you-oo!
My belov-ed, what can I do-oo?'

His spread his hands in supplication, and his lips shook.

'You break my heart
But still my love is only for you.'

His body seemed to sink a little as he allowed the note fade to silence.Those few who had never seen this performance at other parties now lifted their hands to applaud but even as the first clap sounded, Paddy Dundon's voice burst through, this time adding a crying tone, a tender leaf-thin tremulo.

'Catariiii, a-Catariiii'

Some of the younger lads stared at each other in disbelief. Gussie, making sure first that his dad wasn't looking in his direction, scrunched his face like a madman and mimed along. Ritchie had to look away to stop himself from laughing.

'Under the moon and stars beside the ocee-on
You said your love was ever mine.'

Once more Paddy Dundon let his voice sink towards silence but this time the crowd braced themselves, knowing what to expect and, sure enough, he delivered a heartrending howl.

'I'm caaalling! Caaaalling for you-oo!
My belov-ed, what can I do-oo?'

Then he stood, leaping almost from his chair, and stretched a hand towards some far-off place.

'Though we're apart,
My love is a-always for you-oooo.'

Paddy Dundon held the note as his head and body sagged. his right hand pressed to his breast. Then silence. He sank, with downcast eyes, back in his chair. Peadar Crowley led the applause which grew and grew, although it was hard to distinguish between the sincere ovation of the majority and the derisive whoops of a few smart lads. Mary Storan looked Ann with a smirk. 'There's no one else like him.' Her old pal knew exactly what she meant. When the crowd finally calmed down, Paddy Dundon abruptly pointed a finger in Fonsie's direction.

'My Noble Call is for the man of the house.'

Such a command could not be denied. Mikey Storan shouted from the hall.

'Go on Fonsie, your own song, "Alfonso Spagoni".'

Ann was thinking, what else would he sing, sure he only knew the one song? Accepting his fate, Alphonsus Strong, the shy host, sat up straight and half-sang half-talked his music-hall party-piece, 'The Spaniard Who Blighted My Life'.

'List to me while I tell you, of the Spaniard who blighted my life.
List to me while I tell you, of the man who stole my future wife.
It was at a bull fight that I met him. He was giving a daring display,
But when I went outside for some nuts and a programme,
The dirty dog stole her away. Oh yes! Oh yes!
The dirty dog stole her I guess.
When I catch Alfonso Spagoni, the toreador—'

Everyone roared. 'La-la laaaa! La-la laaa!'

'With a mighty strike I will dislocate his bally jaw.'

'La-la laaaa! La-la laaaa!'

Mikey and Mary Storan took to the floor, clicking their fingers and doing some kind of a Spanish dance, as everyone swayed and clapped along. The pair of them were such fun; Ann couldn't imagine having a party without Mary and Mikey. This was what she loved about these nights, everyone joining in, everyone with their own party piece and their own way of performing, old friends and neighbours of all ages, making their own fun with what little they had. Hadn't she met Fonsie at a do like this nearly twenty years ago? Surely there would always be sessions like this.

'Yes, when I catch Spagoni
He will wish that he'd never been born.
And for that special reason
My stiletto I fetched out of pawn.'

By now the whole party had crowded into the back room. The walls were ready to burst. What a great New Year's Eve. As Fonsie sang the chorus for the last time, everyone clapped to the beat.

'I'll find this bullfighter, I will – I will
And when I catch the bounder, the blighter I'll kill
He shall die! He shall die!'

Full-throated roars shook the new house.

'He shall die-didley-eye-die-die-die-die-die-die-die!'

'He shall die. He shall Diiiie!'

The crowd waited their moment, allowing Fonsie's featherlight tenor to hold cleanly on the high note. Every time he sang this song he had the same moment of memory, sitting on the coal-cart with his father, old Nell pulling them along slowly as usual, and his father smiling down at him lilting gently, 'die-diddley-I-die-die-die', and encouraging his little boy to join in.

'Ohhhhhh! I'll put a bunion on his Spanish onion, when I catch him bending tonight.'

'Olé!'

'Good man Fonsie.' 'I love that one.' Fonsie sat down, his shy smile wide.

stopped. Zing! The pair of them were [illegible] couldn't [illegible] having [illegible] and [illegible]. Flo were [illegible] about these [illegible] were the [illegible] old friends and neighbours of all ages, smiling, [illegible] little [illegible] had [illegible]

Yes, what fun [illegible]

[illegible]

[illegible]

By [illegible] the whole party had crowded into the back room and [illegible] were [illegible] for the [illegible] in the [illegible]

[illegible]

[illegible]

[illegible]

[illegible]

[illegible]

[illegible]

[illegible]

[illegible]

[illegible]

1962

Five: January 1st

Two hours into the new year, Gavin Bloom was wandering aimlessly around the packed function room. He felt oddly empty, disconnected from the party atmosphere, too exhausted to dance and too restless to sit and relax. In the midst of all this drunken happiness he felt somehow unnecessary. Perhaps that was why he was so quick to get involved when, wandering towards the bar, he saw a drunk man in a gorgeously tailored tuxedo swing a slow fist at Baz Malloy's chin.

Baz had been sitting near the bar with his young camera crew enjoying a few calm aftershow drinks. Because he was the only one who had ever worked on live television before, he felt particularly proud of what his boys, Joe, Murph, Mick and Eoin had achieved, especially when, after the broadcast ended, director Ed Loebwitz bestowed on them his most extravagant accolade: 'A clean show, guys.' Baz enjoyed the dry humour of the understatement even though he tended to be more lyrically inclined when describing the night's work. To witness a live television camera crew working in unison was, he said, to experience a silent ballet of great precision and beauty, whose artistry was all the more pure because the performance was unseen and unheralded by the viewing public. Its sole purpose was to make those in front of camera look good. The crew still slagged Baz whenever he spoke in these terms, but that only encouraged him to express himself even more hyperbolically. He was amusedly aware that when he first arrived back from Manchester many of his new colleagues in TÉ assumed, from his vocabulary and physical demeanour that he must be queer, but his technical virtuosity quickly won their respect; indeed, in the case of some young cameramen, awe bordering on adoration. Nothing pleased Baz more than the fact that, nearly two hours after the end of transmission, his younger colleagues were still consumed with the pride of their achievement. The crew relived the broadcast as a series of complex behind-the-scenes moves and adjustments, of minor mishaps, near disasters and triumphant details. There was the moment when fat Tommy, the cabler, had to go down on his stomach and wriggle along the floor so he could reach out and snatch away a cable before a disastrous collision with Eoin's camera pedestal. Even better was the moment when the boom mike nearly whacked Baz on the head as it panned round at speed. His camera was on-air at that moment and he was in the middle of a difficult pivot, so he didn't see it flying towards him, but luckily he spotted and correctly interpreted Gavin Bloom's frantic hand-warning just in time and somehow managed to duck down and pop back up without interrupting the flow of his camera move. The rest of the crew assured Baz that it was like something out of Buster Keaton. They were still laughing when the stranger spoke to them. He was dark eyed, wearing a monkey suit so expensive and well cut, it might have made him look elegant if he wasn't having so much trouble staying upright.

'Are you all right for a drink there, lads? Great job tonight. Have to hand it to you. Top class. The BBC couldn't have done it better. What'll you have?'

Baz answered for everyone. Decisively. 'No, we're fine.' The man in the stylish monkey suit pulled a wad of notes out of his pocket and gestured to the barman. 'Ah, come on, seriously, what'll you have?' Baz shook his head and raised an eye to the others. Did anyone know who this fellow was? He obviously felt himself important enough to issue compliments and buy drink. Someone from the Broadcasting Authority? Baz was taken by surprise when the man suddenly lurched towards him. His whiskey breath was now well in range.

'Here's my question. Will it change things, lads? Television I mean. 'Cause we have to get the fucken place moving, don't we?

And we're doing our best but, you know, it can't be left up to us to do everything, yeah? I mean, fair's fair.'

'We' and 'us' seemed to confirm that the man was someone of importance in Teilifís Éireann, but to Baz he was just an annoying drunk.

'You're right, fair's fair. All we want is to do the work and then be left in peace to enjoy a nice quiet drink. All right?'

The Drunk lurched closer, staring at Baz. Now, almost eyelash to eyelash, his breath was lacerating. Apart from feeling a touch nauseous, this was the first time it occurred to Baz that he might be in some kind of physical danger. Just as he saw the approaching fist, the man seemed to stumble backwards, and there was Gavin Bloom holding him by the shoulders and laughing.

'Mind yourself there.'

It was only after he dragged the man back that Gavin got a close look at the face and realised who he was. Having heard so many outrageous stories about Dom, especially where drink was involved, he knew, from the glitter of aggression still in his eyes, that a brawl was not yet out of the question. Baz and his boys looked like they might be up for it too. Gavin adopted his most jocular peacemaking tone.

'Lucky I caught you. Imagine if we had a distinguished member of the government doing himself an injury, tonight of all nights.'

He looked directly at Baz as he said 'member of the government'. Just to make sure his colleague got the message.

'I don't know if you had a chance to introduce yourself to our number one cameraman, Baz Molloy. I hate to embarrass him because he's very modest, but you should know Baz left a big job with Granada Television just to come back home and work with us.'

Gavin was relieved to see Dom attempt a smile.

'Oh. I see. One of our returned emigrants?'

'Exactly. Determined to help the Nation in its hour of need, aren't you Baz?'

Baz couldn't help being impressed at how quickly the Drunk could switch from street gutty to slurred but genial party host.

'Well, welcome home. There you go. You're proof my friend… proof that, thanks to our policies, the national landscape is changing. And now television will change things even more. You've probably seen this happen in England already.'

Knowing that the Drunk was an important politician only encouraged Baz to keep needling.

'That's true. Thanks to television everyone now knows what a terrible government they have and can't wait to get rid of them.'

The Drunk's answering chuckle was neither warm or sincere. Baz saw rage flash once more across his eyes and prepared to shield himself from a flying fist or even a head-butt. Instead, the Drunk's hand merely stretched out to pick up his whiskey and polish it off before replying in a self-consciously jokey tone.

'Ha ha, very good, yeah. Very nicely put. Touché. But you see, the point about that is, the Tories are mired in the past. They don't know how to use television. Unlike Kennedy, for example. He knows what it's all about. The political party that has someone who can shine on camera like Kennedy is the party that will own the future, aren't I right?'

'And would you be like Kennedy, by any chance?'

'We'll have to wait and see, won't we?'

Even though the answer was politely spoken Baz sensed he was just one sneering remark away from that head-butt. Or a kick in the balls. Gavin had the same feeling and interrupted quickly.

'Well, my colleagues and myself will always do our best to make everyone look good on camera.'

Dom smiled, stared, licked his upper lip slowly, then picked up a fresh drink.

'I look forward to that.'

After he lurched off. Gavin shook his head at Baz.

'That was very bold. You enjoyed giving him the lash, I could tell. Have you a notion how notorious he is?'

'Not a clue.'

'A brilliant man by all accounts, but desperate in drink. Oh, and look – see the divine creature he's after falling against? That's his missus. And the little lizardy fellah she's dancing with, now surely you know him – what?'

'As you said yourself, I'm a recently returned emigrant. These gombeen men mean nothing to me.'

'Ah well, to be fair now dearheart, these particular guys are a cut above gombeen men. They're more – oops! and down we go.'

Dom had keeled over.

Baz, a little repelled, couldn't help watching as the little lizard man and the divine woman tried to get the Drunk back on his feet. She grabbed him as if he was a bold child and started brushing his expensive suit with her free hand. He pulled away roughly, executed his own little *pas de chat* and fell again, laughing.

'So, that's the hope of the nation,' said Baz and went back to his pint.

*

Francis woke. It was not the noise of the party that woke him, nor Martin's little snores. Francis woke at some time every night. If they forgot to close up his cot he could climb out and trot into the other room and creep in between his mother and father. Sometimes they let him stay and he would wake there in the morning. Sometimes he heard his mother's voice tell his father to bring him back, and his father would carry him to his cot. On other nights when he woke, he would kick away the blankets, get to his knees, and then stand up, tall enough now to lean on the side of the cot. On these nights he just stood silently until his eyes got used to the dark and he could see what he already knew was there; two beds, the big bed with the shapes of Ritchie and Gussie, and the small bed with the shape of Martin. Sometimes he could see a face. He listened to his brothers breathing. He could stand looking and listening for a long time. This night, as soon as he woke, he knew it was different. It was dark, yes and he was in bed and Martin was in bed, but the big bed was empty. Where were his big brothers Ritchie and Gussie? He could see the sky outside. He could hear things outside as well. Francis knew a lot of words now, like 'bed', 'sleep', 'dark', 'night', but he didn't have words for what he heard now. He was still too young to say 'singing' or 'voices'. And 'bells', even though he heard them every day. Sometimes he imitated their sound – 'Bong!' There were so many words he didn't know yet. Every day he heard more and more and more from his mother and father and brothers and sisters and everyone. Then at night it all stopped. But not tonight. Why was that? Francis looked at Martin asleep and listened to all the cheerful voices singing outside. He didn't cry. He didn't mind being alone and silent. Listening.

1963

Six: November 20th

Michael Liston's facial expression was permanently sour and people found his manner unsympathetic but, as far as Dom was concerned, any man who'd suffered the tragedy of losing his wife in childbirth and had to bring up three kids on his own deserved to be cut a bit of slack if he wasn't always the life and soul. He wouldn't win many votes if he ever ran for election, but Dom found him a loyal and useful backroom boy. His advice was usually worth listening to and, right now, Dom needed a sensible, sympathetic ear. In his car, on their way to the meeting, Michael Liston didn't interrupt as Dom told him the whole story. Or, at least, as much of it as he could remember.

'You see the problem was, it wasn't me driving at all, really. My old friend Dummy had taken possession of the wheel, laughing probably, mad eyes on him. I swear Michael, the first thing I knew about it was when I recovered consciousness and found myself looking through a cracked windscreen at what appeared to be the inside of some class of a shop. Then I noticed a trickle of blood on my cheek but I wasn't feeling any pain. That came later. Oh Christ, yes! A migraine that made me want to chop my head off to get a bit of relief. But at that moment, no pain. Dummy. I'm thinking, what hole are you after landing me in this time? Now I should say that, as far as the shop and the damage was concerned, that was all sorted out the next day before I came home. I made sure to meet the owner personally, migraine or no migraine. One of God's gentlemen. He recognised me all right but, once he saw I was speaking to him very much from a kneeling position and waving a chequebook in his direction, he was more than happy to abandon any notion of causing trouble. It could happen to the best of us, was his fine broadminded Dubliner's view as I put my signature to the agreed figure. So that part is all grand. No complications there at all. No… my concern is more this little niggle I have in the back of my mind. I mean, it mightn't be a problem at all. It's just, as I say, a little niggle about my encounter with the Garda who arrived on the scene.'

Dom went silent as he tried again to recall exactly what had taken place. Michael Liston waited.

'You see, I can't really remember what was said. That's what worries me. If my Garda friend spoke to Dummy rather than Dom, Christ only knows what exchanges might have occurred, as they say. I've tried to recall, you know, what was the general atmosphere. Was it, you know, cordial or…'

Dom gestured helplessly. Michael supplied the euphemism.

'Strained?'

'Well, yes. The trouble is, something tells me it might have been. I think. Look, I can't be sure.'

'But you're not worried he'll bring charges?'

Dom laughed spontaneously at that. Michael joined in.

'Ah no, nothing like that. Just… you know the way word goes around. I'd prefer if Lemass didn't get to hear about the incident at all. Wouldn't look good, would it?'

'Should be easy enough to find out where this Garda is stationed up in Dublin and have a quiet word if need be. You want me to do that?'

This was exactly what Dom hoped Michael would say. Had it been a local Garda this would not be an issue, they wouldn't even be talking about it. The fact that it happened in Dublin was the only slightly unsettling element. Better if Michael took care of it. Dom nodded and left it at that. He was probably worrying unnecessarily.

This morning they were meeting a builder-man at the new Inter-Continental hotel, which had opened in the town just in time for the Kennedy visit a few months before. Dom didn't know the man but according to Michael he had a proposal that was bold and forward-thinking. Builder-man lived in Birmingham and intended travelling on the overnight ferry to Rosslare and then driving to the hotel. As they turned into the parking area Dom spotted a dark green Wolseley with English number plates and a dirty big Irish head behind the wheel. 'It that our man? Fill me in quick. What's his name again?'

'Gabriel Guiney. Emigrated from Annascaul in the forties and worked his way up from labourer to builder to sole director of Guiney Developments. Doing plenty of business in the Birmingham area. Lots of big housing contracts. Told me when he saw Lemass on the front cover of *Time* he figured maybe he should be taking a look at what was going on back home.'

'And he's one of our own, you say?'

'Well, he's been in England for twenty years but his late father was dyed-in-the-wool. Canvassed for Tom McEllistrim in North Kerry all his life.'

'Can't say fairer than that.'

As they got out of the car Michael suggested to Dom that Guiney might be more at ease if, instead of having the pow-wow in the busy hotel lobby where every dog and divil passing would notice them, he might talk more freely if they went for a stroll in the fresh air along the riverbank. A bit more discreet all round. When the suggestion was put to Guiney, a nod indicated that this idea was acceptable. Michael said he'd go for a pot of tea and leave them to it.

As soon as they reached the path along the river Dom tried to get the ball rolling with a bit of banter about Kerry football and was rewarded with another nod. His comments on British cars in general and Wolseleys in particular elicited no more than a couple of grunts. Dom, his heart beginning to thump out a warning rhythm, cast about frantically for any subject that might excite a response from the other man; emigration, the sights of London, showbands, building sites. Finally, when he heard himself rhapsodising about the beauty of the river on this unusually golden winter morning, Dom knew it was way past the time to shut up. He began to wonder if Guiney intended to make any verbal contribution at all to this encounter. He could not fathom why the man he was increasingly thinking of as 'this Kerry hoor' wanted to meet him if he wasn't going to open his mouth. His demeanour seemed typical of a certain breed of Irish emigrant. Years spent in the fleshpots of London, Birmingham and Manchester had not added so much as a whiff of urbanity to his stunted personality, but merely deepened and solidified his peasant spirit. Surely success in business and, from what Michael had whispered, considerable prosperity, ought to have taken some of the Kerry muck-savage out of the man? Apparently not. It hadn't even improved his dress sense, which had the look of a farm labourer uneasily encased in his Sunday best. If his three-litre Wolseley spoke of wealth it did so only in a wary whisper; a car that took care not to announce itself. No flash Jags or Bentleys for this son of Annascaul. Still, Dom respected Michael Liston's opinion and his impression was that the man had an ambitious plan to transform the landscape of the city in a way that could create a lot of jobs and homes for thousands of future grateful voters. Dom only wished the Kerry hoor would show some sign of getting down to business so that he could call a much-needed halt to his own babbling. He was getting a pain in his chest from the stress of it.

They had begun to run out of pathway. Only meadowgrass, reeds and water remained in front of them. The edge of the city. Beyond the marshlands, just out of sight, Shannon Airport. More than anything, right now Dom needed a drink which, given his recent misadventure, was probably not a good idea. It suddenly occurred to him that maybe that was why wily Michael had suggested the walk by the river. Was it his way of keeping Dom away from the temptations of the hotel bar?

Without warning, Guiney opened his mouth and spoke. Not a grunt or a mumble but full sentences which, to Dom's surprise, developed into quite a sustained monologue. Despite what seemed like conscious efforts on the part of the old emigrant to hammer his accent into some harder, flatter, duller shape, it retained a surprising amount of its natural Kerry music. The effect was curious: like a star tenor trying not to stand out in a chorus of amateurs.

'I've been coming back t'Annascaul all these years, since 1948, on account of my mother. She's still going strong, thank God, but there's little else would have brought me home, to be straight with you, until lately. I began to notice something in the air round about. We all know the Irishman has always craved his little house. There's been verses wrote about it, good and bad, which was of little consequence, seeing as no one could afford the purchase. Not in my growing-up years, anyway. But the last few of times I've come home, I heard some of the unlikeliest characters talking about owning their own house as if t'was a serious proposition.'

'That's no surprise to me at all. Things are changing here. And very fast.'

Guiney pointed.

'Over beyond there's fifty hectares of farmland, just at the city limits as they are presently constituted. I've looked it over carefully from every aspect. I know of no parcel of land better fit for the purpose hereabouts, or in Cork or Waterford or Galway, for that matter. Oh, I've looked. I can do houses, semi-detached, three bedrooms, garden front and rear, with every modern convenience you can think of, ten to an acre. Twelve hundred new homes at no more than three thousand and four hundred pounds each. All in. A young couple looking to get married or a young family would only need six hundred pound for a deposit and a twenty-year mortgage. They'd have a fine home with all the facilities of a modern city on one side of them and one of the most beautiful counties in Ireland on the other. The airport is only a stone's throw away if it's foreign holidays they're seeking or they want to greet a relative arriving from the States.'

It seemed like a much-practised speech. To Dom's experienced ear it had the rhythm of something written down and learned off by heart. Then Guiney made an observation that chimed with Dom's acute political radar.

'And of course, all the people working out beyond in Shannon would probably prefer to live here in the city, if they can get there and back easily. I believe there's already a scheme for a dual carriageway.'

Dom thought about twelve hundred brand new semi-ds, housing two thousand or more voters of the most satisfactory kind; happy prosperous ones with jobs and sprouting families. The Kerry hoor might be on the money after all. Give an Irishman a chance to own his own place, he'll jump at it. Three thousand and four? Not a bad price. If the man could do it. They'd sell all right. And more. In a few years there could be four or five thousand families with their own new house and garden in the city. Six hundred was a sum within the reach of a lot more people now as long as they felt secure in their jobs and were no longer afraid they might have to take the boat. Dom saw himself as a man who could give people that confidence. Before long they'd be returning to Ireland in droves, depending on how well Shannon developed. More jobs, more services. More income from rates and taxes.

He put a halt to his mind's mad gallop and looked at the Kerry hoor, who was silent again. Transmission over, apparently. Was he paid by the word or what? Dom presumed he was waiting for a response. The cute Kerry hoor had carefully prepared his little speech because he knew that, for a scheme as big as this, no other local politician was worth a bag of shite. Dom was the only man to talk to, the coming man, destined to be a government minister sooner rather than later. Without his say-so, there would be no re-zoning, no planning permission, no political support worth squat, no matter how good the idea was; not in this constituency anyway. The proposal needed careful thinking about.

'Well, you've certainly given me food for thought, Mr Guiney. Have you plans I can examine?'

'Of course I have. Detailed ones.'

The talking was done. As they walked back to the hotel parking area Dom now found the silence agreeable. This charmless man's big notion was growing on him. And, after all, he was one of their own. As good as. They shook hands without words, just a dignified manly nod, and parted. When Dom got back into his car he could see the question in Michael Liston's eyes and was tempted to tease him with a Guiney-like silence but he couldn't manage it.

'Well, Michael, I certainly wouldn't want him out knocking on doors canvassing for votes on my behalf but I think we should take a closer look at his plans.'

'I'll sort that out with him so.'

Michael Liston waddled over. He stayed talking longer than Dom expected. Suddenly Guiney seemed to be all chat. Then he pulled a bag from the back seat of his car and handed it over. When Michael came back to the car Dom noticed an ugly smirk on his face as he opened the bag to show what was inside. It was a bottle of duty free Black Bush.

'He thought you might like this. Bad timing on his part, ha? Although he wasn't to know about your recent little incident.'

Dom wouldn't have minded a capful all the same. Instead he just smirked back at Michael Liston as if drink was the last thing on his mind.

'Beware of cute Kerry hoors bearing gifts.'

'Indeed. A token, he says to me. You're right there, says I. Just a token.'

They both offered a non-committal salute in the direction of the Wolseley as it drove off. It occurred to Dom that if Guiney Developments was doing so well, the company might like to show its support for the Party in a more substantial way. When he said this to Michael. It was clear from his reply that he'd had the same thought.

'I think that's a definite possibility. And a fine idea.'

*

Francis wondered why his godmother, Auntie Mary, had collected him from school today. She wouldn't tell him. 'No reason,' she kept saying but her smile told him there was a reason. As soon as he turned the corner on his road and saw someone way up on the roof of his house he knew what was happening. That was his dad and they were putting the aerial up for the television. He pulled on Auntie Mary's hand but she wouldn't let go until they had crossed the road at the grotto. Then, laughing and coughing, with the cigarette still in her mouth, Mary watched him hare off like a mad thing. If he fell over now there'd be tears.

Francis could see his mam outside at the gate and hear her shouting up at his dad to make sure that the aerial was secure and wouldn't fall down on their heads if it got windy. Ritchie and Gussie were there too, holding the ladder steady. Why weren't they at school? Francis looked along the roofs at the line of aerials from his house to the next and the next. Now there was one on every roof in their row. Ever since Mrs Tuite at Number 69 had put one up ages ago, their house had been the only one without an aerial. It looked much better now. Even though none of the aerials was exactly the same, he liked the way there was a proper line of them with no gaps. The Bensons, one. The Reidys, two. His house, three. The McMahons, four. The Hacketts, five and the Tuites, six. The whole row.

'Mam, look at all the aerials in a row.'

'Shut up Francis. Ritchie, Gussie, are you holding that ladder steady for your father?'

'Yes, Mam.'

'There's a great view from up here, Ann. I can see the spire of the Redemptorists.'

Auntie Mary arrived, still laughing.

'Well, the questions started as soon as he saw me waiting for him and then the pulling and dragging for me to let go of him once he spotted Fonsie.'

'Oh, you were privileged. Sure he won't take my hand at all these days. He's gone too independent, that fellah. Did you behave yourself in school today? Fonsie! Will you come down, I'm nervous looking up at you.'

'No, Mam, he has to check the picture first to see if he's done it right.'

'Shut up Gussie. Fonsie! Do you have to do something with the television set?'

'Yes, but I can't be up here and down there at the same time.'

'Well, I'm not touching it.'

'Gussie, you know how to tune it in, don't you?'

Gussie knew everything about television. His mam asked could she trust him not to break it and his dad said again he couldn't be in two places at the one time, so unless someone else was going to climb up on the roof… Gussie was already gone inside. Francis followed him. Was he really going to see television on in his own house? Auntie Mary had a television but it was never turned on when he was there. She always said it was too early. His granny had no television. The only place he had ever seen television on was in the window of a shop called RTV Rentals, but his mam always dragged him past it, saying they were only robbers, charging five and six a week for the rest of their lives. Bernard McMahon from next door, who was four months older than Francis, said television was brilliant. There were American cowboy films with gunfights and funny cartoons, but he couldn't bring him in to show him 'cause his mam wouldn't let him 'cause it was only on at night. Television was something that got everyone all excited. Francis had never seen his family so excited. Ever since his mam told them all that she had saved up and bought a television, Ritchie and Gussie and Marian and Martin talked about nothing else. Especially Gussie. Television, television, television! He was like a mad lunatic about it. When it arrived yesterday in a big box, his mam warned them all not to touch it. Only she and Dad were allowed to go near it. If anything happened to that television they were not getting another one. His mam told them again that she had saved up sixty-two pounds and ten shillings to buy it because they wouldn't throw money away on rent like others were doing. Francis knew she meant the Reidys and the McMahons, who were renting. He knew as well, from the way she was talking, that sixty-two pounds and ten shillings was an awful lot of money. A bar of Cadbury's was 3d. So four bars was a shilling and there was twenty shillings in a pound… Francis stopped thinking about that because it was getting hard to add up in his head and anyway Gussie had turned on the television and he wanted to see what would happen next.

When his dad took it out of its box last night, it looked like a much bigger television than the ones he had seen in the shop. It was so heavy Ritchie had to help his dad lift it. His mam had cleared everything off the chest of drawers against the wall and they put the television on top. It was cream coloured and on the side there were knobs and buttons and near the bottom in a circle. Francis spelled, P-Y-E, with a big Y like a tree.

He heard Gussie say Pie, like a steak and kidney pie. That's how you said it, but what did it mean? Now Gussie was twisting the big round knob. The television made a noise and Francis saw jumpy lines. Gussie ran outside. Francis stayed looking at the television. In the glass part he could sort of see his own face looking back at him like a ghost. He could hear Gussie shouting.

'There's lines and it's hissing. What will I do now?'

Hissing. That's what the noise was called. Then Francis saw something change on the television. Now there was no hissing and the lines were different kinds of lines. Gussie ran in, looked, and ran out again, roaring.

'Nearly, it's nearly there.'

The television changed again and now there were no lines. There was a kind of a picture like a photo but it was just all shapes in grey and white and black with writing in the middle: 'T-E-I-L-I-F-Í-S É-I-R-E-A-N-N'. Francis knew the words because he had heard people say it over and over again. He could say it, 'Telefeesh A-ran'. Gussie ran in, shouted, 'Yes!!' and ran back out shouting, 'It's there, it's there.' Now his Mam and Ritchie and his Auntie Mary ran in too. His mam said, 'Don't touch it, leave it alone until your father sees it.'

'Well, Ann, at long last. You won't know yourself now with the telly. Listen, I'll leave you to it.'

Francis heard his godmother shout, 'Good luck Fonsie, well wear,' to his dad as he climbed down the ladder. He came in and looked at the television.

'Well. That seems to be fine.'

'Are you sure, Fonsie?'

'Well… that's the test card. I suppose we won't know for sure until the programmes start.'

'So what'll we do in the meantime? Turn it off or leave it on?'

His dad thought about this. Francis thought please, please leave it on.

'Well, if we leave it on it's using up electricity, but at the same time, we'll know it's working.'

'But I can't be keeping an eye on it all the time.'

'It'll be all right. No one will touch it, sure you won't? Gussie?'

'No, I won't. What would I want to touch it for?'

Mam seemed to be satisfied with that and just said, 'You'd better not,' as she went out to the scullery. Everyone else stayed staring at the television. Then Dad said he'd better get back to work. He told Ritchie to bring the ladder back to Mr Benson. When they were gone, Gussie sat on the couch. Francis sat next to him.

'What time does it start?'

'Six o'clock.'

They stared at the television. Francis had a lot of questions in his head. He was just going to ask what PYE meant when Gussie said, 'Do you know why that's called a test card?'

That was another question Francis wanted to ask.

'No, why?'

'It's a special card they made so you know your television is working. If you can't see the test card then there's something wrong and you have to get it fixed.'

'Where does television come from?'

'Donnybrook, Dublin 4.'

'Where's that?'

'Dublin, I said.'

'Where's that?'

'Oh shut up.'

Francis was sorry Gussie had told him to shut up. He liked it when his brother told him things. Gussie knew lots of funny things. He was the only one of his brothers who told him things. Francis stayed quiet, hoping Gussie would get in a better mood and start talking again. After a while he did.

'We have only one channel but in England and America they have loads of channels.'

Francis wanted to ask what a channel was but he was afraid that Gussie would get moody again so he just listened.

'And in America television is on all day. It's ridiculous, only starting at six o'clock.'

Francis knew that word. His mam often said 'don't be ridiculous'. He decided not to ask Gussie why television only started at six o'clock but it sounded ridiculous all right. He had to go to bed at eight o'clock, so that meant he'd only see it for two hours. They stared silently at the test card. Francis hoped his brother would speak again and tell him something else he didn't know.

*

'The task I am about to ask you to consider undertaking will, if you take it on, allow you a direct role in some of the most extraordinary changes taking place in our Church.'

Fr Mullaly was pleased with the impact of his opening salvo. He certainly had the full attention of his listener, a man who should be very much au fait with Church affairs and understand how the death of the former beloved Pope and the election and coronation of Paul VI had changed matters. While the new Pontiff had publicly signalled a continuation of the path envisioned by the gentle John XXIII, Fr Mullaly perceived in Paul VI a different kind of intelligence at work. Instead of the fulsome and generously innocent spirit of his predecessor, there was now a practical, subtle, administrative mind at the helm; a strategic mind. In Father Mullaly's view, this was exactly what was needed to enact with precision and clarity John's beautiful but somewhat unfocused vision. It was as if the Almighty, in His wisdom, had arranged it so. First, He offered his faithful a beatific breeze that blew away the cobwebs and dead wood of the nineteenth-century Church, then, at precisely the correct moment, He replaced that refreshing, invigorating but unsettling wind with calm; clear-eyed and efficient calm. If Father Mullaly had been pleased with how earlier events had helped change his fortunes, he was now convinced more than ever that the latest development was the harbinger of some further significant personal advance. Humility did not allow him to name, even to himself, what this might be, but he strongly sensed that God had placed him in this parish at this time for a reason. The first step, it seemed to Father Mullaly, was for him to be a practical advocate of the new dispensation, indeed to lead the way in enacting change. Though he had loved and revered John, he felt more of an intellectual bond with Paul and looked forward, with enthusiasm, to enabling and personally administering the important changes he knew were about to be decreed.

This was why he had requested a meeting with Mr Cormac Kiely, a man highly regarded by the devout laity of the diocese; a father of seven children with impeccable qualifications in his field. He seemed the ideal man to help Father Mullaly carry out his great plan. As the parish priest sat in a pew awaiting his visitor he surveyed the church interior, noting, not for the first time, how little there was to recommend it; drab and cheaply constructed to a dull formula, its fixtures and fittings were uniformly tasteless. For the last four years Father Mullaly had yearned to alter this and that, but another wiser instinct had warned him that piecemeal improvements were pointless and the achievement was always more impressive when the raw material was unpromising. So he had waited patiently, watching the great drama in Rome unfold. Now, he felt, was the moment to act.

Mr Cormac Kiely arrived precisely on time. Fr Mullaly noticed other immediately positive signs. Though the architect was older than the parish priest, his voice and handshake were diffident and respectful. He did not sit until invited to so do. By the time Father Mullaly began his prepared opening statement he was already confident that this was his man for the task. Sure enough, Mr Kiely's first response was not just supportive but perceptive.

'Of course any call to be of help to the Church is an honour. From what you have just said, would I be right in guessing that this task might be, in some way, connected with the work of Vatican II?'

Father Mullaly was impressed. That Mr Kiely had moved so quickly to the heart of what this meeting was about was inspiring. Clearly he did not resemble the general run of parishioners here at Our Lady of Consolation. This man's deference did not come from bovine docility but, rather, a deep appreciation of Church traditions and the inescapable logic of its hierarchical structures. Mr Cormac Kiely had clearly been following, in as much detail as an intelligent layman could, the profound work of Vatican II. He might even have heard mention of the document Father Mullaly now decided to name.

'Pope Paul is about to promulgate Sacrosanctum Concilium, the practical effect of which will be far-reaching, changing the experience of worship for, if I may so express it and very much between ourselves, Mr Kiely, even the most passively ignorant of our flock. If I may quote from memory a short passage which is particularly germane to our conversation today: "The rite of the Mass is to be revised in such a way… that devout and active participation by the faithful may be more easily achieved."'

Fr Mullaly saw that Cormac Kiely clearly understood the profound implications of the Pontiff's text.

'Father, are you saying it is really going to happen? In our lifetime? That we are actually talking about –'

He paused, looked at the altar and opened his palm towards it in what Father Mullaly interpreted as a graceful and reverential gesture.

'The priest facing the people?'

'That is exactly what I am talking about and, Mr Kiely, believe me, it will happen more quickly than any of us would have dared to prophesy. Which is why I ask you here today. I want you to design a refurbishment of this church, a refurbishment that will reflect, affirm and indeed celebrate the new dispensation. I want Our Lady of Consolation to be the first church in the diocese, perhaps in the country, to represent physically, archtecturally, the theological developments advanced by his late Holiness Pope John and about to be decreed by his successor, Paul. Do you think you are the man for the task?'

Mr Cormac Kiely said it would be an honour, and then delighted Father Mullaly even more by immediately asking quite a profound question.

'If the priest is now to face his congregation during the liturgy instead of turning his back as has been the practice for centuries, how will that alter the relationship between pastor and flock? Isn't there a danger that barriers might be broken down in a way that might not be appropriate or healthy?'

Cormac Kiely had cut right to the heart of the matter. There were subtle dangers involved in these profound changes. Father Mullaly was all too aware after fours years in charge of this parish that many of his flock had minimal education and only the most basic grasp of their religion. Pope Paul's proposals were of such consequence that ignorant people might misunderstand and possibly abuse the new dispensation. It was, he observed tactfully to Mr Kiely, up to those who understood better and more fully appreciated what was happening to guide their less-educated fellows very carefully. In this instance an architect might have to shoulder, if it was not too great a burden, a measure of theological responsibility. Father Mullaly's inclusive smile, as he spoke those words, was returned with warm understanding by Mr Kiely. They would get along very well together. Before leaving, the architect delicately broached a practical matter.

'In considering possible ways of doing this, Father, should I have a particular budget in mind? I have found that it is always better to know the financial restrictions from the beginning.'

Father Mullaly appreciated the question. He had given some thought to this himself.

'Well, of course we're not building St Peter's Basilica.'

Both men smiled.

'It is a refurbishment of a small parish church. However, neither is it merely repair work. Let us think of it as, first and foremost, a task of Divine significance and I will be emphasising this to my parishioners when the question of serious fundraising arises. Also it has been noticeable – I'm sure you have seen this in your part of town – that, over the last couple of years, the employment prospects of the men of the parish have greatly improved. Many now have more money in their pockets and my perception is that this situation is likely to continue and indeed improve further – would that be your view?'

'It certainly would, Father. I am of the strong opinion that our unfortunate little country may have finally turned a corner.'

'Exactly. So, to answer your question, we won't let budget considerations restrict more sacred priorities. I am confident that, in the context of their own increasing prosperity, the generosity of ordinary parishioners towards the important work of the Church will be all the greater. I certainly intend to make it so.'

*

It was dark by the time Marian Strong came home from school. She was thrilled to see the television turned on, but thought it was very funny that Gussie and Francis were just sitting staring at the test card like eejits. 'How long have you been waiting?' 'None of your stupid business,' was the only answer she got for her trouble. Marian told them that it didn't start until six o'clock and the Angelus would be the first thing on, she had seen it over in Pauline Cosgrave's. Gussie just said, 'Shut up will you!' Marian said that in Pauline's house they all knelt down for the Angelus. When Gussie shouted at her again, with an awful word this time, Marian turned and went straight out to the scullery and told her mam that Gussie had no manners and he was giving out to her for no reason. She was delighted that her mam went into the back room straight away and said, 'Leave Marian alone, you. Now, get some coal and light the fire.' Gussie marched through the scullery in a temper. Marian whispered as he went past, 'You're stupid, looking at the television when it's not even on.' Then she ran into the front room and slammed the door in case Gussie came after her.

Now Francis was on his own, waiting. How long more? From the front room he heard Gene Pitney on the record player. It was the only LP Marian had and she was always playing it. He thought about what he was going to see when the television started. He thought it might be like the pictures in his storybooks, only everyone would be moving and talking. He wished it would start. When was six o'clock? Gussie came back in with a bucketful of coal, lit the fire really fast and ran out to put the coal-bucket back in the shed.

Of course, as soon as he was gone it all started. First there was music and a different picture came up; a kind of a big cross and the words Teilifís Éireann again. Francis shouted, 'It's started, it's started!' His mam came in, calling everyone. Gene Pitney was turned off, Ritchie and Martin thumped down the stairs and Gussie rushed in, wiping his hands on his jumper. Francis heard a voice say: '*Teilifís Eireann anseo agaibh.*'

He knew this was Irish. He had started learning some words in school. Teilifís Éireann was Irish television. He also knew what '*anseo*' meant because when Miss Barrington called out his name at the start of school every day he had to say '*anseo*'. That meant 'here' or 'here I am'. So '*Teilifís Éireann anseo*' meant 'Irish television here'. But what about the other word that sounded like 'a-gwiv'? Francis didn't know what it meant, and there was no point in asking his mam because she'd just say 'shut up and don't be always asking questions'. Now the television had a picture of Holy Mary kneeling in front of an angel and a bell was ringing. His mother blessed herself. Everyone did the same. Then she started praying.

'The angel of the Lord declared unto Mary.'

All the family answered, except Francis: 'And she conceived of the Holy Ghost.'

The bell kept ringing. They all had their hands clasped and were staring at the picture on the television.

'Behold the handmaid of the Lord.'

Again, everyone except Francis knew what to answer. He was annoyed that he didn't know. Why had he never heard this prayer before? He thought he knew all the prayers.

'Be it done unto me according to Thy word.'

Then they said the Hail Mary. He knew that all right. Then his mam went down on one knee and stood back up.

'And the Word was made Flesh.'

'And dwelt among us.'

After another Hail Mary, his mam started to say a long bit on her own. She said it very fast so it was hard for Francis to understand all the words until near the end.

'... through the same Christ Our Lord. Amen. In the name of the Father and the Son and the Holy Ghost. Amen.'

They blessed themselves and at that exact second the bell stopped and the picture changed. Francis saw an old man with a serious face.

'Good evening. Here is the news, read by Charles Mitchell.'

Francis knew what news was. His mother was always saying it if she met someone or someone came to the house. 'Any news?' Then they would talk about people. His mam liked doing that, but not as much as his Aunt Mona, who knew everything about everyone. His dad said, 'Here comes the news of the world,' whenever he saw her walking up the road and his mam always laughed. Francis thought Charles Mitchell was like his Aunt Mona. He knew about loads of people. He said Pope Paul had spoken to a crowd in St Peter's Square. President Kennedy had made a speech. Francis remembered that President Kennedy was in Ireland ages ago before they went to Ballybunion on their holidays and before he started going to school. Some of the people

Charles Mitchell talked about had funny names. Francis liked the way they sounded. U Thant, Krus-choff, Mak-ar-ios, Athan… Athanag… agoros. The man whose name was really hard to say had a big black hat and huge grey beard. He looked like he was hundreds of years old. He looked older than Grandad Robert looked when Francis went in to see him dead. Charles Mitchell had a deep voice. He smiled when he said goodbye. His mam said, 'Hasn't he a beautiful speaking voice?'

Then a nice woman looked at them smiling and said that all the children would be happy now because the next programme was… and she said something that sounded like 'Daw-hee Locka'. Everyone stayed watching. Francis saw the words 'Daithí Lacha'. He knew Daithí was Irish for David because David McCarthy was in his class and Miss Barrington called him Daithí MacCárthaigh, but he didn't know what 'Lacha' was. The story was about a big duck who wore stripey underpants or maybe they were swimming togs. Was he Daithí Lacha? But he didn't move or speak. It was only like pictures in a book and a man's voice told the story in Irish so Francis didn't understand it. Gussie said it was stupid and his mam said if he didn't like it he didn't have to look at it.

After that a programme called *Bat Masterson* came on. Gussie said, 'Oh, this is a cowboy film, it's brilliant.' It started with music and words on the screen. B-A-T spelled Bat so Francis knew the other big word must be Masterson. Then he saw more words, STARRING GENE BARRY. He could say Gene because it was the same as Gene Pitney on the cover of Marian's LP but he didn't know what the other words were. There were cowboys riding around on horses. They were very mean to a poor old woman. Then Bat Masterson came. He looked different from everyone, not like a normal cowboy at all. He wore a shiny sparkly jacket and had a walking-stick that was gold on top. His hat was different too. The bad guys laughed at him. Francis thought they were going to kill him but Bat won in the end because he was clever and he could talk better than any of them, so he made fools of them. By the end Francis really liked Bat

Masterson. The best thing was that he was different from all the other cowboys.

His mam suddenly said, 'Oh my God, is that the time? Marian, lay the table for the tea.' She went out into the scullery but everyone else stayed watching the television. The next programme showed a bird in a hedge hopping from branch to branch. Then there was another bird. And another. A man's voice was talking in Irish. Francis couldn't understand him. Gussie said he hoped there was something better coming on after this stupid thing. His mam came in and said, 'I'm turning that off if you don't sit down and have your tea.' They all ran to the table and tried to grab chairs facing the television. Francis wasn't fast enough. he had to sit with his back to it. His mam said stop turning round, so he gobbled his bread and jam and drank his tea fast. Martin could look straight past Francis at the television and he kept saying things like. 'Oh wow, look at that. Oh Francis, you're missing it!'

'I'm finished now Mam, can I look?'

'Put your crockery in the sink first.'

Francis took his cup and saucer and plate and ran out to the scullery. When he came back, the nice woman was talking again.

'Now it's time for the lady who puts a smile on everyone's face. It's Lucille Ball in *I Love Lucy.* His mam was very happy when she heard this.

'Oh, Lucille Ball. I have to watch this. She's great. She's pure mad.'

His mam sat down on the couch and Francis sat next to her. She put her arm around him as the happy music started. STARRING LUCILLE BALL. It was the second time he saw the word STARRING. He wished he knew how to say it.

'I'll let you watch this so, but you're going to bed as soon as it's finished.'

Ritchie asked who was Lucille Ball and his mam said she used to be in loads of films years ago. A woman with fair hair opened her front door. Francis heard people clapping. She was holding a pair of shoes in her hands and came into a room. It was huge, bigger than their whole house. The woman went on tiptoe as if she didn't want anyone to know she was there. Now Francis heard people laughing but he couldn't see them. Then a man came in from the kitchen and said, 'Lucy,' and she jumped like she got a big fright. Now people were laughing and clapping. Where were all these people? Were they in the house too? Lucy and the man took no notice of the people laughing, they kept talking to each other. Francis couldn't really understand what they were talking about, but his mam and Gussie and Ritchie and Marian thought it was funny. Francis kept wondering who were all the people on the television laughing that he couldn't see. His mam squeezed his shoulder and said, 'Lucy is funny, isn't she?' Francis said yes.

Fonsie Strong heard laughter as he came in the door. When he looked into the back room he saw the strangest sight. The whole family was sitting together, all looking in his direction and laughing. Of course he quickly realised that he was standing next to the television.

'Fonsie, look who's on. Lucille Ball. She has her own programme.'

Fonsie couldn't sit down because he was filthy from work so he stood near the fireplace and watched. Lucy was in her kitchen opening the fridge. Francis asked, 'What's that?'

'A fridge.'

'What's a fridge?'

Fonsie thought to himself it was bad enough before, but now with the television there would be no end to the questions from that child.

'Shh, I'll tell you after.'

Francis knew his dad would forget. He said the word in his head so he would remember it. 'Fridge.' And 'a-gwiv'. He would ask Miss Barrington these words tomorrow.

Now Lucy dropped the bottle of milk and it went all over the floor and she started crying. She scrunched up her face and she sounded like a baby. Francis thought that was funny. Then the man came over to her and went shh shh like she was a little baby who wouldn't stop crying and that was funny too. Everyone was laughing now, his mam and dad and Ritchie and Gussie and Marian and Martin and all the people on the television that Francis couldn't see. Then the man said, 'Oh Lucy, it's no use crying over spilt milk,' and the people on the television roared laughing and started clapping. Francis didn't know why.

When the programme finished his mam said she was sick from laughing and his dad said, 'Very good, very nice.' Francis knew what his mam would say next but he hoped she wouldn't. 'Come on now, bed.' His dad went upstairs to wash himself as his mam pulled Francis towards the door. He said, 'Please Mam, can I stay up a small while?' But his mam said he'd seen more than enough for one night and his dad, climbing up the stairs, said the television would still be there tomorrow. Francis wanted to start crying but he knew that would only make his mam really angry and she might bring the television back to the shop and then everyone would blame him, so he didn't.

He had to wash his hands and face in the bath because his dad was at the sink. Francis liked the smell of Swarfega. He asked his dad could he have some but his dad said that he wasn't old enough or dirty enough. His dad was funny sometimes. Then his mam tucked him in and told him when he was five he could stay up later. 'When am I five?' His mam just said good night and turned off the light. After a small while Francis got up and crept out to the top of the stairs to peep down but the door of the back room was closed so he couldn't see the television. It wasn't fair. He went back to the bedroom. The words he didn't know the meaning of came into his head again: 'a-gwiv', 'fridge'. What was that other word he saw twice? He got his pencil and copybook out and tried to remember. He wrote down S-T-A-R-I-N-G and got back into bed. Just before he fell asleep he remembered another thing he had to ask Miss Barrington. Where is Dublin?

1964

Seven: May 28th

The officials had managed his entrance with marvellous ease. He had been guided expertly and discreetly to the podium, where he saw a hand stretch to shake his and then a face came close enough for him to make out the smiling features of the Speaker of the House. 'You are welcome, Mr President.' The Speaker then drew his hand expertly towards the Deputy Speaker, who took it and shook firmly. Then Éamon turned and reached out to find the lectern. Resting his clasped hands there gave him an anchor and he could be confident that he was positioned correctly for the microphones.

The reception from the distinguished audience was above and beyond. Éamon could not help but be flattered at the persistence of the ovation which went on for surely several minutes and seemed unlikely to abate until, eventually, the Speaker had to employ the gavel. Gratifying indeed, but it made him somewhat more apprehensive about what was to come. He would be speaking without notes. What use would they be to him after all? It helped his concentration to know that the Congressmen and Senators were seated in a wide semi-circle around him, even though, as he peered left and right, it was like viewing an image, almost washed of colour, through a rain-spattered screen.

As he received what he estimated was his third spontaneous round of applause, Éamon wondered how long he had been speaking. Surely it must be twenty minutes at least. He felt a little tired. There had been some stumbles and hesitations but he was satisfied that his voice had remained strong and, on the whole, he didn't think he had thus far forgotten anything of importance. But it was time perhaps to get to the heart of the matter. Not many Statesmen were honoured with an invitation to address the joint Houses of Congress. Éamon did not wish to outstay his generous welcome.

'An Irish poet, thinking some one hundred and twenty years ago of the role he would wish his nation to play, addressed her in these words:

"Oh Ireland be it thy high duty
To teach the world the might of moral beauty
And stamp God's image truly on the struggling soul."

President Kennedy…'

He knew this was the moment that everyone in the chamber was waiting for; to hear in what tone and context he would invoke the now-sacred name. Éamon had given a great deal of thought to this part of his speech, knowing it would be quoted in the *New York Times* and heard in newscasts the length and breadth of the nation.

'President Kennedy, in his address at Amherst College, thinking of the future that he would wish and that he foresaw for America, said he wished an America whose military strength would be matched by its moral strength, the moral strength of its people, its wealth by their wisdom, its power by their purpose, an America that would not be afraid of grace and beauty. An America in short, he said, that would win respect not merely because of its strength but because of its culture…'

Éamon thought of the cheering crowds as he drove with him down O'Connell Street barely a year ago, their hungry love for this graceful, cultured emigrant son. He had stood to acknowledge them, safe that day amongst his kin, waving and smiling his golden smile. Their aspiration, their future.

'… I am sure that that is the America that you would want, as it is the Ireland that we would want. But these things can only be secured by undeviating pursuit of the higher ideals that mean the full life of the people. I… Mr Speaker… I would like to confess and confess freely that this is an outstanding day in my own life. To see recognised as I have here, in full, the recognition of the rights of the Irish people and the independence of the Irish people in a way that was not at all possible forty-five years ago –'

The applause sounded heartfelt. Éamon waited until it had died before allowing one small, sentimental perhaps, but sincere, addition.

'I have longed to come back and say this to you.'

Eight: October 10th

Dom woke beside his Beauty on the morning after the worst day of his life. When he got back from Dublin late last night he had briefly entertained her with a lighthearted version of events. In his retelling the whole farrago might have been a court case straight out of Somerville and Ross. But it was not easy to hide his self-disgust so, pretending to be exhausted, he escaped to bed early. After a couple of Alka-Seltzers and a good night's sleep surely he would be Happy Dom again.

The most depressing thing was how little premonition he had had beforehand of how badly the thing would affect him. When the Chief Whip whispered word earlier this week that the date for the General Election had been decided so they needed to get this drunk-driving business out of way as quickly as possible, Dom said he couldn't agree more. Luckily, no journalist had got on to the story yet but this particular Garda was proving oddly impervious to all manner of persuasions. The Chief Whip wondered, was he a Blueshirt? Dom said he had no idea.

'Did you say something that really got up his nose?'

'I wish I could remember.'

'Maybe he's just one of these balubas you know, with a bit of a chip, delighted with himself at catching out a member of the government. Fellahs like him are dangerous to have in uniform. A good slap is what he needs.'

At that moment Dom couldn't have agreed more.

'Anyway, for whatever reason, the bollocks is determined to drag you into court. So it'll have to be done, one way or another.'

A couple of days later when Michael Liston explained the plan of action to him, Dom had laughed out loud. It was smart, it was brazen; a great stroke. He couldn't have come up with better himself. Soon this miserable business would be all over and he could concentrate on getting ready for the election. There was good news on that front. Michael Liston mentioned that an exceptionally large donation from an enthusiastic supporter, Guiney by name, had swollen Dom's election war chest. Perfect timing.

So, up to about half-four yesterday, the world was looking just fine and dandy; right up to the moment Dom looked Garda Drury in the eye. The bit of hugger-mugger, waiting in Liston's car a hundred yards from Green Street courthouse, had been a laugh. They watched the exodus at four o'clock. He recognised a few of the journos heading off for the weekend; casually strolling away from a front-page scoop. If they only knew. This was fun, the stuff of legend. Dom wondered who had come up with this wheeze. Surely not some Legion of Mary sourpuss in the Justice Department? Lemass himself? He must have given the go-ahead at least. At about four-fifteen, when the street was deserted and anyone who might make life difficult had gone home, Seamus Maguire, Senior Council and long-time Party stalwart, a thin man in a fat profession, came walking with intent towards Michael Liston's car. He slid in next to Dom. The gravity of his tone could not disguise his pleasure at the caper. He would allow a few months' grace and then begin to feature it as one of his prime after-dinner anecdotes.

'Are we ready for our ordeal?'

'Have I a choice?'

'Just so it's absolutely clear to you what is about to happen. This will be a normal court case in every sense. Justice will be done and seen to be done. The fact that it will be seen by rather fewer people than usual is accidental and incidental. We will enter a guilty plea and I will then invite you to grovel to the court. I presume you've prepared a short oration admitting egregious error of judgement, highlighting your generous financial reparation to the businessman concerned and expressing a sincere hope that you will never again have cause to appear on such a grievous charge, or indeed any charge.'

'Absolutely.'

'You will then submit to a vigorous tongue-lashing from his Honour just for the records. There'll be a fine. And then we all go for a drink. Clear?' Dom nodded. 'Let's go.'

Just six pairs of eyes gazed at Dom when he walked into the courtroom. His own solicitor Nestor, two court officials, the State legal team Finnegan and O'Donnell and, sitting behind them, a Garda. Not having met the man since the night of the car accident, which meant, in effect, that he had never met him at all, Dom hadn't a bull's notion what Garda Michael Drury looked like. This, presumably, was he. Not an obvious bitter old Blueshirt type. Younger than he expected, with strong green eyes in an open country face. No more than thirty. Dom felt the first twinge of unease. The emptiness of the press and public galleries began to seem odd, creepy. Maguire motioned him to sit and nodded to Finnegan, who nodded to one of the court officials, who opened a door behind the judge's podium and looked in. The official held it open for a few seconds, then the judge appeared. Dom did not recognise him nor, when his name was announced, did it mean anything to him. 'District Justice O'Murchú presiding.'

It all proceeded exactly as Maguire predicted. He stood and entered a plea of guilty on behalf of his client. Counsel for the State accepted the plea. Maguire said that his client would be very grateful for the opportunity to apologise for his lapse and put his sincere remorse on record. He craved the indulgence of the court in this matter. Justice O'Murchú graciously allowed him a short statement. Dom thanked the court and abased himself for several minutes, in a manner he thought abject enough to satisfy even a Presbyterian elder. Justice O'Murchú, a Catholic and an alcoholic, acknowledged the fulsome sincerity of Dom's contrition, while recoiling from the original lapse of judgement. He then enjoyed listening to himself deliver what Dom thought was, even by the standards of a district court judge, an extraordinarily sententious finger-wag. His thoughts drifted elsewhere. It occurred to him that proceedings were almost at an end and it was clear that Garda Drury would not even be asked to present his evidence. He, the only reason they were all present, was being ignored by everyone, even the State's legal team. Was he sitting back there regretting his hubris or burning with resentment at being outwitted? Dom could not resist the temptation to sneak a look. He casually adjusted his sitting position, shifting more to his left and crossing his legs. It now required only a slight, seemingly careless, turn of the head to bring his adversary into view. When he did this he got a little shock. Garda Drury was already looking at him and did not flinch or falter when their eyes met. In the couple of seconds Dom managed to hold his gaze before turning away, he read a particular emotion in those green eyes. He could even put a simple word on it: disappointment. And clearly he was the source of this disappointment. It had not occurred to Dom until now, but could it be that the young Garda had never had any malice, bitterness or animosity towards him? That he had done nothing more than follow the law, believing that Dom was the kind of decent proper man who would expect and want justice to take its normal course?

Now, the voices in the old high-ceilinged courtroom sounded hollow, its emptiness an accusation. Dom, who loved an audience, who prided himself on his ability to woo people to his side, had conspired to keep them away. Dom, the great debater, had allowed the contest to be fixed so that his only opponent was silenced. A shiver of what Dom recognised as shame made his heart sore.

Justice O'Murchú rose. They all stood. Court adjourned; case concluded. Dom hadn't even heard how much the fine was. Garda Drury was first to leave. Alone. Maguire seemed to relish what had just taken place.

'Excellent. Justice served, the media rabble outfoxed, and the boy in blue handed the dunce's cap, which, frankly, fitted him better than his own. Drinks, gentlemen? The Brazen Head?'

His Beauty stirred and opened her eyes. Her smile was

innocent, her yawn contented. She poked him in the ribs. 'Good, you're awake. I wouldn't mind breakfast in bed.' This suited Dom. It allowed him escape her loving gaze until he could persuade himself that he in any way deserved its comforting warmth.

*

Ritchie kept his eye fixed on the ball as number 8 moved into the penalty area. The tackle would have to be clean and perfectly timed. Ritchie slid in, felt the ball at his toe and poked it clear. Number 8 went over like he'd had the legs cut from under him, but Ritchie kept his cool, stayed on his feet, got to the ball first and had a quick glance round. Number 6 for Ballynanty Rovers was steaming towards him. Ritchie didn't think he could beat him, but he had just enough time to make a decent pass. It had to be either Tony Coughlan, far out on the left wing, his arm up, screaming, or dink it right to Frankie Horan standing in the centre circle. Ritchie could hear trainer Dick O'Dea roaring but there was no time to figure out what. He knew the simplest, neatest, most sensible thing to do. He leaned left, shaping to send the long ball to Tony. Sure enough, their number 6 was fooled. As he ran at Ritchie, he shifted slightly to block him on the left. Ritchie, with no need to look again, sidefooted the ball ten yards right onto Frankie Horan's toe. Off went Frankie on his bike and Ritchie jogged backwards to his defensive position. Job done for now. He heard a couple of admiring comments from some of the bystanders. 'Good lad, safe as houses.' 'Mr Dependable.' St Dominic Savio won the game 2–0, which put them into the under-sixteens semi-final. There was a lot of shouting and singing as they changed their clothes over at the railway wall. Kevin Finn, of course, acted like he'd won the game all on his own when he hadn't even scored a goal. Dick O'Dea went round tapping fellahs on the head and saying, 'You did the biz,' which was his favourite compliment. Ritchie said thanks to La-La Donohue who always minded the bundles of clothes for them during the games. Poor old La-La. Ritchie thought it was lousy the way some of the fellahs imitated him behind his back, even though Ritchie himself sometimes asked La-La particular questions that would make him say things that sounded funny because of his speech defect.

'What did you call the ref today, La-La?'

'Hi challed him a what whucker.'

La-La enjoyed people laughing when he said 'what whucker' because the poor fellah thought he was being funny, so Ritchie told himself that was OK. It wasn't being nasty like some of the other fellahs, imitating his drag leg and getting him to feel himself with his twisted arm and making dirty noises. That wasn't nice. Especially when La-La was so loyal to the club. He hadn't ever missed a Dominic Savio match. The only thing Ritchie didn't like about La-La was the way, once in a while, he'd stand too close, talking, while Ritchie was trying to get changed. There was an awful stink off him and it always made Ritchie think of how sweaty and smelly he must be after the match and how there was nowhere in Cals Park for players to wash. Also he sort of didn't like the way La-La seemed to stare at him sometimes as he took his shorts off. It wasn't only him, he did it with other players too. Some didn't stay as quiet as Ritchie about it.

'Jesus Christ, back away there La-La, what are you trying to do, pull my wire or what?'

If Dick heard any talk like that he always took La-La's side.

'Hey, enough of that now. Lay off. Laurence only wants to talk to you about the match.'

That's why Ritchie never shouted at La-La when it happened to him. Dick was in charge and he knew how to handle things. As far as Ritchie was concerned, if more people listened to Dick the team would be a whole lot better. Even though he'd played with all these lads since under-twelves he didn't pal around with them. His mam had warned him from the start, especially about some of the fellahs from Hogan Road, and she was right. Ritchie just liked to dress and get out of Cals Park fast after a match, so he could go home and have a wash. As he pulled himself over the wall and headed up the railway line he heard Dick shouting, 'Training Wednesday night, Strong-boy.'

Everything was going well for Ritchie just now. They won the match today, his inter-cert results had turned out a bit better than he expected and, best of all, when his gang went to the Stella last Saturday, the night after the results came out, he finally chatted up Gretta Lehane. Ritchie was surprised how it happened. They all got on the dancefloor together because Brendan Bowyer was going mad onstage as usual, singing 'Kiss Me Quick'. Next thing, there was Gretta, smiling right at him. Ritchie thought she was beautiful, with long black hair and dark eyes. Her whole face was really pretty but every time Ritchie thought about her in the last week he remembered that he hadn't been able to take his eyes off her tits. She was only fifteen but they were really perfect and, whatever kind of blouse she'd been wearing, they jigged up and down when she was dancing. Especially to Brendan Bowyer. Tonight all his gang was going to see *Kissin' Cousins* at the Savoy. Peter Malone told him that definitely Gretta Lehane would be there and he should ask her out, which was easy for someone like Peter to say. He could play lead guitar and he knew everything about every band and every record. He could say things like Brendan Bowyer's version of 'I Ran All the Way Home' was better than The Impalas' original. His father gave him money to have LPs and 45s posted over from America way before they came out here. He thought Manfred Mann was better than the Beatles. He said 'Do Wa Diddi' was the best single of the year and should have been number one. Peter was starting a band and wanted Ritchie to be the drummer but Ritchie hadn't a hope of being able to buy a drum kit. Even with his summer job, after he gave his wages to his mam he only got back enough to go to the Stella once a week and once to the pictures. If he had a girlfriend, he didn't know what he'd do. That made him even more nervous about Gretta Lehane. What if she let him kiss her? Or let him do more and then wanted to go out with him? Still, more than anything, he hoped she'd be at the pictures tonight.

The key was in the front door but the house was silent when Ritchie went in.

'Mam?' There was no answer but she must be around somewhere. Having a lie down maybe? His dad had probably taken Francis and Martin out with him because they drove her mad sometimes, especially when they were hanging around the house all day. If he went upstairs to wash himself he might disturb her. Ritchie stood in the hall listening, not knowing what to do next. Then he heard a distant voice. 'Great drying weather, isn't it?' Mrs Reidy from next door. Then he heard his mam's voice. 'Oh, you couldn't ask for better, thank God.' His mam sounded cheerful. Ritchie was relieved. He went to look out the back window at her taking down washing from the line. The sheets were shiny white in the sun and the wind wrapped them around her as she took the pegs off. Ritchie saw an envelope on the table addressed to him and he knew straight away from the logo in the corner that it was from Krups. He picked it up.

The letter had been opened.

Ritchie's anger was like what happened when he blushed. It rose in a second and there was nothing he could do to stop it. He heard his mam's voice chatting away to Mrs Reidy, happy as anything. He started to try and force himself to be calm, telling himself his mam had only opened the letter because she saw it was from Krups and she was just anxious to find out what it said. His mam only wanted what was best for him, that was all, and she was anxious to see him fixed up now that he was finished school. Ritchie managed to push away his anger and felt better again. He stared at the letter, afraid to open it.

Of all the interviews for apprenticeships he had gone to in the last couple of months, this was the one he most wanted. His mam kept going on about the Germans, how reliable they were and Krups was a very good name and they paid very well and they took care of their workers and it was perfect because the new factory was only ten minutes' walk from their house. On the form he had to choose which trade he was interested in. When he asked his dad about it his dad said, 'I don't know,' as usual, then said, 'Well, you're very careful about doing things the right way.

And you've a good eye. You're very precise about things. You like things to look proper.' Thinking about what his dad said, Ritchie began to think he might like to be a carpenter. But his mam said she didn't see what a company that made electrical goods would want with carpenters. 'What will they want plenty of?' she asked. Ritchie thought about this and put down 'machinist'. His mam said that was more sensible.

Mr Schneider, the German man who talked to him, was a football fan too and supported Shalke 04 because he grew up in that part of Germany. He shook Ritchie's hand and said they would write to him soon. Though his mam kept asking him afterwards, he hadn't a notion if he had a chance or not. Mr Schneider had said nothing that gave away anything. Not like MacNamara down at the joinery, who had kept saying, 'You're just the sort of youngfellah we need,' and 'I'd say we can fix you up all right.' Then Ritchie heard nothing for ages until his Aunt Mona told his mam that the son of a friend of MacNamara's had got the position. 'Sure that's how it works Ann. It's all pull.' At least Krups did what they promised. Today, four weeks after his interview, here was the letter. Ritchie was afraid to look at it. Now he saw his mam coming in with the basket of sheets. She looked really happy. So did that mean that it was good news? Ritchie knew there was nothing she wanted more than to see him settled in a good trade. So maybe it was good news? Now Ritchie was glad his mam had opened the letter. He could hear her in the scullery, humming. She sounded in great form. Next thing she came out into the hall.

'Jesus, Mary and Joseph! You're after giving me an awful fright. Why didn't you tell me you were home?'

Ritchie saw her look at the envelope in his hand. She couldn't keep the smile off her face. Ritchie was sure now it was good news.

'Well, did you read it?'

'Not yet.'

'Well, go on so.'

Ritchie felt annoyed again, for just a second, that his mam didn't even mention that she'd opened his letter, let alone apologise. Then he made himself forget about that. He pulled out the sheet of paper and opened it. The letter was only two sentences. It started 'Dear Mr Strong'. Ritchie had never been called Mr Strong before, except in a sarcastic way by some of his teachers.

> Dear Mr Strong,
> We wish to offer you a position as apprentice machinist beginning work on Monday Oct. 19th 1964. Please confirm by Wednesday Oct. 14th, at the latest, that you wish to accept the offer.

That was all. The signature was a squiggle but below was typed:

> M. Schneider
> Head of Personnel

Ritchie looked at his mam and he thought her eyes were a bit watery. Was she going to cry? He had never seen her crying.

'Now, love. Isn't that great news? All my prayers to St Joseph the worker. I told you. Krups! You won't do better than Krups.'

Then she reached out and hugged him. Ritchie thought this day was one of the best days. His mam smelled of washing. Then he got a whiff from under his arm. He needed to scrub himself really hard.

Afterwards, sitting on the side of the bed drying himself, he thought of something that made him feel even better. If he was starting work on Monday week, then he would get his first real pay packet the next Friday. He knew that, as an apprentice, it wouldn't be much, but it was guaranteed, every Friday as long as he did his work right and kept his job. And he would be paid more after a year and more the next year and so on and so on until he qualified in four years' time. It was nice knowing what was ahead. He opened a drawer in the dressing table and took out a small box. He got a key out of his pocket, opened the box and looked at the money inside; a pound note, a ten-shilling note and some silver. He took out a half crown. In case he got off with Gretta Lehane tonight.

1965

Nine: March 20th

Eyes never look old. Sitting deep in their ruffled bed of skin, the Taoiseach's eyes were as alert and knowing as when he was a twenty-year-old sitting in the first Dáil back in 1919. But, Dom thought, now there was greater wisdom, understanding. And sadness. The question he's just asked allows for no avoidance or circumlocution. The answer can only be I will or I won't. Dom accepted the Taoiseach was right to put it to him so clearly, of course. It had been coming a long time. Subtle hints had not worked.

Mea culpa, Boss.

Was it Lemass had sorted the court case? Dom would love to know. He'd never tell, of course, not even with the tiniest quiver of an eye or crinkle about the corner of the mouth would there be the slightest indication. Not even now with the two of them sitting securely alone. In a way it was the greatness of the man. That's why he loved him and wanted his forgiveness so much. The day he was born, Lemass was already out there fighting for Ireland's freedom. Dom would do anything to serve him. He wanted to shout at him, 'For Christ's, sake put me out in the front line. Please! I'll bite legs for you, by Jesus I will. I'll send those pampered Blueshirts limping back to the law library whining like wounded pups if you'd only give me the chance.' Of course, maybe Lemass would have done exactly that long ago if only Dom's drunken antics didn't keep preventing it. It was hard to explain that the man who got up to so much mischief wasn't really Dom, it was Dummy. Dummy, the dangerous lunatic who erupted out of him at certain moments when Dom was off his guard. Dummy caused all the serious trouble.

Lemass was an intelligent man, a subtle man. He hadn't spoken in generalisations, telling him to cop on or get his act together or prove his loyalty. No, he had just asked for this one specific thing. Promising the world was easy, promising faithfully to do one thing was hard. Could Dom honestly reply with a yes? Maybe there was a good side to the fact that he was being issued with an ultimatum right now at the start of the general election campaign. It meant the Taoiseach saw him as still in the game. If he was washing his hands of him, this meeting wouldn't be happening. The question wouldn't have been asked at all. Dom looked straight at Lemass, who seemed content to wait patiently for an answer. He desperately wanted to calm his brain and order his wild thoughts. Sometimes he wished he could just say out loud precisely what he meant.

'You're wondering, Taoiseach, can I answer yes truthfully? Truthfully, not just convincingly. Jesus, I can say it easily enough, but can I stick with it? Let me explain how things happen. The first few sips and the night is alive, the laughter is loud and the women are beautiful. Then, as I knock them back, a phantom hand flicks the switch and Dummy sidles up beside me, whispering, "Let's make mischief." If only I could control that switch. Why is it that as long as the last drink has done me no harm I think the next one won't either. Like in the Coffee Dock, when was it? Was it the night of Kennedy's funeral, that far back? I was flying it until Charlie pulled that PR one into the gents to try and ride her and left me trapped on my own with Hanley who, of course, insisted on telling me about his latest column. In detail. I ordered another round and played the usual little Hanley game, feeding his ego with bon mots and Dáil corridor gossip. More drink, more Hanley. Trapped on my own with a self-obsessed, self-important, self-righteous, self-loathing peasant intellectual, it really would have been no fault of mine if Dummy had made his appearance at this juncture. But somehow I just about stayed on the sunny side of the street. Hanley never realised how narrowly his fat nose had escaped the caress of my fist. Charlie finally returned and I'd love to able to describe to you, Taoiseach, the look of satiety on your son-in-law's lizard face, but that isn't what you want to hear from me right now, is it? And of course he had to gild the lily by spreading out his legs and adjusting the crotch of his trousers as he sat down as if to suggest that his mickey was so red raw he had to avoid the unpleasant sensation of mohair tickling it. It was only then that Hanley realised what shenanigans had just taken place in this classy Dublin 4 men's convenience. Well! The excitement of being in on this latest bit of ministerial scallywaggery as good as gave him a horn. He squealed like a tickled pig when Charlie ordered a bottle of Krug to be sent to the table of the Lady in Question. Even as I ordered something extra large I should have known that this would the one to send me off the deep end, but you see, that's the mystery of it. With the benefit of hindsight it all seems so obvious. Thinking about it now, Taoiseach, here in the solemnity of your office, with the spring sunlight warming me and those wise eyes coolly awaiting my reply, of course I know exactly what particular moment intermingled with what particular Jameson and ice to cry havoc. It was the gall of Charlie. It was the way he turned casually to Hanley, having picked up on the tiny part of the tail-end of a very long sentence that he happened to hear as he returned from his tryst, and then have the brass neck to *comment* on it, *opine* when he had not endured, as I had, Hanley's insufferable pontificating. Oh yes! That was the final straw. I drained my glass and there was Dummy, his arm on my shoulder, not yet roaring at this stage, just scanning impatiently for a waiter to supply his urgent needs and quietly enumerating all the things that got his goat. The dull look of satiated pleasure on Charlie's lizard puss, for one. Hanley's lumpen head, for two. Dummy considered whacking it into some more attractive or, at least, acceptable shape. Where the fuck was that waiter? Unfortunately the Abbey Actor who brushed against Dummy at that moment and made an amusingly cantankerous remark got his timing all wrong; not, by all accounts, for the first time. He didn't know what hit him, big an' all as he was. I realise now of course – hindsight again – that the unfortunate man was not to know that what had got up Dummy's nose had nothing to do with him at all. *Mea culpa. Mea culpa.* And another mess to be sorted out. I was surprised, to be honest, that the man remembered the incident the following morning. From my intermittant forays to the Abbey, it seemed to me the actor in question often had trouble remembering even his own lines. It stuck in my gullet that they had to get that sanctimonious old Presbyterian prick Blythe to intercede on my behalf. Was your hand in that too, Taoiseach? I really wanted to say nay to that, but what are called wiser councils prevailed. To be fair, it wasn't that big of a settlement in the end but I accept that if I'd said sorry at the time and bought the old ham a drink it would have been a lot cheaper. My fault again, sir.'

Dom steadied his thoughts, hoping that his silence hadn't become embarrassing. How long had it been since Lemass asked the hard question? Only seconds, hopefully. Dom did not want to seem hesitant. He wanted his answer to sound determined and sincere.

'I will do it, Taoiseach. I will stop drinking. Entirely.'

*

It was eight o'clock and, though still not quite dark, there were no children playing on the green or anywhere on Rowan Avenue, which was very unusual for a Saturday evening. There were no mothers out chatting. Even Mrs Canty was not leaning out of the window of her upstairs flat surveying the goings-on below and calling out greetings to any of her neighbours who passed by. The street and the green were empty and silent. Everyone was inside watching television. The Eurovision Song Contest was on.

Fonsie liked the fanfare that began the programme and thought the trumpets' tone was very pure and uplifting. When the presenter came out, smiling, Ann said she was a lovely looking girl but why had she cut her hair so short and that necklace was just ridiculous, much too old for her. The presenter said welcome to Naples in three different languages. Ritchie thought she had a really sexy voice. Gussie thought it must be because the programme was transmitted live by satellite that she sounded so crackly and far away. Marian was already starting to feel nervous for Butch Moore. Did he know the whole of Ireland was waiting to hear him sing? Marian would just die if she had to do that. Martin laid his head happily on his mam's shoulder. He loved it when the whole family sat down together like this to watch television. It was like a party. Francis sat on the floor at the end of the couch, half hiding behind Ritchie's legs. He did this because he thought if he kept out of the way and said nothing, his dad might forget that he was only allowed stay up until after the Irish song.

Ann said the presenter had a beautiful speaking voice, and she must be very well educated, the way she could switch from her own language to English or French without even thinking about it. Listening to her talk about the huge television audience, not only in the eighteen countries taking part, but in other places too, Fonsie suddenly felt very proud that Ireland was involved and that, by sitting down together, the whole family was part of this big occasion. He hoped that Butch Moore wouldn't let them down. Ann seemed to read his mind.

'I hope Butch doesn't get too nervous.'

Marian leapt to Butch's defence, remembering something she had read in *New Spotlight* magazine.

'Of course he won't. He's always really relaxed and smiling and friendly.'

'I'd say we'll come last.'

Fonsie wondered why Gussie always had to try and cause a row. Marian would be better off ignoring him instead of rising to the bait.

'We won't come last.'

'Well, we'll see.'

'Yes, we'll see.'

'Remember who said it first, when it happens.'

'Except it won't happen.'

Marian hadn't really been a fan of Butch Moore until recently. Even now, if she had to choose, she would have to admit that Gene Pitney was still her favourite. But Gene wasn't Irish and he wasn't Ireland's first ever representative in the Eurovision Song Contest and Butch Moore really was good looking and his smile was lovely and the more often Marian heard his song, the more she liked it.

The presenter said that the order of singers had been decided by drawing the names out of a hat and Ireland was fourth. That made Francis very sad. He knew now that if his dad really made him go to bed straight after Butch Moore, then he would miss most of the contest. When the first singer was introduced Martin asked where was the Netherlands and Ritchie told him it was where Holland was. Francis wanted to ask how could Holland and Netherlands both be in the same place but then he remembered to say nothing and not draw any attention to himself. The British song came after the Netherlands. Everyone knew it already from the radio. Ann said Kathy Kirby had a very powerful voice and it was a good catchy song. It might be a winner. Then came another female singer from Spain called Conchita. She was very dramatic and did a little dance as she sang but none of the family thought she had much of a chance. And suddenly the moment arrived; Ireland was next. Fonsie liked how, for each country, the presenter introduced the conductor of the orchestra as well as the singer. He thought that showed proper respect for the musicians. He was surprised when he heard the name of the conductor for Ireland. Ann looked surprised too.

'Who's Gianni Ferrio, Fonsie?'

'I don't know, it sounds like an Italian name. Well, I'm sure he'll do a good job, Italians have a great musical tradition.'

When the presenter said, '"Walking the Streets in the Rain", *canta* Butch Moore!' and he walked out onto the stage smiling and looking as cool as anything, Marian felt her heart race. The dramatic piano chords and drumroll that began the song had a similar effect on everyone else. If hearts could be heard, their combined beating would have drowned out Butch and the entire orchestra.

For the next three minutes the Strong family shared silently the same fretful hope: that their fellow Irishman would survive his ordeal. Each found their own special reason to wish him success.

Ritchie's was the simplest. Butch Moore was Irish, that's all there was to it. It was true that when Butch and his showband performed at the Stella a couple of months back neither Ritchie nor Peter Malone nor any of his friends had bothered to go see him, but that was different. Now he was far away, in another country, singing for Ireland, so of course everyone should be cheering for him.

Gussie would give anything to do what Butch Moore was doing right now – being on television performing in front of millions of people. Or, even better, he imagined himself operating one of the cameras, steering it around the studio looking for the best shots, or one of those people with headphones giving signals, making sure everything was perfect because it was live and if something went wrong everyone would be laughing at them, thinking they were eejits.

Marian was afraid she was going to be sick, she was so nervous for Butch. She had to stop herself letting out a little cry when, as he sang sadly about the tears of the rain falling, it seemed to Marian that he turned and looked straight at her. She loved the way he patted his hand on his thigh in time with the music. That was really sweet.

Fonsie was happy that Butch Moore was singing so confidently but he wished he'd stop tapping his hand on his thigh like that. It made him look like he couldn't keep a proper beat. 'Walking the Streets in the Rain' wasn't really Fonsie's sort of song but the orchestration was very good. Maybe, maybe it would do well. People liked sad ballads.

Martin didn't like the song, even more so because his stupid sister looked like she was going to burst out crying listening to it, but he still hoped Ireland would win because everyone would be happy then, his mam especially.

Ann liked everything about Butch Moore. He seemed to be a very well brought-up young man, his hair was neat, he didn't act like he was full of himself, he had a lovely smile and his voice was very pleasant. Francis was hardly listening to the song at all because he was getting more and more nervous. Was he really going to be sent to bed after this? He wanted to see the rest of the show more than anything.

When the song ended and the audience applauded, Ritchie and Marian and Martin and even Gussie all cheered but Francis just hid himself at the side of the couch praying that, with all the excitement, his dad would forget he was there. The German song was next but nobody paid any attention because everyone, except Francis, was talking about how good Butch Moore had been, how he didn't look a bit nervous and he had hit all the high notes perfectly. Austria, Norway, Belgium and Monaco followed. Half the countries had performed and Francis still hadn't been sent to bed. He kept looking at the clock on the fireplace. It was nearly ten past nine. He had never been up so late before. It wasn't so much the songs he liked listening to as all the different languages and wondering how they came to be. It was easy to work out why French people called Ireland *Irlande* but why did they call Britain *Royaume Uni*? Or why did the Italians call a singer *canta* or a conductor *maestro*? Francis thought *maestro* sounded much better than conductor.

It was Sweden that caused all the trouble. When the singer was introduced Francis liked the sound of his name, Ingvar Wixell, but he turned out to be a fat old man going bald who sounded more like the singers on his dad's old opera records. Francis thought the song was awful. When he noticed that Martin had fallen asleep against his mam's shoulder he thought of a funny thing: that it must have been the old bald man's voice that put him to sleep. Just as the song ended and his dad was saying that Ingvar Wixell was easily the best singer so far, his mam, smiling, spoke very quietly. 'Fonsie, look at this. Fast asleep.' As his dad stood up and went to lift Martin, Gussie said the same funny thing that Francis had already thought.

'I'm not surprised he's asleep after that boring song.'

Francis laughed. His dad looked over at him and he knew what was going to happen.

'Come on, Francis. You too. It's way past your bedtime.'

'Ah no, please!'

His dad took Martin into his arms and started to carry him to the door.

'Look at the time. You were supposed to go to bed ages ago.'

Francis looked at the others but no one cared. Ritchie just smiled at him. Tough luck. Gussie waved and said, 'Nighty-night Francis,' in a funny voice. Marian just kept looking at the television and his mam said, 'Don't start now, do what you're told.'

Upstairs, as he undressed, miserable, Francis watched his dad trying to put his brother to bed without making a sound. The way he placed him down, anyone would think Martin was going to break into little pieces if he wasn't careful. Francis thought it was funny because he knew that if his big bully of a brother was kicked around the room like a football he still wouldn't wake up. His dad lifted the blankets and covered Martin really gently like the birds did to Snow White on 'Walt Disney Presents'. By now Francis was in his pyjamas, waiting. He'd have to lie in bed, wide awake, listening to snoring while the others were all enjoying themselves watching the Song Contest. It wasn't fair. His dad whispered, 'Now, careful getting into bed. Don't wake him.'

'But I'm not sleepy. Can't I stay up just for a small while?'

'No.'

'But I've no school in the morning.'

'You have Mass.'

'I promise I'll get up in time for Mass.'

Even in the gloom of the bedroom Fonsie could clearly see his youngest son's wide-awake begging eyes. Did the child never give that brain of his a rest? Fonsie knew already that when Ritchie and Gussie went to bed later he'd still be awake and as soon as they came into the bedroom he'd be sitting up asking them what happened and who won. What was to be done with him? He wasn't a bad child, but the constant talk and all these questions couldn't be good for him. Fonsie heard soft footsteps. Ann stuck her head in the door.

'Are they all right?'

'I'm not sleepy, Mam.'

'Of course you're not. You're never sleepy. Oh here, let him come down for a few more minutes, Fonsie. He'll only end up waking Martin and then they'll be fighting.'

Fonsie sighed. He thought it was wrong. The child was too young to be staying up so late, but he would never argue with Ann in front of him.

'Come on, so. Quiet now.'

Francis jumped at the chance. He ran past his mam and dad down the stairs. The others paid no attention to him when he came into the room, except for Ritchie waving him out of the way when he passed in front of the television. They were all staring silently. A girl was singing. She had blonde hair and, Francis thought, looked nearly as young as Marian. Where was she from? He didn't dare ask.

From the moment France Gall came onstage Gussie wondered why Irish girls never looked like that. Even though she had this innocent-looking face with a pretty spot on her cheek and big eyes like a baby's, there was something else about her. She probably wasn't any older than he was but Gussie would bet money she wasn't a virgin. He wondered if Ritchie thought so too, but he wouldn't know how to ask his brother things like that.

Ritchie and his friends had started calling sexy girls birds. France Gall was a real bird even though she didn't even have big tits. He wouldn't mind going out with her. Would he prefer her to Moira Harrington? He'd only been out with her four times so not much had happened yet, but he definitely preferred her to Gretta Lehane, who called it off after two weeks. His face went a bit red when his mam and dad came into the room, because his mam looked directly at him as if she could read his thoughts. But she only wanted to know what country was on now. 'Luxembourg,' he told her. Ann said in God's name what kind of a dress was the girl wearing, it was more like a slip. Fonsie thought it wasn't much of a song or a singer. She sounded to him like a child practising scales. Marian said it was catchy but maybe not her favourite. Ritchie and Gussie said nothing. It was the quietest they had been all night.

After the songs the voting started. Francis liked the big scoreboard with all the names on it. He could see Ireland up near the top, except it was written *Irlanda.* He started looking at all the names and trying to say them and work out what the English name was. Ann kept saying wasn't the presenter really brilliant, the way she could talk away to all those people all around Europe in any language. It was very disappointing that Britain gave Ireland nothing and Ann said she hoped that Ireland would give them nothing either if that was the way it was going to be. On and on it went and, after thirteen countries had voted, finally, the woman from the Portuguese jury said, '*Irlande, trois points.*' The family cheered even more when, straight after that, good old Italy gave Ireland the top vote; five points. Then Yugoslavia gave three more points. Butch Moore had suddenly gone from last to sixth place but by now it was obvious who was going to win: the little blond girl from Luxembourg. Ritchie and Gussie were delighted. The composer was called onstage to get his award. Francis repeated his name to himself: Serge Gainsbourg, Serge Gainsbourg. Then the presenter asked France Gall to sing the winning song. Ann said she was a lovely young girl all right but, really, that dress! It made her look like she was on her way to bed. Fonsie said that coming sixth out of eighteen wasn't bad for a first go. Butch Moore had done his best but sure, who was to know what people would vote for when something as silly as that Luxembourg song won.

But from the moment the strings launched a reprise of the agitated intro and the percussion rattled in to give the song its restless insistent pop beat, Ritchie, Gussie, Marian and Francis all started jigging about. They couldn't help themselves. Ann and

Fonsie didn't understand what it was had got hold of them. It was all just silly noise as far as they were concerned. But their children felt the pulse of it. Even though they hadn't a clue what the words of the song meant, France Gall's sexy legs and pouting face and naive little girl's voice stirred them to yell and sing along with its relentless pop beat.

La la la la la la la,
la la la lala la laaaa!
la lala la lala lala la
lalala la la lala LAHHHH!

Ten: June 14th

Ann opened her eyes with a small comfortable moan to see Fonsie's face, leaning sideways, looking at her. He pointed at the bedside locker where he had placed the cup of tea and the small plate with two slices of toast. Without moving her head from the pillow Ann could smell the butter melting on the toast and see steam rising from the cup. Fonsie smiled and gave her shoulder an affectionate squeeze. 'I'd better be off.' He was gone before Ann's head cleared enough to remember that it was his first morning in the new job and she hadn't wished him luck. Still, the thought of it cheered her up. At last reliable weekly wages; twelve pounds a week until the builders' holidays started. Maybe even some overtime.

Ann, suddenly awake, sat up. She loved that first mouthful of toast, the luxurious saltiness of the melted butter, still warm. It would be a few seconds before the tea was cool enough. Her brain began to sift through the family budget, which would be a lot worse if she hadn't pushed Fonsie into asking around about other work. He'd have just kept tipping away at the coal, out all hours, coming home black as the ace of spades, earning half nothing in the summer. You have the lorry, she'd kept saying to him, maybe there's a better use for it, let people know you're available. And wasn't she right? Of course, he was so obstinate and so slow to move himself that she had to keep on and on at him. Then, when he told her that O'Neill's, the builders' providers, needed any amount of extra deliveries done for some big housing development on the road out to the airport and they'd offered him regular work for the summer, did he as much as mention that this was all a result of her pushing him? Not a hope. And imagine wondering if it was the right thing to take the job because he didn't want to let down his regular customers; a few people, living up to twenty miles outside the city, looking for a bag of coal once every four weeks in the summer. Maybe. If he was lucky. Honestly, that man! Was it any wonder she suffered from migraine?

Ann steered herself away from stressful thoughts. The tea was lovely and through a small gap in the closed curtains she could tell it was a bright sunny day. The money end of things was looking a bit better now for the rest of the year. Fonsie was going to earn at least sixty pounds more than he'd usually bring home in June and July. Ritchie would soon be starting into his second year in Krups and he'd promised to give her another two pounds a week on top of the thirty shillings he already brought home, which would mean that she'd have another – what was it? – about twenty-four pounds more. With Gussie leaving school after his exams that was his fees saved, but not really, because Marian was starting secondary school in September, so hers had to be paid now. Thirty-two pounds. When the time came for Martin to go to secondary then she'd be paying two fees at the same time. It never ended. But at least for this year, as far as she could calculate, she was about eighty pounds better off. Maybe Gussie would bring in a few bob as well once he sorted some kind of apprenticeship for himself. She wondered if Fonsie could have a word with whoever was building those houses about starting him off as a bricklayer or a plasterer? Pity the poor owner of the crooked house Gussie would build. Ann smiled as she pictured such a thing. Still, he might learn. He was no fool, if he'd only get his head out of the clouds. If it wasn't films and television then it was that camera he said he was saving up for. Ann was determined to make him start thinking seriously what he was going to do with his life. Whatever it was, hopefully it would mean a bit extra coming into the house before the end of the year.

Ann finished her tea, snuggled in under the blankets again and began to dream a little about what she might do with the extra money. The list in her head was long: new wallpaper for the front room, bunk beds for Martin and Francis to make a bit of space in the boys' room and her dream, a twin tub washing machine, an automatic. The knob squeaked, the door crept open and an eleven-year-old head peeped in cautiously. Even in the murky light Martin's baby-blue eyes looked nervous. What had he done? Or what lie was he about to tell?

'Mam, are you awake?'

'I am now. Come in and open the curtains.'

Ann sat up again as the room brightened. It really was a lovely day. It would be just gorgeous in Ballybunion today. She looked at the clock. Ten minutes to nine.

'Why aren't you gone to school yet?'

'I'm going now. But I wanted to ask you something before I went. Dad said to ask you.

Of course he did, Jesus, couldn't Fonsie ever just say no? And why had he left the house without making sure that Martin had already gone to school? Did she have to do everything?

'Ask me when you come home for your dinner. Now go on. Hurry. You're going to be late already.'

'Can I go to the pictures today after school?'

'I told you, ask me at dinner-time.'

'But Eddie Hassett told me his mam said he'd only be let go if you let me go, so I have to tell him this morning so he can tell his mam when he goes home at dinner-time.'

'Eddie Hassett? And who else?'

'Martin Casey.'

'And who else?'

'That's all.'

'What about Tony Cuddihy?'

Ann had warned Martin again and again about hanging around with that lanky redheaded troublemaker.

'No.'

'No what?'

'No, just Eddie and Martin.'

'What are you going to see?'

'Ah… *Mary Poppins.*'

Did he think she was a complete eejit? The thought of that trio of galoots trooping in to see *Mary Poppins* would make the cat laugh. Martin's face even went a bit red as he said it. Suddenly, clever Ann had an idea that would give her a much-needed break this afternoon and make sure that Martin really did go to *Mary Poppins.*

'All right, you can go. On one condition. You have to collect Francis from school and bring him with you.'

Ann enjoyed the look on Martin's face. 'Ah no Mam no.'

'It'd be a nice birthday present for him. He'd love to see *Mary Poppins.*'

'Yeah, but Gussie told him he'd bring him.'

'Gussie's in the middle of his exams. He won't be going to any pictures for weeks.'

Ann was delighted to see Martin had no answer for her, though he was trying his best to think of one.

'Ah, Mam!'

'You're going to be late for school as it is. If I have to get out of bed to you –'

As she pulled back the blankets, Martin was already out the door. He spoke from the landing.

'OK, OK so, I'll take him.'

'Grand. I'll give you the money at dinner-time. Now run.'

Peace followed the door slam. There was even birdsong just outside the window. Ann was delighted with her little scheme. It would give Fonsie a good laugh when she told him tonight. Killing two birds with one stone. She'd have some free time this afternoon to get a few bits done, not to mention some blessed peace and Martin would have to go to *Mary Poppins.* He and his pals could either like it or lump it. Ann would know everything that happened because Francis would be all talk afterwards, describing every tiny detail of what he saw and what he heard. Sometimes she dreaded him arriving in from school, yap yap yap. Sister Goretti said this, Sister Goretti said that, questions, questions, questions. Vaccinated with a gramophone needle was

Mary Storan's joke. She had the right attitude, she just knocked great fun out of him. So did Ann sometimes, but he really could wear you down. It never stopped. Where did he get it from? Could he not just accept whatever he was told? Did it always have to be why this and why that? Anyway, with the pair of them at the pictures this afternoon she could get out of the house, call over to have a look at Mona's new Hoover Keymatic – money no object with Mona, of course. And maybe if she had time after that she could take a little run into town and have a look at those bunk beds in Cannocks. That would be nice.

*

Sister Goretti was looking around as if she was trying to make up her mind who to pick. Francis waved his hand and shouted, 'Sister, Sister!' the same as all the other boys, but he was sure already that it would be him. The first time Sister Goretti had said that his answer was the best in the class it sounded nice but he didn't really understand what that meant. He did now. It meant smiles all the time. It meant Sister Goretti pointing to him after other boys had given the wrong answers so that he could say the right one. It meant whenever he asked a question he would be told it was a very good question and he was a clever boy for asking it. He had never heard that before he came to Sister Goretti's class. It meant a big tick on his test and two marks after excellent, which Sister Goretti told him were called exclamation marks, which she then explained were like a sort of a cheer. One was a hurray and two meant a really big hurray. Francis liked the way exclamation marks changed how a word looked. Excellent!! He tried it with other words and it worked. Hello. Hello! Hello!! Me. Me! Me!!

And, of course, being the best meant that he was picked for special jobs. Francis liked being picked by Sister Goretti. Sometimes he was a bit afraid to show how much he liked it, but this time he didn't mind because everyone else seemed to want to be picked too. They all had their hands up. Except for poor Rory Hogan sitting in front of Francis. He only put his hand up a tiny little bit and didn't wave it. And kept his head down. Francis wondered why he didn't want to be picked. Was it because his head was a funny shape? Was he too shy? Or did he just think that she would never pick him anyway? Francis forgot all about Rory Hogan when he heard his name called.

'Francis Strong.'

As he walked to the top of the class Sister Goretti took a piece of paper from her desk, folded it up and held it out to him.

'I want you to take this up to Sister Ignatius.'

Everyone was afraid of Sister Ignatius. She taught the biggest girls. Marian was in her class and she said that nobody ever did anything wrong, they wouldn't dare. But Marian also said that she liked her, which Francis couldn't understand. He much preferred smiling Sister Goretti to grumpy old Sister Ignatius.

'Do you know which classroom it is?'

Francis nodded. Upstairs was where all the big girls were. Second, third, fourth, fifth and sixth. Boys weren't ever allowed up there. If he was meeting his sister after school he always had to wait for her to come down. It must be a really important message if he was being sent up there. Sister Goretti put her hand on his shoulder and walked with him to the classroom door. She pointed down the corridor.

'That stairs is the quickest way. When you get upstairs it's the third room on the left, the same as the hand you write with.'

She took his hand and held it up for a second. Francis liked that. He was the only boy in the class who wrote with his left hand and it made him feel special. Martin used to write with his left hand too, but he didn't any more because a nun, who was gone from the school now, Sister Magdelene, used to hit him on the knuckles with a ruler until he learned to use his right hand. Martin kept telling him that bad things like that were going to happen to him in school but they never did.

Francis felt really excited going up to where the big girls were. He wondered what the message was. He wanted to open it and read it but he was afraid to get caught. The corridor upstairs looked exactly the same as downstairs. There wasn't a sound.

Francis stopped outside the third door on the left and knocked. He heard a growly voice. He knew it must be Sister Ignatius. Even though he had never spoken to her, he had heard her talking to other pupils in the corridor. And seen her. She looked much older than Sister Goretti because she was bent over and her face was really white like paper, but she could move just as fast and never had to raise her voice. When she appeared in the corridor everyone suddenly became quiet and walked more slowly and stood up straight.

'*Tar isteach.*'

Francis opened the door and stepped in. The first thing he noticed was all the eyes that turned silently to look at him. Every single girl in the class. It was like a picture he had seen in a storybook of the forest at night, all black except for loads of owls' eyes staring. He couldn't see his sister. He stopped where he was. The eyes made him feel like they were going to get him.

'Yes, what is it?'

Francis was glad to be able to turn away from all the eyes.

'Sister Goretti said to give you this.'

'Well then, *tar anseo*, come here – *dún an doras*.'

Francis stepped forward then turned and went back to the door. As he closed it he heard Sister Ignatius.

'*Lean ar aghaidh a chailíní*.'

When he turned again not a single eye was on him apart from the old nun's. All the big girls had their heads down, staring at their books. He didn't dare look for his sister Marian now. He began to walk across the classroom. Then he noticed the smell. Since his very first day in school Francis knew the convent had special smells. The boys' toilets had a smell that made his eyes sting but there was a nicer smell that he breathed in the first time he walked through the front door. It was everywhere. A long time after, he found out that this smell came out of a big tin and was rubbed into all the floors. His mam told him it was just polish the same as she used at home, but it wasn't. He smelled his mam's tin of polish and it was a bit like it all right, but not the same.

Sometimes older boys stayed back after school and were given cloth to wrap around their shoes. Then the nuns put the stuff on the floors. They called it wax and the older boys skated up and down making the floor shine. Francis' class did it this year and he thought it was great fun, even though his mother said who did those nuns think they were, making slaves out out the children.

Sometimes a boy in class was even more smelly than wax. One day Padraig Leddin told Francis that there was a smell off him. He nearly started crying because it was true. The reason was, even though he ran, he didn't get to the toilet on time. He hoped that no one would notice but once Padraig Leddin said it then other boys sitting near him said it too and made faces. When the bell rang Francis ran out of the class and out the big door and all the way to the gate and didn't stop. Some of the boys had followed him shouting 'Smelly Strong' after him but they couldn't catch him. That was last year before he went into Sister Goretti's class.

But the smell in Sister Ignatius' class was something he had never smelled before. It wasn't a bad smell but it wasn't a nice smell either. What was it? Was it like any other? He sniffed and tried to think of all the smells he knew; dirty smells, sweet smells, the smell of something nice cooking, burning smells, cleaning smells, the smell of the dustbin when it was full. This was not like any of them. He didn't know if he was supposed to like it or not. He looked at Sister Ignatius. Her head was down, reading the message, so the veil hid her face. She was just a black shape. The smell wasn't coming from her. Nuns never had a smell. Did no one else notice it? Francis looked at the big girls. So many of them sitting all together like this looked very strange. The boys hardly ever saw the big girls. They had their *sos* at a different time and they finished school half an hour after him. In this little room they looked all crushed together, loads of hair, red and brown and black and then the blue of their uniform. He couldn't see any faces because they all had their heads down in case Sister Ignatius gave out to them. They were writing or maybe just pretending to write. Loads of right hands scratching like a giant funny hairy blue machine. Underneath the desks looked even more strange. There were huge bare knees, some were stuck together, some were apart with skirts falling between them. One hand kept scratching a knee. Another hand was fidgeting inside a skirt. Some feet were sticking out, some were tucked in with ankles crossed. It was like when his dad took him hunting for periwinkles on the rocks in Ballybunion and Francis saw a world of crawly things hidden in the pools, floating and wriggling and clinging.

'Are you looking for your sister?'

Sister Ignatius' voice gave Francis a scare. She was folding the paper up much more carefully than Sister Goretti had done and speaking at the same time.

'Marian Strong, *seas suas.*'

Marian stood up. Francis saw her face go pure red.

'There she is and I hope when you are twelve you'll be as good a pupil as she is. *Suigh síos a Mharian.*'

Marian sat and hid her face behind the girls in front of her. Francis noticed that Sister Ignatius' voice seemed a bit softer as she handed him the message.

'Now bring that very important message straight back to Sister Goretti, won't you?'

'Yes, Sister.'

'*Maith an buachaill.*'

Sister Ignatius wasn't as nice as Sister Goretti but she wasn't as bad as he'd feared. As soon as Francis closed the door of the classroom he noticed that the strange smell was gone. Along the big girls corridor, down the stairs and all the slow way back to his classroom he sniffed, but the only smell now was the smell of wax that the nuns used everywhere. He breathed it in easily. Francis liked walking along the corridor like this carrying the message safely for Sister Goretti. He loved school. He wanted to ask about the smell in the big girls class but, though he didn't exactly understand why, he knew he wouldn't.

*

SHANNON VIEW
GUINEY DEVELOPMENTS
Phase One

As he drove onto the site Fonsie thought he had never seen anything like it around the city. The last time he'd been out this way it was all fields. He had a coal customer, poor old Martin Fitzgerald, who died towards the end of last year. Fonsie guessed that his farm was probably part of the site. The land had been cleared in every direction and foundations were already in at this end. Where had his old cottage been? The landscape had already changed so much it was impossible for Fonsie to figure it out. There were men at work everywhere he looked. Wasn't that a great thing? Badly needed. He even recognised the odd face and saluted them as he drove along the makeshift road to the site office. A youngfellah in a suit gave him his docket but when Fonsie asked him where the cement should go, he looked at him as if he had two heads. Fonsie explained.

'I haven't delivered here before.'

'Well, I don't know. Ask the foreman.'

'Who's that?'

'Ah… can't think of his name. Big fellah. Don't worry, you can't miss him.'

Fonsie walked around in search of the foreman. One of the labourers told him his name was Gerry O'Grady and, funnily enough, he also said that Fonsie couldn't miss him. In the end Gerry O'Grady found Fonsie before Fonsie found him. At least he assumed that's who was roaring at him. The man never introduced himself.

'Hey! Is that your lorry up there?'

'Yes.'

'Well, what's it doing there? It's not going to unload itself.'

'I was looking to find out where to unload it.'

'Really, and why didn't you ask instead of wandering around the site like a spa?'

'Sorry.'

'Look, the cement doesn't get delivered, the concrete doesn't get made. The concrete doesn't get made, the foundations don't go in, and so on. You see what I'm getting at, Sham? Sinking in slowly, is it? I've fellahs sitting around pulling their wires 'cause they're waiting for O'Neill's to deliver.'

'I see what you're saying. So where do I unload?'

'Not up there.'

'All right but –'

'Well, get on with it so.'

Fonsie looked around nervously, not sure what to do or say. He didn't move quickly enough for Gerry O'Grady.

'Jesus, Mary and Joseph, do you think this is all I have to do all day? Hold your hand and show you how to do your job?'

'No, but if you can tell me –'

'Look around you. Open your eyes. Do you see any cement mixers? Do you see bags of cement near them cement mixers?'

'Right. I have you.'

'Well, get on with it so. And I tell you, the next time I'm on to Josie Hoare I'll be asking him to send someone with a whole brain to do the delivery.'

Fonsie went back to the lorry feeling a bit shook. He didn't know why men like Gerry O'Grady felt they had to act the bully-boy all the time. There would always be people like that, he supposed. He reversed back down the track to where two large cement mixers were in operation. Four men were shovelling, two more went back and forth with buckets of water and four others wheeled barrowloads of wet cement away. One man seemed to be supervising. Fonsie pulled in.

'Is it all right to unload here?'

'I couldn't care less where you unload.'

'Is this the right place?'

'Is this where you were told to go?'

Fonsie knew every question asked would only get another question back so there was no point in asking any more. Also he was aware that Mr Hoare had told him to be back by twelve to load up again. It had seemed like plenty of time but now, with all this messing, he was going to be late. He started to unload quickly, noticing how much easier it was to handle bags of cement compared to bags of coal. A hundredweight of cement seemed less bulky, much softer against his back and of course cleaner in its sealed bag. This part of the job would be very handy compared to what he was used to. He wasn't too surprised that the smart-alec supervisor just stood looking at him as he humped bag after bag, but when the other lads stopped what they were doing while they waited for a mix to be ready he sort of thought that some of them might offer to lend a hand, just to speed things up. But no one lifted a finger.

*

Francis wished it was Gussie taking him to the pictures. At least he'd talk to him, telling him all sorts of things about Hollywood and film stars. Martin just stared out the bus window saying nothing. When the bus stopped outside Powers small profit store, Martin got up and said, 'Come on.' Francis had to run after him to keep up. It was raining. By the time they got to the Lyric they'd be soaked. He followed Martin down Wickham Street, then down Roches Street, then up Catherine Street, then Francis was surprised when Martin turned at the next corner. This wasn't the right way. *Mary Poppins* was on in the Lyric. The Lyric was across the road from the Dominicans' Church. Martin was still walking fast. Francis stopped and shouted after him. Martin turned and said, 'Come on,' again. Francis told him it wasn't the right way. Martin walked back to him.

'We're not going to *Mary Poppins*, we're going to a different picture and you'd better not tell Mam. Come on.'

He grabbed Francis' hand and pulled him along. Francis nearly started crying but he knew if he did that it would only put Martin in a worse temper and he mightn't take him to the pictures at all. He could see a bright red sign that said 'Royal'. Now he could see the names of the pictures.

DOUBLE BILL
THE FACE OF FU MANCHU
DRACULA

They ran in out of the rain and Martin dragged him over to where the posters for the films were in a glass case. 'Wait here.' Francis watched Martin go to a fat woman with blonde hair who was sitting behind glass reading a magazine. There was a little hole in the glass. She didn't look at Martin when he pushed in the half crown Francis had seen his mam give him at dinner-time. The fat woman handed back a ticket and some money. She still didn't look at Martin. He came back and pointed at the posters.

'Stay here. Look at those. I won't be a sec.'

Then he went through a swinging door. There was no one else around except the fat woman reading the magazine. The rain was pouring down now. The man on the poster looked like he was staring down at Francis. He was a Chinaman with a big funny-shaped hat holding a huge pointy knife over his head. His eyes were red and his moustache was hanging down like two rat's tails. There were words all around him.

Obey Fu Manchu ... or every living thing shall die!

The exclamation mark was huge. Underneath, Francis saw another exclamation mark after more words but it was smaller.

The face of Fu Manchu

The most evil man the world has ever known!

He looked evil. All over the poster there were drawings of girls tied up and girls being attacked by Chinamen with pointy knives. The other poster had a picture of a man's face as well. He had big staring eyes and he was showing his teeth like a growling dog. There was shiny red blood coming out of his mouth. A girl, much smaller, like a doll, was holding her hands up and screaming. Francis read the words in big red letters.

Christopher Lee is
Dracula.

Francis noticed something. Christopher Lee. The name was on the other poster as well. Christopher Lee as Fu Manchu. Christopher Lee is Dracula. Francis looked from one face to the other. Was the man with the dog's teeth and the one with the rat's tails the same person?

'So is this the baby brother, yeah?'

'Are you coming to see *Dracula*, Squirt?'

Martin was back with two other big boys. They looked even older than him. One had a long skinny face and was smoking a cigarette, the other had a head like an orange. Francis didn't know who they were. They didn't live on Rowan Avenue.

'It's very sca-a-ary.'

'You'll wet your pants.'

Martin grabbed him by the shoulders.

'Now you promise you won't tell Mam? Promise.'

'I promise.'

'You're to hide behind us when we go in. If they catch you they'll throw you out because you're too young.'

Francis wondered who 'they' were. He was just going to ask when Martin said, 'And keep your mouth shut for once.'

'How much have you, Macker?'

Francis wondered why Orange Head was calling Martin 'Macker'.

'A shilling.'

'What are you getting us?'

'What do you want?'

'I want an ice-pop.'

'Yeah, me too. We'll sneak him in when her back is turned.'

Martin went up to the fat woman behind the glass.

'Hey Missis, four ice-pops.'

The fat woman looked up from her magazine. She made a face for some reason, then wriggled off her high stool. When she had her head down in the ice-pop fridge the boy with the long face pushed Francis through the swinging door. On the other side there was a long narrow empty corridor. They all waited for Martin. Francis wished he would hurry. He didn't like these big boys who were laughing and whispering things he couldn't hear properly. Martin came in with the ice-pops. He gave them one each. When he gave Francis his, he pointed to a door at the end of the corridor.

'When we go in there, right, stick behind me and don't let the fellah with the flashlamp see you. OK?'

'Who's the fellah with the flashlamp?'

'Look, just shut up and do what I tell you.'

Orange Head went first and pushed open the door. Francis grabbed the back of Martin's jumper and followed him in. Long Face walked behind with a hand on Francis' shoulder. His cigarette was in the same hand and the smoke curled up into Francis' nose. It was dark on the other side of the door. Francis heard loud music and voices. He knew it must be the picture but he was afraid to look and kept his face pressed against Martin's back. His ear felt the heat of the cigarette. He heard Martin talking to a man. Was this the fellah with the flashlamp?

'We were in already.'

'Yeah well, they'll be no more goin' in an' out, do you hear me? Or out you go for good. No more messin'. You shouldn't even be let in to this picture at your age.'

Then they started walking. Francis hung onto Martin's jumper. Long Face behind kept pushing him forward, the smoke from the cigarette still going up his nose. On one side Francis could see people sitting in seats staring up at the picture. When they stopped walking Francis was very glad that Long Face took his hand away because he was afraid that the cigarette smoke was going to make him sneeze. Then he saw light from a flashlamp shining on a row of seats.

'Go on, get in there and not another squeak out of you, do you hear me? And you shouldn't be smoking at your age.'

Martin and Orange Head stayed where they were, whispering to the man with the flashlight. Long Face suddenly pushed Francis past them to the seats.

'Sorry sir, we won't go out again.'

'I know you won't. Go on. Shift.'

'Have we missed much of the picture, sir?'

'Get in there and shut up, don't be annoying me.'

There was only one man sitting in the row. He stood up to let them pass but he never took his eyes off the picture. Long Face pushed Francis on to his knees.

'Stay down for a sec.'

Francis kept his head low. He heard squeaks and thumps as the bigger boys tipped their seats down. He could hear the sound of the picture as well. A man with a deep voice was saying, 'I do not drink wine.' When he got a tap on his shoulder he looked up. Martin was sitting with his feet up on the back of the seat in front of him.

'OK, come on.'

Francis sat and peeled the paper off his ice-pop. He could just see the picture over the top of the heads of people in front. It was huge. Much bigger than the television. The man had grey hair, staring eyes and a deep voice. He wasn't showing his teeth yet but Francis knew he was the man on the poster.

It was Dracula.

The time went by so fast Francis couldn't believe it when the picture ended. He never thought about *Mary Poppins* once. *Dracula* was excellent with three exclamation marks. Even though sometimes during the film he heard Martin and his friends muttering, he wasn't interested in what they were saying and when they started laughing he didn't wonder why. Even when, out of the corner of his eye, he saw Martin smoking, he forgot about it a second later because Dracula was coming to Lucy's bedroom. She backed away as he walked towards her. Then he closed the door and she screamed. Francis wasn't afraid of Dracula at all. He wanted him to win. The only time he really got a fright was when the flashlamp suddenly shone at them. Francis was sure the man had caught him. He hid behind Martin and peeked but all he could see behind the flashlamp was the black shape of a big head with a hat on it like a policeman's hat. The voice wasn't whispering this time. It was like a dog growling.

'Cut out the blackguardin' or you're out that door, do you hear me?'

Then the flashlamp swung away and the man went to shine it on someone else at the back. Francis couldn't believe the man hadn't seen him. He said it to Martin and he whispered, ''Cause he's a blind old bastard,' and the other boys laughed. Francis didn't say anything about the bad word because now Dracula, in his tomb, had suddenly opened his eyes wide, listening. He knew they were coming to get him. Francis hoped they wouldn't. Near the end he guessed that Van Helsing would make a cross out of the candlesticks just before he did it. Once he did that, Dracula didn't stand a chance. He turned into dust and blew away in the wind.

All through *The Face of Fu Manchu* Francis couldn't stop thinking about Dracula. The way he stared at people, the way he stood so tall, the way he walked and swished his cloak, the way he made everyone obey him without as much as lifting a finger. The way he was like an animal. The way he was always alone. Francis didn't like Van Helsing. His voice sounded mean and he was full of himself, talking all the time about defeating evil. Francis just wanted to see *Dracula* again. He wished he knew the words to say what the story made him feel. He liked looking at Dracula. There was something about him, as if he knew something. A big secret. Fu Manchu wasn't the same at all. He was just a bad man. Francis was glad that he didn't win. When it was over he wished he could stay and watch *Dracula* again but Martin stood up and said, 'Come on.'

The rain had stopped and the sky was red and black. Martin's friends kept asking him was he scared, would he have nightmares tonight, what if Dracula came to get him? Francis thought they were really stupid. They wanted to go to somewhere called Donkey's but Martin said he had to bring the Squirt home. It was only when the other boys were gone that Francis suddenly thought about *Mary Poppins.*

'Mam will be asking us about Mary Poppins.'

'Just tell her it was brillo.'

'And what else?'

'Nothing else. Just say nothing.'

'But she'll ask me.'

'No she won't.'

Francis didn't believe him. When he thought of his mam asking him about *Mary Poppins* he got really frightened. She'd find out that he hadn't seen it and she'd never let him go to the pictures again and she'd kill Martin and then he'd get Francis back. He stopped walking. He could feel tears coming.

'I don't want to go home. I don't know what to say to Mam.'

Martin tried to tell him again and again just say brillo and that would do but Francis knew that if Mam asked him any more questions he'd go all red and wouldn't know what to say. Now Martin started to get angry again and told him he'd better not tell. Then, suddenly, he grabbed Francis' hand and started walking back towards town. They went through the People's Park. When they got out the other side Francis saw the big clock and the Dominicans' Church, where the Lyric was. Was Martin going to bring him to see *Mary Poppins* now? They stopped outside the Lyric and Martin pointed at pictures in glass boxes on the wall.

'Now look at those. Look. That's Mary Poppins there. Now you can say you saw her flying or something and you won't be telling a lie.'

Francis looked at the pictures. There were one, two, three… eight. He looked from to the other. He saw Mary Poppins, he saw a man with a black face like his dad when he came home from work, but this man wasn't a coalman. He had a brush and he was up on a roof. Francis got it; he cleaned chimneys. There was another man all dressed up in a stripy jacket dancing with Mary Poppins, but then Francis saw it wasn't another man, it was the same man as the chimney sweep. Like Dracula and Fu Manchu were the same man. In another picture there were two children with cartoon animals all around them. Then Martin said, 'OK, have you seen enough?' and before Francis could answer Martin grabbed his hand and pulled him away.

When they got home his mam was in very good mood. Marian was setting the table for tea and Dad was there too, all clean, watching *Newsbeat* on the telly. He was never home this early usually. There was a nice smell from the oven.

'I made bread-and-butter pudding for the tea. So how did ye get on?'

Martin said fine and, when he was asked what did he think of *Mary Poppins*, he just said, 'Ah, boring.' and went into the front room to play records.

'Did you enjoy it, love?'

Francis said he loved the picture, meaning *Dracula,* so it wasn't a real lie.

'Was it very funny?'

Francis didn't know what to say for a couple of seconds. Then he thought about one of the photos he saw outside the Lyric.

'All the men dancing on the roof looked funny. They were cleaning the chimneys and then they all started dancing.'

His mam opened the oven and checked the bread-and-butter pudding.

'Lovely. And did you like the songs?'

Francis really wanted to tell his Mam all about Dracula but he knew he couldn't do that. So he thought about the other photos of *Mary Poppins* he saw. Then he started talking and talking and talking.

'Yeah, they were singing on the roof as well. Then Mary Poppins came down out of the sky with her umbrella and then she met the man who was cleaning the chimneys and dancing and singing and he said can I go out with you and she said you have to wash yourself first because his face was all dirty from the chimneys and he said OK and then he was all clean with a stripy jacket on and Mary Poppins got all dressed up as well and she had a new umbrella and they went to the park and they started dancing and singing and... and... and oh yeah there was a boy about my age and a girl too with Mary Poppins and the man and then there was all these animals like in a cartoon. They were jumping and dancing around the boy and the girl and then they all went up on the roof and it was dark and they all got dirty from the chimneys and they were laughing.'

As he spoke, his mam took the bread-and-butter pudding out of the oven and put it on the table. It smelled nice. She took down bowls and from the way she said, 'That's lovely,' as she started filling the kettle and then called Marian to come and give her a hand with the tea, Francis knew she wasn't listening to him any more.

It was OK. He and Martin wouldn't get into trouble. He hadn't told.

1966

Eleven: January 26th

'Am I right in thinking that's the end of James Connolly and Tom Clarke?'

Gavin Bloom stepped away from the crowded smoky set of the devastated General Post Office so that he could speak quietly to the director of *Insurrection.* Louis' reply was precise as usual.

'Not quite. We need the pick-up shot of Volunteers lifting Connolly from bed to stretcher.'

Gavin was annoyed with himself. He hated forgetting any detail.

'Sorry, yes of course. But Tom Clarke is wrapped, check?'

'Yes that's right. Now I don't think we'll get the pick-up done before lunch Gavin, so I propose –'

'Yes, dearheart, just a sec…'

Gavin interrupted because, surprisingly, Louis seemed to have forgotten something: the tradition of formally announcing when an actor had finished on a shoot. Gavin would now enjoy reminding him.

'Is there a problem, Gavin?'

Unless it's a problem that you can't be bothered to thank one of your actors, darling, who has given his all for several weeks now, Gavin thought but did not say. 'No problem. Just a moment, sir.'

He stepped through the main entrance of the General Post Office and clapped his hands to get the attention of seventy or so grubby, exhausted and wounded Irish rebels. But before he made his announcement Louis spoke down the cans.

'Oh Gavin, I think now is probably the best time to announce that Jim is wrapped and thank him formally for his magnificent performance.'

It was one of those rare occasions when Gavin Bloom was speechless. As everyone on the set looked at him, waiting for instructions, Louis spoke again.

'Sorry, did you hear that? Tell Jim I'm coming out on the gantry, would you?'

'Yes, yes. Got that, sir. All right everyone, we are happy with that last take, which means that the first of our 1916 heroes, the daddy of them all, Tom Clarke, aka Mr James Norton, is officially wrapped. Well done, Jim. Fantastic work as always, sir.'

Everyone in the studio clapped and cheered. Gavin shook hands with Jim and, covering his microphone, whispered.

'Look up to the gantry. His Serene Highness has emerged from production control to acknowledge your contribution.'

Jim Norton waved up at Louis and offered a mock-formal incline of the head. Then he grinned at Gavin and the sparkle in his eyes suddenly betrayed the handsome young actor hiding behind the white moustache, thinning white hair and glasses of the aging 1916 hero. Gavin was caught by surprise. Having grown so used to seeing Tom Clarke ill and world-weary, he had almost forgotten that Jim Norton was nearly thirty years younger than his character. Since production began, Gavin had more or less lived on this enormous set, a replica of the General Post Office in 1916, as they recorded scene after increasingly moving scene of this drama series. Quite genuinely, he had begun to forget about the actors Jim, Ronnie, Declan and Eoin, and instead saw only the legendary heroes of Irish nationalism, Tom Clarke, James Connolly, Joseph Plunkett and Patrick Pearse, made flesh and blood and voice. Only the day before, during a scene in which James Connolly dictated to a female Volunteer his final dispatch to the troops, Gavin had been unable to hold back the waterworks. Luckily Louis' decisive, 'Splendid and… cut,' down the cans reminded him just in time that it was only dear old Ronnie Walsh tugging at the heartstrings. In fairness to all the thesps, they were really doing the business on this one, acting their thick woolly socks off day after day but, thinking about it afterwards, Gavin still couldn't make up his mind if the scene was just sentimental old tripe and it had been completely unprofessional to get tearfully involved like that or was there something deeper, more profound happening within himself? Which thought immediately prompted the answering thought: Deep, darling? Me, darling? Profound? Never heard of the word.

The simple truth was that, although everyone working on the production was fully aware that the scenes they were acting out each day in Studio One had actually taken place, less than three miles away, in the GPO on O'Connell Street, it was only now, as the final tragic scenes were being recorded, that this fact of history was prompting a powerful emotional response from actors and crew. These real-life heroes had offered up their own lives. And was it because of their sacrifice that Gavin and his colleagues had the freedom to play-act in Studio One?

Louis decided that time would be better used if they took an early lunch. They would lift James Connolly from bed to stretcher after the break. Gavin was the last to leave Studio 1 and recognised a familiar melancholy mood creeping up on him: that last-day feeling. Tonight would be the big one, the scene he had been anticipating nervously for some time. They would set fire to the General Post Office and the plan was that Patrick Pearse would stand lonely amid the burning ruins, contemplating the end of his dream for a free Gaelic Republic, before walking away through the smoke. They could be in for a long night. It might go according to Louis' meticulous schedule or it could turn into an unholy mess and they'd all have to hightail it from a blazing Studio One. Gavin was confident that Eoin O'Súileabháin, who could be a moody fucker but a glorious actor when he felt like it, would hold the moment brilliantly, but the rest of it was a logistical nightmare. He thought it was hilarious that Louis had brought over an English pyrotechnical expert to create the fire. 'They burned us out in 1916 dearheart, now we're bringing them over to do it again.' Gavin imagined that even if the whole place went up in flames, Louis would still be issuing crisp instructions.

'Track in two, CU Pearse on one, standing by with wide shot three. More smoke!' Gavin had insisted that the Dublin fire brigade should be on hand in case of any accidents. Once this scene was shot, then the great adventure would be over. He knew already he'd feel a little lost. More than anything he loved being in the thick of a big show and this was the biggest Teilifís Éireann had ever done. He loved working with and being around actors. This bunch were a handful but truly wonderful. He loved being so busy that he didn't have time to think of other things. Things out there beyond the studio walls.

*

Mary Storan asked Mikey, if she persuaded Ann and Fonsie to go to *Carry On Cowboy* tonight, could he get them in free? She knew he'd say no problem but she always made sure to ask because, sometimes, depending on who was doing the tickets, it could be a bit awkward. Mary had this notion in the back of her head that Ann could do with a good night out and a laugh. She looked completely worn out when the Storans called round as always on St Stephen's Night and Mary could see it was more than just the usual tiredness after Christmas. Ann, of course, hid it with her best smile and was full of happy talk and joined in the sing-song as usual but Mary wasn't fooled. She'd known Ann Casey far too long. And there was something about the way Fonsie tiptoed round her even more than usual. Mary hadn't got to the bottom of it that night and what with one thing and another hadn't seen Ann since, so a night out at the pictures seemed like a good way of giving her a bit of a lift. Mikey had told Mary that it was the best Carry On yet and Sid James was brilliant in it.

The key was in the door of number 66 and Mary was about to shout 'Hello!' as she opened it when she saw Ann, with a big smile on her face, peeping into her own front room. Mary was so surprised she didn't speak for a second and, next thing, Ann spotted her and put her finger to her lips which, of course, meant that Mary Storan had to do the opposite and speak. 'What is it?' Ann went shhh! and waved for her to come and look. Mary still asked. 'What's going on?' Ann pulled her closer to the front room door, whispering, 'C'mere. Look. This is the latest. Don't laugh now.'

Mary didn't know what in God's name she was about to see but, whatever it was, she could tell Ann thought it was great gas. The front-room door was only open a tiny bit so she had to look in with one eye. Francis was standing in front of the good cabinet, facing the far wall. He had his head bowed, doing actions with his hands and he was muttering to himself. For a second Mary couldn't figure what he was wearing over his white shirt and then she worked it out. He had knotted two stripy green towels together at two corners and put his head through the gap. It sat on his thin shoulders like a gown. Then Mary copped on. It was meant to be a priest's Mass vestments. Of course. Now she noticed the twine tied around his waist and rosary beads hanging from it. Francis lifted a silver cup high above his head, still muttering, She had to turn away and cover her mouth to stop herself from laughing out loud.

'That's one of Marian's Irish dancing trophies, isn't it?'

'Killaloe Feis. Under-fourteen jig. Did you ever in all your life? And you saw what he's using for the blessed Eucharist?'

Mary looked again. Francis' head was now bent down. He was holding a broken-off piece of ice-cream wafer close to his lips and whispering. Mary tried her best to hear him. '… speak but the word and my soul shall be healed.' Then he put the wafer in his mouth and genuflected. Mary felt Ann pulling at her arm. She followed her to the scullery and closed the door so they could laugh.

'Well, that's the best yet. How long has that been going on?'

'Only since Christmas. I suppose it was all the Masses and carol services we went to and then Fonsie's mother gave him one of the new missals in English. I thought, ah for God's sake, what kind of a present is that to give a six-year-old, but he's after proving me wrong now. Loves it. He has the whole thing off by heart already.'

'You're not serious.'

'I swear to God. I mean there's words he couldn't understand but he knows how to say it all off. The priest's part and all the responses.'

Mary lit up a fag. Ann put the kettle on.

'Does he do a sermon and all?'

'I swear to God he does.'

'No!'

'Oh yeah, talking away to the furniture. All about Christmas you know. How Baby Jesus came to save us.'

'Well now, have we a priest in the making?'

'I was thinking that. I mean, here we are laughing but you know, none of the others ever did that, not even Gussie and he was a bit of a play-actor too.'

Mary blew a perfect smoke ring.

'Do you know what, Ann? I must be a better godmother than I thought I was.'

'Well, maybe so now.'

'Ah go 'way, I'm only joking.'

'I know, but I mean still. He's mad about you. Weren't you the first person he showed the crib to. Even before he brought it home here.'

Mary knew in her heart that this was true and she really had been touched when Francis did that. On the day he got his Christmas holidays he called in to her flat on his way home from school. He was carrying a big box. Look what I won, Auntie Mary. She could tell he was made up over it. It was a beautiful big crib with thick black paper all crumpled up, sprayed with snow and a shiny gold star stuck on top. It had lovely painted figures, Jesus, Mary, Joseph, the shepherds, the wise men, a cow, a donkey, sheep, the whole farm. Straw even. Mary told him it was absolutely gorgeous. How had he won it?

'We had a Christmas spelling test and Sister Goretti said whoever came first would win a prize and I got twenty out of twenty and no one else did and Sister Goretti said I could have two shillings or the class crib and I said the class crib.'

'You chose the crib instead of the money?'

And his face had been so innocent when he answered her, as if to say of course, Auntie Mary, what else would I do, that, straight away, she'd gone for her purse and taken out two shillings, warning him not to tell his mam, because Mary knew Ann would kill her for giving him money and probably make him give it back. Francis promised and, somehow, Mary felt sure that, even though he never shut up talking from one end of the day to the other, she could trust him not to say anything to Ann about the two shillings.

'I couldn't get over it. I mean it's a much nicer crib than our old one and he's mad about it but, honestly, when I was his age I'd have taken the two shillings like a flash.'

'I'd have taken sixpence.'

'I don't think it even occurred to him.'

Then Mary got a surprise when Ann added, 'Mind you, he wasn't so holy that he didn't take the two shillings when I gave it to him.'

'You gave him two bob?'

Mary nearly said 'as well' but stopped herself in time. Ann sounded very proud as she spoke.

'Ah yeah, I mean when he was telling me the story didn't I nearly start crying and I thought, God help us, wasn't he so good to do that? There was Sister Goretti testing him, holding out the two shillings for him to take and still he picked the crib. Because he loved baby Jesus, he told me. I mean, he deserved some kind of a reward for that. So I just thought it was only fair that he shouldn't lose out on the two shillings.'

For a tiny moment Mary wondered. Surely Francis could not have known that by choosing the crib instead of the two shillings he would end up with the crib and four shillings. No. Ah no. It wouldn't have crossed the child's mind.

'Imagine all the same, if he did become a priest?'

Mary blew a big cloud high in the air.

'Well Ann, at least we'd have an "in" with the man above and, God knows, we could do with it.'

Mary Storan wasn't one of those women who prayed for a priest in the family. She certainly couldn't imagine her Shamie becoming one and, in all honesty, wouldn't want him to be, being her only boy. Maybe it was different for Ann with four boys. Thinking about it, Mary was a tiny bit tickled at the notion that herself and Mikey would get some of the credit for her godson having a vocation. They'd be cock of the walk at his ordination. What a laugh! In all seriousness though, she was relieved to find Ann in such good form today. Whatever had been troubling her seemed to have passed and that could only be a good thing.

*

Miriam Hartnett, a young design assistant on *Insurrection*, passed Gavin in the corridor. 'Lona at reception is looking for you. She said there's someone waiting to see you.'

Gavin wasn't expecting any visitors. Lunch break was short enough and, with such an intense afternoon and evening ahead of him, frankly, he was in no mood for distractions. Who the hell could it be, anyway? Though tempted to ignore the message, he couldn't resist walking down the corridor to the double doors leading to reception and having a sneaky peek, but opening one of the doors slightly and putting an eye to the gap didn't provide him with an answer. There was no one standing around and the reception desk itself impeded his view of the seated area. He could just about see a head of wavy hair, which wasn't even sufficient indication whether the person was male or female. The sensible thing, given that he was a busy little bee today, would have been to turn round, go back upstairs to the canteen and let whoever it was go and shite. But Gavin was curious. He went to the internal phone on the wall just inside Studio One and called Lona at reception. Gavin explained that he was very busy and, before deciding whether or not to meet this person, needed to check out on the QT who was looking for him. Lona replied almost in a whisper.

'He says his name is Brendan Barry… Hello Gavin? … Did you get that?'

But Gavin had already dropped the phone and run back to the double doors. Again he opened one a fraction and peered through. Lona had put down the phone and was calling out 'Mr Barry'. When the young man stood up Gavin instantly remembered the pale taut delicate face. His brown eyes were just as sad and – Gavin could not summon up any other word – beautiful as he remembered them. Remembered and thought about many times over the last while. Brendan Barry. Gavin saw him smile his shy smile. His natural timidity was beguiling. So it had been that night last April. Gavin remembered how Brendan Barry's easy charming hotel-manager banter had very gradually lurched and stuttered. In the end neither of them had been able to decide what the next move should be, what words needed to be spoken.

When Baz Malloy, walking towards TV reception, saw Gavin peering through a tiny gap in the double doors he was amused because he had just been caught indulging in a little mild voyeurism himself. Over the last few weeks on the set of *Insurrection*, he had become increasingly attracted to the design assistant, Miriam, but hadn't yet had a chance to test if the feeling was in any way mutual. A couple of minutes ago, as he turned onto the corridor, there she was, walking a few yards in front of him. Just as he made a decision to catch up with her and attempt to start a conversation, Miriam went into the Ladies. Baz stopped outside the door, staring at it in frustration. Then it suddenly opened and a woman he didn't know gave him a very odd look as she emerged. He walked away quickly, telling himself, another time. So what was Gavin up to? Who was he spying on? He tapped his shoulder to surprise him but wasn't remotely prepared for the reaction he got.

'What the fuck! What do you fucking think you're doing, Baz! Jesus!'

This was so unlike Gavin that Baz just raised his palms, said, 'Sorry!' and moved quickly into the reception area. He heard the double doors slam behind him. What was that all about? What had Gavin been looking at? Apart from Lona at the desk, the only other person in reception was a fair-haired young guy who was leaving. Was it him? They reached the exit at the same moment and the young guy politely held back to allow Baz go first.

Gavin, on the other side of the closed double doors, was furious with himself. Where had that snap come from? What made him issue the lash like that? He would apologise to Baz later. At least it forced him to make a decision about what to do next. Acting on that decision was harder. It helped to imagine Louis' voice issuing directorial instructions. 'Open the door. Now go talk to him would you, please Gavin, thank you.' Walking into TV reception he composed his opening line, a cheerfully relaxed greeting, 'Well Mr Barry, how's the hotel business?'

Gavin had noticed Brendan Barry moments before he met him for the first time in a packed hotel lobby after a live outside broadcast during last year's election campaign. He was, literally, a face in the crowd. Gavin and the rest of the crew were leaving the function room where the election debate had happened. The usual circus surrounding Teilifís Éireann's trips down the country was in full swing. Apart from programme participants and audience members, the lobby was jammed with local hangers-on who descended on the hotel just to be part of the glamour and excitement. Gavin loved outside broadcasts. Live audiences largely made up of simple folk, television virgins, their mouths agape at the goings on, were a gift to a sophisticated floor manager with a silver tongue. Gavin felt it more or less incumbent on him to treat them to his most extravagant performance. As far as he was concerned, in these situations he was the public face of Teilifís Éireann. As the audience never saw the actual director of the show, who was tucked away in a van somewhere outside the venue, it was inevitable that they frequently assumed Gavin was king of it all. Of course he would never make such a claim, not by nod or wink or hint but, somehow, people seemed to form that impression. Perhaps it was the way he strutted freely about the set and with a gesture, a graceful motion of his hand, instructed the famous presenter, John O'Donoghue, when to speak and into what camera. Perhaps it was because it was Gavin who, with simple mime, exhorted the audience to applaud or commanded them to be silent and respectful. At any outside broadcast there was a percentage of the audience who would remember nothing of the programme itself, because they spent the entire evening observing Gavin's behind-the-cameras *tour de force*. So, after the election debate had ended, he already knew that a gaggle of awe-struck locals would be waiting to approach him, nervously eager to discover more about the secrets of television. As he emerged from the function room he immediately noticed this particular face pushing towards him through the melée. It was crystal clear that the bright innocent brown eyes were fixed on him, but it was only as the young man emerged from the scrum of bodies that Gavin saw how trim and immaculately suited he was. The hand Gavin shook was spotlessly manicured, its grip strong and determined. Yet the eyes remained shy.

'Hello. I'm Brendan Barry, the night manager.'

Gavin wondered for a second was the young man putting on a joke voice? It was a strange mismatch; the delicate features, the soft eyes behind longer-than-usual lashes seemed to clash with an accent as flat and rasping as any local low-life.

Brendan Barry congratulated Gavin on a top-class, professional production. He said the hotel was thrilled skinny that they had been chosen to host the broadcast and hoped everyone was happy with the accommodation and facilities. Gavin managed no more than an agreeble nod as Brendan Barry scarcely drew breath. He had been up to his eyes since coming on duty but managed to nip in a couple of times during the broadcast to see what was happening. Very impressive. A-1, the whole operation. Gavin was the name, was it? Brendan Barry said he spotted it on the credits at the end. Anyway, the way Gavin had co-ordinated everything was just spot-on. The ordinary Joe Soap probably wouldn't realise how complicated that end of it was, but Brendan Barry thought Gavin had done brilliant, absolutely mighty. Flattered as Gavin was, he was also thirsty. He pushed towards the bar.

Brendan Barry, still talking, stepped ahead to ease his way. He had also caught a fair bit of the programme itself on the TV set they rigged up in the bar for the occasion and, from what he saw, it seemed to him that, as far as the debate itself was concerned, Dom had really stuck it to the rest of them. He wondered if Gavin agreed, from his professional persective? Gavin asked if he was a government supporter, then? Jay no, not at all. Brendan Barry seemed surprised by the question, although in fairness he would admit that Dom was a regular in the hotel and a colourful character. An awful man too, sometimes. Brendan thought he should mention that it might be just as well to keep out of his way later on tonight, if previous experience was anything to go by. Very enjoyable sometimes though, to watch Dom's antics from a safe distance.

Although Gavin agreed with Brendan Barry that tonight, on a panel of local opposing candidates, Dom had been the undoubted star turn, he explained to him that, as a Teilifís Éireann employee working on a political programme during an election campaign, he was precluded by the Broadcasting Act from making any comment that revealed a bias. Even as he said this, Gavin thought it sounded far too pompous, so he added that even if the particular politician mentioned did indeed wipe the floor with the rest of them and even if it was Gavin's professional opinion that this particular politician understood much better than anyone else on the panel how to use television, he had to keep these opinions to himself. Brendan Barry grinned and asked did that mean he couldn't agree with him that Dom had the best answer of the night when he told the old Fine Gaeler, Russell, that 'moral indignation is only envy with a halo'? Gavin said definitely he could make no comment on that, nor could he comment on how smart Dom was to mention that he'd be on the edge of his seat at Dalymount Park in a couple of weeks' time, roaring on the local team in the FAI cup final. He got the biggest cheer of the night when he said that. In fact the only thing Gavin was allowed to say – and, with perfect timing, he reached the bar at that moment and rapped the counter – was, 'Drink please!' Brendan Barry laughed and insisted on getting the order himself. He ducked in under the bar, served up the gin and tonic requested and refused payment. He seemed to stare at Gavin as if about to say something. Then, quite suddenly, excused himself: 'Sorry, up to my eyes.' For a few seconds Gavin's eyes followed the younger man's rapid yet elegant progress through the sweaty crowd.

Three times more over the next few hours, Brendan Barry returned to where Gavin sat with other crew members. On the first two occasions the young manager appeared to address the general group, politely enquiring if everything was to the satisfaction of the Teilifís Éireann contingent. Though the words were directed at them all, Gavin could not help but feel that the eyes were not. Brendan's childlike gaze returned to him again and again and, it seemed, lingered. Having received increasingly boisterous assurances that they were all having a whale of a time, he bowed ever so slightly and politely left the group. Gavin had to stop himself gazing after the departing figure.

On the third occasion, Brendan Barry appeared out of nowhere. Gavin felt a hand graze his shoulder and looked up to see him leaning forward, his fringe flopping over his right eye. He was close enough to speak quietly and be heard by Gavin alone. Close enough to notice his scent. Discreet, expensive.

'Just thought you'd be interested to hear. I got it all wrong about the bould Dom. He's been on red lemonade all night. Like a lamb over there in the corner.'

Gavin stood up to take a look at what was, apparently, the unheard of spectacle of the notorious Dom sober in a bar late at night. More importantly, this move also allowed Gavin to turn away from his colleagues and stand close to Brendan.

'Listen, we're closing the bar so we can get rid of the gougers. Run 'em out of Dodge. There's a few of them acting the langer. But don't worry, we'll keep serving ye all once they're gone.'

'Thanks. You're very good to think of us…'

He hesitated. Brendan did not move away. His angelic smile

had a passive but expectant quality. It encouraged Gavin to continue.

'We might even get a chance to have a proper chat when things have calmed down for you?'

The reply came without hesitation.

'That'd be mighty.'

Gavin watched Brendan move energetically around the bar, targeting particular clusters and politely urging their departure. He motioned the bar staff to start collecting glasses. He ignored increasingly desperate pleas for one more lousy drink. In what seemed to Gavin an amazingly short time, the great mass of bodies had been cast out and the lurching, heaving mob was reduced to a few privileged boozers. Apart from genuine residents, including the television crew, all that remained were the election candidates and their particular friends.

As the next hour passed, Gavin, despite drinking more or less continuously, remained alert. The ritual dance he had nicknamed the Outside Broadcast Tango began. Around two o'clock Mr Senior Cameraman and Miss PA became the first to fall together. Very soon after, Mr Sound Supervisor sidled in the direction of Miss Hair and Make-up. Rather more subtly, Madam Director, having animatedly solved the nation's problems with young Mr Researcher, suddenly yawned, stretched, checked her watch and announcing sleepily that she'd better get along. Less than five minutes later young Mr Researcher resisted all pleas to stay for just one more, claiming that he was 'totally fucked'. Maybe not totally yet, Gavin thought, as the lift door closed and carried the sleepy lad to his chosen bed.

By now the lobby was so quiet Dom's voice could be heard from a distant corner blabbing out a production line of anecdotes. The hangers-on contributed regular bursts of laughter. Gavin stood and meandered. For no particular reason, he told himself. When he saw Brendan Barry go behind the unattended reception desk to answer the phone it suddenly seemed the right time to collect his room key and head for bed. Gavin approached, holding himself as steady as possible. Brendan Barry put down the phone, looked up and smiled.

How long they stood talking across this barricade it was impossible to recall. Thinking about it now as he walked through the double doors to television reception all Gavin could remember was the odd, but delicious, sense that, for whatever few seconds or minutes, it had felt like they were entirely alone. Which, of course, was not the case. Dom and his acolytes were still rattling along and there were drunks lounging about. But what his memory really held onto was how the silent language of eyes and smiles and little gestures had created a private wordless universe which had nothing whatsoever to do with the trivia of their spoken conversation because, in the end, what might have been said never was. When the moment came, the moment when there were no words left to say other than those that might smash through a barrier less visible but rather more recalcitrant than the reception desk between them, neither Gavin nor Brendan Barry had been able to summon up those words, even though, in his strong memory, Gavin could see Brendan's face inviting him to speak. He was equally convinced that his expression had encouraged Brendan to do likewise. Instead, eventually, lamely, the encounter ended with, 'If you're in Dublin at all…' scribbling his name and the TÉ number on a scrap of paper, underlining the extension number as if to underline the sincerity of his interest.

'I'd be delighted to show you round the studios… have a coffee.'

These, it transpired, were the last words spoken before the desk girl arrived back and Gavin, smiling a polite good night, took his key and turned towards the lift.

Brendan Barry was no longer in TV reception. Gavin slowly turned 360 degrees as if he was expecting him to pop up out of nowhere. He caught Lona's eye and made a questioning gesture. She looked surprised in her entirely uninterested way.

'Oh. Where's he gone? He was here a minute ago.'

'No matter.'

Lona resumed pretending to be busy and Gavin stared at the revolving exit door. So. Gone. So. That was that. OK. Probably just as well, what with the hectic afternoon and evening Gavin had ahead of him. Lunch-time was speeding by and the thing to do now was go upstairs to the canteen. Gavin tried not to look like he was either hurried or anxious as he turned instead through the revolving door. Once outside he walked a few casual steps before he started trotting. The figure of a man he presumed was Brendan Barry was just about visible, almost at the Nutley Road exit. Gavin would have to get a lot closer before calling his name, otherwise he would seem a bit frantic and draw unnecessary attention on himself. But finally he had to shout out, or it would have been too late.

Brendan Barry turned and, recognising Gavin, smiled in immediate and open delight.

*

Across the road from the Carlton Cinema, Ann, Mary Storan and Fonsie sat in the lorry waiting for Mikey. The women huddled together for warmth, still laughing at bits from *Carry On Cowboy.* Mary had a soft spot for Sid James, especially that dirty laugh, a bit like her own, she said and laughed. She'd never have thought he'd make such a good cowboy, though. Jim Dale wasn't her cup of tea at all, to be honest. Ann said, ah no, Jim Dale was nice but Charles Hawtry was her favourite. He made her laugh just looking at him. She asked Mary if he reminded her of anyone. Mary said no. Ann said wasn't he very like Seánie Madigan, who did the dame in Panto Frolics every year. Hadn't he the same, she didn't know what to call it, funny way about him.

'That's because Seánie Madigan is one of those, the same as Charles Hawtry.'

'Ah, Mary, don't be saying things like that. Anyway, I wasn't talking about that, I was talking about their acting, you know, their expressions. The way they… I don't know, it's hard to explain, but they're very funny.'

'I'm telling you it's because they're both nancy-boys Ann. Sure

I saw Seánie Madigan coming out of Todds one day and I swear on my late mother's soul he was wearing eye-shadow.'

'No!'

'I'm telling you.'

'Go 'way, I don't believe that.'

Ann didn't want even to be thinking of those sort of things. All she was trying to say was that she thought Charles Hawtry was funny in the Carry Ons and, in the same way, Seánie Madigan was funny in the panto. She told Mary that Gussie, for his first Christmas present since he started earning, had taken Fonsie and herself on a night out to see *Dick Whittington* and they had a great laugh. Mary said that was very generous of him but Ann just made a face and said it was typical Gussie, everything had to be a big show. When he brought them to Naughton's on the way home didn't he want them to sit inside and have their fish and chips off plates. And of course he drove them mad singing his favourite bits from the songs in the panto over and over. There was one about all the tax on drink. She couldn't remember how it went. She asked Fonsie who said, 'Huh?' because he hadn't been following the chat. He had been thinking that maybe he should start the engine and get a bit of heat going in the lorry while they were waiting for Mikey and wasn't Mary great, the way she always put Ann in a good mood and made her forget her troubles.

'Fonsie, are you listening? What was that song that Gussie thought was so funny. About the tax on the pint. What's this it was to the tune of?'

'Oh… ah… yes. "Black Velvet Band".'

'That was it. "Black Velvet Band". Can you remember any of it?'

'I should be able to, we had to listen to it often enough. It went aah… let me see…

"The more that the price of a pint goes up,
The more you will see it go down."'

'That was it and Seánie Madigan pointed his thumb in the air for the first bit and then put it down his mouth for the second bit, you know like he was drinking, do you understand?'

Mary Storan said that was very clever all right. She was sorry now that she hadn't gone to see the panto and, in fairness to him, Seánie Madigan was always a brilliant Dame. Oh he really was, said Ann. Even if he is a big old nancy-boy, said Mary, and Ann poked her, laughing.

Mikey arrived, saying there was no need to wait, he'd have enjoyed the walk home. He sat in and put his arm around Ann and said isn't this a grand tight squeeze? Fonsie said he hoped Mary didn't mind having to sit on the water tank between the two seats. Mary said not at all, wasn't it warming her bum very nicely? and they all laughed. As they took off Ann suggested that a few chips from Naughton's would be the perfect way to round off the night.

*

In room 522 of the Dublin Intercontinental hotel, Brendan Barry laid his head in the curve of Gavin Bloom's neck and shoulder, curling his legs and arms tightly around as if determined not to let him escape. Gavin stroked his wavy hair and smooth neck, reaassuringly. Was their frantic breathing loud enough to wake sleepers in nearby rooms? Gavin felt Barry's breath hot against his collarbone. He enjoyed the sensation just as, to his surprise, he felt completely at ease with the muscularity of the body clinging to him. In his imagined script of a drama like this, slipping away quietly would be the next item on the running order, dearheart. But no, as it turned out, emphatically no. The darkness and the stillness were added blessings because he was exhausted. He had talked enough all day, to Louis, to crew, to actors. At a certain point late tonight he had begun to wonder would they ever go for a take or just endlessly rehearse this final sequence with its slow complicated developing crane shot, tracking, seemingly floating, through the smoking, burning GPO until the moment when Commandant Pearse entered frame dramatically, from below camera, and walked slowly towards the centre of the blaze to his mark. As the clock ticked towards midnight Gavin had became increasingly tense and his tone more abrupt, bordering on aggressive. He just wanted to wrap and get out of there. Yet, when the take finally happened and the fussy little pyrotechnics expert from London had set the place ablaze and arty Baz had added his unique poetic touch to the camera move, Gavin, standing by to cue Eoin O'Súileabháin for his entrance, had still been able to forget everything except the moment, the drama. And of course, once O'Súileabháin walked on, he was mesmerising, somehow managing to convey with his body alone the nobility, tragedy and, it seemed to Gavin, a little of the insanity of Pearse. Was he standing there contemplating, sadly, desperately, in the collapsing ruin of the GPO, the failure of his dream of Irish freedom or was he preparing to step gloriously into the fire of martyrdom? Everyone's concentration remained unwavering. The seconds passed. Gavin heard Louis whisper 'wonderful wonderful' down the cans. He let the scene run, perhaps hoping for some extra unexpected moment of magic. The silence was as intense as Studio One had ever experienced. Would he ever call 'cut'? Out of the gloom Gavin spotted a stagehand's anxious hand-signals. Then he saw. Oh Christ! Smoke and flame had crept up the pillars and were now dangerously close to the lighting grid. He whispered to production control.

'Louis, are you happy with the take?'

'Hmm. Oh yes, yes absolutely. Eoin is magnificent, isn't he?'

'Good, because I think the studio might be about to catch fire.'

Gavin broke the spell with a loud. 'A-a-a-and Louis is happy. We're all happy. That's a wrap! Well done, Eoin, absolutely fabulous. Well done everyone and off the set immediately, please. NOW! Fire brigade, please!'

He reassured Louis, who came running out on to the gantry, that the fire was under control and everyone was safe. Then, as if at the flick of a switch, this production, which had consumed him for months, indeed the 1916 Rising itself and all its dead heroes, counted for nothing any more. Gavin Bloom quietly sidestepped the hubbub of hugs and embraces he would normally have been leading and orchestrating. He now had only one focus, one anxiety. Already he was late for his rendezvous and Brendan Barry was in Dublin for one night only. Even though Gavin ran to his car, and drove too fast, in his heart he was already convinced that it wasn't going to work out.

Yet, astonishingly, against all logic, everything was OK. When Gavin hurried into the Coffee Dock at the Ballsbridge Inter-Continental, sweating, apologetic and mildly hysterical, Brendan Barry was waiting calmly, seemingly unfazed by any delay. He simply suggested, quite brazenly, that they go straight up to his room. They did. What Gavin had not expected was how such an easy, charming, accommodating man afterwards became this lonely clinging child. Fortunately, he found the inconsistency appealing. Tonight at least. Gavin felt the need to speak, even if only in a whisper.

'Do you think we're the only two in Ireland?'

'Hmm?'

'You know, right now, together, like this?'

'Fellahs?'

'Yes.'

Brendan sounded amused. 'I doubt it.'

'But sometimes you'd think there was no one else in the whole country, wouldn't you?'

'Sure you work in Teilifís. Everyone says it's full of poofs.'

'Ah yeah, I know. And it seems that way. But things aren't always as they seem. I mean, look at me. Twenty-seven and this is my first time.'

It was impossible not to hear the genuine surprise in Brendan's voice.

'Are you serious?'

'Yes. Oh I've seen the inside of Bartley's and even had the odd flirt but… no.'

Brendan squeezed tighter and yawned.

'Well, that's even nicer then.'

Gavin wondered why, having talked for Ireland all day, he couldn't stop himself talking now.

'It's hard to know what anything means, isn't it? When I first noticed that people thought there was something different about me, I didn't know what that was because... well, I was just me. What made it more confusing was some people liked me and some people hated me for the same reason. Then I find myself with a baby and even though I'm not even sure if I want one, suddenly a lot more people seemed to like me again 'cause they're thinking, oh, it's all right, he enjoys acting like a queer but he isn't really, it's all just for a laugh, a bit of an act. He's just... flamboyant. But of course I'd already started thinking maybe I wasn't just flamboyant 'cause I was noticing men all the time now and not only the obvious queens but all sorts. I couldn't stop. Even when I was out with little Alice and her mother I'd be taking sly glances at fellahs passing. One day I was staring at this young couple in the canteen and one of the crew at my table says to me, 'You're a married man you dirty dog, keep your eyes off her,' not realising that it wasn't her I was looking at. Brenda saw through me, though. Alice's mother. Not that she ever said the words. She could see I was just sort of drifting away from her. Avoiding. Spending more time at work. Going away on too many outside broadcasts. And even when we were together nothing much was happening any more. Anyway... So she left. We didn't even have a decent row about it. "I'm not really what you want, am I?" was all she said and I couldn't argue with that.'

Gavin had never spoken out like this, never shared such intimate thoughts with another person. When he fell silent again, the steady rise and fall of Brendan's relaxed breathing made him realise that, in fact, he still had not.

Twelve: February 1st

Dom loved being a man among men. Eight months after becoming a minister he still felt the tingle, the thrill, the horn, to put it crudely, every time he sat down for the weekly cabinet meeting; togging out for Ireland's first fifteen. And he loved Seán Lemass, who had gone out on a limb, made an act of faith, perhaps even played loose with the law, to put him in this position. Sober Dom had promised, 'Cross my heart and hope to die,' that he would repay that faith. Unlike some others he could name at this table right now. He tried to listen carefully as Lemass dealt with the main item on the agenda today; the schedule of official events commemorating the fiftieth anniversary of the Easter Rising. As ever, the Taoiseach focused on detail – dates and times, places, lists. Matters of fact. A stranger would never have guessed that the man talking had, at seventeen, been in the thick of it, fighting in the GPO alongside those who subsequently became martyrs and saints. At seventeen the only people Dom had fought were classmates in Clongowes; handbags at ten paces. It had never been proved either way if, during the War of Independence, Lemass really had been one of Collins' hitmen, the notorious twelve apostles, yet every time Dom was tempted to rubbish the rumour, it would occur to him that it wasn't poets or hotheaded idealists who were best fitted to walk into a house by dawn's early light, put a gun to a man's head and blow him away. If patience and calm control were what was required to be an assassin, then Seán Lemass might well be your man. And if he had helped change the history of Ireland back then, it seemed to Dom he had done it again forty years later, perhaps to greater effect, without ego or bombast, offering a vision of economic transformation in the same cautious, dull tone with which he was now outlining a plan to use Croke Park as the venue for the big commemorative pageant.

Looking at those grouped closely around the Leader, Dom amused himself by framing them as a modern, rather grubby, version of some Dutch old master; a sort of tableau vivant of betrayal. Jack and Neil sat closest to the Taoiseach, both employing their weapon of choice, the pipe, perfect for puffing, plucking and pointing. Haloes of smoke hung above them. Look at us, the pipes seem to declare, we are symbols of unhurried intelligence, owned and operated by weighty men who can be trusted with the reins of power. Next was Charlie, the young genius, the lizard son-in-law who knew how to hold a cigarette with style. Did Lemass really trust him? After all, Dom, who was his pal and, even since sobriety, still enjoyed his company above all others, certainly wouldn't trust him. At least George, sitting next to Jack, made no bones about his ambition to succeed Lemass, although of course he didn't see it as ambition, more like entitlement. When Dom's eyes flicked to Dr Pat he felt the old sore, the long-time local rivalry, pinch and torment him. His inner voice savagely mimicked quiet, harmless, loyal Dr Pat's modest locutions. 'Who me? The leadership of the nation? Ah no, no, no. What am I but a quiet, gentle, empathetic, highly intelligent rural physician turned reluctant statesman? Me, born to serve? … Well, of course, should the Nation call, should the people cry out, who am I to deny them their wish?' Dom was convinced that every one of them was praying for Lemass to depart the scene as soon as possible. He knew the rationale exactly, he had heard Charlie actually put it in words. Having won the Party a third election in a row, there was no way he could win them a fourth. So, because whoever took over would need as much time as possible to prepare for the next battle, the sooner Lemass moved on the better.

Dom did not support this. He wanted his beloved boss to go on and on. The main reason, the decent reason, was that he considered him to be a truly great Taoiseach, but there was a less decent reason. Dom didn't fool himself that personal ambition played no part in his thinking. He was just glad that, as it happened, ambition and loyalty to Lemass were comfortable bedfellows. Dom didn't see a fourth victory either. Common sense told him it wasn't possible to keep beating the odds. People got sick of the sight of you sooner or later. After defeat in, say, 1969, Fianna Fáil would then need a different kind of leader, an inspirational one to restore them and lead them triumphantly back to power at the following election in 1974 or thereabouts. Dom allowed himself to think he might become this leader. All going well, he could end up Taoiseach at fifty-four, a perfect age for the job. Even thinking about it gave him heartburn. To turn this ambition into a reality it would not be enough for him to traipse along as an averagely competent minister like so many of this lot. The thing to do was pull a rabbit out of the hat, something that would set him apart, make the whole Nation love him even more than the Party hacks did already. As the cabinet meeting continued to discuss banal details of 1916 commemorative events, Dom's thoughts drifted about like the smoke from his colleagues' pipes. Exactly what form might his rabbit take? What would his Big Idea be? He knew it was out there somewhere, waiting for him. As long as Lemass stayed put, he had time on his side.

*

The expression on Fr Mullaly's face made Mr Cormac Kiely think of the celebratory excitement of the duet 'We Did It' from *My Fair Lady.* Needless to say, he cast the smiling parish priest as Colonel Pickering, with himself playing Professor Henry Higgins. The temporary partitions had been removed and the completed extension to the Church of Our Lady of Consolation could now be viewed from every angle. Cormac Kiely was confident that the snag list would be a short one. Next Sunday, Fr Mullaly had told him, the bunting would be out, the Papal Flag would fly alongside the tricolour, all local dignitaries, including the city's recently appointed government minister, would be present and the Bishop would join with him and his curates in concelebrating the new vernacular mass to mark the successful completion of the church renovation. While Cormac Kiely fully recognised the value of a big finale, he also hoped that Fr Mullaly appreciated how deeply considered his design was, from a theological as well as an architectural viewpoint. He had done his homework thoroughly, assiduously studied relevant documents from Vatican II as well as drawing inspiration from Le Corbusier and Gibberd. He had eschewed entirely the cruciform shape of the old church, the hard lines and angles, the railings that copperfastened a rigid separation of Priest and People, replacing it with the softer embrace of a large octagon, full of stained glass in the brightest colours to suffuse the space with heavenly light. The seating flowed naturally from the pews in the old nave into the new extension, gathering in a circle round the altar area so the congregation would feel like guests at a feast. The freestanding altar was of granite, symbolising simplicity and strength. All these innovations were a source of deep pride to Cormac. From their earlier conversations he had reason to hope that Fr Mullaly would pick up on many of these subtleties. As the parish priest stepped on to the altar area he smiled at Cormac.

'No railings. It feels strange but, I have to say, profoundly satisfying. No more barriers between priest and flock.'

Precisely, Cormac thought. Fr Mullaly stepped onto the second and then third level where the altar table and tabernacle were. He stood centre-stage, as Cormac like to think of it, facing the main body of the old part of the church.

'Raising the altar table a further step was an inspired suggestion on your part. It feels perfect, well done.'

Cormac acknowledged the compliment, though he was aware that the extra elevation had been Fr Mullaly's own suggestion. Something about ascending to the table of the Lord, he remembered.

'I hope that next Sunday, when the parishioners see this for the first time, they will appreciate your work, Cormac, not perhaps the intellectual complexity of your achievement, but at least they might, at a simple level, recognise something of its elegance and concede that all the collections and bingo nights and fund-raising of the last few years have been well worth it. I certainly think so.'

Cormac nodded modestly. He noticed Fr Mullaly was now staring towards the back of the church, presumably looking at the old organ loft, which had been sealed with reinforced glass to create a 'crying area', an idea imported from churches in the US. No doubt Fr Mullaly was enjoying the thought that, at last, his homilies would not have to compete with a wailing chorus, a particular hazard in a parish like this where there were so many small children, and mothers had little choice but to bring them along. However, when Cormac turned also, he realised that it was not the crying loft that had drawn the priest's attention. It was a thin little boy standing in the aisle at the back. Fr Mullaly's tone hinted he was not pleased to be interrupted.

'Yes, what is it?'

'Sister Goretti said I had to come and see you, Father. Father Tierney told me you were here.'

'Sister Goretti?'

'Yes. About my first Holy Communion.'

'Oh yes. What time? You're early?'

'Sister Goretti said three o'clock.'

Cormac couldn't help checking his watch. Exactly three o'clock. The child's hair was carefully brushed and his clothes looked like they might be the best his mother could manage.

'Yes, yes. Well unfortunately I have very important business to deal with at the moment. I'll arrange another time with Sister Goretti.'

The boy looked so disappointed that Cormac was touched. Quietly, diplomatically, he whispered to Fr Mullaly.

'You know, I have a number of minor things to check for my snag-list. I'd be happy to take ten minutes on my own. Then we can finish our discussion?'

'Well, as long as it suits you, Cormac. In fact I think I did promise Sister Goretti I'd talk to this little fellow.'

Fr Mullaly went to the back of the church and sat the boy down. As Cormac moved about, checking details, making little notes, he was conscious of the distant voices, one deep, one light, first one, then the other. It sounded in Cormac's ears like a mildly comic duet with the rhythm of question and answer. From the way it flowed back and forth it seemed the boy knew his part very well. If anything, he had the larger role. They went on longer than Cormac expected. He had finished his checklist long before Fr Mullaly dismissed the boy. As he was leaving, it occurred to Cormac he might be useful for a particular test.

'Little boy, before you go, could you do us a favour? Sorry, what's your name?'

'Francis.'

'Francis, have you a good pair of lungs on you?'

The child looked puzzled.

'Can you project? Do you mind shouting?'

Francis smiled and shyly shook his head. Cormac pointed up to the crying loft.

'Well, you'd be doing Fr Mullaly and me a great favour if you went up there and shouted your head off. Do you mind?'

'It's all right, Francis. It would help us.'

'Shout as loud as you like.'

Francis went up the stairs. When Cormac and the priest stepped onto the altar and turned, they saw the child, his hands pushing against the reinforced glass, his mouth open, in what looked like a sustained howl.

But they could hear nothing.

'Amazing, Cormac. That's absolutely splendid.'

Fr Mullaly gestured and the boy come down. Cormac noticed that the priest seemed preoccupied, staring after him as he left the church. Finally he spoke.

'You know, when sent to a parish like this, one hopes that, however unlikely the possibility may be, one will uncover a diamond in the rough. Well, Sister Goretti requested I see that boy because she feels strongly he is more than ready for his first Holy Communion; very bright, very pious, with understanding beyond his years. She told me an interesting story to illustrate this. The boy came first in the Christmas spelling test and she offered him a choice of prizes, a two-shilling piece or the class crib to take home. Well, apparently without hesitation, he chose the crib.'

'Very devout. But I don't understand. Is there some difficulty?'

'A technical one. As you know, the church deems seven to be the age at which a child has sufficient reason to be allowed take the sacrament of Communion. This boy won't be seven until June and first Holy Communion happens in May. Sister Goretti would like me to make an exception.'

Out of nowhere Cormac felt a spasm, a dart of jealousy. By coincidence, his youngest daughter Gráinne would be seven in June also. She was clever and devout as any child her age but she wasn't even in the Holy Communion class. It had been long decided that she would make it next year. Why should this boy be any different? Fr Mullaly was still talking about him.

'I asked him his Catechism. He answered everything correctly; original sin, the difference between venial and mortal sin, he named the seven deadly sins, all the sacraments, he understood what contrition and penance were all about, he explained the Resurrection, the Ascension, sanctifying grace and actual grace, Judgement Day, Heaven, Hell, Purgatory, Limbo. When he recited the Confiteor and the Our Father and the Creed he didn't sing it off in a meaningless way like most boys his age. He said it with proper emphasis and reverence.'

Cormac Kiely recognised his own reaction as foolish jealous anger. This was silly, he told himself. Yet he knew already that, when he got home this evening, he would be asking his daughter to say the Creed and making sure she knew it properly. Fr Mullaly was still speaking about this boy.

'I even went beyond what a first Holy Communicant would

normally be expected to know and asked him questions about temptation. I wouldn't even expect you to know the answer,s let alone a six-year-old? What is temptation? The child answered precisely. "Temptation is anything that incites, provokes or urges us to offend God." I asked what is the best means of overcoming temptation? Can we always resist temptation? Is it a sin to be tempted? He could answer them all.'

By now Cormac had heard enough about this boy, who seemed to have entirely distracted Fr Mullaly from the important matter of his church renovation. Did he think this child was some saint in the making? Cormac now regretted allowing Louise to persuade him to wait another year before sending Gráinne to school. She would have been just as ready for Holy Communion as this little brat. He couldn't stop himself making one last mean – he knew even as he said it how mean it was – and destructive comment.

'I've just discovered something unexpected about you, Father. Having experienced the remarkable complexity of your intellect through our work on this marvellous project –'

'Well, thank you.'

'I'd never have thought you would let the heart rule the head. Particularly with regard to the Holy Sacraments.'

Fr Mullaly seemed to take this on board. He nodded, thoughtful. The architect steered the discussion away from the child, back to the fine details of his renovation but, even though they talked for another hour and he received many more compliments for his achievement, Cormac Kiely never quite felt he succeeded in recapturing Fr Mullaly's full attention.

*

Too much coffee. Far too much Hanley. It was after midnight in the Coffee Dock and no sign of Charlie or Brian or anyone who might rescue Dom. For some time now he had been wondering if all the favourable mentions in the famous column, all the oleaginous myth-making was worth the time spent and tedium suffered indulging the tenacious ego that once again, was keeping him from his bed. Tonight it was the presidential election in June that served as the trampoline on which Hanley could bounce the enormous arse of his opinion.

'As a perspicacious man, Dom, tell me this: have they lost their grip at party headquarters, putting Dev up again? I know, I know, you don't need to explain the thinking, 1916 hero, fiftieth anniversary, I know all that.'

The trouble was Hanley knew fucking everything. And insisted on telling Dom everything he knew, even about Dom himself. But if he stopped indulging him, what then? Could he survive without the fairy dust of Hanley's approval in his weekly column?

'The man is eighty-four and blind as O'Carolan! He's not just yesterday's man, he's the day before yesterday's man. Does anyone in Fianna Fáil watch the *Late Late Show*? Has anyone been looking at what the kids are up to in the beat clubs?'

Dom drew some amusement from the disturbing image of balding piggy-eyed Hanley, who had probably never been young, infiltrating beat clubs to do a little research into what the kids were up to.

'They're going wild for the likes of Jagger while Dev probably thinks Butch Moore is a pernicious influence. That's if he even knows who Butch Moore is. Ye're on a hiding to nothing with this. If Dev wins then the country loses. It means we're still backward as bejasus with the oldest head of state in the known world. He's older than Mao or Tito! If Dev loses it's humiliation for an aging national hero and a massive embarrassment to the Government.'

'He won't lose.'

'He might lose. I think he will lose. And I'm getting whispers in my ear that he doesn't even want to run.'

Dom knew this to be true and loathed himself for being so weak as to offer Hanley a tiny nod of the head by way of unattributable confirmation. Jesus! This was pathetic. He had given up the drink, why couldn't he beat this other addiction? Sucking at the media teat. How long more would tonight's incarceration continue before he could legitimately make an excuse and leave without causing offence and tantrums and probably a thinly veiled reprimand in next week's column?

'And the laugh of it is, the madness of it is, the perfect solution, the ideal candidate is staring you all in the face.'

With a repellent combination of canine eagerness and feline arrogance, Hanley's jowly grin begged the question. Dom knew the choice was either a knuckle sandwich to wipe that look off his face, or just give in and ask.

'And who would that be?'

'Lemass.'

'Lemass?'

'Lemass.'

'For President? Give up being Taoiseach? Why?'

'Oh I know, sure I'd have him as Taoiseach for another thirty years, but that ain't gonna happen, as the man says. He's getting on, no more than the rest of us, although of course, compared to Dev, he's but a leppin' foal. But don't you see the advantages of sending Lemass to the Park? They are several and significant. First of all, in crude election terms, you'd be on a winner. He'd sail in, no question, right? Secondly it would allow Dev to do his bit of wreath-laying this Easter, attend a commemorative Mass or three and, finally, with dignity, drift away, undefeated, into the dusk of a well-earned retirement. Thirdly, if I was looking for someone who might do something interesting with the constitutional abomination known as the Presidency, then Seán Lemass would be the man I'd choose. And finally… it paves the way for a dynamic young Taoiseach. Someone with Big Ideas.'

Now it hit Dom where this was coming from. Hanley was parroting Charlie's script. Did the Lizard son-in-law seriously think that by some miracle this would actually happen? That Lemass would shuffle off to Áras an Uachtarán and Charlie would, in the blink of an eye, succeed him as Taoiseach? Wishful thinking. The trouble with people like Charlie was that they thought power was all about political manoeuvring, being the smart cookie. But Dom was genuinely surprised at Hanley thinking the same way because, buried somewhere under that butter-basted ego, a proper, serious brain lurked. Had he become so besotted with the Lizard that he had lost the capacity for independent thought? If so, Dom would have to keep his own counsel in future. Come up with a Big Idea in silence.

Thirteen: March 18th

Sister Goretti said that the big 1916 poster with the Proclamation of the Irish Republic on it had been sent to every school in the country. Sister Goretti said the Proclamation was the most important event in the history of Ireland and it happened fifty years ago this Easter. Francis had asked his dad if he remembered the 1916 Rising but, before he could open his mouth to answer, his mam said, 'The cheek of you, neither of us were even born until years after the Rising.' The nuns had hung the poster on the wall near the main door of the school and Francis couldn't pass by without stopping to look at it. He had even started learning the Proclamation off by heart. He stood in front of the poster for a couple of minutes every day until he had learned another small bit. Francis found it easy to remember things like poems and songs, his Catechism and even how to say Mass. If there was a word he didn't understand, he was good at guessing how to say it. Already he could remember loads of it.

> TO THE PEOPLE OF IRELAND. IRISHMEN AND IRISHWOMEN: In the name of God and of the dead generations from which she receives her old tradition of nationhood, Ireland, through us, summons her children to her flag and strikes for her freedom. Having organised and trained her manhood through her secret revolutionary organisation, the Irish Republican Brotherhood, and through her open military organisations, the Irish Volunteers and the Irish Citizen Army, having patiently perfected her discipline, having resolutely waited for the right moment to reveal

> itself, she now seizes that moment, and supported by her exiled children in America and by gallant allies in Europe, but relying in the first on her own strength, she strikes in full confidence of victory. We declare the right of the people of Ireland to the ownership of Ireland and to the unfettered –

Francis understood every word until 'unfettered'. Then straight after that were more hard words like 'sovereign' and 'indefeasible' and 'usurpation'. The sentence with 'usurpation' in it was very hard to learn and every time he tried to say it all off from the start he always got stuck there.

> 'The long usurpation of that right by a foreign people and government has not extinguished the right, nor can it ever be extinguished except by the destruction of the Irish people.'

It got a bit easier after that. He had never seen the word 'asserted' before but he could guess what it meant. And 'sovereignty' was like 'sovereign' so, by the time he read 'sovereign' a second time. he'd guessed that it must have something to do with being free.

> '... We hereby proclaim the Irish Republic as a Sovereign Independent State and we pledge our lives and the lives of our comrades in arms to the cause of its freedom, of its welfare, and of its exaltation among the nations.'

Francis wished he could pledge something to God and Ireland but he didn't know what. Yesterday he wore a shamrock and a badge with a harp on it. His dad took him and Marian and Martin to the St Patrick's Day parade. It wasn't as good as the big parade in Dublin that he saw on television later, with the high-school bands from America but still, they stood in the rain cheering all the local floats from Mattersons and Krups and Spaights and the CBS pipe band and the Boherbouy brass band. They were proud of their city and proud to be Irish. Since he'd first heard about the 1916 Rising, Francis had prayed every night that Ireland would always be free. He also prayed that he would be allowed to make his Holy Communion soon. He wanted to do more but he didn't know what. Learning the Proclamation was something. The sentence he learned today was easy.

> 'The Irish Republic is entitled to, and hereby claims, the allegiance of every Irishman and Irishwoman.'

He didn't know what 'allegiance' was. He would ask Sister Goretti. He was more than halfway through now. He hoped to learn the whole Proclamation by the Easter holidays.

On the top part of the poster there were photos of the seven leaders of the Rising who were executed by the British. Sister Goretti liked Patrick Pearse best of all and talked about him all the time. She told the class he was a teacher who owned a very special school called St Enda's and he loved young people. He was a poet as well and he wrote poems about the beauty of Ireland. He was a very good Catholic and when he was a small boy he made a promise to God that he would give his life for Ireland. Every time Sister Goretti talked about him her voice changed into a slow whisper. Francis wanted to like Patrick Pearse as much as Sister Goretti but for some reason he didn't. He wasn't sure why. Was it because in the photograph he turned his face away? All the other 1916 heroes looked straight out. That's what people were supposed to do when their photo was being taken. He was always told look at the camera and say 'cheese'. His dad was always caught with his eyes closed, which was funny. Why did Patrick Pearse look away and only show one side of his face? Francis asked Sister Goretti about it and she said it was a mystery, but maybe his mind was on more important things like the freedom of Ireland and he wasn't bothered about posing for a photograph. Francis asked his godmother Mary and she said she hadn't a clue but his godfather Mikey said it was because he had a pig in his eye. Francis didn't know what he meant and his godmother said don't mind that fellah he's only acting the eejit and his godfather said no I'm serious, he had a pig in his eye and he was too embarrassed to let people see it. He told Francis to think about it and, later on that day, Francis got it. Pig. Sty. Patrick Pearse had a sty in his eye. He asked his dad if that was true and his dad said he couldn't be sure but he had heard some story along those lines. After that, every time Francis looked at the photo of Patrick Pearse he tried to imagine the other eye. Had he turned his face to one side because he was afraid everyone would be laughing at the sty in his eye? Some of the boys laughed at Dickie Fennessy, a boy in senior infants who was cross-eyed, so maybe Patrick Pearse was right to turn away. Still, it didn't make Francis like him any better. His favourite 1916 hero was Seán MacDermott. He didn't really know why but he always ended up looking at his photo more than all the others. Was it because of his sad eyes? Sister Goretti said Seán McDermot had polio when he was a child and he walked with a limp. Francis wanted to know more but, because Sister Goretti talked about Patrick Pearse so much, she hadn't much time to say anything about Seán MacDermott or any of the others. All she said about James Connolly was that he was injured during the Rising and he couldn't stand up, so the British had cruelly executed him tied to a chair. She said Tom Clarke was the oldest. That was easy to see, with his white hair and moustache and glasses like his Grandad Robert who was eighty-two when he died. Francis couldn't imagine him going out with a gun to start a war. But looking at the photographs of the leaders of the Rising, Francis couldn't imagine any of them being soldiers, not like the ones he saw in the *Victor* or *Hotspur* anyway. Except James Connolly. He looked tough enough but even he was a bit too fat. He looked like Uncle Seán Enright with his moustache and beer belly. Tom Clarke was too old and Seán MacDermott had a limp and Sister Goretti said that Tomás MacDonagh and Joseph Plunkett were poets like Patrick Pearse. They were all dreamers and poets she said. And martyrs. But then Francis thought, maybe that was the reason everyone said they were so brave, because they went out and fought even though they weren't any good at it. Francis didn't like fighting even though he was tall for his age, and he was useless at throwing stones. He'd never have the courage to go into battle like that. Not even to save Ireland? Well, maybe, if he had to, Jesus would give him the courage.

'Francis, have you any notion of coming into class?'

When he looked around he noticed that there was no one left in the corridor except himself. He saw straight away that, though Sister Goretti had her serious face on, she was only pretending to be angry and was smiling underneath because she knew he wasn't doing anything bad, only thinking about the heroes of 1916.

'Sorry, Sister.'

Sister Goretti clapped her hands for attention as she followed Francis into the classroom.

'We've found our lost sheep daydreaming in the corridor. Now, would the class like to tell Francis what we're doing next? We're learning what?'

'A new song.'

'Exactly. And what is it called?'

'"God Save Ireland".'

'Very good. OK, Francis? "God Save Ireland", there's the words on the blackboard. So, boys, sing each line after me. And two, three, four…

'High upon the gallows tree swung the noble-hearted three.'

'Not too bad. Once more.'

And the class tried again. Sister Goretti taught them all kinds of songs but recently they were always about Ireland and 1916. They had learned 'A Nation Once Again', 'Kevin Barry', 'The Foggy Dew', 'Deep in Canadian Woods', 'The Tri-Coloured Ribbon O' and the National Anthem, which she said was called '*Amhrán na bhFiann*'. Francis liked today's song, especially the chorus, because Sister Goretti encouraged everyone to sing it out as loud as they could and even the crows in the class cawked at the tops of their voices:

'"God save Ireland!" said the heroes,
"God save Ireland!" said they all.
"Whether on the gallows high
Or the battlefield we die,
Oh, what matter when for Erin dear we fall!"'

Soon it was dinner break. As everyone ran out of class, Sister Goretti called Francis back. She held up an envelope with a very serious look on her face.

'Now, Francis. This is a note for your mother. Promise me you won't open it.'

'I promise, Sister.'

'I know you won't. And don't worry, it's not bad news, it's good news.'

'Is it about my Holy Communion, Sister?'

Sister Goretti smiled and the way she smiled, Francis knew it had to be.

'Your mother will tell you everything.'

She handed him the envelope.

*

Ann stirred a big spoon of Bisto into the minced meat and onions. Her shoulders and neck still felt stiff and two doses of Mrs Cullen's Powders hadn't got rid of the headache. She couldn't put up with it any more. It was happening too often. There was only one thing for it and that was to go see the doctor as soon as the dinner was over with. She hated sitting in that dispensary, but what choice had she? At least there was only Marian, Martin and Francis to cater for today. They'd better behave themselves or she wouldn't be responsible for her actions. Martin and Marian arrived home first. Ann told Martin to wash his hands and stay out from under her feet. She gave Marian margarine and told her to mash the potatoes and then set the table. There were a few more minutes of peace and quiet until Francis burst in, shouting 'Mam! Mam!' and waving an envelope at her. It was all Ann could do not to give him a clatter.

'Sister Goretti said to give you this. I think it's about my Holy Communion, Mam. Mam!'

'All right, all right. Put it down there, can't you see my hands are full? I'll read it in a minute.'

'I can open it for you. Please, Mam.'

'I said put it down there and get out.'

'But Mam, Sister Goretti said.'

'I warning you, Martin.'

'I'm Francis.'

'Don't you correct me. Now get out and wait for your dinner!'

Even though he put down the envelope and went out of the scullery, Ann could still feel him standing in the hall staring in. It made her want to scream. She dished up the savoury minced meat.

'Marian, be a good girl and put the mash and the beans on those plates and bring them in, would you.'

Ann picked up the envelope. 'Mrs A. Strong. By hand.' Out of the corner of her eye she saw Francis edging to the doorway like a dog hoping to be invited in.

'I'm not opening this until you go and start your dinner.'

For a second she thought he was going to dare her, then he turned away and went into the back room. Ann looked at the envelope. A collection for some charity probably. Money for something anyway. it was always the same.

> Dear Mrs Strong,
>
> Happy news! Fr Mullaly has agreed to a special dispensation which will allow Francis to make his first Holy Communion this May. It's a great privilege. Fr Mullaly thinks Francis is a very devout and intelligent boy. This also means that Francis will be moving on to the Christian Brothers in September. Father Mullaly has arranged for him to meet Brother Skelly this afternoon to decide which class Francis is best suited for. I am confident he will get into the 'A' stream.

Brother Skelly will be in room five upstairs in the Old School building. If you cannot go today please send him back to school as normal and we will try to arrange another appointment.

Searbhónta Dé

Goretti.

Despite her headache and her annoyance at the way this arrangement was thrown at her out of the blue like this, not to mention, all of a sudden, the extra cost of a new suit for Francis, Ann couldn't help welling up at the thought of him getting his wish to make his first Holy Communion this year. And getting a special dispensation! If Sister Goretti and Father Mullaly thought so much of him, that must be a good thing, surely? CBS wasn't too far from the dispensary, so she could drop him off on her way. Ann went into the back room and was glad to see that, excited as Francis was about this letter, it hadn't affected his appetite and he had managed to make a fair hole in his dinner. By some miracle he didn't go wild when she gave him the news, but his eyes and mouth opened wide and Ann could tell he was more excited than he had ever been in his life, which was saying something. Marian said that's brilliant, and Martin said he'd better buy him something out of all the money he was going to get for his Holy Communion. Ann told Francis that instead of going back to school today he had to go see Brother Skelly in CBS. She could tell that was a big shock. Martin started laughing and said Smelly Skelly would murder him. He was the worst of all of them. Smelly would grab him by the hair at the back of his head and twist it like this. Martin tried to grab Francis' hair but he jumped off his seat in time. Ann told him to sit back down and finish his dinner and if there was another word out of Martin she'd take his plate away. Francis sat. Then the questions started, the endless questions. Why did he have to go in to see Brother Skelly? Was it for a test? What things would he ask him? On and on and on, standing outside the bedroom while Ann got into her best clothes for the doctor. How would he get there? How long would he be there? On and on, he didn't even shut up while she was washing his face and hands and putting on a clean vest and shirt. Would Brother Skelly ask him questions in Irish or in English? Would there be a spelling test? On and on, down the road to the bus stop, at the bus stop, on the bus. Would Brother Skelly ask him his Catechism like Fr Mullaly did? What day was his first Holy Communion? If he was making his Holy Communion did that mean he had to make his first confession too? Telling him to shush because everyone was listening and the conductor was getting annoyed only shut him up for a few seconds, then it all started again. Ann's head was lifting off her by the time the bus stopped near Sexton Street. Of course he wouldn't hold her hand and as soon as they went through the main gates he started running ahead, even though he hadn't a clue where he was going. He stopped at the main door of the grey three-storey building and looked back at Ann, who just walked past it.

'Smart as you think you are, you haven't a clue where you're going. Now just calm down and stop racing ahead. Take my hand.'

Upstairs in the old school building two other boys were waiting with their mothers outside room five. Ann now felt a bit mortified that she was leaving Francis on his own. She spoke loud enough to be heard.

'I've a few messages to get but I won't be too long and Brother Skelly told me if I wasn't back when you were finished it was all right for you to wait here for me. Do you understand, love?'

'Will you bring me back something from the shop?'

Ann saw the other two mothers smile at that. They seemed nice. She threw her eyes up.

'The usual.'

'Oh sure, my fellah's the same.'

'We'll keep an eye on him for you.'

'Thanks very much.'

By the time Ann was back on the street, her neck and shoulders were knotted with tension. The headache hadn't got any worse but it wasn't easing, either. She hurried down Tanyard Lane and on to Gerald Griffin Street. She prayed silently that there wouldn't be a big queue for Dr Greaney. She hated waiting in that ugly old building. Everyone in there always looked poor and miserable. When she got inside she looked down the wide gloomy hall before sitting down. There were six doctors' offices, three on each side, with long wooden benches sticking out for patients to sit on. Doctor Greaney's was one of the worst queues. Seven people ahead of her, could she have no luck? Two of the other doctors had only one person waiting. It really drove Ann mad that patients weren't allowed choose the shortest queue. Doctor Greaney was the name on her medical card and it didn't matter if there were a hundred people waiting outside his door, Doctor Greaney it had to be. Her sister Mona, who didn't qualify for the medical card because she had only one child, had to pay for everything, but at least it meant she could choose her own doctor and go to a proper surgery and change him if she didn't like his attitude, as she had done a couple of times. Knowing Mona, she'd never put up with Dr Greaney, who could be a bit abrupt. But Ann had no other choice. She joined the queue.

*

It seemed to Francis that he was waiting for ever. The other two boys had each been with Brother Skelly for a long time. The second boy came out with a funny look on his face and he wouldn't answer his mother when she asked how he got on. Francis couldn't help remembering what Martin had said about Brother Skelly. Had he grabbed the hair on the back of that boy's head and twisted it? When Francis was called in, the first thing he noticed was a long leather strap swinging slowly from a belt. He looked away from it up to Brother Skelly's big face. His hair was white and his skin was white. His teeth were yellow. There was hair growing out of his nose. But he was smiling.

'Sit down there, Francis.'

Francis sat where he was told in front of a big desk. Brother

Skelly went round to the other side humming diddley-idle and sat down as well. He hummed for a few more seconds, looking straight at Francis and then suddenly spoke in Irish.

'*An bhfuil aon Gaeilge agat a bhuachaill?*'

'*Tá Gaeilge agam a Bhráthair.*'

'*Go maith. Cad is ainm duit?*

Brother Skelly knew his name already so Francis guessed he wanted to find out if he could say the Irish version.

'*Proinsias is ainm dom.*'

'*Agus cén aois a bhfuil agat?*'

Did Brother Skelly already know he was still only six? Had Fr Mullaly remembered to tell him that was all right? He couldn't tell a lie but he hoped it wouldn't get him into trouble.

'*Tá me sé bliain d'aois.*'

'*Agus cén mhí a mbeidh do lá breithe?*'

'*Mí Mheitheamh. Beidh mé seacht ansin.*'

'*Go maith. Agus an bhfuil tú ábálte aon phaidir a rá i nGaeilge?*'

Francis nodded. He could say lots of prayers in Irish. Brother Skelly waved a hand at him.

'*Lean ar aghaidh mar sin.*'

He decided to say the Hail Mary.

'*S'é do Bheatha, a Mhuire, atá lán de ghrásta, Tá an Tiarna leat. Is beannaithe thú idir mhná, agus is beannaithe toradh do bhroinne, Íosa. A Naomh Mhuire, a mháthair Dé guigh orainn, na peacaigh, anois agus ar uair ár mbáis.* Amen.'

'*Go hanna mhaith.* Well done. And are you as good at the maths? Do you know your three times table?'

Francis did. Brother Skelly then asked him his six times table, his nine time tables and his eleven times table. Then he spoke very fast.

'If I have eleven apples and I give you six and you give three to your friend and he gives me back one, how many apples do I have?'

'Six.'

And your friend?'

'Two.'

And yourself?

'Three.'

Brother Skelly sat back and laughed.

'*Maith an Bhuachaill.* There's many a fellah I caught out with that one. Now do you like reading?'

'Yes, Brother.'

Brother Skelly handed him a piece of paper.

'Try that for me. Have a look at it first if you like.'

Francis looked at it for a few seconds. The only word he didn't understand was 'hath' and but it looked easy to say. He began:

'The beauty of the world hath made me sad,
This beauty that will pass;
Sometimes my heart hath shaken with great joy
To see a leaping squirrel in a tree,
Or a red lady-bird upon a stalk,
Or little rabbits in a field at evening,
Lit by a slanting sun,
Or some green hill where shadows drifted by
Some quiet hill where mountainy man hath sown
And soon would reap; near to the gate of Heaven.'

Brother Skelly took the sheet from him and asked him to spell 'beauty', 'field', 'quiet' and 'mountainy'.

'*Go hanna mhaith.* Now. Soon you'll be making your first confession and Holy Communion. Are you looking forward to that?

'I am, Brother.'

'Of course you are, but no good even thinking about Holy Communion unless you make a good confession. What is confession?'

Francis knew he had say the exact answer from the Catechism.

'Confession is the telling of our sins to a duly authorised priest, for the purpose of obtaining forgiveness.'

'Why does the priest give us a penance after confession?'

'The priest gives us a penance after confession that we may satisfy God for the temporal punishment due to our sins.'

'Very good. And don't worry, I won't be giving you any penance after this. So, tell me Francis. You're a fine tall lad for your age, do you enjoy sports?

'Yes, Brother.'

'Are you a good hurler?'

'I don't know, Brother.'

'Well, we'll find that out soon enough when you come to us in September. Very nice to meet you, Francis.'

He wrote something down while he was talking then stood up and went to open the door. Francis was sorry it was all over. He liked sitting there with Brother Skelly answering questions. This was even better than in class because he didn't have to wait and give others a chance before Sister Goretti picked him. As Francis left, he thought again about what Martin said. His brother must have been telling lies, or maybe he just didn't know how nice Brother Skelly was?

*

They were all gone: the woman who said hello to everyone who arrived and asked them what their trouble was but never said a word about her own; the smiling girl who told her she was seven months gone; the young mother with two small children and a baby in a pram who was afraid the baby might have croup; the chubby boy with his arm in a sling who went red every time anyone said anything to him; the elderly woman who coughed all the time and whose voice was so frail that even the woman next to her couldn't hear anything she said and just answered yes, yes all the time. That woman had, like Ann, dressed up for the occasion and looked embarrassed to be in the dispensary. Finally the rough-looking man who just sat with his head down saying nothing to anyone had gone in and Ann was next. Four more had arrived after her. Surely it couldn't be much longer? Her headache was now less aggravating than the discomfort of the bench and the anxiety of waiting.

Dr Greaney was writing at his desk when she came in. He nodded to a chair then continued. Ann sat and placed her medical card on the desk. When Dr Greaney finished writing he picked it up.

'Now Mrs... Strong. I don't think I've seen you in a while. What's the trouble?'

As Ann began to explain he turned to the filing cabinet and opened a drawer.

'I've been getting these headaches, doctor, on and off since before Christmas. I usually find Mrs Cullen's Powders great but not this time. It starts back here around my shoulder blade and then all the way up my neck to the back of my head. It's not even the pain so much, but it just won't go away.'

Dr Greaney was looking at a file as he spoke.

'It could be hypertension. Perhaps you're under a lot of stress? Ah yes, I remember. The last time you were here with your daughter. November last year. Everything all right there now?'

Ann knew he was politely referring to Marian's monthlies. They had just started and she'd been having cramps and seemed a bit nervous about it all. Ann had also quietly hoped that Dr Greaney would know better how to explain the whole thing to Marian. The poor child had been mortified.

'Yes, she's grand. No more problems –'

'Good. We'd better check that blood pressure. Take off your jacket and blouse, please. Just this arm will do.'

Ann did as she was told. Dr Greaney wrapped the cuff around her upper arm.

'Now, take a couple of deep breaths and relax.'

Ann didn't like the choking feeling on her arm as the cuff squeezed. To take her mind off it she talked.

'You were asking me if I'm under much stress. Well, I don't know, maybe I worry too much about little things. I know we're very lucky in lots of ways and there's people much worse off than we are, I mean, my eldest two now, Ritchie and Gussie, both got jobs straight away after they finished school. And Marian loves school and she's great to help out at home, she's no bother at all. Martin does get into trouble a bit I suppose but, as Fonsie my husband says, if he doesn't like school he doesn't like school and there's nothing much we can do about that. But you see that's where Fonsie and me are different. He's cool as the breeze, you know, takes things as they come and that's well and good but, sometimes, I just wish he'd shift himself and do something –'

'Ah,' said Dr Greaney suddenly, looking at the reading. 'Hmmm. Right.'

He walked round to his desk, sat and began writing. Ann waited for him to say something. What had he found out? Was it serious? Dr Greaney looked up.

'You can get dressed again. Now Mrs Strong, your blood pressure is higher than it should be. Quite high, actually. The headaches are a symptom. I'm going to start you on something, but it's important that you avoid unnecessary stress also. Your husband doesn't put you under too much pressure, I hope?'

From his look, Ann guessed what he meant.

'No. Absolutely not. Fonsie? No.'

'Good. A lot of husbands do you know. Begin immediately, take one today, then one twice a day. I'm giving you enough for thirty days. We'll see how things are then, all right?'

He handed Ann the prescription and her medical card as he opened the door. The next woman was in straight away. The door closed. Too late now to ask any questions. High blood pressure. How serious was that? Avoid tension. Thirty days. See how things are. What then? Ann stared at the prescription. It was just a scribble. Feeling more agitated now than when she came in, Ann joined the long queue for the hatch. Her hope had been that Doctor Greaney would just give her something stronger for the headache and that would be that. But now she had something that didn't sound like it would be easy to get rid of. Was it something that could kill you? Her mother had died of a brain haemorrhage. Blood pressure. High blood pressure. Now she could imagine the blood thumping along her shoulders up her neck. So that was what it was. Pressure. Maybe it was lucky she had done something about it. Maybe she'd caught it in time and this prescription would sort it out.

She noticed the clock on the wall and that didn't do her blood pressure any good at all. It was after half-three. Oh, Sacred Heart! She had left Francis at quarter-past two. He was probably waiting ages. Would he be all right? Was he getting worried? He wouldn't wander off, would he? How long was this going to take? At the top of the queue Ann saw a hand appear from the hatch and take a prescription. Then there was a long wait before the hand appeared again with the medicine in a bag. There were at least a dozen people ahead of her. It was all Ann could do not to scream.

*

Brother Skelly came out of his room, locked it and told Francis he had to lock the main door of the building also. Was someone coming for him? Did he have a brother in the school? There was a bowsie called Strong in fifth class, was he a relation? Francis didn't want Brother Skelly to think bad things about him because of Martin, so he just said that his mother was on her way to collect him. At what time? Francis could see from the clock on the wall that it was only a few minutes before three, so he said three o'clock. Brother Skelly said that was all right so, but he'd have to wait outside.

When Brother Skelly had gone away Francis sat on the step looking all around him. This school was much much bigger than Our Lady of Consolation. There was a huge yard in front of him, wide and very long. At one end near the main gate was the huge grey building he and his mam had passed when they came in and at the other end were barriers. There was building work going on behind them.

Francis stood up and walked around the empty yard, thinking about all the classrooms and the hundreds of boys behind all those windows. Thousands, maybe. He'd love to peep inside, see what they were doing in the classrooms, but he was afraid he'd get caught. The windows were too high up anyway. He knew there were boys at this school all the way up to Leaving Cert. Ritchie was here until after he left when he was sixteen. Gussie the same. So Francis could be here for ten years or maybe even more. He liked the thought of that. He moved closer to the barriers and looked up at the big sign.

Department of Education Project.
SCOIL ÍOSAGÁIN
GUINEY DEVELOPMENTS

There were little gaps between the barriers. He peeked. It was hard to tell if it was one huge long building or lots of small ones. Whatever it was, it looked fantastic. There were loads of men going in and out of the entrances, carrying things, and big machines putting tarmacadam on the ground and men behind with rollers. There were men on ladders putting stuff on the walls. Through the windows, inside, Francis could see men hanging doors. Each bit of the building seemed to be built on stilts, like huts in Africa he had seen on television, only much bigger. The workers were walking around underneath. There was an entrance at the bottom and two floors over that. Francis thought that they must be the classrooms. Each little building was attached at a corner to another little building exactly the same, also built on stilts with an entrance and two floors on top. And another the same, and another and maybe more. The gap he was peeping through was too small for Francis to see all the way. How far did it go? Was this a whole new school? Imagine if in September he was put in a class in this span-new building? It was like they were building it especially for him. Francis got completely lost looking at this world of big tough men on the other side of the barrier, all pushing and pulling, lifting, carrying, pressing, hammering, shovelling. All their hair and faces were grey from the dust. Machines rattled and drilled. The men kept shouting bad words. There were two who seemed to be in charge. They had special jackets on and didn't lift anything. They did most of the roaring and one of them seemed to like pushing people around as well. It looked like a hard, dirty, angry life.

A lorry came from somewhere and stopped. It was carrying

lots of toilet bowls and sinks. It wasn't really like his dad's lorry because it was too big and new but it made him think of his dad and then, suddenly, his mam. He had forgotten all about her. Where was she? Maybe she was here looking for him? He turned around. There was no one else in the yard. Just as Francis was wondering what time it was now, a loud bell rang. A few seconds later doors opened in every building and boys appeared and pressed against each other in the doorways before spreading out into the yard like something being squeezed out of a tube. Francis couldn't believe how many there were and how quickly the yard filled up. The noise even drowned out the sounds from the building site. It seemed to Francis that he was the only person there who wasn't talking to someone or laughing or shouting in groups, trying to make themselves heard above the other boys. And the sound was different from the sound he heard every day in the yard of Our Lady of Consolation. It was louder because there were more pupils but there was something else different, too. Francis listened and then he realised what it was. The voices sounded deeper and lower because there were no girls, just hundreds of boys, most of them much bigger than Francis. Some of them were so big they were more like men. Standing in the middle of this crowded chaos of boys, Francis felt no fear. The opposite. He couldn't wait to be part of it.

*

Ann was anxious but she didn't panic too much about having to push through mauls of rowdy youngfellahs going in the other direction until she got to the Old School building and discovered it was locked. Francis wasn't waiting outside. Where was he? Had he gone looking for her? Had he left the school grounds? Had he felt afraid of all these bigger boys and run off? Had someone hit him? It was all her fault. What if he was knocked down by a car? That awful dispensary. Looking wildly around she saw Martin with some of his pals wheeling his bike out, but he was too far away to hear her shouts. As she started running towards him he cycled off. Boys kept pushing past her, had they no manners?

Ann kept thinking she'd spotted his head of hair but there were lots of boys with mousy short back and sides. The poor child was all alone somewhere. He didn't know anyone. He had never been here before. He must be terrified. As always in a crisis she muttered a prayer: 'Oh St Gerard, please don't let me down. I'll do the nine first Fridays if you send my little baby back to me safely.' A hopeful thought came into her mind. Was Brother Skelly looking after him? What would he think of her keeping him waiting for so long? She'd be mortified. Maybe he'd brought him to the Monastery building? Ann wasn't sure where to find it but it was a chance at least. She looked around for a teacher who might direct her but there were none to be seen, just noisy boys. The yard was emptying very fast now. Two older pupils, who looked about fifteen, were talking quietly as they came towards her. They seemed well-behaved and respectable. She called them. 'Excuse me lads do you know where the Monastery is?' They pointed and when Ann turned to see where she should go it was like a miracle because they seemed to be pointing directly at a thin mousy-haired little boy, standing all alone, looking around.

Apart entirely from the shock they got, Ann's shriek made the two schoolboys think the lady must be a bit loopers. Especially as, without waiting for them to speak, she just ran off. They looked at her wild dash for a second, but, being more far interested in their own affairs, just made faces at each other and walked on. They did not witness the delirium of the reunion and the intensity with which the mother embraced her child.

*

When Fonsie got home from work he found everyone taking their ease. Because *Get Smart* was on, he barely got a nod from Martin and Francis when he looked into the back room. There was no one in the scullery but there was a plate of liver, turnip and potatoes waiting to be reheated. Marian and her pal Pauline Cosgrave were in the front room doing their French ecker and listening to Pauline's new Beatles record at the same time. Fonsie asked if they were playing 'Help!' because learning French was so hard? Marian said ha ha very funny and told him Mam was having a lie-down and she was to heat up his dinner for him when he came in. It would be ready in about fifteen minutes. He didn't ask any more questions in front of Pauline, but went upstairs straight away while Marian went to the scullery to turn on the oven. The truth was, Fonsie was surprised that Ann was having a lie-down at quarter-past eight. Trying not to let the bedroom door squeak as he opened it, he sneaked his head in. He heard Ann's breathing and he could just about see her shape. He whispered, 'Are you asleep?' No answer.

Fonsie went to the bathroom and stripped down to his vest and underpants. He gave himself a good scrub with Swarfega as usual, then washed himself more thoroughly with soap. He kept thinking about Ann. It wasn't like her to be in bed at this hour. Was it one of her headaches? He decided that, as it sounded like she was in a deep sleep, he could chance going back into the bedroom for clean clothes. He picked up his bundle of work clothes and, checking first to make sure there was no one on the landing or coming up the stairs, he stepped out quickly and slipped quietly into the bedroom. He could see into the chest of drawers by the light from the landing and plucked out the first shirt, vest, socks and underpants that he put his hands on. He stripped off silently and dressed. The wardrobe was nearer Ann's side of the bed and the door was a bit stiff, so he would have to be more careful getting clean trousers. As he tiptoed forward, he noticed the bottle on the locker beside the bed. Curious, he took another couple of cautious steps closer and reached out to pick it up. He brought it to the door so he could see better. It was a prescription bottle full of little white tablets. He read the label: BETALOC, take one twice a day. Very cagily, Fonsie eased down on the edge of the bed near Ann's legs. She was lying on her side turned towards him. He put a hand on the quilt and could just about feel her body underneath. Why hadn't she told him she was going to the doctor? It must be something more serious than the odd headache if she'd been given these pills he'd never heard of. Were they some kind of sleeping pills? Not for the first time, Fonsie felt he hadn't done enough. A vague unease he had been carrying for some time now began to take shape as guilt. Ann had been on at him all the time lately about how hopeless the coal business was, that she was sick of looking at him, coming in at all hours, filthy dirty. And she worried constantly that he'd end up with arthritis or back trouble or lumbago. So he'd been glad to tell her that O'Neill's wanted him again this summer, starting at the end of May. Ann said that was something, at least. What Fonsie hadn't told her was that the boss, Mr Hoare, said there was so much building work going on he'd be happy to offer him a full-time job. As usual, Fonsie had hummed and hawed and ended up putting the man off. He knew if Ann found out about it she'd make him take it and she'd be right, of course. O'Neill's was an easier, cleaner job. Most important of all, he'd earn better money. So he never mentioned the offer to her. The thing about it was, as far as Fonsie was concerned, he knew that if he took that job he'd end up being told what to do all the time – at work as well as at home. He'd have two bosses in his life, O'Neill's and Ann. Dirty and damp as it was, the coal work was his own, at least. He loved being out, tipping around on the lorry, deciding for himself where to go that day and when to call a halt. But he didn't mean to make Ann worried and sick.

BETALOC? What was it for? Well, Ann would tell him when she woke up. At least she seemed to be getting a good sleep. And whatever was wrong, the doctor was taking care of it. For a long time Fonsie sat at the edge of the bed in his underpants, listening to Ann's steady breathing, his hand resting on her still body. He completely forgot about his dinner, slowly drying up in the oven's low heat.

Fourteen: April 15th

His name was Francis. Francis was so surprised to hear his own name on the television that he didn't hear what Francis' last name was. He asked Marian, who was watching the programme as well. She said she wasn't sure, it sounded like Sheehy-something, a long name that she had never heard before. Francis Sheehy-something had a beard and glasses. He was Irish but he wasn't one of the Volunteers. He wasn't part of the Easter Rising at all. He was just walking along the street and saw people smashing shop windows and stealing, so he tried to stop them. Then an awful thing happened. Francis couldn't believe it. He was arrested by the British army and he said, 'Why have you arrested me? I did nothing.' But the English officer didn't care. He was pure mad. He made Francis march on the street with his soldiers and said he'd shoot him if any rebels shot at them. Then the mad officer saw young boys about Martin's age out walking and he shot one of them in the back for no reason at all. Then he made Francis and all the other soldiers kneel down and say a prayer. He told God if Francis died it would be because he deserved it. Then he took him back to the barracks and had him shot by a firing squad. For no reason at all. Francis couldn't believe that such a bad thing could happen in Ireland.

Insurrection was the best programme he had ever seen on television. He preferred it even to *The Virginian.* It was like a war film, only better, because in war films it was always the English and the Americans who were the good guys, but in *Insurrection* the good guys were Irish. They talked like his dad or his uncles. One gang of Volunteers was as brave as Davy Crockett at the Alamo. Five or six of them were locked up in this house and they had to stop the English getting across a bridge. They killed hundreds before the house was set on fire. One of them was delighted with himself because he shot loads of English soldiers and he said, 'It's a great day for the Irish.' Then he didn't say anything after that. He didn't cry out or anything but when his friends looked at him a few seconds later, they saw that he was dead.

After watching *Insurrection* every night for six nights, Francis had changed his mind about his favourite 1916 leader. James Connolly was definitely the best. His hat was a bit like a cowboy hat. He led the charge when they attacked the General Post Office and he gave all the orders when they took it over. He was really brave and he got shot twice and, even after he couldn't walk any more, he made them bring his bed to the most dangerous place so he could still help with the fighting. Because he was too sick to write, he asked this woman to type a letter for him. He thanked all the rebels and said well done to all the men and women for being so brave. When he said, 'Never was a cause so grand,' Francis heard sniffs behind him and looked around. Marian, who was doing the ironing while she watched, had put down the iron and was rubbing her eyes. Francis didn't laugh at her because he was nearly crying himself. Why had Sister Goretti never told them all these things about James Connolly?

Tonight's episode was the saddest of all because the English set the General Post Office on fire and the Volunteers had no chance any more. There was smoke and flames everywhere and all they could do now was try and escape. They all went running into a dark street. James Connolly had to be carried on a stretcher. Old Tom Clarke said goodbye to Patrick Pearse, who went back into the Post Office and stood all on his own with the burning building falling down around him. Then he bent his head down as if his heart was broken. For a second, Francis thought he was going to throw himself into the fire, even though he knew already that wasn't how he died. He wondered if the real Patrick Pearse had thought about doing that.

After the episode ended, Francis couldn't stop thinking about it. He'd felt like he was right there in the burning Post Office. Even though he knew they were all just actors, the same as in American pictures, it was different for some reason. But why? Maybe it was because of the way *Insurrection* had television reporters with microphones interviewing the rebels and the English, as if it was happening today and this was the news. On the first night he saw it, Francis had been completely confused because there were reporters in modern clothes talking to people from 1916 in old-fashioned clothes. But, bit by bit, he got used to this and now he thought it would be brilliant if television presenters really could go back in some sort of time machine and meet all sorts of people from the past. He'd like to do that.

It was great the way the actors looked exactly the same as the photographs on the poster in school: Tom Clarke, so old and white-haired, James Connolly with his round face and big moustache, Seán MacDermott's sad eyes and Joseph Plunkett with those funny glasses on the end of his nose. Best of all, Francis found out that Patrick Pearse didn't have a sty in his eye. There was nothing wrong with his eyes at all. He was exactly the way Sister Goretti talked about him, his face very serious all the time and he was always making long speeches. The actor spoke just like Francis imagined Pearse would speak. In the first episode when his mam saw him she said, 'Oh, that's Eoin O'Súileabháin. I love him, he has a beautiful voice.' In the second episode, when the rebels took over the General Post Office, he went outside to say the Proclamation and Francis was able to recite the whole speech along with him. Silently. Now, even though he couldn't wait for the next episode tomorrow night, he was sad, because he knew the ending already. The English would win and the leaders of the Easter Rising would be executed.

The strange thing was, lying in his top bunk later that night, thinking about all the people who died, he was most sad about Francis Sheehy-something. It was really unfair what happened to him. He didn't fight anyone. He didn't even have a gun. He just spoke up for himself and he was shot for it.

If Francis Sheehy-something had said nothing and gone home, he'd have been all right.

*

After hearing the depressing news about Miriam Hartnett, Baz Malloy could not stop thinking about her. He even considered not going to his friend Sheelagh's for dinner that evening, but then decided that the combination of her famous beef in Guinness stew and the inevitable competing monologues of her usual gang might be a comfort and a distraction. It proved much harder than he thought, however, to dislodge Miriam from his mind. When Bob, who Sheelagh liked to call 'my intermittent inamorata', praised Baz for his fine work on *Insurrection*, it only served to remind him of that last night of production, which had been the first time he almost spoke to Miriam. As Bob moved swiftly from compliments to his real purpose in mentioning *Insurrection*, which was to attack it for not being 'Irish' enough – 'The thing would have been much more authentic and moving as an Irish language drama or at the very least bilingual' – Baz stopped listening, remembering instead how, as everyone was departing Studio One that January night in search of drink, giddy with a sense of achievement, Baz had lingered on the smoke-filled set, not from some sentimental reluctance to leave the production behind, but because he had spotted Miriam and others from the design department gathering props and clearing furnishings. Having missed one opportunity during lunch-break that day, he wondered if now was the time to talk to her. She moved about the set, delicately free-floating. Her loose top, gypsy skirt and full hair seemed all of a piece. The special-effects smoke hanging in the air created a mood of soft-focus enchantment. Unexpectedly, Miriam turned to walk in his direction with a pile of props in her arms. She would pass within inches of him. Baz managed a smile and she smiled back. Was it his imagination or did she slow down a little as if expecting him to speak? But he was unable to think of a single thing to say and so, still smiling, she flitted by. He turned and watched her disappear out of the studio.

A flapping arm pucked Baz from his lonely reverie. Jim, extravagant in word and gesture, was elaborating on why he hated the Abbey Theatre's new building. Sheelagh, playing devil's advocate, said that, in fairness, it was only just finished. It hadn't even opened yet.

'But Sheelagh, my love, have you seen it? It looks like a mausoleum, which might actually be apt, as it will house a company of dead actors.'

Jim's unceasing soliloquy boomed on but not even his clarion tone could keep Baz from his sad obsession. He had allowed a second opportunity with Miriam to pass him by on a Saturday two months ago. After working on a *Late Late Show*, Baz and the crew had had a few drinks in hospitality and then, as happened so often, they'd ended up in a house in Donnybrook. He didn't even know whose it was. Word had gone round in Madigan's and everyone turned up with bags of booze. Baz, nudging through the crush, was surprised to see a very welcome face smiling up at him from a crowded couch. 'Nineteenth Nervous Breakdown' was playing so loudly that people either had to shout or not bother to talk at all. It made his night to see Miriam's beautiful mouth shape, 'Baz! How are you?' Infuriatingly, there was no room on the couch, not even on the arm. He lifted his bottle in greeting instead and so did she. As he was considering his next move, a young cameraman, Brian, arrived at his side and started yabbering in his ear about how much he loved working in TV, especially live TV, and how all his pals were impressed that he actually worked on the *Late Late Show*. Baz hadn't the heart to tell him to go away and, instead, it was Miriam who left. With one of the bastards sitting with her on the couch.

Baz was briefly distracted from the misery of this recollection by the sight of tall Peter, standing on his chair, swaying and wobbling as he repeated a filthy joke he had heard at this morning's editorial meeting involving Archbishop McQuaid, an altar boy and a choc-ice. Peter's outrageous stories normally made Baz laugh, but tonight he could do no more than affect an interest and, long before the punch line, his mind had drifted back to the last time he had seen Miriam, in the canteen less than three weeks ago. Noticing a free seat opposite her, he decided to seize the moment. Her smile and invitation to sit down seemed genuinely enthusiastic. So here they were. At last they might talk. As it happened, Baz mostly listened, but that was fine, too. Pure joy, actually. Having already been attracted to her looks and style, he was now seduced by her voice. It had the colour of Galway with none of its throwaway aggression. He also loved her attitude. Miriam told him she'd already discovered that television just wasn't her bag. Great to have the regular few bob and all, but the beast was so all-consuming she had no head space left to do the stuff she was really into. Which was, you know, proper painting. She wanted get her hands dirty. Fly away and do nothing else. Was she pure mad, like? He said no, definitely not, and meant it. Even as Baz was formulating the precise words he would use to ask her out, Alf, Miriam's department head, appeared out of nowhere. 'I have to steal her from you, Baz.' Why was his tone always so insinuating? 'Miriam can you drag yourself away? Mini crisis in Studio Two.'

And that was the last time he saw her… How foolishly casual he had been to assume that other opportunities would arise, that they'd bump into each other around the studios, he'd spot her in Madigan's, or they'd end up working on the same production.

Sheelagh was poking Baz in the ribs.

'Baz, you work there, too. Do you agree with Deirdre or Eoin?'

Not knowing what Deirdre and Eoin were bellowing at each other about, Baz had no idea who to support. Neither, he suspected. If only to banish depressing thoughts, he attempted to tune in. Deirdre was quietly determined to make herself heard despite Eoin's rasping heckles.

'The uncomfortable truth is that making television programmes is actually very easy–'

'Fucking reactionary bullshit!'

'Most producers know they're on to a handy little number

and are just too lazy to rock the boat in any way, shape or form. There's no conspiracy –'

'What do you know, working in fucking light fucking entertainment – ?'

'– and that's why, yes, that's why most programmes are so bland.'

'No! It's because of censorship. The Broadcasting Authority is stuffed with government hacks and the executive is swarming with Knights of Columbanus. What you have is a planned Church/State pincer movement designed to crush free speech and hard questions and it's the responsibility of all producers to fight back by any means possible.'

Baz wondered if there was any chance he could get drunk enough to pass out. Then the pain might go away. At Sheelagh's table there was always no end of controversy, argument, meaningless shouting matches; talk, talk, talk; what the Irish were famous for, after all. But yet the few simple words to Miriam that might have made a difference had eluded him. Now it was too late. A few hours ago, running into Alf as he left Studio One, Baz had heard more wretched words.

'Where will I find someone as talented as Miriam at such short notice? – Oh Baz, didn't you know? I am surprised. She left us at the end of last week. Needed to go find herself in the wilds of Connemara. A cabin of clay and wattles, I presume.' That infuriating relentless insinuating tone! 'Unlike you and I, Baz, Miriam might be that rarity, a true artist.' But then, as if only at that moment comprehending how genuinely Baz was affected by this news, Alf's tone became surprisingly kind as he added: 'I'm sure I can find her new address, if you want to try and contact her.'

Jim had fallen off his chair. Bob and Deirdre were trying to pull him up. Eoin was singing 'Joe Hill'. Sheelagh asked Baz was he feeling all right – he seemed a bit lost in himself tonight? He said he was fine, just a bit whacked.

Fifteen: May 14th

Even the fact that the lorry wouldn't start and had to be pushed didn't dent Ann's sunny mood on the morning of Francis' First Holy Communion. Lily Duggan's only boy, Tommy, across the green and Katy Tuite's youngest, Jacinta, were also making their First Holy Communion, so the idea was that everyone would walk to the church together. But, what with one thing and another, by the time the Duggans and the Tuites were ready to go, the Strongs were not, which was typical, although to be fair to Fonsie, it wasn't his fault this time. Ann had spent too much time making sure that Francis looked as good as she could make him and so wasn't ready herself yet. She said, 'We'll just have to take that bloody lorry, God forgive me,' and told Fonsie to tell her neighbours to go ahead and she'd see them at the church. She gave him two rosary beads in little purses for the children and warned him to be sure to tell Jacinta Tuite that she was looking lovely. As he went down the stairs, Ann called after him to find a rug to throw over the seat of the lorry to keep Francis' suit clean.

Finally ready, the three of them sat in the lorry and the engine spluttered, but with no real intention of starting. It was quarter to eleven. Before Ann even opened her mouth to comment, Fonsie leapt out. She looked at Francis and automatically fixed his fringe. He seemed to be off in another world. Was he nervous? Was he praying? He had been very good but very quiet all morning. In the side mirror Ann saw Ritchie, Gussie and Martin come out of the house with Fonsie. Then Mr Reidy from next door appeared. They all went to the back of the lorry while Fonsie came to his door. Here we go, Ann thought. She had been through this many, many times. Fonsie said, 'Right,' and they all started to push. As the lorry moved, it slowly passed old Mr and Mrs Ryan, who were standing in their garden enjoying the free entertainment. Ann called out through the window, 'Look at us in all our finery,' and Mrs Ryan said, 'Oh, I hope it starts, and don't forget to bring Francis in to see us afterwards.' The lorry was now moving fast enough for Fonsie to give it a go. He jumped in and threw it into gear. Ann held onto Francis with one hand and the door handle with the other as the lorry lurched and coughed and nearly got going, then died. Fonsie jumped out and shouted, 'Straight away again.' Ann looked at her watch, surprising herself that she was staying calm enough to work out that if it started this time they would still get to the church with a few minutes to spare. Lately, she had been more relaxed about lots of things. Dr Greaney said the Betaloc seemed to be working and had given her another prescription. Francis, who seemed to be enjoying the hullabaloo now said, 'Will I get out and push?' 'And ruin your suit?' Ann said. They were rolling now faster than before. Fair dues to Mr Reidy for coming out to help – he wasn't always the friendliest neighbour. As they went past the grotto Ann blessed herself for good luck and Fonsie jumped in again. This time, after three big lurches, the engine roared and took off. In the side mirror she saw the lads standing on the road waving after them, laughing and gasping for breath.

As they were now on time, Ann made Fonsie park the lorry at the top of O'Donoghue Avenue out of sight of the church. She wasn't going to scramble out of this old jalopy and fix herself in front of the whole parish. They would walk the rest of the way. She checked Francis' hands, straightened his suit jacket, licked a handkerchief and wiped his chin, fixed his fringe again and then they were ready to walk on. Sister Goretti and Sister Pius were marshalling all the boys and girls outside the church. When Sister Goretti saw Francis approach she smiled and came to them. Ann could tell she was made up to see Francis. Such a lovely nun, so sweet and young, she found it hard to disguise the fact that he was her favourite.

'Well now, here you are, Mrs Strong, Mr Strong. Are you all excited? And Francis, aren't you looking handsome?'

'Thank you, Sister.'

'Now you leave him with us and get yourselves a good seat. The procession will be starting in a couple of minutes. Come with me Francis, there's a nice little cailín I want you to meet.'

Even though it was Ann's fifth time bringing a child to First Holy Communion, she loved it every time, and each new ceremony brought back memories of before. Once again a shiver of spontaneous happiness washed through her when the organ began and the line of children entered, each boy and girl holding hands, singing:

'Oh Mary we crown you with blossoms today
Queen of the Angels and Queen of the May.'

The line of girls was a long white floating ribbon. Some of the dresses were exquisite; broderie anglaise was still a favourite, but the georgette was lovely too, and many of the veils sat on their little heads like wisps of cloud. God's sweet angels. Of course a couple of stupid parents had put their little girls into full-length dresses, which just looked absolutely ridiculous. What were they trying to do, turn them into little women? As far as Ann was concerned, a Holy Communion dress should end just at the knee, with a white buckled shoe, ankle socks, a short delicate veil and a little handbag made from the same fabric as the dress to set it all off. And there were so many here today who were just perfect. How shy and innocent Marian had been when she made hers. Ann was eight months gone with Francis that day.

It wasn't just that she had four sons, but Ann always thought the boys looked even more sweet and angelic than the girls. Maybe it was because she was so used to seeing them on the street rolling in dirt and roaring. Maybe it was because she had been washing her sons' dirty underclothes for nearly twenty years. Maybe it was because so many innocent boys grew into drunken goats, but somehow, on this day, with their silly smiles, or solemn faces and their cheeks rubbed into a rosy shine, with their skinny white knees spotless and their brand-new suits in dark blue and dark green and charcoal and brown and the way they held their heads up and walked tall, somehow each of them seemed to Ann to become something else, no longer a little mammy's boy and not yet a strapping lad, but some special angelic creature, a friend of Jesus. Maybe she just felt this more about Francis than her older sons. She had a feeling that this day was special for him in a way that was different from the others. Although maybe that was all in her head on account of what Mary Storan had said about him becoming a priest. Looking at him, with his eyes fixed on the altar as he passed by, he seemed much the same as the rest. She had chosen a very dark brown suit with a thread of green, neat and smart. His hair never looked right and he wasn't as naturally handsome as Martin, who was growing up to be really good looking, but definitely Francis looked the best he could today. And so tall. No one would ever know that he was the only child there who wasn't seven yet. She had warned him not to show off about that to anyone.

Some parents seemed to spend even more money on the boys 'clothes than on the girls'. Ann saw one little freckled fellow with a mop of red curls in a russet-brown suit that must have cost the earth, with a green tie and tan leather shoes. But, in fairness, she thought it suited him down to the ground. She wasn't so sure about the fair-haired boy in the cream suit and matching dicky bow. It was too pretty. They were making a bit of a cissy out of the child. And of course, there were always the stupid parents who let them wear long pants. Francis had mentioned it once, saying that some pal in his class was getting a suit with long pants, but Ann had cut him off in no uncertain terms and he hadn't mentioned it again. One by one the children sat into the front pews that had been reserved for them, girls on the left, boys on the right. The hymn ended, everyone sat down and Fr Mullaly began. Ann was disappointed that Fr Tierney, the lovely curate who ran the parish bingo on Sunday nights, wasn't doing the Mass. She had never warmed to Mullaly and he drove her mad, always going on and on about money for the church renovation, although now that it was done, she had to admit it was very bright and airy and this new Mass in English was a bit more cheerful than the old Latin one. Of course, that only might be because she always went to Fr Tierney's mass. His sermons were very kind and he was always saying nice things about mothers. His own mother was probably very proud of him.

Finally the big moment arrived. Fr Mullaly spoke the words that changed the bread and wine into the body and blood of Christ.

Transubstantiation. Francis thought of the word as the bell tinkled. Then they all said the Communion prayer good and loud just as Sister Goretti had told them. They got a signal from Fr Mullaly to stand up calmly and walk forward reverently to receive Jesus for the first time. The organ began and everyone sang:

'Soul of my Saviour sanctify my breast
Body of Christ be thou my saving guest
Blood of my Saviour, bathe me in thy tide
Wash me in water streaming from your side.'

Fr Tierney was also giving out Communion, but Francis hoped Fr Mullaly would come to him because, on the day he had answered all those Catechism questions and said the Ten Commandments and the I Confess and the Our Father and the Apostles' Creed, Francis had noticed a look on the priest's face that made him feel very special. He wanted to see that look again when Fr Mullaly placed the Body of Christ on his lips. At the end of their conversation that day he had asked Francis if he understood what a vocation was. Francis said yes and then Fr Mullaly told him he should pray very hard and ask God if he had one.

'Deep in thy wounds Lord, hide and shelter me
So shall I never ever part from thee.'

Fr Mullaly arrived to him and raised the Blessed Host. Francis opened his mouth, put out his tongue, lifted his head and looked past the Host to the priest, but his eyes weren't on Francis as he said Corpus Christi. They were somewhere else. Father Mullaly was thinking of something else entirely and moved straight on to the next boy as Francis felt the dry host stick on his tongue. He closed his mouth, thinking of Sister Goretti's repeated warnings not, on any account, to allow his teeth to touch Christ's body. As he walked back to his pew he carefully chewed the host between his tongue and the top of his mouth until he could swallow it. Jesus was inside him.

Francis knelt down and closed his eyes. What would happen now? Did having Jesus inside him mean that he wouldn't sin any more? He'd like that, because he wanted to be good, but also because he'd got a big shock the evening before when he discovered that he didn't like confession. He wasn't sure why. He knew from his Catechism it was a way of cleansing himself of his sins and becoming all pure again. That sounded nice and he'd been looking forward to his first Confession but last night he found out that he didn't like kneeling in this dark box, and he didn't like the way the Fr Mullaly sat, a black shadow on the other side of the grille, listening. He only got three Hail Marys for his penance, but after saying them he didn't feel any different. It wasn't like having a hot bath when, even though his mam had to chase him sometimes to get into it, he loved the feeling afterwards of being all dry and clean, sitting in front of the fire wrapped in a big towel. Confession wasn't like that at all. There was something about it – Francis wished he knew the exact word to describe his feeling – something like 'nasty'. Even the church had looked strange and red with the late-evening sunlight creeping in the new windows. Before making his first confession, Francis had knelt in a corner and made a thorough examination of his conscience. He went through each of the Seven Deadly Sins. Wrath. Sister Goretti told them that meant anger, but Francis preferred Wrath. It sounded like something bursting out that was so strong it could knock down a big skyscraper. He had never felt wrath, but he admitted to himself that he got angry all right: with Tommy Duggan when he wouldn't pass the ball; when his sister Marian corrected him about his table manners or bossed him around, telling him to wash his hands; with his mam and dad and he answered them back. He got angry most of all with Martin and, even though often it was Martin's fault for being a bully, he knew that sometimes, because of his anger, Francis was mean and sly and used words in a certain way to get Martin into trouble with Mam. He would confess all that. Sloth was laziness. Francis didn't really think he was lazy, but he knew that sometimes he didn't tidy things and his mam had to do it so that was probably a sin all right. Avarice, Sister Goretti said, was greed. Straight away his conscience put a picture in his mind of the morning he collected the bottle of milk from the doorstep and, instead of shaking it to mix up the cream with the rest, he sneaked into the scullery and poured the cream from the top into his Corn Flakes before anyone else came downstairs. That was stealing from the rest of the family, which was very bad. And, he had to admit, it wasn't just once. He had done it a few times. Sometimes he even got up earlier than everyone else deliberately to do it. Francis wondered did that make it a mortaler? The Catechism said a mortal sin was committed 'with full knowledge and full consent'. He felt very guilty about it.

Envy was a deadly sin that really confused him. He definitely felt it sometimes towards boys in class who got pocket money and were able to buy their own sweets and chocolate and lemonade. But he never did anything bad because of Envy. So was it a sin to have the feeling? He'd confess it anyway, just in case. After all, he had nearly seven years of his life to confess, so there had to be a lot of sins. Gluttony. The cream on the Corn Flakes was definitely gluttony. So was the day he got sick in his dad's lorry. It was very soon after last Christmas. His mam was in bed with a headache so his dad took him out delivering coal. Everywhere they stopped people were really nice and gave him lemonade and biscuits. One man gave him a slab of Cleeve's toffee and a nice old woman gave him a bag of Colleen assortment. As they drove around the countryside, every time his dad wasn't looking, Francis ate another sweet. Next thing they were all gone. Suddenly there seemed to be loads of potholes in the roads and the lorry was bumping up and down a lot more. His dad looked at Francis' face just before it happened and he stopped the lorry really fast and reached over to open the door. Francis barely got his head out as he vomited everything he'd eaten that day. Thinking about it now, the word gluttony was just like the way some of the dark liquoricy vomit had gone glob! against the door of the lorry and then started slowly going down. Glug… glug. His dad didn't give out to him really, but he did shake his head when he saw the empty bag of Colleen and said, 'Your eyes are bigger than your belly,' and that was true. He would have to confess that, too. Sister Goretti told the class they didn't need to worry about the next deadly sin at all: Lust. She was sure none of them had committed that sin. They didn't even need to know what it was.

So he made his Confession and told plenty of sins, but now, kneeling with his eyes closed after his first Holy Communion, with Jesus inside him, Francis had to admit to himself that he had not confessed his biggest sin of all: Pride. He knew this was his biggest sin because it was the thing he was told all time: 'You're so full of yourself.' 'Mr Know-it-all.' 'A big show-off, that's all you are.' 'Why do you have to be such a notice box?' 'What makes you think you're different to everyone else?' Of course, not everyone said things like that. His sister Marian didn't, nor his godmother and definitely not Sister Goretti, who praised him for knowing things. But still, it seemed to Francis he heard it all the time from loads of people. He tried to work it out. It wasn't a sin to be clever, he was sure of that. So was it a sin to show you were clever? Did God make some people clever as a test, to see if they would commit the sin of Pride when, really, he wanted them to say nothing and pretend not to be different? Francis knew in his heart that sometimes he liked being the centre of attention, and showing off, and trying to be funny but really just being cheeky, and it would be better if he didn't do that. He understood why sometimes people just got sick of listening to him and wanted him to shut up, but did that mean it was a sin of Pride to say the things that were in his head? Francis would have liked to ask these questions in Confession, but when the curtain whooshed back and he saw the black shape of Fr Mullaly's head bent down and heard him say, 'Tell me your sins, child,' he knew from his voice that the priest didn't want to hear any questions. So he did not speak about Pride. Did that mean he made a bad confession?

Today was much happier. He liked the feeling of kneeling here asking Jesus to help him think things out, listening to the echoey sounds of people shuffling along the aisle receiving Communion and the choir singing 'Sweet Sacrament Divine'. Even the coughs were gentle. There were no babies wahhhling because they were all up in the new crying gallery. Francis knew that today it would be easy for Jesus to keep him free from sin because there were so many nice things happening. After Mass, Gussie would be waiting outside with his brand new 8mm ciné camera he'd brought home only two days ago. He was going to make a film of Francis on his big day. Then, as a special treat, Mam and Dad were taking him to a restaurant for the first time in his life: the Hong Kong Chinese Restaurant in William Street. Then his mam would bring him to visit everyone; his godmother Mary and godfather Mikey, all his aunts, Mona and Una and Bernadette and Marg. They would go to his granny and neighbours and other friends of the family. Everyone would be saying what a good boy he was and how nice he looked and they'd give him money. In class all week the boys were talking about how much they might get. Padraig Leddin said he was told that anyone who gave less than half a crown was really mean. David McCarthy said his brother collected twelve pounds and five shillings last year but no one believed that. Francis thought if he got even four pounds he'd be very very lucky.

The hymn ended and Father Mullaly's voice broke the spell. Francis opened his eyes and sat down. 'Mass is ended. Go forth in peace.' 'Thanks be to God.' Everyone stood up for the final hymn. 'Hail Holy Queen Enthroned Above'. He looked around and could just see his mam and dad's heads much further back. His dad was smiling and his mam had a huge smile and gave him a little wave with her fingers. Francis made a funny face as he waved back.

Sixteen: June 17th

'People are waving, a hUachtaráin.'

The President immediately lifted his hand and, with a tiny motion of his head, acknowledged the greetings.

'We are just passing the new church of Saints Peter and Paul. It looks very impressive. There's quite a crowd gathered outside.'

Éamon felt the Presidential Rolls swing right, so he knew they were now driving up Portlaoise Main Street. The car eased to a dignified processional pace as Colonel Seán continued to speak softly.

'There are people gathered on both sides but most of them are on your left, sir.'

Éamon faced the left passenger window and waved at the moving blur. It was no longer possible for him to distinguish even the shapes of people at this remove, but he believed they were there. They still came out on the street to salute the President. He even heard a few 'up Dev' cries. Portlaoise in the constituency of Laois-Offaly. It had voted well for him this time.

The car began to speed up again. The blur changed form. Éamon felt Colonel Seán's gentle staying hand on his shoulder.

'We're on Grattan Street, leaving the town now, a hUachtaráin.'

Moving ever closer to his heartland. The county of his childhood and the beloved county he had represented for so many years, the counties that had stood by him once again when Dublin and so many other places had not. Two weeks since the election result and he could not dislodge the great boulder of shame that pressed down on him. To win, as he had, by less than one per cent, was no victory. To be returned to office in this humiliating way was to be handed a seven-year prison sentence.

At his own request, a whisper every few minutes informed him of some landmark along the route. This gentle aide-memoire, along with the relaxing motion of the Rolls, helped him to live the twists and turns of the journey. His labyrinthine knowledge of the Irish hinterland and his still precise memory allowed him to see everything. Approaching Mountrath he knew a sharp left turn would be followed by a straight run to the fine square where, in 1932, he had addressed a crowd of several thousand. When the car veered right again, he saw the little bridge that brought them to the outskirts of the town. A whisper of 'Borris-on-Ossory' and straight away he saw himself, forty-five years ago, slipping out the back of the Leix County Hotel in the middle of the night to evade capture.

Having left the flat plains of Laois, he knew that, ahead of them, the proud Silvermines Mountains were rising up behind the lush grasslands of the Golden Vale, dotted with milch cows. As he waved at the crowd that Colonel Seán assured him had gathered along MacDonagh Street in Nenagh, another town of pleasant memory in the constituency of Tipperary North, Éamon requested that they abandon the main road and continue instead along the narrow lakeside drive that wound its way down to sweet Killaloe, allowing him to enjoy again the calm beauty of Lough Derg. Though he never said this, not even to Sinéad, he suspected that the journey of his inner eye was a far lovelier thing than the Ireland he would encounter now if the blessing of sight was still on him. How many more cars and trucks cluttered the road? His ears told him of that change; he would hate to have to put his eyes on it. And building everywhere? He had heard so much about this great boom and the benefits it brought, but it had not been given to him to see any of its achievements. As far as Éamon was concerned, he was well spared the vulgarity of factory buildings and garish hotels where once there had been only the pleasing slow motion of grazing cattle or the natural beauty of hedgerow with fields of beet or cabbages beyond.

Why had he agreed to run again? So many times he had asked

himself, even before the election. Sinéad had been as forceful as she had ever been in counselling against it. His own body told him no. He resented An Taoiseach for putting pressure on him. 'Isn't it time for someone younger?' he had said to Seán, and then something he never expected to admit aloud: 'I am eighty-four and there is a great tiredness on me.'

What Éamon wanted now was either to take a pleasant nap or enjoy, somewhere to his right, his mind's eye view of Lough Derg, glorious in the June sunshine. But he could do neither, tormented as he was by the nagging anger. 'You won't even have to campaign, Chief.' Seán had said to him, again and again. 'It's the Golden Jubilee and you're the only 1916 leader still living. They'll be glad of the chance to vote for you, this year of all years.' Which, of course, turned out not to be the case. Half of them tried to vote him off the stage. He realised now that, far from being venerated as the living embodiment of the great Rising, a new generation blamed him for, as they saw it, evading the firing squad. In the end it did not matter how many graves he visited or wreaths he laid or monuments he unveiled or commemorative Masses he attended, there were those who could not forgive him for having survived when so many sanctified heroes had given their lives.

'We're just turning in to Scoil Íosagáin now, a h-Úachtarán. As you know, it's an entirely new primary-school building and the Christian Brothers are immensely proud of the modernity of the design. The architect chose this raised modular structure as a solution to the problem of building on a long but very narrow site. The theme of his design is building blocks, as in the first steps of education…'

Éamon had already commited these notes to memory but he appreciated Colonel Seán's whispered reminders. Some day soon he really would need them. He resolved to shake off this melancholy mood. It had not been such a bad day so far. The journey had been pleasurable and the opening of a new school was truly a cause for celebration. There was nothing more important than the education of the nation's children.

'... Oh, and the Minister for Education will also be attending.'

Ah yes. Dom. He had finally achieved high office. Éamon was a little surprised that he had stayed the course, remembering how impatiently ambitious he had been when first elected. Arrogant, privileged; a Jesuit boy, of course, and written all over him, too. But he could always make Éamon laugh. It was his saving grace.

The air outside was warm and the light very bright. Was the new school building before or behind him? To his right or left? He would never see it and the modernity of the design meant he was unable to create a reliable image of it in his head. A dark shape appeared before him and was introduced as Brother Scully, the Superior. Because he greeted the President in Irish, Éamon was enthusiastic in his reply, congratulating the Brother warmly not only on this latest achievement but on the great work of the Christian Brothers for so many years. He expressed the hope that, in this fine new school, young boys would learn to be proud citizens of Ireland and bring honour to their native city. Brother Scully thanked the President for his sentiments and said it was indeed a privilege for the Order and the pupils and the city to have the nation's greatest living hero present today. Then, one after another, a dozen or more black shapes stepped forward and were introduced by name. Éamon knew there was no point in trying to remember any of them. He could not see these Brothers and was unlikely to speak to them again. Finally Colonel Seán's discreet hand guided him towards another looming shape:

'The Minister for Education, a hÚachtaráin.'

Éamon remembered that Dom did not have much Irish, so when he felt the powerful insistent grip, it amused him to offer the Minister a lengthy salutation in his native tongue and so force him to summon up what little store he had in reply. Dom, for politeness and form's sake, welcomed him with his school Irish. Briefly. '*Dia dhuit agus fáilte, a hÚachtaráin.*' Then he continued in English, eyeballing Dev directly as he did so, even though he was virtually one hundred per cent certain that the old Chief couldn't see sky or sea these days.

'And can I say how delighted I am to welcome you here today. And how appropriate that you should be opening a new school in the county where you grew up and received your earliest education.'

Dom was gratified at the 'hear-hears' from the little group crowded around them. The old man's hand was ice-cold, the grip flaccid, tired. But, aware of press cameras clicking, Dom held on and even used his other hand to rest lightly on Dev's shoulder, implying greater intimacy.

'And, of course, congratulations on your recent historic victory. I can safely say that, in this part of the country, it was never in doubt for an instant.'

Cheers and applause for that one. Well pleased, Dom allowed the long-suffering Colonel Seán to take charge of shepherding Dev to the podium.

'Nice work. Those photos will look great.'

Suddenly Michael Liston was beside him. Dom nodded towards the President and his aide-de-camp.

'Thanks. I'd say most soldiers would gladly take their chances in Katanga rather than suffer the drudgery of that job. Like a Labrador, guiding him from one Republican grave to another, wreaths, twenty-one-gun salutes, day after day after day. Jesus.'

'He'll deserve whatever pension and perks come his way, all right.'

Dom noticed the boy at Michael's side and realised it must be his youngest. What was his name again? This was ironic. Michael was usually the man who'd whisper a name in Dom's ear when needed. It must be two years since he last saw the boy. Growing fast. He hunkered down to his height.

'Well, hello youngfellah, do you remember me at all? … No, sure, why should you? The last time I saw you, I had more hair and you were only half the size you are now.'

'Tomorrow's my birthday.'

'Matthew, I told you not to be saying that.'

That was it. Matthew. Dom relaxed.

'Ah sure, why wouldn't you want to tell me about your birthday, Matthew? Isn't it a very important day? What age will you be?'

As Dom spoke it hit him, but too late to shut up. Of course. Poor Eva died giving birth to him. No wonder Michael didn't want the youngfellah reminding people. Did Matthew know his birthday was his mother's anniversary? Surely not.

'Seven.'

Was it really seven years since Eva Liston died? Dom knew from Michael's manner not to say anything. Not so much as a whisper about it. Instead, discreetly, he took out his wallet and found a crisp clean orange note.

'Well, Matthew, seven is a very important age. Here's something for your piggy-bank. Do you have a piggy-bank?'

Eyes lowered, the boy nodded. Jesus, he was a morose child. Not even the prospect of ten bob could wring a smile out of him. Michael Liston pressed on his shoulder.

'What do you say?'

'Thank you.'

'Don't mention it, Matthew. Tell me, what do you think of this new school? Would you like to be a pupil here?'

Matthew didn't seem to know what to say to that. He looked up at his father. Dom was surprised at the odd shiftiness in Michael's eyes, the evasive tone of his reply. The question hadn't been a serious one. Dom would have been surprised if Michael intended sending his child to the Christian Brothers.

'It's a lovely new school. But ah… Matthew and I… we're off to Dublin aren't we?

This was news to Dom. Michael moving to Dublin? He hadn't mentioned it.

'Well, that sounds brilliant, Matthew.'

Matthew nodded but didn't look thrilled about it. The child was definitely a long cold drink of water. As Dom stood up, Michael muttered in his ear.

'No big deal. The twins are going to uni in the autumn, so they're off my hands and I thought it was time to give Matthew a go at boarding school. It's near Dublin, so it's better if I'm close by.'

Dom suspected it was more a case of Michael wanting to go to Dublin and dumping the child into a boarding school to suit himself. There was definitely some other agenda. Michael Liston was always three steps ahead. It was what had made him so valuable to Dom over the years.

'I was going to talk to you about it. Maybe you might introduce me to a few people in Dublin, get me started.'

'Of course. Say no more.'

Michael nodded. He seemed oddly uncomfortable, as if he had been caught out in some way, so it was a relief when an eager young Christian Brother approached to tell the Minister that Brother Scully was anxious to get the ball rolling. Dom took his seat on the platform next to Dev, who seemed to ignore him. Was he in a snot, or just lost in thought, preparing his oration? Or dozing? When Brother Scully began proceedings, Dom inclined his head towards the speaker and gazed thoughtfully, as if listening intently. He was looking forward to tomorrow's press coverage. There should be lots of smiling pictures and, with any luck, the reports would create the impression that Dom had carried a hod and personally plastered the walls. Launching a new school was the best kind of publicity, even more so when the building was so impressive. Guiney had delivered on the construction end, to be fair to him, but the design was the big surprise. It was innovative and exuberant. Not adjectives he'd ever have imagined himself using where the Christian Brothers were concerned, but credit where it was due. Even though the memory of Father Coveney's sneering tone still stung, he wouldn't ever have considered swapping Clongowes Wood and his Jesuit education for the dreariness of a Christian Brothers day school in this tough old city. Even though the pupils in the audience today were hand-picked and scrubbed, they still had the whiff of deprivation about them. What chance had most of these poor little hoors? Their fathers either had lousy jobs or no jobs, so most of these lads would never get beyond primary school anyway, because their parents couldn't afford the fees, pure and simple. Some families had so many kids they could end up with five children all of secondary school age. Where would they get the money to pay for them? They'd be forced instead to make terrible choices, pick the brightest and pay for him to stay at school as far as Inter Cert while the others were put out to find some kind of work. That was the inevitable rhythm of a school like this. How many of these grinning galoots sitting in front of him, would get near the Leaving Cert? Dom realised that the answer made him genuinely sad. He liked the poorer classes, he admired all kinds of things about them, their ability to get on with things in a rough and ready way, their distinctive use of language, the native wit and the hilarious malapropisms. He loved the banter in the pubs and on the street. But Dom was not self-deluding. He was glad he wasn't one of them.

Could a shiny new school like this make a difference to the underprivileged? If these young gougers looking up at him actually enjoyed their few years in primary school would that make them more inclined to want more education, even with the dreaded Christian Brothers? A bright, well-designed building like this surely helped make education more interesting, happier? Dom spotted Michael Liston's son in the crowd, his dark head bent low. Certainly happier than whatever fate awaited that poor motherless child in boarding school. If, as Minister, he built more schools like this one, would education start to seem more attractive to poorer children? Dom was beginning to feel a twinge, a tickle of excitement. A massive school-building programme, a nationwide effort. Could this be the seed of his Big Idea? Would this capture the popular imagination? A new school every week! Not a bad banner line. Imagine all the positive publicity if he was personally opening a school a week.

Dev suddenly stood, unaided, and stepped carefully to the lectern. Now boys, Dom thought, you think the leather strap is frightening. You think no one can inflict torture like a Christian

Brother. Well, after you've listened to Dev making a speech, you'll understand what cruel and unusual punishment really is.

'Brother Superior, Minister, ladies and gentlemen, boys… As I journeyed here this morning to attend this marvellous event I was thinking with what… delightful temperate weather Almighty God has blessed us today, and what a worthwhile task lay before me, for there is nothing so worthwhile as education. It is the key to true happiness. For remember, boys, happiness is not something you can hold in your hand, it is a… a condition of the mind and if we are chronically dissatisfied and discontented, that puts an end to our happiness. And there is much to be happy about. We have here a wonderful little country. We have not here any of the extremes of temperature, the tornados and cyclones… and blizzards which afflict other parts of the world… earthquakes…'

Perhaps Dev's slow, stumbling delivery had sapped Dom's enthusiasm but, when he resumed thinking about his school-building idea, the air seemed to have gone out of the tyres. Too costly, too slow. By the time sites were found, designs commissioned, planning permission acquired and, of course the Church consulted – Oh Christ! – three or four years would pass before a sod was turned anywhere. What good would that be to Dom? The next election would come and go and he'd have nothing to show the voters but an office full of architectural drawings. Forget it. Yet he knew he was on to something. If only there was a simple, clean way to make a big splash. Force people to sit up and pay attention. The children of the poor were leaving school too early. That was the nub of it. They were not getting the education that was their due.

'… but thankfully, we are now a free, independent people. Free to make our own laws and free to decide our future…'

Dev's words resonated and suddenly the simplest of phrases presented itself to Dom: Free Education. There it was. The catch-cry of a Big Idea, at least. Two words that required no further explanation. Dom would give the children of Ireland free education. It was astonishing he hadn't thought of it before. Of course he hadn't a clue how he'd do it or what it might cost. For the moment he didn't even want to think about that part of it. In case it put him off.

Seventeen: September 10th

The first thing that Francis thought about when he woke up was Ian Barry's yellow cardigan, which was the brightest yellow, and his tartan trousers, which were the shortest trousers he had ever seen on a boy. They were more like underpants. They made his legs look so long compared to Francis and the other boys, who all wore trousers almost down to their knees and long socks nearly up to their knees. Ian Barry had ankle socks. They were white. And shiny black shoes with a buckle. Out of the hundreds of new boys in the yard last Monday he was the one that Francis couldn't stop looking at. Even the way he walked was different. He seemed to bounce along, his arms swinging gently and the curls at the end of his sandy hair hopping up and down as he moved. Francis saw some other boys staring at him too and heard one of them say 'Fancy Pants' and his pals laughed.

There were noises from the bunk underneath Francis, little squeaking sounds. Was Martin having a nightmare? It sounded like he was tossing and turning and trying to catch his breath. Francis looked over at Ritchie and Gussie who were still asleep too. Ritchie was turned towards him, his head on his arm, one leg hanging out the side. He was breathing quietly. Francis knew he had an important match today. Ritchie told him that, if they won, Krups would be top of the inter-firm league with only three games to go. He was going to watch the match on his way to the library. Ritchie always did his best and never made a mistake. Francis liked watching him play.

Gussie, on the flat of his back, mouth open, let out a big snort and turned to the wall, pulling the blankets with him. He had told Francis he might bring him to see *The Heroes of Telemark* this afternoon. Gussie was really looking forward to seeing the film because Richard Harris was in it and he had met Richard Harris for real. One day, ages ago, he came home from work all excited, saying, 'Guess who sat himself at the bar in the departure lounge all on his own because his flight to New York was delayed?' No one knew. 'Richard Harris,' Gussie said, 'and I served him and he started talking to me. He asked how was life in the old town these days and he said he'd love to get home more often. He'd been off in Norway making a new film.' Until Gussie said 'film' Francis didn't know who Richard Harris was. Now he wondered if he'd ever seen him in a film.

'From New York he's flying to straight to Hawaii to make another film. He said to me "It's called *Hawaii*, funnily enough."' Gussie laughed. 'He said it was a tough life but someone had to do it.' Gussie laughed again. 'You know the way he looks big on screen? Well, sitting at the bar right in front of me he looked huge. Powerful. There's something about him, all right. He really stands out. Even if you'd never seen any of his films you'd know there was something special about him. But he was as nice as anything. Real ordinary, you know.'

Francis had never seen Gussie so excited. Ever since he started working in the bar in Shannon Airport, he often talked about famous people who flew in from America, but he had never spoken to any of them and, from the things Gussie said about them, none of them sounded very nice. But Richard Harris seemed to be different. Even though he was stuck there for three hours waiting for his flight he never complained once. And even though he drank like a fish, he never got drunk. He just got friendlier. And he wanted Gussie to serve him all the time. Vodka, he drank. After Gussie served him a few times he said, 'Ah, just give me the bottle, for Jaysus' sake,' and Gussie knew that Ollie, the head barman, couldn't give out to him for letting him have the bottle because he was Richard Harris. Then he poured himself a big glass and asked Gussie loads of questions about himself, and even though Ollie was always telling the trainee barmen to keep their distance and not bother the customers, Gussie knew that it was all right to talk because Richard Harris wanted him to, so he did.

What Gussie, despite frequent repetitions of the story, never told anyone, not his friends, nor his workmates, nor family, nobody, was how, after many jokes and anecdotes, Richard Harris asked for a second glass to be put on the bar counter. As he poured a reckless measure into it he asked, 'Am I right, my friend Gussie, in thinking you are an Augustine and not an Aenghus?' Gussie, who had always been embarrassed at his name, just nodded, expecting to be teased. But Richard Harris' blue eyes looked kind as he said, 'A remarkable man, your namesake, a profound philosopher and the author of a prayer that every poor benighted Irishman should commit to memory and murmur at every available opportunity. Do you know what the prayer is? Do you know what your namesake famously begged of God?' Gussie hadn't a clue. He shook his head and Richard Harris just stared at him for a long time before he spoke. '"God, make me good – but not yet." What about that ha?' Then he smiled, lifted his glass and pushed the other one towards Gussie. 'So, a toast, young Augustine. Never mind that old fucker' – seeing Gussie look towards Ollie, who was spying on him from the far end of the bar – 'Do your own thing. Never be afraid to do your own thing. Pick it up there. Join me in a toast. "God, make me good – but not yet."' As Richard Harris swallowed, Gussie decided he'd better knock his back and the burn inside him made his eyes water even as Richard Harris' laser blues fixed on him like a brother, and his laugh was cracked and full and warm. To be enfolded in such giant charisma was more intoxicating than the vodka.

But Francis and the rest of the family only heard about the huge tip placed casually on the counter when Richard Harris' flight was finally called. Francis still remembered how Gussie had taken the folded up note from his pocket as he came to that part of the story and opened it slowly to show them. Twenty pounds!

'Imagine, growing up around here and ending up a huge Hollywood star.'

Since that day, any time Richard Harris' name was spoken, Gussie always said those same words.

'Imagine, growing up around here and ending up a huge Hollywood star.'

No wonder his big brother was dying to to see *The Heroes of Telemark*. Today was his first day off since it came to the Savoy. He would definitely go this afternoon and maybe he really would bring Francis with him. Sometimes Gussie said he'd do things and then he'd change his mind or just forgot to do the thing he said, but Francis never really minded that because then Gussie, all of a sudden, would do a really nice thing and it would be a brilliant surprise. Like one day, a long time ago, when Francis was much smaller and Gussie was still going to school, he came flying up the road on his bike and, without telling Mam or anyone, just grabbed Francis, lifted him on to the bar of his bike and carried him off. He wouldn't even say where they were going. Next thing they arrived at Sarsfield Barracks. There were hundreds of people there, all pushing up against the railings staring into the barracks field. Gussie hoisted Francis onto his shoulders and then he saw the most surprising thing; a crashed plane. It looked huge, nearly half the size of the field. It was tipped over on its side with one wing broken and the other wing up in the air. There were soldiers and Gardaí all around it. 'What do you think of that?' Gussie said. 'It's a Constellation. The pilot had to crash-land. It's a miracle it didn't blow up.' Francis didn't know why Gussie had cycled home to collect him and bring him to see this, but he was delighted he had.

His two big brothers were so big now their bed looked tiny. Two lumps, his mam called them. Francis was glad she saved up and got bunks for him and Martin. It was even better than having his own bed because he was so high up. From underneath he heard a moan and then Martin went completely quiet. Had he woken up out of his nightmare? Francis wanted to see but he knew if he peeped over and Martin was awake he'd say something and then Francis would answer back and then Martin would start kicking him from underneath and then Francis would throw something down at him and then it would turn into a real fight. But Francis didn't want anything to happen today that would get him into trouble. His mam was allowing him to go to the library this morning on his own for the first time, which he really wanted to do because he was hoping to borrow the book that Ian Barry had shown him. Ian Barry's book wasn't from a library; it was his own. He said his daddy bought it for him in Dublin. Francis had never known anyone who called his father 'daddy'. He had heard English children say it on television all right but Ian Barry definitely wasn't English. He sounded just like all the other boys, which was surprising because Ian Barry looked so different from everyone else with his yellow cardigan and his funny tartan pants.

If everything worked out for Francis today then first, he'd see Ritchie winning his football match, second, he'd find the book he was looking for in the library and third, Gussie would bring him to see *The Heroes of Telemark*. He'd never be lucky enough to do all three things, though.

*

Sitting in bed in the Dublin flat, three pillows propping him up comfortably, Dom read to his Beauty the speech he intended to deliver that night to the National Union of Journalists at their annual dinner. It was the first time he had heard his words spoken aloud and, even though the setting was incongruous and his delivery flat and quiet, it seemed to him that the shock of its content still screamed out. Mother of fuck! Sweet holy divine Christ! Was he really going to say this tonight? In front of that crowd? Announce to a bunch of journalists a radical new policy without first informing anyone in his department or any of his Party colleagues? He had talked to Lemass, of course. But Lemass did not instruct him to make this speech. Lemass hadn't even read the speech. In fact Lemass, the oldest fox, did not want to know that such a speech existed. And yet if Dom had not had that conversation would it ever have occurred to him to take this action? He couldn't say for sure.

He had enjoyed a certain illicit pleasure in composing the speech, but reading it aloud to his favourite audience of one was sobering, a cold, early-morning watersplash. What did she think of it? Afraid to look at her face, he kept his head down and the words flowing in reasonably good order, but with nothing like the pitch and roll, the colour and cadence he would summon up in front of a crowd. The last sentence was spoken without flourish, the manuscript set down and Dom turned to pick up his cup of tea from the bedside locker. Only then did he dare look at her. She was nodding. Agreeably, surely? The smile was encouraging too, as was her hand reaching out to squeeze his. But was she ever going to speak? And would her words give him the sort of confidence he needed to proceed, or leave him guessing, as Lemass had done? Over the last few weeks, since his meeting with An Taoiseach, Dom had parsed and analysed their conversation until he was blue in the face, but all he was left with was an intuition, a whisper on the wind, a brief meeting of eyes that seemed, in the moment it occurred, to be a hint of encouragement, nudging him to determine his own future, whatever that might be. To be his own man.

Throughout their conversation Dom had felt himself inspired. He had not only explained his scheme cogently, he had begun to feel more confident of its simplicity and – yes, possibly – even greatness. He made himself passionate about its focus on justice and fairness, he was at his most coaxing when he advertised its vote-winning potential, he grew sentimental and, in a most unlikely turn, spiritual when he offered the plan as a worthy tribute in this special year to the dreams and plans of the 1916 martyrs, so many of whom were teachers and poets. What could be more appropriate than to give the children of the Nation free education? Finally, he became slyly and ruthlessly political.

'The Blueshirts are about to publish a policy document on Education they've been preparing for the last year. They'll seize the agenda and we'll spend all our time answering questions about their proposals. It'll be "why are we not doing this, why are we not doing that?" You don't want us on the back foot do you?'

'No.'

'This will prevent that.'

'Only if you get to announce your policy first.'

'That's exactly what I want to do.'

'And that's why I'm saying don't bring it to cabinet.'

'So you won't support me.'

'It doesn't matter whether I support you or not. Imagine the reaction if you present such a proposal to cabinet. Erskine will want to know why he can't get that kind of funding for Health and Social Welfare. Charlie will ask why is he having to stand firm against the farmers if there's cash in the coffers to finance free secondary education.'

'It won't be as costly as they think it will – '

'I'm telling you what will happen in cabinet once you open this for discussion. The reality of it. And even if you get the support of every other minister, there is no chance in the wide world that Finance will just hand over the money. They will put every obstacle in your way. They'll say that before such a scheme can be announced officially, as policy, there will need to be an investigating sub-committee, or a feasibility study, or a departmental audit. Memos will fly back and forth and the months will become years. You'll end up tearing your hair out and wishing you never had the idea in the first place.'

'But you can force the issue. You have the authority.'

Silence and a shake of the head. Dom smothered his anger. Who was Lemass trying to fool? If, truly, he wanted this to happen, he could make it happen. He'd been doing this sort of thing patiently and determinedly for forty-five years. If he didn't like the idea, why couldn't he be honest and just say so?'

'So I should forget about it?'

'Are you listening to what I'm saying? If you want this to happen, don't bring it to cabinet.'

And despite more wheedling from Dom, An Taoiseach merely said the same thing again. And again. Precisely the same sentence.

'If you want this to happen, don't bring it to cabinet.'

Dom began to divine that Lemass was sending him a different message, one that could never be spoken, not even closeted alone like this. Something that could never be said to have been said. He had no real idea what that message was until, just as he was leaving, Lemass asked, apparently apropos of nothing, 'I hear you're guest speaker at the journalists' do in a few weeks time. You'd better have some good jokes to keep that crowd happy.'

'Don't I know.'

'Or at least something interesting for them to chew on.'

Dom looked closely, but the old man's grey eyes, resting deep in their soft wrinkled beds, gave nothing more away.

'If you deliver this speech tonight –'

At last his Beauty was speaking, with a face so serious, so intense, her hand gripping his shoulder.

'– I will be more proud of you than I've ever been. And you know that's saying something.'

The kiss was spontaneous and passionate. It was going to be all right. He would go ahead. Fuck them, he'd do it. She pulled back from his lips only to hold his gaze.

'You know, don't you, love, that what you're going to say tonight and what you're going to do should have been said and done in this country a long time ago. But it never was. So now you'll be the one to make it happen.'

*

Francis gazed at his library book as he walked along the railway line to Cals Park. *Francis and Clare: Saints of Assisi* by Helen Walker Homan. His first library book. He had never even heard of a public library until Marian brought him there last week and he didn't believe her when she told him he could borrow all these books for free. There seemed to be thousands of them. When he picked this book the woman in the library stamped a date on it and gave it to him. Marian told him he had to bring it back by that date or he would be in big trouble: 17th September. So he was bringing the book back five days early. Francis hoped that would show the woman in the library what a good reader he was and then she would let him take another book out. The reason he had read the story so fast was because it made him feel really good. Francis of Assisi was one the best-loved saints in the whole world, gentle and humorous, always singing. He loved birds and animals and he devoted his life to the poor. The picture on the front cover of a very kind man in a brown robe with a big bald patch on his head was just like a statue Francis had seen before in the Franciscan Church, but there was another picture at the start of the first chapter that surprised Francis. Every time he opened the book he looked first at this picture. Now as he walked along the railway line he was looking at it one more time. In the picture, Francis of Assisi is only seven and he is in the street of the town, laughing, as birds fly around him. He looks like a very rich little boy with long dark hair and a cloak and a kind of skirt and strange-looking pointy shoes. A beautiful lady in a long dress is sitting nearby. She is his servant and she is minding him. When Francis looked at this picture he thought of Ian Barry.

The shouts of football supporters made him look up. He realised that he was after walking past Cals Park because, staring at the picture, he'd forgotten everything else. He closed the book, walked back, left the railway line, and climbed over the wall. There were five football pitches in Cals Park and this morning there were matches on in all of them. Francis saw Ritchie's team, Krups, straight away because he knew they wore all white. The team they were playing, Mattersons Meats, was in yellow and blue. It was a dead easy game for Ritchie. He was in defence and Krups were attacking most of the time. Soon they were three goals up. Francis noticed a baldy man near him holding a fat boy's hand. They both looked very fed up so he guessed that they were cheering for Mattersons Meats. Even though he wanted Ritchie's team to win, he felt a bit sorry for them. When Krups scored a fourth goal, Francis looked over again and he saw the man let go the fat boy's hand and take something out of his pocket. He bowed his head and started muttering. Francis realised he was holding a rosary beads. The man tapped the fat boy's arm. The fat boy turned away but the man grabbed his arm and pulled at it. Then, acting like he didn't want to, the boy took a little purse from his pocket, opened it and pulled out a rosary beads. He bowed his head too. Francis looked around to see if anyone else had noticed the two of them praying. It seemed very funny to him, but then he thought about Francis of Assisi. Even though the library book said he loved jokes, Francis was sure the saint wouldn't be laughing at the father and son standing on the sidelines with their heads bowed. And what if Mattersons suddenly scored a goal because of their prayers? How would Francis feel then if he was laughing at them? The father kept nudging his son to give the response to the prayer. The fat boy's face had gone all red and he kept looking up to see if anyone was staring at him. But the people all around them were only interested in the match. Even though he seemed bigger because he was fatter, Francis began to realise that they were both about the same age and that made him feel sorrier for the boy. He was glad the baldy man wasn't his father because he seemed to be a bit mad. Suddenly the crowd went Oh! and then Ooooh! as one of the forwards for Krups beat the last defender and his shot flew past the goalkeeper. The fat boy's father stopped praying for a couple of seconds and he squeezed his son's shoulder. Then, when the ball struck the crossbar and went wide, he let go, blessed himself, and started praying again. Francis knew that if he didn't stop staring at them he'd start laughing again, but as soon as he turned away he saw La-la Donoghue staring at him. La-la waved his good hand, and came limping fast towards him. As he came near, Francis put the library book inside his coat. He wasn't afraid that La-la would grab the book but he might ask him questions about it and Francis knew they'd be stupid questions, or else he might want to hold the book and then he'd probably drop it in the mud or damage it in some way and Francis didn't want to get into trouble with his first library book.

'You aw Whitchie's bodda, awnt you?'

Francis nodded.

'Whitchie is a good whutballa.'

'He's very good.'

'I thee all hith mathses. Nominick tSavio and Khwups and all.'

Francis had met La-la three times since the first time Ritchie had introduced him and noticed that he said the same things every time.

'Have you theen all hith mathses?'

'No, not all.'

'I theen all a them. He'th a very good whutballa.'

Francis thought that St Francis of Assisi wouldn't mind if La-la said the same thing all the time. He'd be very patient and call him Brother Laurence and invite him to join his mission. But thinking about what St Francis would do didn't stop Francis wanting La-la to go away and when, after another fifteen minutes and two more goals for Krups, La-la was still standing very close to him and saying that his brother was a great footballer and he had seen all his matches, Francis decided he wouldn't stay any longer. Anyway, if he went to the library straight away that would give him more time to find the book that Ian Barry had shown him and still get home in time for Gussie to bring him to see *The Heroes of Telemark.* To make sure that La-la wouldn't trail after him he just said, very quickly, 'I have to go. 'Bye,' and ran. It was only when he got out of Cals Park and looked back to make sure that La-la wasn't limping along behind that he remembered the baldy man and the fat son. Were they still praying, even though the score was now six–nil?

Francis walked through People's Park, getting more nervous the closer he got to the big old grey library. When he finally reached the entrance he stopped and looked at the dark inside, sure now that something would go wrong. Someone would tell him it was all a big mistake and he shouldn't have been allowed take the book about St Francis in the first place and he certainly couldn't take away any other book. Books for free? Who did he think he was? Now he wished he hadn't begged his mam to let him come here on his own. He wanted to turn around and go home but he had to give back *Francis and Clare: Saints of Assisi.*

before the 17th, so he might as well do it now. At least they'd know he was a good boy for bringing it back early. If they were nice then he might ask if they had the book that Ian Barry showed him and could he take it out? Francis took one step inside. The door to the adults' library was straight in front of him. He could see people through the glass wall walking around, taking books from the shelves and looking at them. The door to the children's library was around the corner past the big stairs. Francis stepped forward far enough to take a look.

Behind the high counter just inside the children's library was a woman with a ponytail and glasses. It wasn't the same woman as before. Francis couldn't tell if this woman was nice or not. There was no expression on her face. A girl who looked about nine or ten came to the counter with a book. The woman with the ponytail smiled at her, opened the book and stamped it just like the other woman had stamped his. Then the girl just walked out with it, and went past Francis into the adults' library. He looked through the glass and saw her go to a woman and show her the book. The woman smiled and squeezed her hand. Francis decided to give it a try.

He went into the children's library, put his book on the high counter and waited to see what would happen. The woman opened the book and looked at the date stamped on it, then she started going through a big box of cards. She picked one out. The card had a pocket with another little card inside. She took out the little card and put it into *Francis and Clare: Saints of Assisi*, closed it and added it to the pile of books behind her. Then she said, 'Is your mammy with you? Is she in the adult section? Or your daddy?' Francis didn't know what to say. His mam and dad had never been in the library, as far as he knew. The woman looked at the card with the pocket and said, 'What's your name, little boy?' Francis' voice was only a whisper. 'Francis Strong.' What trouble was he in now? The woman said, 'OK. So are you here on your own, Francis?' He nodded. 'That's grand. And are you taking out another book today?' Francis whispered, 'Can I?' Suddenly the woman smiled. 'Of course you can, love. Sure isn't that what we're here for? There's your card. Mind, don't lose that now.' The card had his name and address on it in Marian's writing. So what she'd told him really was true. As long as he had this card he could borrow books whenever he wanted. Francis thought of the book Ian Barry had shown him. 'Do you have *The Mystery of the Pantomime Cat* by Enid Blyton? A Five Find-outers mystery.'

'Well, there's any amount of Enid Blytons. So we might. Let's have a look.'

Francis followed the nice woman. He prayed she would find *The Mystery of the Pantomime Cat* because yesterday Ian Barry had came up to him in the schoolyard and said, 'Have you read this?' On the cover of the book Francis saw a drawing of a fat policeman scratching his head looking at a man in a cat costume. *The Mystery of the Pantomime Cat* by Enid Blyton. Francis was completely surprised that Ian Barry had talked to him because he had wanted to talk Ian Barry ever since he first saw him in the yard on the morning they started in CBS when he didn't even know his name. He had been really happy to find out they were in the same class, 2A, but was sorry he wasn't put sitting next to him. He looked at Ian Barry a lot in class and listened to his voice when he answered the teacher's questions. He seemed to be very clever, but everyone in 2A was clever. That's why it was 2A. After only a couple of days Francis knew he wasn't the best boy in the class like he used to be in the convent school. He still hadn't talked to Ian Barry but he had heard other boys saying things about him in the yard. They all called him Fancy Pants. One boy who knew him from before said he was an only child and his mother made all his clothes for him, that's why they looked so mad. The next day, Mr Finucane, their teacher, was asking if anyone in the class had ever won competitions or prizes. Joseph Quinn said he had medals for running and Tommy Madigan said he had come first in grade two piano and Ian Barry said he was a champion Irish dancer. Some of the boys laughed at that but Mr Finucane said, '*Cúinas*!' very angrily, and then told Ian Barry that was a great achievement and he hoped he would keep it up. The next day when Francis was leaving school he saw Ian Barry walking ahead of him. He didn't exactly follow him because they were both going towards the big gate anyway, but he did slow down a bit so he could stay behind him and watch. There was a woman waiting at the gate who hugged him and held his hand as they walked away together. Francis thought she looked much younger than his mam. He started walking down the street behind them even though it wasn't his way home, but then he stopped because suddenly he felt afraid that Ian Barry might look around and see him and for some reason he didn't want that to happen.

No one else in 2A was collected after school. Francis would be really embarrassed if his mam waited for him at the gate. Did Ian Barry mind? He didn't seem to. From the way he acted in school he didn't seem to mind about anything, even when other boys said bad things about him and made sure he heard. He just bounced along smiling, his curls hopping. Francis had already talked to lots of boys in his new class and he didn't know why he wasn't able to start talking to Ian Barry, but he just couldn't do it. That's why it was so surprising when it happened the other way around and Ian Barry talked to him.

During *sos* Francis had been looking at Brother Hagan, thinking how glad he was that he hadn't ended up in his class, 2E. Brother Hagan was the scariest-looking brother. Hedgehog, everyone called him, because his head was shaved around the sides and the thick black hair on top stood up. Every day, for the whole *sos*, he marched his class around the yard like soldiers: *Clé, Deas, Clé, Deas, Clé!* They were not allowed to play at all, just *Clé, Deas, Clé!* Suddenly, Ian Barry's face was right in front of Francis, asking him something and he didn't know what to say because he had never read the book he was showing him and he didn't even know what the question meant: 'Do you prefer the Five Find-outers to the Famous Five?' Francis wanted to lie. He wanted to show off in front of Ian Barry. He felt his face go red. Then he said, 'I don't know.'

'Oh. But you like reading, don't you?'

How did Ian Barry know that? What else did he know about him?

'I do.'

'You're the best in our class at reading. In my old school I used to be the best at reading but you're better than me.'

Francis remembered that the day before, when Mr Finucane asked boys to read from *Aesop's Fables* out loud, he had let Francis read much longer than anyone else and said '*ana-mhaith*' when he finished. That was why Ian Barry thought he was a good reader.

'I thought I preferred the Famous Five until I started reading this. My daddy bought it for me in Dublin. I only started it yesterday and I'm up to page ninety-four already. Do you want to read it? I'll give you a loan of it when I'm finished.'

Francis said, 'Yes, OK.' and Ian Barry smiled at him. Then the bell rang and they had to go back to class, but after school he came over to him again and they walked together towards the big gate. Ian Barry started telling Francis all about the Five Find-outers, Larry and Daisy and Pip and Bets and Fatty especially, who was the cleverest, and his dog Buster and Mr Goon the policeman who was really stupid and funny. But when they were near the gate Ian suddenly said goodbye, see you Monday and ran off. Francis saw the same woman waiting. She kissed him and took his hand. Ian didn't look back as they walked away.

Because Francis had liked *Francis and Clare: Saints of Assisi*, so much, he had been thinking of getting another Vision Book from the library. There was one about St Francis Xavier called *Francis of the Seven Seas*, and *St Anthony and the Christ Child*, and *Saint Ignatius and the Company of Jesus*. But after talking to Ian Barry, he'd decided to borrow *The Mystery of the Pantomime Cat* instead. If he got it on Saturday he could read most of it before school on Monday and talk to Ian Barry about it.

'Here it is. Plenty of Enid Blyton there to keep you going.'

Francis looked to where the nice woman was pointing. There was a shelf full of books by Enid Blyton. She must be an amazing writer to write so many. Had Ian Barry read all of them? If he had, Francis would never catch up. The nice library woman picked up *The Mystery of the Pantomime Cat.*

'Will I stamp this one for you?'

'Yes please.'

*

At seven-thirty that night, in the Royal Marine Hotel, the Minister for Education made a speech that succeeded in surprising an entire roomful of journalists. Only one had been honoured with any kind of prior warning. Indicating the script in his hand, Dom had whispered to Hanley before dinner began. 'I'm following your advice, by the way. Thank you in advance. Oh and don't worry about taking notes. I'll give you this copy when I've finished.' There was a smirk and a giddiness about him that convinced Hanley that the Minister was about to announce something sensational and, though he had no idea what the speech contained nor which of his wise words had prompted it, Dom's whisper had made him feel part of a very great secret. Intimating to everyone else in the room that he was thus privileged was not a difficult task, even in so limited a time-frame. By the time dessert was served, Hanley had moved through the fair, gliding from table to table, visited the gents, hovered at the bar and, by means of winks and whispered phrases heavy with import, such as, 'Go easy on the sauce until after the speech. You're going to need a clear head.' 'I hope your lads can make space on tomorrow's front page. You'll be looking for it.' 'Let's just say it involves a rabbit and a hat.' 'You know our Dom. The surprise would be if he didn't surprise us,' he succeeded in raising anticipation amongst his colleagues for what was to come, while at the same time amplifying his own reputation as the man with inside knowledge. Several who wrote for the Sunday papers even thought it worthwhile to step out and phone their offices to warn the night editors that something particularly newsworthy might be arriving later on. Like Hanley, these correspondents implied that they knew more than they were willing to say at that moment.

Quite early on in the Minister's speech, it became clear that what he was about to say would indeed be a big story. By the time he spoke his final sentence and received what, by journalists' standards, was unusually sustained and heartfelt applause, several reporters were hurrying to commandeer a phone, gather their thoughts and file a story they were now certain would be the Sunday morning front-page lead. Back in the function room, Hanley, applauding with the rest, felt like a cat who had got not only the cream but the keys to the creamery. Accepting admiring glances from those colleagues who he permitted to catch his eye, he congratulated himself for being the one to have nurtured this Minister and given him the *spriod*, the balls to get up on his hind legs in such a forum and speak, over the heads of the cabinet and the government and the Dáil, directly to the people. Announcing policy in this way was unprecedented and brave. That the policy should be so far-seeing and radical was the capper, as far as Hanley was concerned. Though several years younger than Dom, his pride in him at that moment was paternal.

The Minister's announcement would be the first thing Charles Mitchell would tell the country on the TV news the following day, it would be the front-page lead in every Sunday paper and on Monday in every daily paper. There would be editorials, all favourable. In the week following, the main topic of conversation would be this daring new plan for Free Education. As the applause finally ended and Dom sat down, he understood very well what he had done. With one speech, one idea, one political act, he had placed himself right at the centre of things. But it was not possible for him, at this moment, to predict his fate. What events would unfold? Who would emerge as friend or enemy? His hands tingled, his brain swirled like rip-tide at Lahinch, his heart was a galloping drunk, knocking over tables, crashing to the ground. Boom de boom de boom de boom de! The words lying silent on the pages, still crushed in his hands, could never convey the intoxication of the experience; hearing himself speak them, sensing the receptiveness of his audience. It would never be possible to recreate the hush that crept, cautious as a black cat, through the room or how, as word followed word, whispered comments and coughs and clinks simply evaporated, until only breath-held attentiveness remained, with Dom as the fulcrum. He loved it.

'I am fortunate in entering office when there is a consciousness as never before of the vital part education must play in the future of a nation, not just for economic and technological advancement, but in the making of the social man, the complete person. Ireland is unshackling itself gently from the chains of the past. Education will pay a key role in deciding what our future will be.

'But in this special year of 1966, this year in which we honour the teachers and poets who fought to establish our independence, seventeen thousand children who finished primary school in June will receive no further education. Seventeen thousand. One third of the school population. And it is not just this year but every year that so many of our young citizens are condemned to a life of unskilled labour or unemployment or emigration. And we all know that the principal reason for this is not because further education will not be of benefit, nor because there is a lack of desire for it. It is because so many of our people cannot afford it.

'This is a dark stain on the national conscience.

'Apart from certain exclusive establishments, the general run of secondary schools charge fees of around thirty pounds a year for each pupil. It is not, on the face of it, an exorbitant sum. However, when the necessary extra costs for books and equipment are added, then forty-five pounds a year at least is needed to keep a child in secondary school. When, as in so many Irish families, there are four or more children, all at school-going age, then these annual costs can multiply to something more like two hundred pounds. This, in a family whose total income might not be much more than a thousand a year, becomes an intolerable burden. What choice does a hard-working parent have in such circumstances? Especially when the alternative is that their child, instead of being a cost to the family, can leave school to find some sort of menial job and actually bring money into the home. But in our society it is the weakest who will always go to the wall. Without education, these children will not have the necessary tools to prosper in the future.

'We must also acknowledge that while there are many parents who are happy to endure privation so that their children receive the education they perhaps did not, there are also some who, having never experienced the positive effects of education themselves, see no value in it for their own family. But should the children suffer because of such a view?

'I think it is one of the greatest tragedies of our history since independence that we have not found the means to check this terrible loss to the national potential for economic and cultural advancement.

'I believe this is a situation that needs to be tackled with all speed and determination. The world of tomorrow will give scant attention to the uneducated and we will be judged by future generations on what we did for the children of our time.

'What we need, and what I want, is to remove for ever the financial barrier to further education. I want every child in this state to have the opportunity to pursue education to, at the very least, Intermediate Certificate and, preferably, to Leaving Certificate level.

'I want free secondary school education.

'In considering how to achieve this, it has been important for me to find the simplest, speediest and most effective means and so, tonight, I wish to announce a new scheme for free education which will operate as follows. From the beginning of the next school year, September 1967, I will be requesting secondary schools to abandon fees. In return, these schools will receive from the state an agreed sum of money for every pupil they enrol. There will be no means test involved. All parents who want their child to continue in education simply have to send them to a school that has opted for my scheme.

It is my fervent wish that the vast majority, if not all, of the schools in the state will avail themselves of the opportunity presented by this scheme and that, by the end of this decade, every child in the state and as a consequence, the state itself, will enjoy the benefits of free education.'

Eighteen: September 13th

The smoke from five pipes scented the air of the cabinet room. Six other ministers were lighting up cigarettes as Dom sat and took a large sheaf of papers from his briefcase. These, he planned to tell the meeting later, were a sample of the letters and telegrams he had received enthusing about his new scheme. Considerably less than half of the impressive pile were as he claimed, but Dom hoped that by showing what appeared to be huge popular support for his initiative it might offset some of the tornado of criticism he was nervously anticipating. Jesus! If his fellow ministers could see his shuddering heart it would make a liar of his calm, smiling face. In the perfumed smog drifting around the table it was hard enough even to see faces. The raw truth was that there was little Dom could do to influence how the discussion would go. It was all up to Lemass; how he decided to manage things. The letter he'd sent Dom yesterday and copied to the Department of Finance had given no hint that An Taoiseach had known anything about the matter beforehand. Very laudable scheme. Very bad idea to have announced it without first bringing it to cabinet. Very serious situation. Did that mean he was going to sit back and let Dom be flayed alive?

Lemass did not bother to pretend there was anything else of importance on the agenda. Straight away he invited reaction to Dom's speech. There was no pause or delay. Mick was in like flynn, apoplectic: 'What… what… what… what was the Minister thinking of, giving out money like snuff at a wake? We… we… we can only spend what we have. Would Dom like us to… to… to raise more taxes to pay for his flights of fancy?'

Erskine was less aggressive but his tendentiousness really got Dom's goat.

'It is a long tradition that policy is made by cabinet, not by individual ministers. I don't think it can ever be correct to depart from such an honourable practice. It is, in my considered view, a retrograde development. Think about it, Dom, if all of us around this table today acted this way, then Government would simply collapse. You see the principle I am attempting –'

Dom pretended to listen with interest, thinking blah blah blah and had difficulty hiding a smirk when Neil, every inch the no nonsense Northerner, ruthlessly cut across Erskine's painfully kind reprimand. Unsheathing the pipe from his mouth, he jabbed it malevolently in Dom's direction.

'Let's call it what it was. A solo run. It's been tried before, God knows and it'll be tried again. And smartly done, to give you your due, Dom. The question is: should you be let get away with it? The answer is: not this time, my friend.'

When George spoke, his tone was, as usual, all sweet reason and concern.

'Obviously the policy, in itself, has merit and, if brought to cabinet for discussion in the first instance, might well have met with all our approval…'

There was a word to describe George. What was it again? It was on the tip of Dom's tongue.

'… Ironically, because he chose to bypass cabinet, Dom has made it less likely that his scheme will ever go ahead.'

Oleaginous, that was the word. Dom found Frank's loud honest rage refreshing by comparison.

'Look, it's as simple as this. We can't have policy made on the hoof, especially by way of a bunch of journalists, of all people! If you want my opinion, there's only one way to nip this in the bud. You have to go out on the plinth, Dom, and tell those same journalists that your speech was intended to reflect your personal view and nothing else. Of course, you'd love if at some future date, when it's appropriate, the government might consider your scheme. Sorry if the speech gave the wrong impression. And so on.'

Dom, appreciating the weight of Frank's influence in cabinet, realised that this was a moment of extreme danger. What if others rowed in behind this specific suggestion? As everyone paused, puffed and considered, Dom looked towards Lemass at the far end of the cabinet table. So far An Taoiseach had just listened, let them all rage on. But if he didn't intervene now the mood of the room might well be to make Dom recant, let him look foolish and politically inept.

Lemass, with no discernible expression on his face or in his voice, turned to Jack and asked, 'What's the view in Finance?'

With those words Dom heard the soft plash! of a lifeline thrown into choppy waters. He realised that Lemass was deliberately shifting the focus away from Frank's proposal, knowing that while placid Jack would certainly report dismay from on high in the department, these complaints, filtered through his mellow Cork sing-song voice, would sound more like sorrow than anger, a crestfallen shake of the head rather than Frank's *Götterdämmerung*. Dom sympathised with Jack in this situation. The poor eejit and his harmless wife had flown back to Dublin on Sunday, from what was presumably a restful little holiday in Turkey, to see headlines announcing a new government policy he knew nothing about; a scheme that would probably cost his department millions. If Dom was in his place he'd be shoving a red hot poker up the offending arse and refusing to remove it until the culprit begged for forgiveness and promised never to speak out of turn again. But soft Jack was not a man for that kind of response. Certainly he relayed his department's strong view that controlling budgetary policy would not be possible if ministers announced enormous expenditures like this without prior discussion, yet the lilt in his voice seemed to suck the poison out of the attack. Listening to him was like taking tea in the Bishop's parlour on a winter evening, when the dreary complacence of the episcopal monologue conspired with the gathering dark and the heat of a great log fire to enervate the listener.

As Dom noted how, with every soft sentence, Jack was lowering the temperature of the discussion, he tried to get Charlie's attention and signal that now was the time to begin the fightback, but the lizard eyes were focused unblinkingly on the Minister for Finance. A cold, hard thought slapped Dom on the cheek. Was Charlie not going to speak up for him? Was he hoping he would fail? Jealousy? The farmers were riding him hard and his stock was the lowest it had been since he first became Minister, whereas, if the Free Education scheme went through, then Dom would be cock of the walk. That had become clear these last few days: the headlines, the gushing editorials, the telegrams. This morning, when Dom swanned into Leinster House, there may not have been a smile and a well done from everyone, but, certainly, every eye flicked admiringly in his direction as he passed. Charlie would be preternaturally aware of all this, and enraged by it. Obviously he'd never speak out directly against his friend Dom – would he? – but why had he not spoken at all so far?

'I take on board everything that Jack and others have had to say, but surely it would be remiss of us not to acknowledge that the reaction of the press and public has been very good.'

By Jesus, Dom thought, the Lizard has timing all right. Charlie's tone was languid, disinterested, but all the more effective for that. Having kicked the ball high in the air, he let faithful Brian off the leash to chase it.

'Very good? You couldn't buy coverage like that. Three days of it. The editorial in the *Irish Times* was practically euphoric. The teachers' unions have all come out in favour. This is political gold, lads. We'd be out of our minds to turn around now and –'

'No one said it wasn't a popular idea. That isn't the point –'

George got no further. Charlie's interruption was imperious.

'Precisely. Popularity, important though it is, is not the point. This is entirely a question of principle. Do we, as a cabinet, as a Party, believe in this policy? The primacy of cabinet government has been emphasised here today. So, leaving aside for a moment the mechanics of how this policy came to public attention, shouldn't we, rather, be asking ourselves a more fundamental question? Do we think free education is the right thing for the children of the Nation?'

Now Lemass spoke.

'Charlie is right. It is a fundamental question. Especially, if I may say, in the year that's in it.'

The 1916 card. Laid on the table quietly and decisively. The fiftieth anniversary. Honouring the dreams of dead heroes. From that moment the game was won. There was more spluttering, of course, but leavened now with references to how meritorious the scheme was and how impressive the public enthusiasm for it. By the time Lemass asked Dom to make his contribution there was only a house of straw left to blow down. Dom was gentle. He tossed his critics a *mea culpa* about his capriciousness, his injudiciousness, two of his many flaws which little by little he sought to mend. Perhaps his enthusiasm for the cause had made him forgetful of proper procedures. The opportunity to get one over on the Blueshirts which, he hoped his colleagues would concede, was most certainly what had happened, had perhaps been too tempting. It would be a terrible pity if such excellent political advantage were to be lost by backing down now. Especially as the voters seemed so enthusiastic for the scheme. He held up his sheaf of letters and telegrams. And after all, the whole idea of free education had been discussed in the department before – Dom had the document with him as it happened – and, in principle, had met with the approval of his predecessor. He turned to Dr Pat who, somehow, had managed not to speak throughout the discussion.

'So, in fact, Paddy should get a lot of the credit for this policy. He would have introduced something similar to my scheme had he continued as Minister for Education. In the end it was purely a question of timing, isn't that right, Paddy?'

What sinful pleasure it gave Dom to force Dr Pat to agree with him while silently ramming home the message: 'You talked about it, Paddy-boy. I did it.'

Lemass summed up.

'We all agree that announcing policy in the way Dom chose to do is not acceptable. I think there is also general agreement that his scheme is one that meets with our approval and, it seems overwhelmingly, that of the general public. However, none of that matters if there is no money to pay for it. So, Jack, are you saying that it'd be impossible for Finance to fund this scheme?'

The framing of the question was sheer genius. What could Jack say?

'No… No. I'm not saying it's impossible. I'll have to look at the costs and –'

'Then let's see how much we can spare. Dom, can you get your estimates over to Jack as quickly as possible? Is everyone happy with that?'

No dissenting voice. It was done. Lemass had played a blinder. Dom was aware that all he had to do now was squeeze as much moolah as he could out of Finance, charm the bishops and the heads of the Religious Orders, and make sure that the schools could handle all the extra pupils that would come pouring in next September. How did that song go? We can work it out.

*

The meeting room in the Mechanics Institute on Hartstonge Street was high-ceilinged and its large sash windows needed repair, so it was always cold, even on the mildest evening. Eight women faced each other, four on either side of a two-bar electric fire. They sewed, knitted, crocheted and chatted. At one end of the group, Mrs Hoare was operating a Singer, their only electric sewing machine. There was a large work table at the other end. This was where Ann Strong spread out the gorgeous silk outer skirt of a wedding dress and considered how best to cut it up.

Fonsie's sister Marg had felt sorry for Ann when she heard that it had rained almost the whole week in Ballybunion and that, really, it hadn't been a proper holiday at all this year. In fact, in many ways it had been worse than being at home, because the children had to be kept amused morning, noon and night. That was why she suggested that Ann come along with her to the Redemptorist Foreign Missions weekly sewing group. Marg thought that at least it would be a break from the young ones for a few hours. A bit of a night out. She didn't put it that way to Ann, of course. Instead she talked about the good work the group did, making the most beautiful vestments for the brave, hard-working missionaries out in Africa and the Philippines. Women with Ann's sewing skills were hard to find, Marg said. When Ann protested that it had been years since she had done any sewing, her sister-in-law said then wasn't it about time she started again and reminded her of the gorgeous dresses she used to make for Marian and her own Mary when they were children. Ann agreed to give it a go.

Within a few weeks she was loving it so much that she wouldn't know what to do with herself on a Tuesday night if it wasn't on. It brought back to her how soothing and relaxing sewing was. The more delicate and intricate the work, the better Ann liked it. Priests' vestments were a challenge, and old Mrs Hoare, who had supervised the group for years, constantly emphasised how vital it was that, no matter in what wild part of the jungle he found himself, the missionary priest should be able to celebrate Mass with proper dignity, which meant having all the correct ceremonial clothing. He needed albs and stoles and chasubles and surplices. Making an alb was the simplest, Ann could run one up on the Singer in a very short time, but stoles and chasubles were a different matter. Silk was much more delicate and expensive and so required the most careful handling. Very few of the women had the patience and precision to hand-sew in gold thread, tiny crosses, leaf patterns and sacred symbols. Any slip and the work done would have to be painstakingly unravelled and begun again. Sometimes a simple mistake rendered the garment unusable. It was Mrs Hoare's firm view that no missionary should be expected to celebrate the holy sacrifice of the Mass wearing flawed or substandard vestments. Marg, who had no talent for sewing and generally confined herself to knitting woolly jumpers, hats and gloves for the regular Sales of Work that raised money to buy material for vestments, was delighted when, on the first night, Mrs Hoare whispered to her, 'Your sister-in-law is a very talented seamstress.' After only a few weeks she began to trust Ann with the most complicated work of all – the chasuble.

Tonight she had given her the old wedding dress to see what vestments could be made from the material. People often offered to donate old clothing to the Foreign Missions Sewing Group but Mrs Hoare generally turned them down. The group was not, she would observe in private, a dumping ground for people's old rags. The only garments even remotely suitable for making vestments tended to be ladies' evening gowns or cloaks. Wedding dresses were ideal, because so much silk and linen went into their making, but they were hard to come by, so it was important that, when the sewing group received one, the best use was made of it. Ann could tell straight away that it would be easy to get as many as five surplices out of the underskirts, but the silk outer skirt presented a problem. There might be just enough in it for one chasuble, but only if she did her calculations very carefully and made no mistakes whatsoever. Ann loved the challenge of making something out of very little and knew what pleasure it would give her to see this old skirt end up as a gorgeously embroidered and braided chasuble worn by a missionary celebrating Mass in some poor little foreign village. She had often seen, in the *Irish Messenger of the Sacred Heart* magazine, photos of priests in spotless white vestments, surrounded by smiling beautiful little black children. It pleased her to think that, in a small way, she might contribute to a scene like that.

Ann was so caught up in her wedding dress problem that for once she took no part in the general chat that was normally such an enjoyable part of the evening. She kept half an ear open and smiled when, as usual, Mrs Liddy spent ages explaining to everyone, in her usual slow voice, what had happened in the latest episode of *The Riordans,* not realising that they had all seen it and didn't need to be told. Ann worked out that she needed to cut the dress into six pieces but it had to be done a particular way and there was no room for error. It should then be possible to restitch the pieces to make the basic chasuble. She was marking out the six pieces, when she heard Iza Clifford's voice calling her name.

'Ann, Ann Strong, are you listening to me? Did you see it?'

'Sorry, Iza. See what?'

'Us on the telly. They showed the Crescent below and the CBS as well.'

'No. When was this?'

'Tonight. On the news.'

Ann was very surprised. The town was hardly ever seen on television, let alone on the news.

'On the news? Why?'

'On account of the Minister for Education coming from here.'

Iza Clifford's knitting needles always seemed to click along in time with her speech. Clickety clickety clickety… 'She wasn't listening to me. You hear didn't a word of what I was saying, Ann, sure you didn't?' … clickety clickety clickety… 'They had pictures of the minister walking along by Crescent College – you know, just around the corner from us here. Rain pouring down, of course, it looked miserable altogether. Honest to God, the one time they show us on the telly and the place looks desperate'… clickety clickety clickety… 'Next thing, there he was, coming out the gates of the Christian Brothers. I was just saying to the girls, my youngest is going there at the moment, but he's doing his Inter Cert next June so this new scheme the Minister is going on about will be no good to me'… clickety clickety clickety… 'and Nora was saying it was the same for her. She has nobody any more and Marg said the same – her last left in June – but Jacinta has two coming up who'll be in secondary in the next few years, so she might get something out of it, at least'… clickety clickety clickety… 'and I was just asking if you had anyone and Marg said you have three. So, is that right? Three, is it?'

Ann had no idea what Iza was on about. Three what? What scheme? It was hard enough trying to concentrate on the job she was doing, but Iza Clifford was looking at her, waiting for an answer. Marg seemed to understand her confusion.

'I told Iza you have three children still at school.'

'Oh yes, that's right, Iza, three.'

'Well, you'll do well out of it, so.'

Once again Ann hadn't the remotest what Iza was on about. Do well out of what? When Mrs Hoare spoke, it only added to her confusion.

'Well now, Iza, none of us doubt the Minister's good intentions. He's a fine man and we're all proud to see a local man in such a high position, but Father Thornton was saying to me this morning that he may be missing an important point and it's this; not everyone is suited to secondary education. There may be a danger with this scheme, that we'd only encourage children who won't get any benefit from it to abuse it and then where will we be? I thought this was a very thoughtful point from Father Thornton.'

Ann knew that all the women loved Father Thornton because, even though he was very intelligent and devout, he was great sport as well. Marg had told her they always had a great laugh at Christmas when he brought them to the Redemptorist community parlour for tea and biscuits to thank them for their work throughout the year. With Father Thornton supporting Mrs Hoare's side of the argument, Ann was very surprised that Iza Clifford did not let it go at that.

'Still an' all, it'll save poor people a lot of money. I paid out thirty-five pounds last year for Peadar's fees. If that scheme was going already I'da saved all that. Think what I could have bought with thirty-five pounds.'

Ann wondered was she hearing properly. Was there some scheme to get rid of school fees?

'With three of them in secondary, Ann there will save herself a load every year. Sure what could be wrong with that?'

Silence. Iza was staring at Mrs Hoare. All the other women now looked towards her. Ann felt she should explain that not all her three children were in secondary school yet, but she was afraid to add to the tension. The clicking had stopped. Mrs Hoare took her foot off the pedal of the Singer and turned to face Iza. Ann could tell from her voice that she didn't like being spoken back to.

'Of course it's a very *well-intentioned* scheme, Mrs Clifford. I have no disagreement with you there. But remember that the priests and brothers and the nuns already keep a very close eye on all their pupils right through primary school, so when the time comes to go on to secondary, they know the cleverest ones and recommend them for scholarships. If a child from a poor family really deserves to continue his education, parents won't be asked to pay for it. Father Thornton assured me that this system works very well and it would be a pity to change it.'

Surely Iza Clifford wouldn't keep arguing after hearing all that? Mrs Liddy suddenly jumped in to say wasn't it great to have someone from the town on the telly all the same. The only other local they ever saw regularly was Terry Wogan, who was very good, at least in Mrs Liddy's opinion. Apart from him, the Dublin and Cork crowd had it all wrapped up, would the girls agree? All the women quickly joined in a pleasant conversation about about which TV presenters they liked and didn't like and the clicking of knitting needles began again.

Ann turned back to her task, but she was still trying to work out exactly what Iza and Mrs Hoare had been talking about. She should try and pay more attention to the news. If she understood them correctly, then did this scheme they were talking about mean that she wouldn't have to pay fees for Marian, or for Martin, who was starting secondary next year? Could that really be true? She had already been thinking about whether it was worthwhile letting poor Martin go on at all. Maybe Father Thornton and Mrs Hoare were right and some children were better off not going to secondary school? But if there was going to be no fees then shouldn't she give him a chance at least? See what happened. As he got older he might get sense and knuckle down. And Marian? With no fees maybe – Ann didn't even want to think about it in case it wasn't true – maybe she'd get her wish and go on and do her Leaving Cert. The first one in the family. No. It couldn't be true.

She must have heard it wrong. For a start, surely an intelligent woman like Mrs Hoare wouldn't be against a scheme if it was as good as that? There must be some catch to it, but she didn't dare ask now in case she started Iza and Mrs Hoare arguing again. She'd find out from Fonsie – he might have heard something. Ann looked at the silk skirt spread out on the table. Better get on with this. She picked up her scissors and stared at the markings. No room for error. With a firm grip and steady hand, she began to cut.

Nineteen: November 5th

Dom was thinking about Lemass, the depths and layers of him, the power of his inpenetrable silence. Had his forty-five years in politics made him this way or had he always been such a man? No one had seen this shock coming. No one. Suddenly an announcement. Out of nowhere. An Taoiseach was stepping down, making way. Not in months but in days. Why? Had he even discussed it with Dev or Frank or any of the old lads? The word was he had not. So why? His leadership was unquestioned, his power undiminished. In the days that followed, Dom's sobriety had been tested as he'd ricocheted between disbelief, frustration, anger, and then, most forcibly and sentimentally, a kind of grief, like Simon Dedalus and the other fellah, Casey, in *Portrait of the Artist*, weeping for Parnell, crying out for their poor dead king. Dom had never before felt such empathy with the pain Joyce described in that Christmas dinner scene. Then, awestruck at the realisation, it had dawned on him exactly why his wily old boss had wanted him to act so quickly on his free education scheme; to force the issue the way he had. Of course. It was because he already intended to step down and he wanted to ensure the scheme got underway before he left. Had Lemass put himself out to do that because he liked the idea so much, or was it pure respect for Dom? Whichever it was, his adoration of the old man intensified. Nothing would ever be the same without him. Who could match him?

Yet as the scramble to choose a new leader began, Dom had acted just as everyone presumed he would and supported Charlie against George, becoming his de facto campaign manager. Of course, the more complex truth was that while he had little time for George, it did not follow that his heart was wholly with the Lizard. His heart, in truth, was as good as broken.

So what about this latest bad news that was bringing him to Charlie's house, with Michael Liston at his side? Dom knew he needed to look and sound upset at the very least and possibly angry as he delivered the hammer-blow. Although, from the expansive and ebullient manner Charlie greeted them when they came knocking on his impressive front door, Dom guessed he had already heard. It would be the Lizard's style to deal with bad news this way. Anyway, it seemed there was no point pussyfooting around this.

'Jack has confirmed. He's putting his name forward.'

In other words, it's over, pal. The shift of Charlie's eyebrow was so slight it could either have meant 'Is that so?', or 'I know that already.'

'The votes aren't there, Charlie, they just ain't there.'

No howls of disappointment or rage. No demand to know the whys and the wherefores, the details of phone calls and hastily convened meetings in Buswell's, and whispered exchanges in the Dáil bar. Dom admired that about Charlie more than anything; his control, his pragmatism. He would immediately understand that, if it was a choice between watching Charlie and George knock lumps out of each other for the next week or slipping Jack in on the nod, then, for most of the parliamentary party, harmless, unambitious Jack was the most sensible option.

'I'm sorry.'

This was not entirely a lie, because Dom genuinely did not want Jack to be Taoiseach. He didn't want any of them. He wanted Lemass back. That's what his own bewildered heart kept telling him. No one could compare. Not Jack, not Charlie, obviously not George. He could say that much with sincerity. 'At least it won't be George.' But that was hardly likely to console Charlie just now.

'Well, should I make a contest of it anyway? We still have a few days to win people over.'

Maybe the Lizard wasn't such a pragmatist after all. Was it going to be necessary to reveal the whole embarrassing truth? That dull old Jack was not just another candidate throwing a hopeful hat in the ring. He was the Chosen One. A part of Dom would take great pleasure in telling Charlie that reluctant Jack had only allowed his name to go forward because Lemass was so determined that his own son-in-law should not be Taoiseach; he had more or less begged him to take the job. Surely Charlie would not want Dom to be specific about how embarrassingly bad the likely vote would be? His word-of-mouth canvass had revealed that, with Jack now in the contest, Charlie would be lucky to get twenty per cent. As Dom considered the most delicate way to frame his reply, Michael Liston fixed his eyes on Charlie and spoke for the first time.

'I think the better option for you would be to concede graciously, having made sure that Jack gets the message, loud and clear, that you expect something in return for your support. Look, we all know Jack has no real future, he's not going to be anything other than a stop-gap Taoiseach. Who in the party gives a fuck about him? Who'd fight his cause for him if it came down to it? Nobody. You know it, I know it. So, fine. With you as, say, Minister for Finance, or, at least Industry and Commerce –'

Charlie interrupted very quickly.

'No. Finance, or nothing.'

'Fair enough. So, with you in Finance, where would the real power be? And remember Charlie, all your plans, all those things you might get done, they won't happen if you fight an election and lose. Jack could toss you some hole-in-the-wall ministry like Defence or… or –'

Dom wondered if he was about to say Education.

'… or the Gaeltacht, for Jaysus' sake! See my point? Don't put yourself out of the game like that. Play it long.'

It was obvious that the Lizard liked what he was hearing. His next words confirmed that already he was slithering quickly through the undergrowth of his disappointment, his eyes now fixed on wide open fields beyond.

'So you're saying stand aside immediately and, Christ between us and all harm, openly support Jack.'

'Yes. Definitely support him. Once he confirms exactly how grateful he'll be after he's elected.'

Dom knew he should be pleased at Michael's intervention. After all, the objective of their visit had been to convince Charlie that his bid to be Taoiseach was doomed. Michael's words seemed to have done the trick. Yet he felt uneasy. A new atmosphere had entered the room. It was as though something intangible but important had been wrested from him. When Michael spoke he had fixed his gaze solely on Charlie. Not once had he turned to Dom for support or confirmation. Not as much as a glance. It was as if he was not in the room. Neither did Charlie look to Dom for his opinion. Instead, as he sipped and considered his options, the lizard eyes focused exclusively on Michael Liston and, after a long period of silence, the tiny nod that indicated approval of the strategy was only offered in that direction. Dom might as well not have been there.

He felt foolishly and unaccountably jealous.

1967

Twenty: February 14th

Francis was pretty glum and he could tell that Ian Barry was too. It felt worse than the end of hols. They had just finished reading their very last Five Find-outers story, *The Mystery of Banshee Towers*. There were no more. Since becoming chums, Francis and Ian had read one every week. Ian's dad had to go to Dublin a lot because of his job and he always brought him back a present of a new Five Find-outers book. Francis would borrow the same one from the library. It was wizard! Reading the same one at the same time meant they could talk about all the twists and turns of the latest during *sos*. They could play out the stories, making teachers and other pupils characters. Mr Quigley, who taught 4C, became PC Goon because, like the silly policeman, he was a bit of a fat sausage with frog-eyes. Whenever the chums saw him in the yard they would put him under surveillance, hoping to catch him doing something silly. One day they were delighted when they saw him picking his nose! Then he flicked the snot away, looking around before he did it to make sure no one was watching, but he never saw the two friends, who were well hidden! They were too clever for PC Goon! Another day they saw poor old Quigley bellowing at two boys in the yard who were fighting, but the boys just ran off because they knew that he was too lazy to run after them. The chums had great fun afterwards, pretending that Mr Quigley bellowed at the two boys like PC Goon.

'Gah! Don't you run away from me! Lawks, you dratted kids. Don't you think you pests can get away with it! I'll give you what-for!'

The chums nearly always picked Brother Hedgehog as the villain. Sometimes they had him writing poison-pen letters like Mrs Moon in *The Mystery of the Spiteful Letters*, or setting fire to things like Mr Hicks in *The Mystery of the Burnt Cottage*. Francis thought Hedgehog was horrid and a beastly toad and hoped they'd discover that he really did have a dark secret but, even though they kept him under surveillance every day and found his footprint and made a drawing of it, they couldn't prove he'd committed a crime. He was too slippery. 'Devious and clever, Pip,' Francis, who was Fatty, said to Ian, who was Pip. 'Devilish. He's a wretch, Fatty,' said Ian. All Hedgehog ever seemed to do was march the boys in 2E around the yard and bark out orders in Irish. Every other boy in the school kept out of his way. If Hedgehog put his evil eye on you, you were in trouble. Older pupils said even if a boy only did a tiny thing wrong, Hedgehog would give out at least four slaps of the leather and usually it was six.

Fatty was Francis' favourite character. Even though he was conceited, he was clever, funny, good at disguises and usually solved the mystery in the end, although sometimes one of the others would say something which led him to the solution. Even though neither Francis nor Ian were plump, they both wanted to be Fatty, so they took turns. Whoever was not Fatty was usually Pip. Neither of them wanted to be any of the others, so they pretended that some other boys in their class were Bets, Larry and Daisy without telling them. For a laugh, sometimes they pretended Gerard Staunton was Buster the dog because he was so scruffy and always seemed to end up rolling around in the yard.

The chums played together every *sos* and when school finished each day they walked together slowly to the entrance gate, chattering happily. A little bit away from the gate, they always stopped and Ian would say goodbye to Francis and bounce off. Francis would wait until he saw him walk away with his mother. The chums never saw each other outside of school, not even at the weekend. Francis' dad brought him to football matches and he knew Ian was always going to Irish dancing competitions. One morning he told Francis that he had just become the Munster Champion, under-ten solo hornpipe. He seemed thrilled about it. Francis asked his mam if any of Marian's dancing cups or medals were for being Munster Champion. His mam said no, that was a very hard thing to win, why was he asking? Francis said no reason, just he had heard that some boy in school had won it. His mam said he must be a brilliant dancer.

In the Five Find-outers books the children were always going to each other's houses and drinking homemade lemonade. Francis wondered what it would be like if Ian Barry came to play in his house, but he knew it was a stupid idea. Imagine Ian's mother walking up their street, holding Ian's hand! Tommy Duggan and Bernard McMahon, who were in 2D and 2E and hardly ever even talked to Francis any more, would see him and be laughing behind his back. Francis was also afraid that if he brought Ian to his house Martin would be there and he'd start making beastly remarks that were supposed to be funny but weren't. His mam would be even worse though. She'd be saying look how neat and tidy Ian is, why can't you be like that? And she'd never give them a pitcher of homemade lemonade and iced buns.

When Francis first started reading the Five Find-outers books, he found some things strange and a bit upsetting. He couldn't understand why grown-ups were calling children 'Master' or 'Miss'. The local shopkeeper, Miss Jolly, always said things like: 'What can I get you today, Master Frederick?' or 'Can I help you, Miss Daisy?' In Curtin's shop around the corner from Francis, Mrs Curtin just screamed at children all the time. 'Wait your turn, you little scut!' or 'You, the boy of the Strongs, take your filthy hands off that counter!' or 'Don't lay a finger on them penny sweets 'til after you paid for 'em.' In the Five Find-outer books the only person who shouted at children was a stupid fat policeman who always got his comeuppance. In the end the adults always listened to the children and told them how clever they were. Francis also wondered how could Fatty afford to take everyone to the dairy and buy them cakes and ice-cream? It was like a different world. Even though they weren't princes or princesses, the children all seemed to have maids and cooks and charwomen. Francis wasn't even sure what a charwoman was, but he knew it was a servant of some kind. Why were there no normal people who didn't have servants but who weren't servants either? Was it different because it was England? Maybe that was why Ireland fought so hard to be independent?

Still, by the time he had finished reading the first book he was thoroughly enthralled by the mystery! Fatty was marvellous! Also, it was thrilling to send Ian messages written in invisible ink or find out if he could escape from a locked room using a sheet of newspaper and a piece of wire. Talking to each other the way the characters talked was great fun too.

'Gracious, you're a marvel, Ian!'

'You're a marvel too, Francis. You're the limit!'

Soon, the world of the Five Find-outers became a completely normal, everyday thing and he forgot how queer it had seemed at first.

The chums had had a grand time but now it was over. They had read all fifteen adventures. Francis didn't want to say it, but the one they had just finished was the worst. He wouldn't want to read any more of them if they were going to be like this one. He wished they could all be as good as *The Mystery of the Invisible Thief*, which was his favourite. He had read that in only one day, starting it while he was walking home from the library and finishing it in bed that night under the covers with a flash-lamp. Francis hoped that Ian wouldn't suggest that they start reading the Famous Five books, because he had already read a bit of *Five Go to Smuggler's Top* and didn't like it much. Could anything ever be as good as the Five Find-outers? The chums sat on the ground under Block F of the new school, staring sadly at their book covers.

'I say, Ian old boy, things are going to be rather dull if there are no more mysteries to solve.'

'Golly what a shame! Do you think that will happen?'

'I jolly well hope not.'

'It would be pretty exasperating.'

'And infuriating!'

'We'll just have to buck up and find something else just as exciting.'

'Topping idea!'

The friends fell silent. Thinking.

Twenty-one: June 18th–19th

On Friday as they were leaving school, Ian asked Francis: 'Do you want to come to a party in my house on Sunday?'

Francis was dumbfounded, flabbergasted. Yes, of course he wanted to. Ian explained how to get there. Three o'clock, he said. Francis was so excited it wasn't until he was nearly home that he remembered something.

Sunday was his birthday.

That didn't have to stop him going to Ian's party. What would happen on his birthday anyway? They might go for a drive in the lorry to Clare Glens and then visit his granny and he'd have to listen to her moaning and giving out. His mam would make a cake, but he could go to Ian's party and still have the cake. He told her about the invitation. She asked him where did Ian live? He said Corbally. That was all right. As long as it wasn't Southill or anywhere like that. She asked what was the party for? Francis realised he didn't know. Ian just said it was a party. His mam said all right he could go, but he wasn't to be telling anyone that it was his birthday in case people thought he was hinting for a present. Francis promised. His mam said did that mean he didn't want a birthday cake? Francis said he did. His mam asked how was he going to eat it after being at a party. Francis said easy. His mam said was he never satisfied?

On Saturday evening she baked a sponge cake and coconut buns. She said the buns were for him to bring to the party, it would be rude to arrive with nothing. Francis didn't want them, it was a stupid idea, Ian's mother would only laugh at him. But he said nothing because he knew his mam would get annoyed.

His mam made him wear his Communion suit for the party so he would look proper and, as he left, she gave him the coconut buns in a brown paper bag. After he got off the bus at Shannonbanks and found the road where Ian lived, he stopped and looked inside the bag. Stupid buns. He was very close now to number 24, which was Ian's house. Maybe he should gobble the buns to get rid of them but then he might be too full to eat all the nice things at the party. He looked around. He was passing number 18. The road was completely empty. He had an idea. No one would see him if he did it fast. He rammed the bag between the wall and the hedge of number 18 and scarpered.

Ian's house was much bigger than his but it wasn't as big as he thought it would be. It was attached to another house on one side. Francis expected it to be all on its own and much more fancy. He recognised Ian's mother when she answered the door. Without her scarf and coat she looked even younger, much younger than his mam. And thinner. She was all dressed up and her hair was very long and shiny. She looked at Francis, then looked past him to the road.

'Is your mummy or daddy with you?'

'No. I came on the bus.'

'Oh. Well. Come in. I'm Ian's mummy.'

Francis followed her in. With her back to him she called, 'Ian, love, your friend from school is here.' When he appeared at the top of the stairs, his mother just walked off into a room. Francis thought maybe she didn't like him. Was it because of the way he was dressed? His Communion suit was getting a bit too small for him. His mam had to let the trousers out. Looking at Ian, who was wearing brand new fancy pants that he had never seen before and a spotless white shirt, Francis felt a bit scruffy.

Ian said to come upstairs. Being an only child, he had a room all to himself and it was as wizard as Francis imagined it would be. He had his own bed in a corner and the wallpaper was bright blue with little animals on it: foxes and rabbits and badgers. There was a shelf full of books and comics. He had all the toys and games that Francis saw advertised on telly – Lego, Scalextric, Subbuteo, the one with floodlighting. He had Matchbox cars, James Bond's

Aston Martin, the Batmobile. He had loads of other stuff too that Francis had no interest in, like Action Man in a pilot's outfit. There were two other boys and three girls in the room already, drinking orange and red lemonade and playing *The Man from U.N.C.L.E.* board game. He didn't know any of them. The boys weren't from his school. Francis saw a little record player on a table behind one of the girls, who was looking through a pile of records. 'I'm a Believer' was playing. Ian said, 'This is Daire and Eoin and Anna and Niamh and Sive. This is Francis from my class in school.' Francis sat on the floor and watched them play. He didn't know what to say to them. The boy called Eoin asked him did he watch *The Man from U.N.C.L.E.*? Francis said he did. Eoin asked him did he know how to play the game. Francis said he wasn't sure. Eoin said it was easy and started explaining the rules. Francis pretended to listen but, really, he was watching Ian, who had gone over to the girl called Sive and was looking through the records with her. Francis didn't know any girls except for his sister and his cousins. There were other girls on his road the same age as him but he never talked to them, except for Tommy Duggan's sister, Val, who was a year older and was always coming over annoying them when they were playing. Ian and Sive seemed to be talking and laughing just the way Ian and Francis usually talked and laughed. They changed the record. Ian let Sive choose. She put on 'Georgy Girl', which Francis thought was a useless song. He wanted Ian to let him pick a record.

A man came upstairs with a large bottle of Shannon Orange and Shannon Red Lemonade in each hand. He said, 'What's going on here? It couldn't be a party, that's for sure, because there's not enough noise. You're supposed to be dancers and there's no one dancing!' The others laughed. They all seemed to know him. Francis guessed he must be Ian's father, even though he looked much younger than his dad. Sure enough, when he asked if anyone wanted more to drink, Ian said, 'Orange please, Daddy.' Then he looked at Francis. 'What's this? Someone without a drink, without even a glass. We'll have to sort that out.' He gave Ian the bottles and went back downstairs. Ian poured orange and red lemonade into everyone's glass. His father came trotting back, pretending to be breathless, with a glass for, 'What's your name?' 'Francis.' 'So what'll it be Francis, orange or red lemonade?' When Francis said red lemonade Mr Barry tossed his long hair back from his eyes and said, 'Ah you're going for the hard stuff. Brave man,' and the others laughed again.

Francis went over to Ian and Sive. They were talking about a Feis and using words he didn't really understand, but he figured out that both of them did Irish dancing and they'd won a competition last week for the two-hand reel. Maybe that was why Ian was having a party? Were all his other friends Irish dancers too? Francis asked Ian could he pick a record, and he put on 'Happy Together'. After that Ian played 'Penny Lane' and then 'Feelin' Groovy'. Then his mother called them all downstairs. She put her arm around Ian's shoulders and told the others to go into the dining room. That was when Francis got two shocks at the same time. A trifling one and a stupendous one.

The first was seeing all the adults in the room. He guessed that they were the mothers and fathers of the other boys and girls. Was he the only one here on his own? Then Francis saw a long table against the wall laden with topping treats. This wasn't a shock, but what was hanging over the table left him astounded and dumbfounded. A long piece of coloured string was pinned to the wall at each end and, in between, gold letters hung from the string. They spelled out

HAPPYBIRTHDAYIAN8TODAY

Ian's father started clapping and everyone joined in as the door opened and Ian made an entrance, smiling, with his mother behind him, her hands still on his shoulders. Ian looked really chuffed at all the clapping and cheering. Francis' mind was racing. Could it really be? Maybe today wasn't his actual birthday. Maybe it was Friday or yesterday or tomorrow and they were just having the party today because it was Sunday. But he really hoped it was today. That would be like a fairy tale. They would be twins.

Ian's father said, 'Time for grub, help yourselves,' and everyone went to the table. Francis wanted to talk to Ian straight away but his mother was with him, one hand still on his shoulder, asking him what he wanted to eat and telling him to hold his plate steady while she put things onto it. Whenever there was a party in Francis' house his mam always had loads of food, but it wasn't as fancy as this. There were no normal sandwiches, only long, skinny little sandwiches with no crusts. There was cooked ham but it was rolled up and stuck on a stick with a piece of pineapple. Hard-boiled eggs were cut in half with some kind of thick cream – like Chef salad cream, only nicer – on top in a spirally blob. There were small round pastries filled with what looked like pieces of chicken and mushrooms in cream. They were hot. And there was ordinary stuff as well, like sausage rolls and pieces of chicken in breadcrumbs and crisps and loads more. As Francis went round the table, filling up his plate, he started pretending to himself that this was all for him too. It was a double birthday party.

Holding his overflowing plate very carefully, Francis looked around for his friend. He wasn't in the dining room any more, so Francis looked in the front room. He wasn't there either but there were photographs of him everywhere in the room. One wall was completely covered with hundreds of medals, cups and trophies. Right in the middle of the wall there was a big photo of Ian in Irish dancing costume with his mother. They were both smiling and he was holding a trophy nearly as big as himself. Francis' sister Marian had won a few cups and medals for Irish dancing but it was nothing compared to this. It was like the cave that Ali Baba entered. It was like the altar up at the Redemptorists. Francis sat on a pouf in a corner and ate, unable to take his eyes off the glittering wall. He had never seen Ian in his dancing costume before but, because of the way he dressed every day, he didn't look so strange in a kilt. It was a kind of purple and over his shoulder was a cape the same colour, pinned to a black velvet jacket by a long pointy brooch with jewels on it. Ian must be a really brilliant dancer if he won so much.

A couple of times Ian's father came in checking that everyone had enough food and drink. He seemed to be in charge of all that, and looked like he loved hopping around, joking and keeping busy. He saw that Francis' plate was empty.

'Is it time for a bit of dessert, ha? Come and have a gander?' He winked. Francis liked Ian's father. He followed him back to the dining room. There were four different desserts. There was red jelly with Neapolitan ice cream that was melting very fast, there was fruit cocktail, there were biscuits shaped like men with Smarties for buttons and, in a bowl, there was something chocolatey that looked like Instant Whip.

'Help yourself, but remember, leave room for a bit of birthday cake.'

He went out to the kitchen and, while Francis was helping himself, Ian appeared again with his mother. She stopped to talk to another mother, stroking his hair all the time. Francis wanted to go over to Ian but he was bit scared of Mrs Barry. He looked up again at the hanging cards.

HAPPYBIRTHDAYIAN8TODAY

And me, he thought.

Because no one else knew him, no one spoke to him, but Francis didn't mind that because it meant he could watch everything as he ate his dessert. He noticed that Ian's mother didn't help with the food and drink. While his father came and went, clearing plates, bringing more food, filling people's glasses and even lighting their cigarettes, Ian's mother just talked to one person for a long time and then moved to someone else and started another long chat. Francis could tell that she was talking about Ian a lot of the time because she was always turning to look at him while she spoke and never stopped touching him. She held his hand, or gently rubbed his shoulders or stroked his hair or sometimes put an arm about his waist and pulled him closer. A couple of times, she brushed the back of her fingers against his cheek. Francis thought she must love him very much, but he wondered why Ian didn't seem to mind that she never let go of him. If Francis' mam was always touching him like that he'd be pulling to get away, but Ian just stood there smiling. Maybe he liked her doing that? When his father came and whispered something in her ear, Mrs Barry finally let go and followed Mr Barry into the kitchen. Ian walked across the room to Francis straight away.

'So, Agent Strong,' he whispered in an American accent, 'have you seen any THRUSH spies lurking?'

Francis laughed. He pointed to a short fat woman sipping tea. 'There's our assassin, Agent Barry. She has a poison-tipped knitting needle in her handbag.'

'She's my grandmother, Agent Strong .'

'Oh. Sorry about that, Chief,' said Francis, just like Maxwell Smart. Then he spoke in his own voice. 'Hey, how come you didn't tell me the party was for your birthday?'

'Didn't I? I must have forgot.'

'And is today your birthday?'

'Yes.'

'The 18th?'

'Yes, why?'

So, it was so. He and his friend were born on the same day. Francis wanted more than anything to tell him now about this amazing thing. OK, he had promised his mam that he wouldn't tell people it was his birthday, but this was different, wasn't it? Surely it was all right to explain it to Ian? But what should he say? Should he just blurt out, 'It's my birthday too, we're like twins.' But would that sound mad? Maybe he should just say, mysteriously, 'I've something to tell you later, Agent Barry. A secret.' That didn't sound right in his head either. Now that the time had come to speak, it was really hard to find the right words. The way Ian was looking at him made him feel – what did it make him feel? He remembered a word. Disconcerted.

'Ian, your daddy's going to bring the cake in now.'

His mother had appeared out of nowhere. Without looking at Francis, she pulled Ian away and, holding his hand, brought him to the other side of the room. Francis was certain now that she didn't like him. Mrs Barry tapped a glass with a spoon until everyone stopped talking.

'No, don't worry, I'm not going to make a speech. It's just that... it's time for Ian's birthday cake!' And she called out 'Brendan! We're ready.'

The door opened and Ian's father marched in, holding up a large square cake covered in pink and white cream with eight candles burning. He started singing 'Happy Birthday to You'. Francis joined in enthusiastically and imagined that everyone was singing Happy Birthday to him as well. At the end Ian blew out the candles with one long breath. His mother held up her hand again.

'Now, would you all like to see a dance from our birthday boy?' Everyone murmured yes oh yes oh yes, as if this was what they had been waiting for all afternoon. Ian's father was already at the stereo cabinet ready to start the music. 'As you can see, he's put the hard shoes on so you know it's going to be a hornpipe.' Ian stepped forward and, suddenly, Francis saw him straighten his back, lift his head and his eyes stared past him to the wall behind. He placed one foot forward. The music began. Ian waited a few seconds and then lifted off.

Francis had seen lots of Irish dancing, his mam loved watching it on the telly, and a couple of times she'd dragged him to a Feis to see Marian. He'd never bothered with it before, but now he was open-mouthed. How light Ian looked and strong at the same time, his whole body lifting in the air as easy as bouncing on a trampoline, his feet rocking over and back, landing on his toes, then clipclopping back on his heels, then kicking high, his back and shoulders straight with his neck stretched long and hands by his side like a young soldier! The crowd began to clap along and Francis joined in louder than anyone, lost in admiration of his friend's talent. When the music ended Ian just smiled and his whole body relaxed. As everyone cheered, two of the girls, Sive and Jean, ran up to hug him. Francis had to stop himself doing the same.

*

It was after six o'clock and Francis knew he should be leaving even though he didn't want to. His mam had told him to be home by half-six for his birthday tea. If only he could have ten minutes to talk to Ian on his own like at *sos*, but it was impossible when he was the centre of attention for everyone. Francis had taken his jacket off in Ian's bedroom earlier. He went upstairs to collect it, glad to have a chance to see his room again before leaving. As he was going in, Ian's father came out of another room wearing a coat and carrying a small suitcase. Francis suddenly felt guilty for no reason and his face went red. His voice stumbled.

'I – I left my jacket. I ha-ave to go – to go home now.'

Ian's father just smiled and said, 'Work away.' Francis went into the bedroom, keeping his head down as if he wasn't allowed even to look around. He grabbed his jacket and followed Ian's father downstairs.

Ian's mother was waiting in the hall looking annoyed. Francis felt like he had done something wrong.

'Right. You're ready. Wait there, I'll get Ian for you.'

She was speaking to Mr Barry, not him. She didn't even look at him. She came back with Ian and he gave his father a big hug. Then, as if she only saw him for the first time, Mrs Barry suddenly started speaking to Francis. He didn't know why.

'Ian's daddy has to go to Dublin. It's his work. He has to go there quite a bit. It's only for a couple of days. We won't know it before he's back, isn't that right, Ian? No time to miss him, even. Just a pity he has to go now. His work starts very early tomorrow so he needs to be fresh –'

Ian's father interrupted her with a kiss on the cheek.

'I'd better head, or I'll be another hour saying goodbye to that lot. See you Tuesday. Good luck, kid.'

He hoisted Ian high and squeezed him. After he left, Francis said, 'Thanks very much for the party,' to Ian's mother but she didn't seem to be listening to him. She was staring at the closed front door. Was she worried that Ian's father had forgotten something? They heard the car reverse fast out of the drive. Francis said, 'See you tomorrow,' to Ian. He had decided that would be the best time to tell him the birthday story. During *sos*.

*

The next day, when Francis saw Ian's mother waiting at the main gate, he was glad he hadn't said anything to Ian after all. He nearly had. A few times. Watching him run to meet her, Francis skulked even closer to the wall than usual so she wouldn't spot him. All day he hadn't been able to make up his mind what way he should tell Ian about how they were sort of twins – as if it was a funny little story, or an astounding discovery, or a special secret. Then something else came into his head too. Ian would definitely tell his mother the story, and she didn't like Francis, so what would she say about it? Would she say he was being very sneaky coming to the party like that and keeping his own birthday a big secret? Would she ask what was wrong with him that he wasn't having his own party? She'd say that was a bit queer. His mam was always telling Francis, 'Don't let people make a fool of you.' What if Ian's mother said the same thing to Ian, 'Don't let that sneaky boy Francis make a fool of you'? And then maybe she wouldn't let Ian be his friend any more. Maybe it was better to say nothing.

Francis crept towards the main gates. His eyes followed Ian, bouncing away hand in hand with his mother. Sometime. He would definitely find a way to tell him sometime.

*

Baz Malloy had the Minister for Education in his viewfinder. Medium close-up. He looked relaxed as he listened to an enraged Oliver J.

'I want to direct the attention of the Minister to "Guests of the Nation", one of the stories in this collection. On page 194 there is a certain word; I will not use it on television. It's a word beginning with B.'

Baz knew the whole country would now be wondering which 'B' it was. Bastard? Bollix? Bugger? Surely not blowjob?

'Now, this type of language might be expected in a low-class pitch-and-toss school, but should not be contained in a book for young children, many of whom are in their first years of preparation for, perhaps, a religious life, or to take their place in whatever profession they are going to follow.'

The Minister did not interrupt the tirade, he just shook his head, and pursed his lips. Baz had to admire how well Dom understood television. He knew that the director would not be able to resist cutting to him for a reaction shot. Sure enough, in his headphones, he heard Eoin call.

'Coming to camera two – and two.'

The red light flashed on Baz's camera, and the Nation saw the Minister shake his head and purse his lips, more in sorrow than in anger. Poor Oliver J, he's completely out of touch, the gesture said.

'And back to camera one.'

Once the shot returned to Oliver J, the Minister stopped the head-shaking routine. The cute hoor knew exactly when he was on the air, Baz thought. By contrast his Blueshirt opponent seemed far too loud and a bit wild-eyed.

'They say teaching has to be modernised, but if this is the type of language to be used in our school textbooks, I am sorry that we did not remain old-fashioned!'

The Minister smiled towards the presenter, his voice sweet reason.

'Well, John, first of all, I should like to point out that in this new school text, *Exploring English*, edited by Augustine Martin, there are, apart from Seán Ó Faoláin and Frank O'Connor, such authors as O. Henry, James Thurber, Saki, G. K. Chesterton, W. Somerset Maugham, Katherine Mansfield, V.S. Pritchett, William Golding, Liam O'Flaherty, Bryan MacMahon, Mary Lavin, James Plunkett, Brendan Behan and Brian Friel. I think the selection is a good one.'

It was impressive; the long list of authors tripped off his tongue without hesitation or reference to notes. The viewers might well think the Minister knew them all personally.

'Frank O'Connor's "Guests of the Nation", the short story the deputy is so critical of, was selected by a committee consisting of representatives of all the managerial and teachers' associations of the secondary and vocational schools, persons distinguished for their knowledge of English literature and highly experienced in the teaching of it. As to why the members decided to include this particular story, I would guess that the merits of the story as a piece of literature outweighed the few vulgar expressions introduced by the author into the dialogue, presumably in order the better to portray the character of the speaker.'

Baz could hear in his headphones murmurs of approval from the control room. On this issue at least, the director and producer clearly thought the Minister was on the right side. The side of Art and Culture. New Ireland versus Old. So why did Baz forebear to cheer for this man of the sixties against the reviled backwoodsman of the forties, Oliver J, the demented but wily old vote-catcher, intent on impressing the Creeping Jesus vote.

'The language in some of these short stories is not suitable for children of twelve and thirteen years. For example "The Trout". I refer to page 170 of the book. There is a paragraph there which I won't subject the viewers to, but which I think is most suggestive. It is a paragraph which should not be put in any short story which is read in schools.'

'I don't know whether Deputy Flanagan has read the whole of this story – ?'

'"The Trout"? As I said, very suggestive. I did not like it.'

'Well then, the saying "*Honi soit qui mal y pense*" was never so appropriate. Does the Deputy, if he has read the story, realise that it is his own vivid and excitable imagination –'

'No. Parents have written to me.'

'If he had read the entire story he would know that this young girl goes into a tunnel to catch a trout and not to catch anything else. If these ideas which the Deputy is putting into Irish minds are all he can find in Seán Ó Faoláin's "The Trout", which many regard as Ó Faoláin's finest story, then I can only say, "God help us."'

This morning Baz had read about young people in Monterey enjoying an open air love-in over the weekend. Meanwhile, on national television, two leading politicians were having a coy debate about whether it was suitable for teenagers to read an O'Faoláin short story that referred to a young girl's sexual awakening in a way that, if Baz recalled it correctly, was so subtle and tasteful as to be virtually opaque. It was profoundly depressing. Why was he contributing in any way to this nonsense? It always bored and frustrated him to work on discussion programmes like *7 Days*; radio with illustrations. He didn't have to move his camera for the entire programme. All that was required of him was to offer either a two shot or – change lens and pan slightly – a single. If he were to lock off the camera on this nicely framed shot of the Minister and sit down to have a smoke, no one would notice. But the reason for his frustration right now was not egotistical; it wasn't that he felt his amazing talents were underused. That would not matter to Baz if the programme content was genuinely challenging, the discussion truly cutting-edge, if it had the potential to change something. But this farce of a fake controversy? A crude word in a Frank O'Connor story? When a whole society needed waking up?

'I know that Deputy Flanagan possibly has ambitions in another sphere and that perhaps he hopes one day to be leader of the Knights of Columbanus –'

'The Minister is –'

'– I did not interrupt you. As far as I'm concerned, John, Deputy Flanagan is quite entitled to aspire to such a great office, though anyone using the Catholic Church for his own material or other advancement makes me vomit…'

Baz looked hard at his viewfinder. Who was this man Dom really? He seemed to hold all the right views, say all the modern things. He was the man who was bringing free education to the children, which was, in Baz's opinion, the most important social advance in the country since he had returned, the one inspired initiative to balance so much failure and inaction. No longer the boastful, arrogant drunk he had encountered all those years ago, could the Minister really be the man the country was crying out for? Its Kennedy? Did he have a bigger better vision to offer? Was he truly worthy of respect? Baz wished he could see behind those smiling eyes.

Scarcely conscious of what he was doing, Baz began to track in very slowly, as though creeping up on the Minister. His face grew larger and larger in the viewfinder.

'I think the ordinary, reasonably minded person who has read this wonderful story by Seán O'Faoláin would not have the slightest qualm of conscience about letting a child read it.'

Baz stared intently at a close-up which was now so big, only Dom's nose and eyes filled the screen. And, at first, behind those jesting eyes Baz saw… nothing. Was there nothing haunting this man, no vision driving him on, no ultimate goal? Could it really be egotistical pleasure and purposeless ambition? A man who just liked winning, who loved the game? A man for whom putting one over on a pathetic old Blueshirt in a pointless debate was as worthwhile as anything else he might do? If something visionary was achieved along the way, well then, that was fine, but no more than a little extra jam on his bread. The longer Baz stared at the big close-up however, the black hole behind the superficial sparkle of those eyes resolved into something harder: an arrogant predatory stare. What Baz saw brought to the surface of his consciousness an anger he had been nursing for some time. What was he doing in this place? Had he been a fool to come home?

Baz felt a hand squeeze his forearm tight. He turned away from the viewfinder to see an anxious Gavin indicating the transmission monitor. Baz was shocked to see that he had tracked in so far that the tip of his camera lens was peeping into the on-air shot. Messy. Only now, as if the volume had been suddenly ramped up, did he hear the rasping in his head phones. How long had the director been screaming?

'Baz, Baz what are you doing? What's the fancy track-in for? This is politics not some fucking *drama*!!! A simple MS. That's all I want!'

Baz pulled back quickly to his original position and framed the Minister once again in a polite unquestioning mid-shot. He looked over at Gavin to reassure him that his little crisis moment had passed.

'I respectfully ask the Minister one question: was it not possible to get, out of all the short stories written by all the great writers of our time, stories for our Intermediate Certificate English that would not be as suggestive as those contained in this book? It is for parents to decide what is best for their own children. I know there are parents who view this book with the gravest concern because of the language contained in it.'

It was clear what was wrong. There was no mystery. Baz was just tired out, television had tired him out. Five years confined in studios, weaving his camera around dramas, entertainment shows, current affairs debates – had it changed or even affected anything? Weren't the same shysters still running the show? Had he wasted his time coming back to Ireland? Baz needed to get out of the studio into the open air. Do something else. Look at his own country again. He thought of Miriam Hartnett, as he had done so often in the last year. She had done the right thing and dropped out. Baz made a decision.

'We're nearly out of time, Minister. Last word to you.'

'We all know that five or ten years from now, world television, to which nothing will be sacred, will be thrown open to us from one or many stations in the sky. It may have seemed to the committee that the responsible milieu of the classroom is, next to the home, the best place to prepare the pupils for what we must expect in the world of such open communication that is coming.'

The victorious Minister and his human punch-bag both smiled as the programme theme played. As soon as the studio lights dimmed, Baz pulled his headphones off and, without saying good night to his crew, walked away quickly. It was part of the protocol of Gavin's job to shake hands with the guests and tell them what a splendid discussion it had been but, instead, he ran after his colleague and, in the corridor outside the studio, called after him.

'Baz, Baz. Are you OK?'

'I'm getting out of here, Gav.'

'Sure. Are you going to Madigan's? I have to be somewhere, but I can have a quick one with you if there's anything you need to –'

'No Gavin, I'm not getting out of the building. I'm getting out. Leaving. I've had enough.'

'You mean… your job?

'Exactly.

'When did you – when did this –'

'Oh, about three minutes ago. It feels good dearheart, believe me.'

*

They lay on the floor in Gavin's flat. 'Waterloo Sunset', the last song on side two, was coming to an end. In paradise. Their lovemaking had lasted almost one side of the album Brendan bought him. He was clinging to Gavin now, fiercely, trying to escape into him, curl up in some place of safety and rest, as if terrified that, should he let go, he would fall into some deep canyon, down, down, like one of those cartoon characters, growing smaller and smaller until finally disappearing, with only a sound effect and a puff of smoke to indicate that he had hit rock bottom. It was always the same pattern, this little lost boy routine. Tomorrow a different Brendan would wake early, leap from the bed, hum his way around the kitchen making breakfast and, as soon as they had eaten, tootle off with barely a hug. Goodbye until the next time he came to Dublin. Which visit Gavin, stupidly, would yearn for.

'A strange thing happened at work tonight.'

'Mmmm.' Not interested.

'Baz Malloy, a friend of mine. I'm sure I've mentioned his name. Cameraman.'

'Mmmm, rings a bell.' A lie. Still not interested.

'At the end of the programme he tells me he's going to leave. He said he'd made up his mind a few minutes before, literally. Just like that. He's been there since the station started. He's probably the best cameraman in the place and, suddenly, he's giving it all up.'

Brendan didn't seem to realise he was supposed to respond.

'What do you make of that, Bren?'

'Hm? Well… I don't know… fair dues, I suppose.'

'Would you ever do it?'

'Leave my job? Sure, if I got a better offer.'

'No, I mean – Baz didn't get a better offer. He's just getting out in order to… to find something else, something better for himself maybe. I'm not sure if he even knows what.'

Silence. Even though Gavin had a very good idea what message the silence was intended to convey, he decided he would not shut up.

'Would you ever do that? You know, I don't just mean your job, but would you ever… leave…' – he couldn't bring himself to say 'your wife.' – '… I don't know. Whatever. Start all over again.'

He felt Brendan's lips kiss his chest and heard a little mock yawn.

'Too tired for talk. Ask me tomorrow.'

'Waterloo Sunset' faded, and there was the usual few seconds of crackle before the needle lifted. Then silence.

Twenty-two: September 30th

'Did you close the door properly?' Since Ann had splashed out on a fridge a couple of weeks ago, Fonsie had said the same thing to the children over and over.

'Yes' Francis said.

'Well, check to make sure. You know it doesn't work if you don't close the door properly.'

Francis did one of his big sighs and checked the fridge door. Marian said, 'Dad, tell him to shake the milk before he takes the cap off, he's always robbing the cream off the top.'

Fonsie took the bottle of milk from Francis and gave it a good shake. The best thing about having a fridge was the cold milk on cornflakes and this morning, because it was his first day back delivering coal after the summer, Fonsie had time to enjoy his cornflakes. Ritchie was gone to work long ago, Gussie was asleep because he was on the evening shift so, after Marian, Martin and Francis were packed off to school, he brought Ann her tea and then relaxed with his own cuppa in the quiet of an empty scullery. This put him in fine form by the time he left to load up the lorry at Tedcastles and head towards Sixmilebridge. With the autumn cold beginning to bite, he had plenty of orders. It would be a long hard day, to be sure, but he could once again take his own time and choose his own route, not like the summer job at O'Neill's. And there was no one shouting orders. Delivering coal he encountered decent people pleased to see him. And, driving from cottage to farm, he could enjoy the peaceful silence in the back roads and lanes of the county.

Ann and the children were on his mind as he trundled along and, in particular, thinking about his only girl, Marian, made the time slip by very pleasantly. It had given him a great lift to see how made up she was when he and Ann had told her a few weeks ago that, on account of not having to pay school fees any more, if she did well enough in her Inter Cert next June then, as far as they were concerned, she could stay on and do her Leaving Cert. If that was what she wanted. Fonsie knew well that of course it was what she wanted. Marian loved school. She was delighted at this news and promised them that she'd work really hard and get good results. Just do your best, they had told her. Since then, getting her to take her head out of the books had been the hard part. Ann said this morning she hoped that Marian wasn't going to start using study as an excuse to avoid doing her share of the housework, but Fonsie was sure she'd never do anything like that.

*

By the time she got the dinner up for Marian, Martin and Francis, Ann wasn't remotely hungry, but she put a small piece of liver on a plate with some mash and sat down, more to take the weight off her feet than anything. She couldn't help looking at Martin more than the other two. Was it her imagination or was he gone quiet lately? She still didn't know how well he was settling in to secondary school. Whenever she asked him how he was getting on he just said 'grand' without really looking at her. So far she hadn't made a big issue of it. There had been enough trouble getting him in there and she knew he'd been mortified that day when she dragged him down to the school, but hadn't it worked out? Hadn't they got to meet the minister and hadn't he made sure that Martin and those other boys were treated fairly?

Ann was a bit mortified herself now, remembering how she'd been like a demon that morning when, out of the blue, the letter from the Brother Superior arrived, saying that although Martin had passed the entrance exam for secondary school, unfortunately there was no place available for him at CBS. The school wished him the best of luck and hoped he would find a place elsewhere. The bare-faced cheek. She'd waved the letter in poor Fonsie's face.

'What are we going to do about this? If he's passed his exams why isn't there a place for him? How do they expect him to find another school and it only a week to the end of the holidays? I thought he was supposed to get free education and now the Brothers won't even let him in the school.'

At first, when Fonsie said he'd write to the school as soon as he got home from work, that seemed good enough, but as the morning passed she had kept picking up the letter and reading it again, making herself more agitated. The letter said Martin had passed his entrance exam, so why wasn't he entitled to a place in the school?

It was when the children came in for dinner and she looked at them sitting together, just like today, that her rage really boiled over. Marian and Francis were all set to go back to school next week and poor Martin would be left out in the cold. What was he supposed to do? Ann had hoped secondary school would be a whole new start for him and he really seemed to be looking forward to it. It was discrimination, that's what it was. She made her mind up there and then. She would go down to the school and talk to the Brother Superior or one of the Brothers. Ann got her coat and scarf and Martin's coat.

'Marian, clear up and do the dishes. Come on, Martin. Francis, you get out in the fresh air and don't be hanging round the house getting in everyone's way.'

Martin didn't know what was going on, but he could tell from the way his mam shoved on his coat that it must be trouble. Where was she taking him? As she pulled him out the door he tried to think what had he done? There were a few things. His mam didn't say a word, but she wouldn't let go of his hand and she had that look on her face that made him really nervous. As they got near the grotto she dragged him across the road, heading straight for the Phelans' house. Oh shit! Up in Baker's field one evening Antoinette Phelan had pulled down her knickers and let Martin, and Malachy Casey, and Tony Hartigan see her gowl. Had she told on them? She couldn't have, she couldn't have! If she had, Martin wouldn't be walking with his mam now, he'd be dead already. She'd have just killed him stone dead. When his mam walked past the Phelan's house and round the corner to the bus stop, Martin was relieved but still confused, because now she smiled at him and at the same time looked like she was going to start crying. She fixed his hair in a nice way, not the way she usually did, dragging at it. What was going on? His mam said nothing and Martin didn't know what to say.

Ann was in such a temper at this stage that she wasn't one bit afraid of meeting Brother Scully or any of them. It wasn't fair. That's what she was going to say to those Brothers. It just wasn't fair and she wasn't going to let her child be made dirt of. As the bus passed the school, she was surprised to see a crowd of people at the main gates. She held Martin's hand getting off the bus and hurried back towards the school. As they got closer, Ann could see that the crowd standing at the gates seemed to be all women and some children. No men. She guessed what was going on. These must be mothers like herself. They'd all got the same letter.

Martin wished his mam wouldn't pull at his hand like that. He could walk across the road on his own. There were other boys from school in the gang of people outside the gates. None of them were looking at each other. They all had their heads down. What trouble were they were all in? Was he going to be blamed in the wrong for something? His mam started talking to some woman she didn't even know. All the women were talking at the same time so it was hard to hear what anyone was saying.

'It's an absolute disgrace!' 'The cheek of them, how dare they!' 'They don't want us to have free education that's what it is.' 'The Minister is in there now talking to them Brothers. He'll sort them out, wait and see.' All the women were raging and Martin wondered what his mam would say about the bad language out of some of them, 'shit' and 'Jaysus' and 'fucken', but she didn't give out to them. Some of the women were rattling the gates, but they were locked and there was nobody in the yard to listen to them except for a man in a brand-new black Vauxhall Victor parked outside the monastery. He was having a smoke, and he just ignored them all. His mam showed a piece of paper to another woman and she nodded.

'That's exactly the same as I got, Missus. Could you believe it? After passing their exams an' all? Is that him, the poor thing? I'd have brung my Declan now, only he has an aul' job for the holidays, so I didn't want him losing out. What have the Brothers got against him, that's what I want to know.'

Even though Ann was still angry, for some reason she felt better knowing that Martin wasn't the only boy to be refused a place. There were more than a dozen women here in the same situation. Some of the poor things even had to bring their younger ones with them because they had no one to mind them; some had babies in prams. How dare the Christian Brothers treat decent mothers that way?

'Here he is,' someone shouted. Martin saw a man in a suit and two Brothers coming out of the Monastery. He knew one; Brother Scully, the superior. The other was a young Brother. Martin had never seen him before. Brother Scully shook hands with the man and went back inside without even looking towards the women and children at the gates. But the man in the suit turned and waved at them. Then he walked over. The young Brother followed him. He had a scared look on his face. Martin thought he'd be useless in class, the kind of teacher they could make a right fool of. Loads of the women shouted at the man in the suit. They called him Dom. The young Brother had a key and tried to open the gates but his hands were shaking and he dropped the key. Some of the women laughed at him and called him an eejit. Even his mam smiled but she didn't say anything.

Ann felt a bit sorry for that poor young Brother. What age was he? He looked younger than Ritchie. He was probably afraid some of these angry mothers would go for him. He finally got the gate open and the Minister held up his hands to calm everyone down. As he walked out, the mothers moved back, dragging their children and pulling their prams and everyone started shouting at the same time but he said, 'Ladies! Ladies!' Ann was one of the first to shut up and she wished that some of the younger mothers, who were very loud, would give the man a chance to speak.

'I know why you're all here. I understand that each of you got a letter this morning saying there was no place for your son in the secondary school.'

Martin got an awful shock. All the women started roaring again and he felt his mam squeeze his hand even more. Was he being thrown out of school?

'Please ladies, please. I have news for you all. I've just had a meeting with the Brother Superior and I'm delighted to be able to tell you that it's all been a very unfortunate mistake. Brother Scully and I have sorted it out. As you know, this is the first year of my free education scheme and even though schools the length and breadth of the country have been very happy to sign up, including CBS here, there was always bound to be what I suppose you'd call teething troubles. One of these is that there are a lot more boys who want to continue in school, I'm glad to say, but of course that also means a lot more classroom space is needed and the good news is that Brother Scully has assured me he will take care of that. Immediately.'

The women cheered and Martin felt his mam pushing him forward as she waved her letter at the Minister.

'What's your name, young lad?'

The Minister's eyes were friendly, but Martin wished he had looked at anyone else except him. It was the worst reddener he ever felt. If he didn't answer, his mam would say this is my little boy Martin or something and then everyone would think he was some kind of a dummy. That would be even worse than his red face. When Martin opened his mouth he could hardly hear himself speak.

'Martin Strong.'

'Well, Martin, I hope you're looking forward to going back to school next week because you and every other lad who passed his entrance exam – every one of you, mind – will get a letter in the next couple of days confirming that you have a free place in the secondary school here. You have my word on that.'

Ann had never ever voted for Dom before, but right then she said a silent prayer of thanks and made a promise that she'd vote for him as long as she lived.

'Do you hear that, Martin? You'll be going to secondary school after all.'

Martin, who until a minute ago hadn't known that he wouldn't be, was just glad that he didn't have to answer any more questions and was even happier when his mam gave him two bob and said he could go to the pictures.

Ann was so thrilled at the way things had turned that, after Martin went off, she decided to call up to Mona, who was his godmother, and tell her the good news. Her sister was delighted, but of course once she started on her own gossip there was no hope of a quick getaway, so by the time Ann got back Fonsie was already home from work, sitting in the scullery finishing his letter to the Christian Brothers. It was on the tip of Ann's tongue to tell him that there was no need, it had all been sorted out, but when Fonsie proudly showed her what he had written, she hadn't the heart to disappoint him after he'd made such an effort. So she just said it was a great letter and would surely do the trick. Afterwards, of course, she realised that Fonsie was bound to find out because Martin would tell everyone what had happened but for some reason he never mentioned it. Not a single, solitary word. So when, a few days later, just as the Minister had promised, the letter came from the school offering Martin a place, Fonsie was delighted that he had sorted it all out.

'Mam, Mam, Mam, Mam. Mam!' Francis' voice dragged Ann back to the present.

'What?'

'Is there any more liver, Mam?'

'No, you've had enough. Anyway, look at the time. Come on, you all have to get back to school.'

As they got up from the table, Ann's eyes met Martin's. It seemed to her that he looked away quickly. Was he still embarrassed about the way he had clutched her hand tight that day at the school gates? She'd never forget how red his face went when the Minister asked him his name. She'd been just about to answer for him but he got it out somehow. Martin was a great one for shouting and fighting out on the green but, for all his show, Ann knew he wasn't as tough as he pretended to be.

*

The dry weather had made it a nice, handy day for Fonsie so far. By five o'clock he had tipped his last three hundredweight of Polish into Mrs Kenny's coal bunker up in Cratloe. If he got back to Tedcastles in time, he could load up again and get to a few customers nearer town. That would make the day well worthwhile. Coming down the hill, he slowed the lorry at Setright's corner just as the bus to Shannon passed by on the main road. Fonsie thought he spotted Gussie on it, but Gussie didn't see him because he was staring out the window, lost in his own world as usual. He was on the late shift in the airport bar so he was probably fed up. He hated working at night. Interfered too much with his hectic social life, Fonsie thought. Gussie was one of those people who never seemed to realise how lucky he was to have a job to go to. Maybe he'd learn.

*

As soon as she got home from school, Marian Strong went to her little bedroom where she could do her English ecker in peace. They were studying 'The Trout' by Seán O'Faoláin and Miss Dillon had set them a question to answer. 'Compare Julia's new understandings about life with her younger brother's view of the world.' Marian made a little list in rough:

> One: Julia wasn't afraid to enter the tunnel like her little brother was.
>
> Two: Julia understood that the trout they found was a real breathing fish who might die if it was left in the tiny secret pool of water. But her little brother thought it was like a magic fish in a fairy story.
>
> Three: Julia didn't believe in fairy tales any more. Her brother did.

By coincidence, as she re-read the story to get more ideas, her own little brother Francis came in, without knocking of course and he wasn't in the room two seconds before he started asking questions. What story was she reading? Would he like it? He looked at her other books. What was *Romeo and Juliet* about? Who was Shakespeare? Marian wondered was Francis like the little brother in 'The Trout'? He was clever in some ways, but there was so much he didn't understand yet. Francis would probably think that he could read the stories in Marian's anthology and understand every word, but he was far too immature to see the hidden meanings because he was still just a child, really, unlike Marian, who was now able to see hidden meanings in stories. It was one of the things she liked most about studying them. That gave her an idea for her ecker. Was this what was happening to Julia in 'The Trout'? Was she discovering hidden meanings in things? Marian scribbled that down in her copybook before she forgot it. She was just going to throw her little brother out, so she could concentrate better, when her mam shouted upstairs, 'Marian, come down and get started on this ironing. Gussie needs a clean shirt for work.'

Even though his sister told him to get out of her room as she went downstairs to do the ironing, Francis stayed behind and picked up the book she had been studying. *Exploring English, an Anthology of Short Stories* by Augustine Martin. The book was open at 'The Trout'. Francis had no interest in fish so he checked the list of titles to see if there was any other story he might like to read. 'An Occurrence At Owl Creek Bridge' sounded good. So did 'The Majesty of the Law' and 'The Green Door'. The name of one of the authors looked mysterious. Saki. Was he from Japan or China or somewhere? Marian was fourteen – would he have to wait until he was that old before he could read this book? He saw a story called 'My First Confession'. Well, he had made his first confession a long time ago, surely he'd understand this easily. As he turned the pages to find it, he was distracted by something he saw on Marian's dressing table; a doll in a long pink dress.

Marian had had it since she was a small girl. He didn't know why she kept it because she was too old to play with dolls now. Francis had never been interested in any kind of doll, but the long pink dress now made him think of something that had been on his mind. The day before he'd been out on the green messing with Tommy Duggan and Ger Doherty and Brendan O'Driscoll. Tommy's sister Val had come over. She was always sticking her nose in and no one wanted her to be there. After a while, when she wouldn't go away, Ger Doherty got really fed up and he said words that shocked Francis. He said, 'Fuck off'll ya!' and Val said, 'I won't, I've as much right to stand here as you and I'm going to tell your da what you said.' That made Ger really angry and he said something even worse. 'Do you want a kick in the mickey, do you?' and he looked like he really meant it. Ger was nearly nine. But Val wasn't scared, she just laughed in his face. She said, 'You can't kick me in the mickey because girls don't have mickeys. You mean you don't know that?'

No one knew what to say.

Ger Doherty went all red and then he tried to grab Val but she ran off and he chased her but she ducked inside her front gate. Francis was afraid to ask Tommy or Brendan if what Val said was true or a lie because then they would know that he didn't know. But how was he supposed to know? Marian was his only sister. She was much older and had her own room and he had never even been in the bathroom at the same time as her or anything like that. Tommy acted like he knew. 'Big fool,' he said about Ger Doherty. So did that mean it was true? But it sounded mad. If girls didn't have a mickey, what did they have?

Now, Francis was looking at the doll and wondering if there was a clue to the mystery under the long pink dress. He heard the front door slam. He looked out the window and saw Gussie leaving for work wearing his freshly ironed white shirt. Francis listened. The only sound in the house were the voices of his mam and sister far off downstairs. He picked up the doll and sat down on Marian's bed. She had long black hair and blue eyes that stared at him. It was an old doll, so the eyes didn't move and the arms and legs went back and forth but they didn't bend. Francis decided to investigate if what Val Duggan said was true or not. He turned the doll upside down and looked up her dress. Her legs seemed very long and she was wearing tiny pink knickers. He would have to take them off to reveal the truth. For some reason he was a bit scared now. He kept the doll steady by holding the head between his knees and, with one hand, held the dress out so there was more room for the finger and thumb of his other hand to reach up her long legs. Just as he caught hold of the little knickers, his mam's voice stopped his heart.

'What are you doing? You dirty thing. You dirty thing! Put that down immediately. Mother of God!'

Francis jumped up and the doll fell to the floor. He could tell from her face and her voice that he had done something awful and he couldn't try to explain why he did it because that was more awful. 'Get out, you dirty thing. You dirty thing!' Francis ran out of the room and down the stairs, his mam's voice shaming him with every step. 'Get out of this house. I don't want to see you 'til your father gets home, you dirty animal! He'll deal with you. Get out!' Francis heard Marian come out to the hall but he turned his face away, grabbed open the front door and ran out.

*

Having spotted Gussie on the bus, Fonsie took it as a lucky sign when, about twenty minutes after that, he saw Ritchie on his Honda 50 waiting at traffic lights. Ritchie saw his dad as well and gave him a big wave and a smile as he drove through. Fonsie knew Ann would enjoy that coincidence when he told her later on tonight. Ritchie wasn't travelling towards home, so he wondered where he was off to. It couldn't be to see his girlfriend, Dolores Spaight, because Ann had told him that she had broken it off a few nights ago. Which was a pity. Dolores, a salesgirl in Roches Stores, had seemed very nice. Of course Ritchie could do no wrong in Ann's eyes, so she had made out that Dolores had treated him very badly, but Fonsie was more inclined to think there was probably two sides to the story. Anyway, from the big smile on his face as he waved, Ritchie didn't seem too put out. He was only twenty, and these things happened.

Ritchie was in a very good mood as he rode to Peter Malone's house. His pal had invited him to come and listen to his latest favourite new album, *Days of Future Passed.* The Malones' small back extension was becoming more like Peter's private music room. It was full of his stuff. He had over three hundred albums – about 295 more than Ritchie had – and probably five hundred singles. He had them all arranged according to when he bought them. Before putting on *Days of Future Passed* Peter told Ritchie how important it was that they listen to all of side one in total silence, which was a bit of a joke, as he was the one who never shut up when they listened to music. So they sat there without as much as a whisper although Peter nearly drove Ritchie spare looking over at him to see how he was reacting and a few times he held his hand up or pointed a finger to draw attention to a particular thing in the music. At first Ritchie was puzzled that none of the songs seemed to end, they just drifted from one to another. Then he got into it and found the whole effect sort of dreamy and relaxing. When side one, ended Peter leapt from his seat to turn the record over. 'Ha? Ha? Whatja think? Ha? Amazing isn't it? Unreal. Ha? Like, they're taking the whole thing onto another level aren't they? It's way out there. An album isn't just a collection of songs any more. That's all gone man, gone. And wait'll you hear, I swear. Side two is savage altogether.' He dropped the needle and sat down again. Ritchie hadn't got a word in. His pal had just assumed that he was knocked out by *Days of Future Passed* as well. Ritchie preferred side two because it had 'Nights in White Satin' on it, the only song he recognised. The album version was longer than the single version, with one of the band saying a little poem at the end. Peter did not jump up when it finished. Instead he just sat back and shook his head. Ritchie thought he'd better make some comment.

'The flute is good, isn't it?'

'Unreal. Unreal. That flute is inspired, man. The whole symphonic vibe is fuckin' inspired.'

They both agreed that side two was definitely worth hearing again. Mrs Malone nearly ruined it by coming in to ask if they wanted their tea but she retreated quicky when her son waved her away impatiently. After their second listen, Peter continued rapping about the album as they collected the mixed grill that his mother had got ready for them and took it back to the room. Ritchie couldn't match Peter's note by note familiarity, so he let him do nearly all the talking while he looked through his pal's other recent purchases. He picked out *Gentle on my Mind*, and asked to play it. He liked Glen Campbell's voice. They played side one but then Peter insisted on playing *Days of Future Passed* again. After that Ritchie definitely had enough of the Moody Blues and suggested going to South's. A bunch of fellahs and girls from the Cecilian's Musical Society came in after rehearsal. Peter and Ritchie knew some of them and managed to get talking with two great-looking birds, Carmel and Áine. Ritchie fancied Áine, the blonde with the happy giggle, so he hoped that Peter was into Carmel. By closing time they were all getting on really well, and the girls said yes when Peter suggested they go on to the 2Club. It occurred to Ritchie that he hadn't told his mam he'd be home so late. What the hell. She'd surely remember to put the key under the mat for him.

*

It was getting dark when a bone-tired, coal-blackened but carefree Fonsie arrived back to find the house in a state of silent misery. The television was turned off, two of his children, Marian and Martin, were at the kitchen table, tear-stained, and there was no sign of Ann. Instead, her sister Mona and Mary Storan were waiting, both looking very heavy-hearted. Words tumbled from four people at once and it was impossible for Fonsie to understand anything.

'Fonsie, thank God you're home.'

'Dad, Mam's in hospital.'

'Bernard McMahon hit Francis on the ear with his hurley.'

'Ann took him to accident and emergency.'

'Hold on, I can't listen to you all. Mona. Let Mona speak.'

His sister-in-law, delighted to be the one to tell all, said, 'Well,' and paused for a moment. Then of course, instead of telling Fonsie what he wanted to know, she started by talking about herself.

'I was at home – this was about six o'clock, now – and I was just about to put Seán's tea on the table when Marian arrived – God help us, she was breathless from running – and she told me that Ann had to bring Francis to Emergency because he was after getting a clatter on the head with a hurley –'

'I saw what happened, Dad, it was Bernard –'

'Shh, Martin!'

'So I came over here straight away. Well, no, first I dropped in on the way to tell Mary, you know, on account of Francis' being her godchild.'

Mary Storan couldn't stay quiet a second longer.

'I got an awful shock, Fonsie. I was thinking what if he's brain-damaged? So of course I said I'd go down to the hospital. Well –'

'And I came here and made these two their tea and at around seven Billy Benson called in to say he'd got them to the hospital all right and hopefully Francis would be seen to very quickly. He said his ear was all red and swelling up like a balloon but, hopefully, there wouldn't be any internal damage.'

'Oh Janey.'

'Oh, that isn't the half of it, Fonsie. Wait 'til you hear.'

'But what happened? Martin, who did you say hit him?'

'I told you Dad. Bernard McMahon.'

'But why? Was it an accident?'

'No, on purpose.'

Marian felt like she'd burst if she didn't say her piece.

'Francis ran out on the green after Mam caught him doing something up in my bedroom, I don't know what, but she was shouting at him and then a few minutes after that Martin came in –'

'– I was after seeing Bernard McMahon whack Francis with his hurley.'

'But what did he do that for?'

'I don't know, I was coming up the road with Malachy Casey. There was a load of them playing hurling on the green and I saw Bernard shouting at Francis and then Francis said something to him and he turned away like this, and that's when I saw Bernard lifting his hurley like this, and he swung it and, I swear, Dad, I could hear the crack off the side of his head. He got him right on his ear. And I ran in and shouted for Mam and then I ran back out to Francis and he was bawlin' his head off and holding his ear and Bernard was still standing there and I was going to go for him Dad, but then I heard Mam screaming and she came running past me and Bernard ran off –'

Fonsie couldn't stop his children's voices tumbling over each other.

'Oh, she screamed at him, Dad, you should have heard her. "You thing you," she kept shouting –'

'– If she'd got hold of him she'd have killed him stone dead –'

'– You thing! You article!'

'– but then she got down on her knees –'

'– and Francis still bawlin' cryin' –'

'– and she tried to lift him up into her arms but she couldn't on her own –'

'– and she shouted at me to go to the phone box as fast as I could and ring 999 –'

'– and she had Francis in her arms and she was bringing him back to the house and Mr Benson came out 'cause he heard all the screaming and he said he'd give her a lift down to the hospital.'

Fonsie knew he'd better go there straight away. Poor Ann was probably at her wits' end.

'I'd better go down to them.'

'Fonsie,' Mona interrupted in her most dramatic voice, 'Francis is here – he's upstairs in bed.'

Mary Storan could see that Fonsie was now totally confused.

'I brought him home. His poor ear is awful sore, but there's no internal damage, thank God. They gave me a cream for it.'

'But where's Ann?'

Mona and Mary looked at each other. Mona spoke first.

'Ann was taken in, Fonsie. She collapsed in Emergency.'

'What?'

'The doctors said it was the will of God she was where she was or they mightn't have got to her in time. Her blood pressure was sky-high.'

Mona remembered the children and dropped her voice to a whisper.

'She was that close to having a stroke, apparently.'

'Is Mam going to die?'

Martin's hard-chaw pals would have been amazed to see the open, frightened face looking up at his dad, looking for reassurance. What was Fonsie supposed to say to him? He felt like he was completely in the dark. Five minutes ago he had walked in the door, looking forward to a wash, a bit of supper, and a sit-down in front of the telly. And now? Mary Storan answered quickly.

'No, Martin love, she's grand. The doctors are looking after her.'

'I'd better go down. Do you mind –?'

'Of course not, Fonsie. We'll be fine here.'

Fonsie was opening the front door when he heard Mona's whisper. She had followed him out to the hall.

'Fonsie, I know you're anxious to see Ann, but you know the way she is.'

What now? What was Mona saying? Was there some other complication?

'And I know you don't want to be doing anything to upset her and… if you arrived into the ward like…'

Now Fonsie understood. Of course. The state of him. He hadn't washed. Mona was right. No matter how sick she was, Ann would be raging if he went to see her looking as black as the ace of spades.

'Oh God, I forgot.'

'Oh course you did. I hope now you don't mind me sticking my nose in?'

'No, no you're right, Mona. I'd better –'

Fonsie ran up to the bathroom, stripped to the waist, and lashed on the Swarfega. It was only when he was in the bedroom putting on a clean shirt that he heard the sounds from another room. Sobs. In his hurry to get to the hospital he had completely forgotten about Francis. The child was obviously in distress. Fonsie was torn but decided he couldn't delay a second longer. He had to see Ann. He tiptoed away from his son's whimpers.

*

Nurse Griffin went out of her way to reassure him. His wife's blood pressure had been stabilised and she had been given something to help her sleep. Nurse Griffin said that's what she needed now, plenty of rest. Fonsie said of course. They were monitoring her heart and blood pressure and everything seemed under control but really – Nurse Griffin's whisper seemed to make it even more serious – she was a very lucky woman. Fonsie said yes, and thanks very much for all she had done. Nurse Griffin said it wasn't her he should be thanking at all but Doctor Rice, who had been brilliant. He had known exactly what to do. Would Mr Strong like to take a quick peek just to ease his mind?

Fonsie stepped into the ward. Nurse Griffin put a finger to her lips but then smiled and left them alone. After staring at Ann from where he stood and listening to her breathing for a minute, he took a chance and stepped closer to the bed. All Fonsie could think was that once again he'd made a right hash of everything. If he could only swap places with her or something, but Fonsie was one of those people who never got sick. He couldn't remember ever missing a day at school or work on account of illness. Feeling utterly useless, he tried whispering a prayer, the Hail Holy Queen. It didn't really make him feel any better. Even if Ann had been awake, he wasn't sure what he'd say except tell her to rest and relax and not worry, as if saying these things would make them happen. Why did she always have to get herself into such a state about things? The same over Martin a few weeks ago. Sure, what good did it do? But again, saying that wasn't much help. Maybe if he hadn't gone back to delivering coal, that would be one less thing for her to fret about. If she ever found out he'd turned down the chance to go full time at O'Neill's it might kill her altogether. If she didn't kill him first.

When he got home Fonsie decided he should chance knocking at Billy Benson's door and thank him for his help. For doing what Fonsie should have been there to do.

'Ah jay, no bother. Sure, it was only the luck of the draw that I was just in the door from work. You were better off not being around, Fonsie, to be honest, because if you heard the roars out of the poor little fellah and seen the state of his ear you'd probably have killed that other little bastard with your bare hands. Have you talked to his father yet?'

'Ah no... no... I thought at this stage better leave it 'til morning.'

'You're right, Fonsie, you're right. Only upsetting yourself. But I'm telling you now, if you get no satisfaction out of Enda McMahon you should bring the Guards in on this and I'll back you up, no bother. You should have seen his ear, Fonsie. It wasn't just red, it was more like a sort of a silver, there was a kind of a spark off it. And poor Ann, I'm sure she told you, the poor thing was in the back of the car, rocking him in her arms and crying and kissing him, She spat on a hanky to wet it and put it on his ear hoping that'd cool it down a bit. Oh, she was in a desperate way, Fonsie. 'Twas all I could do to get her to let me carry the poor youngfellah into Emergency. She didn't want to let go of him.'

Billy Benson finally said good night and God bless. Back in the house Marian and Martin were still up, drinking tea. Ritchie hadn't come home yet – where the hell was he? The telly was on again and they were all watching *Mannix*. Mary Storan said Francis had been very good and quiet, but she wasn't sure if he'd gone to sleep yet. It must be hard for him with the pain. The cream the doctor gave her was in the new fridge to keep it nice and cold; more soothing. Fonsie got it and brought it upstairs.

As soon as the door of the boys' bedroom creaked open, Francis sniffled and turned a sad face.

'How are you?'

'I have a pain. It's tingly.'

'It's probably a bit like an electric shock. It'll wear off. Is it better than it was?'

'A small bit.'

'I'll put some more cream on it for you.'

Fonsie eased the bandage off and opened the pot. The cream was lovely and cold. As his fingers were so cracked and rough, he was extra careful putting it on. The ear looked swollen all right, but it was hard to see how red it was in the light from the landing.

'So, tell me what happened. Who did this to you?'

The McMahons were decent neighbours and Fonsie didn't want to cause a row without being sure of his facts. Francis' voice became more tear-filled.

'Bernard McMahon.'

'Bernard? But I thought you two were pals. What did he go and do a thing like that for?'

'No reason.'

'That's terrible. No reason at all?'

'No.'

'That was a terrible thing to do. Well look, I'll go and speak to his dad about that, don't you worry.' No answer. 'Mr McMahon has probably punished him already. Especially if he knows that Bernard did it for no reason at all.'

No answer. A sniffle.

'Bernard won't have told him anything different, sure he won't?'

Fonsie saw Francis' eyes shift away, then look at him again.

'I didn't hit him or anything, I swear. If he says I did, he's telling lies, Dad.'

'OK. OK. That's all right.'

'All I did was… I… I… I… said something.'

'What if you did? That wasn't a good enough reason for him to give you a wallop with a hurley. What did you say, anyway?'

'I just said… I just said he was stupid.'

'Oh, right. He still shouldn't have hit you, but you know as well Francis, you shouldn't say things like that.'

'But he is stupid.'

'Then maybe that's even more reason not to say it.'

Even in his pain and his sorrow Francis knew his dad was right. He knew it already before his dad said it. He had never ever called Bernard McMahon stupid before, because he felt sorry for Bernard, who was only in 3E and was always getting slaps. But today, Francis had been feeling bad after his mam chased him out and then Bernard started arguing with him about hurling and Bernard hadn't a clue what he was talking about, so, just to be mean, Francis told him he was too stupid to understand the rules of hurling. Boys were always calling each other stupid and worse, but Francis knew in his heart that what made Bernard McMahon really mad was the way he said it. He was scornful. It was as if he was looking down on Bernard.

'You can be too quick with your tongue sometimes. People don't like that, Francis. But look, he was wrong to do what he did and I'll go and talk to his dad. I'll make sure he won't touch you again, but you have to promise to leave him alone too, all right?'

Francis nodded.

'Promise?'

'I promise.'

After his dad left, Francis remembered again the look on poor Bernard's face when he spoke to him as if he was only dirt. That look was why Francis had turned away, already a bit ashamed of himself. Then he felt the side of his head explode and thought he was going to die. He couldn't help wondering if all the bad things that happened today were God's way of punishing him for looking up that doll's dress.

Twenty-three: December 30th

'Francis, watch out! There's a rat under your chair!' Gussie exclaimed mischievously.

Francis didn't even raise his eyes from *The Hooded Hawk Mystery* by Franklin W. Dixon. The best book he had ever read. He was nearly at the end of the most thrilling chapter so far. The Hardy boys had just escaped being caught in a vicious bear trap cunningly hidden under leaves.

'That rat's going to bite your leg, Francis,' chuckled the mouse-haired eighteen-year-old, who loved needling his youngest brother.

'Oh sure, you could put a bomb under him and he wouldn't take his nose out of that book,' wryly observed Mr Strong, a broad-shouldered rugged forty-six-year-old man, with big hands used to tough physical work.

'Eats the books,' his bustling good-natured wife added, humorously throwing her eyes to heaven.

Thanks to this brilliant book Francis had discovered a new word to describe family talk. Banter. On every single page there were more new words, like dilemma and stymied. Right now, the Hardy boys had a big dilemma: how to get over an eight-foot-high electric fence protecting the villains' hide-out. They were stymied.

Out of the corner of his eye he saw Granny Strong purse her lips. She was an angular, hawk-nosed woman with definite opinions on many subjects.

'All that reading can't be good for his eyes,' she declared tartly.

'Nothing better than reading,' interrupted Francis' Uncle Peadar Crowley, who never missed an opportunity to argue with his mother-in-law. 'As our great Minister for Education is always trying to explain to people,' he added emphatically. He knew that Granny Strong hated the government, so he enjoyed praising them even more just to aggravate her. Sure enough, the spirited old lady snorted, but it wasn't tartly this time. Francis thought for a second. Indignantly. That's how she snorted. 'Humph!'

Mrs Strong exchanged a knowing look with her sister-in-law Marg Crowley, a cheery round-faced smiling woman. Both of them had suffered Granny Strong's tirades for many years but, unlike Uncle Peadar, who was bull-necked and bald-headed, they were a little more wary of disagreeing with her so openly. Francis thought it was so clever the way Frank and Joe found some stout saplings in the nearby forest and used them to pole-vault over the electric fence. 'Wow,' he whispered under his breath.

'There now, Isn't it lovely to see that he's enjoying the present you bought him, Marg?' Mrs Strong ventured.

'Oh I'm delighted,' beamed Marg proudly. 'But I can't believe he's nearly finished it already. I only gave it to him two days ago.'

'Once he loves a book there's no stopping him,' Mrs Strong observed.

'Good for him,' Uncle Peadar asserted belligerently, as he sipped his large Crested Ten, which he always drank with half a teaspoon of water.

'Don't say I didn't warn you when he goes blind at a young age,' retorted Granny Strong, tartly again.

Francis figured that the family banter was turning into a fight between his granny and his uncle. Mr Strong hastily intervened.

'Mam, will I put more coal on the range for you there?' Mr Strong was always anxious to keep the peace.

Granny Strong, sitting in her winged chair right next to the Stanley range, squinted at the bright orange flames before replying.

'It won't do any harm, I suppose,' she scowled.

Francis had just finished the second-last chapter and the villain Bangalore had captured the Hardy boys and, with an evil smirk, ordered his minions to flog them. The boys were in a tight corner. Just as he was about to find out what happened next, he was distracted by a familiar buzzing sound on the driveway outside his Granny's tranquil cottage. He puckered his brow thoughtfully and shrewdly guessed that it must be his oldest brother Ritchie zooming in on his 1964 Honda 50. Francis glanced outside to confirm his deduction that it was indeed his tall dark-haired oldest brother who was arriving. He was carrying a passenger. Even though a crash helmet hid the face, Francis spotted a wisp of blonde hair sticking out and, employing his sleuthing skills, decided it was a cinch that the mystery passenger was Áine Kiely, Ritchie's latest girlfriend. A moment later his hunch was confirmed when her face was revealed. Francis liked Áine; she was a pretty, quick-witted and vivacious girl with a carefree laugh.

Mrs Strong, who had been having a whispered conversation with Aunt Marg Crowley, jumped up with alacrity.

'Oh look, there's Ritchie and Áine,' she exclaimed enthusiastically. Although he had been utterly absorbed in *The Hooded Hawk Mystery*, Francis was nonetheless always curious about whispered conversations and what they might mean. Luckily, despite his recent misadventure with his menacing nemesis, Bernard McMahon, his hearing was once again as acute as ever and, while continuing to read, he eavesdropped surreptitiously, hoping to hear clues that would help him work out the puzzle. He had already noted his mam saying what sounded like 'three times' and even though his Aunt Marg was a very experienced whisperer and difficult to decipher, his sharp ears had definitely heard her mutter 'recovery'. From these few words only, Francis had cleverly conjectured that the two women were discussing his mam's recent illness and 'recovery' and his mam was explaining that she was now on three different tablets, 'three times' a day'. If this was the solution to the mystery conversation, however, it only baffled Francis more. Why the whispering? He had heard his mam talk about her blood pressure and her pills and how careful she needed to be after her hospital scare at least a hundred times in the last couple of months. It was no secret. With the arrival of Ritchie and his lively, appealing, blonde girlfriend, the whispered conversation came to a sudden end. Anyway Francis was much more interested in reading the intriguing final chapter of *The Hooded Hawk Mystery*.

Everyone was delighted to see Ritchie and Áine. There was lots of banter. 'Oh, here comes Bonnie and Clyde,' wisecracked Gussie, who enjoyed kidding with his older brother. Even though there was only a year between them, Ritchie and Gussie were very different. Ritchie had dark hair and was more athletic and serious-minded than his lighter-haired, more impulsive brother, Gussie, who loved movies and had his own 8mm camera. He started filming Ritchie and Áine, who giggled infectiously. Their moon-faced thirteen-year-old brother, Martin, stared at Áine with popping eyes. 'Hello Áine,' he smiled shyly. Martin was just beginning to notice girls, although he was much too young to have a girlfriend yet.

'Well, hello and welcome,' said Aunt Marg warmly. 'Lovely to meet you, Áine.'

'This is my Aunt Marg, my favourite Aunt,' grinned Ritchie.

'Oh go 'way you, you charmer you.' chuckled Aunt Marg, who adored Ritchie. Marian and cousin Mary, who were laying out griddle cake, ginger cake and fruit scones on the tea table, got big hugs from Áine. Ritchie spotted Francis in his corner. 'Don't expect a word out of him if he has a book in his hand,' he quipped.

Without looking up or speaking, Francis gave Áine a little wave. The family chuckled.

'Oh don't mind that fellah,' cautioned Mrs Strong. 'Lost in his own world. Gussie, put that camera down! Now, Áine, will Marian get you a cup of tea?'

'Or maybe she'd prefer something a bit stronger, Ann?' suggested Mr Strong with a mischievous grin at Áine.

'She wants to meet Granny first,' Ritchie said in a low voice.

'She'll need something stronger after that all right,' muttered Uncle Peadar under his breath. Aunt Marg just glared at him.

Ritchie had warned Áine how withering the angular old lady's manner could be, but of course, he also pointed out that she was eighty-six years old and a great woman for her age. The atmosphere crackled with tension as everyone waited, holding their breath, to see how the testy old woman would greet Ritchie's new girlfriend. Even Francis looked up.

'I'm so pleased to meet you at last, Mrs Strong,' said Áine in a polite, respectful voice. 'Happy New Year to you.'

To everyone's relief and surprise, instead of the usual disapproving frown, and terse response, Granny Strong smiled at attractive, blonde Áine.

'Well, thank you love, and a happy New Year to you too.'

Aunt Marg and Mrs Strong exchanged a quizzical glance. Áine must be a very special girl if she could charm peppery old Kathleen Strong so quickly.

'And happy New Year to everyone,' Aunt Marg announced enthusiastically. 'Right, I think we're ready for our tea.'

Francis was musing that it sure was going to be a happy new year now that thoughtful Aunt Marg had introduced him to these swell new mysteries. The action and adventure was top-notch, he loved the two boys, though he preferred Joe to Frank, and best of all he was discovering an avalanche of new words and ways to describe things. At the back of the book, it said that all boys from ten to fourteen would love these lively action-packed stories. He was only eight and had almost finished this first one in two days. Although he felt a little gloomy to be so near the end of *The Hooded Hawk Mystery*, he was not too woebegone because on the blue spine was a number: 34. This must mean that there were at least thirty-four Hardy Boys mystery stories and the titles of some of the other adventures sounded intriguing, like *The Mystery of the Desert Giant*, *The Crisscross Shadow* and *The Clue of the Screeching Owl*. He would look for them in the library and in O'Mahony's Bookshop. Although, as each book cost seven and six, he could never afford to buy one himself, he thought ruefully.

Suddenly, he was alert! It was eerily quiet. No one was talking or making a sound. Yet he was sure that the family hadn't left the room. What was going on? He was perplexed. In order to solve the mystery of the strange silence, he looked up from his book, warily, cautiously. Everyone was sitting at the tea-table, but no one was eating. Instead, eleven pairs of eyes stared at him silently, waiting for him to notice. Seeing his look of consternation, everyone laughed heartily! Even stern-faced Granny Strong chuckled. Carefree Áine nearly choked, she was laughing so much.

'We can't start our tea until you put down that book and join us,' teased Mr Strong, his eyes twinkling with merriment.

Sheepishly, Francis closed his book and came to the table. Soon he was enjoying the food and the family banter. The solution to *The Hooded Hawk Mystery* would have to wait.

1968

Twenty-four: March 10th.

Dragging himself from the bed at half-seven on a Sunday morning was not pleasant but, in truth, Dom was looking forward to his busy day. He shaved carefully, relaxed in the knowledge that the face looking back at him was that of the most popular politician in the country. And a genial, intelligent face it was. Big smiles and hearty hellos usually hailed the approach of this face. A favourite, on his way to being a legend. There would be great excitement among the Mass-goers this morning once word went out that Dom would be speaking to them afterwards. Canvassing was an adrenalin injection even on a wretched morning like this, with indigestion scalding him. What politician worthy of the name didn't look forward to being out and about, meeting the people? His driver, PJ, was, as always, ready and waiting with the ministerial car. Before getting into the back, Dom greeted him with a monotoned, 'Grand morning for it,' while lifting his eyes ironically to the impenetrably grey sky. He was rewarded with a smile. An essentially silent man, PJ appreciated dry humour. While Dom would never have been the kind who fancied the notion of servants waiting on him hand and foot, he had often noted with pleasure that his official driver had the awareness and discretion of the perfect servant. The first part of this morning's drive was a fine example. PJ seemed to gauge instantly that silence was best as they went to pick up JP and Mick. When they hopped in, Dom found their jowl-quivering enthusiasm for the day's electioneering mildly tedious. He knew this morning's outing was a thrill for them, not just because they were riding in a ministerial car with the most popular politician in the country, but because their assumption was that, with Dom on board, high jinks and slagging would inevitably be the order of the day. To be fair to them, Dom was aware that, normally, he led from the front in that regard but, for whatever reason, at the moment of their boisterous arrival, he just wasn't in the mood. The Bisodol hadn't done its work and the smouldering irritation was still there. A bit of fresh air and the buzz of the crowd outside Sixmilebridge church would take care of that, he was certain, but right now, he wished that JP and Mick would give it a rest. However, he found himself making an effort to rise to the occasion at Cratloe, where the other Mick waited outside his house as arranged. As PJ slowed down and the other Mick raised a hand in greeting, Dom said, 'PJ, Pull away at the last minute.'

His driver performed the manoeuvre with expert comic timing. He slowed almost to a halt, then, as the other Mick stepped towards the car, his hand already reaching for the door handle, PJ accelerated away and pulled up again thirty yards further on. The lads inside hooted and Dom looked back to see the other Mick trot after them, enjoying the lark as much as themselves.

'One more,' said Dom, and, again Pat jolted the ministerial car forward just as the other Mick arrived. 'Oh, I can see we're in for a day of it,' the other Mick was puffing and laughing as he finally got in.

The men arrived in Sixmilebridge in time for half-eight mass. Dom used this quiet half-hour to think out a few good lines. The congregation seemed gratifyingly larger than would normally have turned out so early. Presumably they had come to hear him.

Outside, Dom forgot any physical discomfort once he began to perform. A wind that'd cut the nose off an eskimo didn't seem to put the crowd off and he felt the familiar confidence and pleasure of knowing that this little audience was on his side, willing him on. When he expressed solidarity with the ordinary working man, they took him at his word. When he mentioned the stresses and strains of women struggling to put food on the family table, he was speaking their language. They cheered when he proclaimed his special love for the fields and hills and little roads round about, potholed though they may be, he said, but his Party colleague Sylvie would, if returned in this by-election, fix that. And of course, when he took a cut at the Blueshirt adversary they cackled like hens. This was what they expected from him, what they were waiting for. Even those who heckled sounded friendly. They were more like the straight half of a comedy duo, feeding him set-ups so he might tickle them with instant punch lines. The beaming red cheeks of JP and Mick and the other Mick told him he was flying it today. It spurred him on to even more extravagant heights. He didn't lose the run of himself, though, and ended his speech with time to spare for handshakes and hellos before the ministerial car swept them away toward pretty little St John's in Cratloe, where they would catch the crowd after half-nine Mass.

By now the sun was making a bit of an effort and Dom was feeling nicely charged. The old heart was responding to the challenge. He began to notice how much growth there was all round, grass and leaves sprouting, hedges bulging. The year was getting into its stride all right and there was so much to be done, but, as far as Dom was concerned, nothing in political life was better raw sport than rattling around these back roads with loyal men, snaring votes. Some of his colleagues, he knew, thought of it as a wretched chore. They despised it secretly, for to despise it openly was political death. Did these fellahs not know how to live? It was one of the greatest things about this little country that no matter how high a fellow rose, he couldn't avoid this direct, sweaty contact with the people. Luckily for Dom, he would find it hard to imagine enjoying political life without it. And of course, when a man could have it both ways... Well, wasn't that where he was right now? Flying high with his feet on the ground. Dom liked that phrase. He imagined that even if he became Taoiseach, he would still enjoy mixing it with voters outside the church gate after Mass.

When they arrived in Cratloe, Mick stuck his head in the back door of St John's and returned to report that the place was full and Holy Communion was well underway. They'd be out in five minutes or so. The tightness Dom felt slowly spreading across his chest was beginning to get on his wick. The thing wasn't going away. Thankfully he'd be collecting his Beauty off the plane at Shannon in the early afternoon. She'd know what to do. She'd sort him out. For now, the only thing was to ignore it. What was it at all? It couldn't be called pain. He tried to take a full breath but, like a fat man heaving himself over a high wall, he couldn't quite get to the top and over the other side. He exhaled impatiently.

As the punters came out of Mass it was obvious they were delighted to see Dom waiting. Cratloe was so close to the border of his own constituency, it had many residents who would have preferred to live on the other side so they could vote for him. Here Dom was in his element, using the best bits now honed from his earlier performance and a few additions tailored for Cratloe folk alone. He had a line about how unfortunate it was that the most beautiful part of his local area had somehow ended up in the constituency next door, but he thanked them for allowing him the privilege of an occasional visit to paradise. They loved that. A big cheer for that. Once again all discomfort was forgotten. Nothing cramped his communion with an audience who not only wished they could vote for him personally, but would have liked to see him become Taoiseach.

Back at the car Mick said, 'Jesus Dom, you gave it some welly out there. Look at you, you're sweatin'.' The lads were high on it all at this stage. The other Mick confidently asserted that if they'd reckoned on a hundred votes out of that crowd before, they were guaranteed two hundred now. The next stop would not yield many votes, but it was important to Dom because it was the Protestant congregation up at Wells Chapel, and he saw himself as a man who knew how to talk to Protestants. He felt they trusted him, even if they didn't entirely trust his Party.

The jolt, when it came, was like a fist inside him pounding his ribcage. Dom now understood what was happening to him. Oh, sweet Jesus no! The jauntiness of the others evaporated very quickly when they saw the way their man sagged forward, the way he couldn't catch his breath, the way his hand leapt to his chest. This was no wind-up. Dom heard JP ask would a sup of water help? He heard the other Mick roar at PJ to pull in there! A frantic animal was inside him now, flinging itself at its cage, determined to burst free. If only his Beauty was here with him, she'd know what to do. Jesus, a few more hours and she'd be home. Hands were all over him now. Voices seemed more distant for some reason. What were they asking him? Of course he could still walk! But, no point in fooling himself, it wasn't easing.

The poor woman who opened the door got an awful shock. Her face told Dom just how bad things really looked. He hoped the lads had enough savvy to know they'd better move fast. He was sitting again. Sinking in soft cushions. The poor lady held the glass as he sipped the water. A doctor, an ambulance, did they know what was needed? He heard Mick jabbering on the phone. Amazingly, the pounding eased as the water trickled down. The eyes looking at him were so fearful he felt he had to offer them some relief.

'That must be Holy water you're after giving me, it's working already.'

They did their best to laugh. Dom did not tell them a numbness was now seeping across his chest and down his arm, nor did he know why the lads talking to him, barely three feet away, sounded like they were bellowing down a long tunnel. He had lost all sense of time. Dom closed his eyes but forced them open again. Had he drifted off for a while? Strange faces were staring at him. Paramedics, thanks be to Jesus! Now they were lifting him up, now strapping him down, now rolling him out the door. He managed to turn his head and saw the lads following, JP's hand still on his shoulder. Dom tried to say something as they watched him disappear into the gloom of the ambulance. Why was it so hard to articulate? Even in the mad bad old days, the drink had never affected his ability to speak out clearly and with command. On the contrary, it had usually facilitated greater volubility and verbosity. But now, as the door closed, Dom wasn't sure what it was he had just said to the lads. Where was his tongue gone?

One paramedic was attaching something to him and he felt the hands of the other press down hard. It was serious all right, touch and go maybe. He'd be laid up a while, there might even have to be something complicated in the way of an operation. His tired mind was already adjusting himself to these probabilities. For now, the thing was to get to the hospital fast. The ambulance was still bumping along the back roads, not yet even at the outskirts of the city when, for the first time, it occurred to Dom that he might die.

No. No. No! His body shuddered. Until this shocking moment, he had not thought beyond illness and convalescence and time lost, precious time. Surely it would be no worse than that?

For some reason Dom could hear almost nothing now and it was getting harder to stop his eyes closing. But at least he could still feel those hands pressing down on him, though not so firmly for some reason. Why wouldn't the fellow press harder? Come on! He would have to tell him to. He would open his mouth and tell him. He would.

*

The cow looked uneasy but he wasn't moving just yet. Baz settled the Éclair Camerette on his shoulder. It felt snug and light, so different from the massive brooding robot that was his old studio camera. It was going to take getting used to, but that was why he was out in a field inveigling a reluctant cow into a camera test. The wet meadow grass beneath him was not exactly a smooth studio floor, either. He was about to find out how uncertain his hand-held operating was. The cow stared at him as he framed the creature rather gorgeously against the background of the distant Atlantic. The Connemara light was magical at this time of the evening. He held the shot rock-solid. Looking in the viewfinder, it was genuinely hard to tell that it was hand-held, but what would happen when he began to walk? He set himself in position and rolled. He had been warned that the Éclair was noisy and it was.

Even the cow seemed to react to the clacking with a lift of her head. Baz held the shot still for a few seconds, then began to circle the black and white beast, training his free left eye to watch what was happening around him while his right eye, pressed against the viewfinder, concentrated on what was in the frame. As he reached the backside of the cow, he stumbled against an unyielding clump of meadow grass. The camera jolted and the shot skewed, but he managed to stay upright and corrected the frame quickly. Then the cow decided she was tired of being the centre of attention and wandered off. Baz improvised and followed her. With the cow's arse and flicking tail now dominating the frame, the shot was no longer as elegant as his original composition, but the energy of the movement, the sense of uncertainty and unease generated by the shaky chase was immediate and exciting. The cow moved faster and so did Baz. In the intensity of the moment all his attention and focus went to what the right eye could see in the viewfinder. His world became the pursuit of this cow. The shot was, at the speed he was moving, increasingly difficult to manage as the camera stirred restlessly on his shoulder.

Then Baz tripped and fell.

As he tumbled, he turned his body to protect the expensive new toy. His left shoulder took the brunt, but at least he could hear the Éclair still noisily running. He cut and sat up, resting it on his lap. It was clear that plenty of practice would be needed but, after eight months without any kind of camera in his hand, this had felt good. It felt like the personal project he had decided to embark on had officially begun.

When he left RTE, Baz had summoned enough courage to send Miriam Hartnett a card and was pleased to get, in return, an invite to drop by if he was in the area. He'd never expected to be still in Rossaveel eight months later, more or less bedded in, but he had gone with the flow. Miriam told him he was healing and that that process should be allowed take its own course. While not the language he would have used, in essence he agreed with her. For a reclusive artist, Miriam was surprisingly easy company.

Her cottage had a radio but no television or phone. Together they read and talked and walked. On the third night after he arrived they made love for the first time. And so it continued, without discussion or overt analysis. No head stuff. Both of them just let it be. Of course, he knew things would not stay this way, but he hadn't made up his mind exactly what he wanted to do.

When Miriam mentioned a screening in Dublin of some documentary about Ireland today, made by a journalist called Peter Lennon who was a friend of her friend Sarah, Baz wasn't that interested. When Miriam mentioned that the film had been shot by a famous French cameraman he became a little more curious, then frustrated because she couldn't remember his name. For Sarah's sake, Miriam wanted to go to the screening so Baz agreed to accompany her on the 340-mile round trip. As soon as they arrived at the Cameo he inhaled that particular Dublin buzz of secret delight. Apparently RTE had refused to broadcast the film so, now that it was officially 'controversial', the in-crowd could not afford to miss it. Baz let Miriam manouvre them through the crush in search of Sarah. After hugs and introductions she remembered to ask the name of the famous French cameraman. 'Raoul Couthard.' Baz was stunned. Couthard had been a hero of his since he first saw *À Bout de Souffle*. He had visited Ireland? When? Shot a film here? How had such a thing come about? Suddenly, his expectations soared.

Luckily, *The Rocky Road to Dublin* turned out to be everything he would have hoped from the genius of *nouvelle vague*. Turning his camera on today's Ireland, Couthard had conducted a giddying smash-and-grab exercise involving a combination of brilliantly observed improvised hand-held sequences in dimly lit dance halls and elegantly composed cityscapes, which allowed him to counterpoint the sad decay of old Dublin streets with the ruthless modernity of Ballymun's new towers. Baz admired the relaxed simplicity of the interviews. Seán O'Faoláin seemed at ease in his garden as he offered a clinical dissection of a society without moral courage, which observed what he called 'a self-interested silence, never speaking in moments of crisis'. Couthard's unfussy observation of a trendy young priest going about his business became, in its understated way, devastating satire. The fatuous cleric probably loved being on camera more than he loved Jesus, and had no idea how ludicrous he seemed. At one moment he was performing the 'Chattanooga Shoeshine Boy' to bewildered patients in a hospital ward, at another he made himself the master of ceremonies and chief entertainer at a parish wedding. Finally, puffing casually on a cigarette, this junior celibate offered his considered views on the dangers of pre-marital sex. Baz loved how Couthard had the wit not to employ odd angles or camera tricks to make the cleric look more ludicrous. He simply pointed it in his direction, knowing the young priest's bloated ego would do the rest. Throughout the film, moments of ordinary Dublin life were captured: looks, glances and revealing details of behaviour. Baz was also amused that Couthard had spotted a phenomenon that Irish people took entirely for granted. There were priests everywhere; in every hole and corner, at every activity, gathering and bunfight.

Baz watched, transfixed, envious, exhilarated, frustrated, enthralled. Driving back to Rossaveel that night, he couldn't stop talking about it. 'Imagine, in six years of national broadcasting, no one working in RTE, including myself, came close to creating what we just saw.' This was the kind of film that had been in his head ever since he returned to Ireland. But Peter Lennon with the help of his French cameraman had got there first. Baz told Miriam that, when the film ended, he hadn't been sure whether he should stand and cheer, or curl up and cry. Couthard had popped over from France for, maybe, two or three weeks, presumably earning little or no money – for surely this film must have been made on a shoestring – yet he had, with casual genius, pointed his camera and penetrated the heart and soul of this society. Miriam said, very simply, 'Well, why not be inspired by it? Go out and make something even better.' Baz was silent for some time after that, but around two in the morning as they crossed the Shannon at Athlone he said, 'All right. I'll try.'

In what was a self-conscious act of homage, Baz managed to find out, with the help of Miriam's friend, what camera Couthard had used and he ordered himself an Éclair Camerette. He didn't, as yet, know exactly what he was going to do with it, what story he was going to tell. It would be something about where his country was at the end of this most bewildering decade. But it wouldn't be an essay, a polemic. Baz wanted the images to reveal whatever story was out there. He didn't have much money, but he wasn't on a schedule either. No one was paying his wages any more. His time was his own.

When he got back to the cottage, Miriam asked how the screen test had gone: 'Will Buttercup get the part?' Baz said the cow's performance was fine but the cinematography left a lot to be desired. He was about to pack away the Éclair when he heard her pass on, almost as an afterthought, something she had just heard on the radio. The Minister for Education had dropped dead earlier in the day. A heart attack. 'Imagine, only forty-seven, the poor fellah.'

'What? Dom is dead?' Miriam agreed it was quite a shock but Baz could see she was surprised at the depth of his reaction, so he told her the story of Dom's significant, if unintentional, role in his decision to leave RTE. Miriam said it was karma. 'You've been thinking about this project of yours. When to start, what'll it be about. Your new camera arrives and the next day you hear this news. The camera was still in your hands when I told you. It's clear as day, Baz. You have to bring it to the man's funeral. See what happens.' Whatever his thoughts about karma, Baz was inclined to agree with her conclusion.

Twenty-five: March 11th

Mr Hennessy was a nice mad teacher. When he took the boys out for hurling practice he wore a hairnet to keep his big head of long black hair from going all over the place as he ran around. Even though he was a lump of a country fellah and always wore a suit, the boys called him Hippie Hennessy. Everyone in 3A liked him. History was his favourite thing to teach, and last Friday he had told them to read all about the Battle of Kinsale in their picture book, STAIR NA hÉIREANN. Francis loved history and had learned off the three reasons why, STAIR NA hÉIREANN explained, the English beat the Irish again in 1603.

1 Snow fell.

2 There were spies in the Irish camp.

3 The Spanish never came.

He had been hoping that Mr Hennessy would ask him the three reasons, but when he saw the look on his face as he came up the stairs, Francis wasn't so sure. Mr Hennessy unlocked the classroom door and threw it open without a word. Then he sat down, opened up the roll book and started barking out the names very fast. The boys of 3A were smart enough to answer '*Anseo*' with no messing, until Padraig Leddin was caught with his head under the desk when his name was called. Mr Hennessy just stared. Silence. Finally Padraig Leddin looked up and realised. His voice squeaked when he said '*Anseo*' but nobody dared laugh. Mr Hennessy kept staring at him for another couple of seconds. Deadly silence. Then he went on with the roll-call. Francis and Ian sneaked a wary glance at each other across the room. What was up with him?

Mr Hennessy slapped the roll-book closed and kept his head down, his hair falling forward. 3A waited in trepidation. It was the first time Francis understood properly what that word meant. After a few seconds Mr Hennessy pushed his hair way back on his head, looked up at the boys and started to speak. But he didn't sound angry at all: just very, very sad.

'Boys, as you know from your history lessons, there have been many great Irish people in the past. We also know that many of them died far too young, sacrificing their lives for Ireland. Well, yesterday another Irishman, who we should all be proud of, went before his time. This man was our Minister for Education. He was a local man, born and bred in this city. In fact, less than two years ago I heard him give a mighty speech down in that yard there at the opening of this very building you're sitting in now. And remember boys, as Minister for Education he wasn't only in charge of this school, but every other school and college in the whole country and I can tell you, he worked night and day to make sure that every boy and girl in Ireland would get a better education. It's because of this man – listen very carefully now – that most of you sitting here are getting a much better throw of the dice than your parents did. Do you hear me now? It's important that you appreciate this. And I'm not embarrassed to tell you lads how sad I feel this morning that such a fine man has been lost to us…'

Mr Hennessy stopped talking for a few seconds. He was at the window now, looking down at the yard. The whole class could see that he was trying not to start crying.

'… so… stand up boys and we'll say a special prayer for the repose of his soul. Oh, and… ah… there's something else I have to tell you and I'm warning you now, I don't want to hear a sound out of you, but ah… the funeral is taking place tomorrow in the cathedral, a State funeral, so, as a mark of respect to his memory –'

Francis knew what Mr Hennessy was about to say and that anyone mad enough to start any kind of a cheer was asking for trouble.

'– the school will be closed and you will all have a day off.'

Mr Hennessy looked around, daring someone to whoop or

even grin, but there wasn't a peep out of anyone and everyone tried to look serious. However delighted the boys of 3A might be at the news of a free day, they were bright enough to keep it to themselves.

Twenty-six: March 12th

Michael Liston gazed at his boy. At eight years of age what did he make of this enormous, important funeral? A nurse had minded him during his mother's burial when he was only five days old. When Michael called to the boarding school at eight this morning, to collect the child, he was by no means confident that, given reports he had been receiving lately about his recalcitrance, he would even want to come. How well did the boy remember Dom anyway? But he was ready and waiting, spotlessly turned out. Father McCormick said Matthew had seemed quite anxious to go to the funeral. Father McCormick thought it was a very good idea to bring him.

Holding his son close, Michael pushed through the crowd around St John's Cathedral. They were allowed inside and directed to a reasonable spot halfway back. Michael could see that most of the dignitaries were now in situ. It was a fair old turnout, by any standards. Dev and Jack and most of the cabinet and the opposition leaders. Anyone with sufficient sense of their own importance had made it their business to squeeze in. Even Dom would have been reasonably satisfied with so much official lamentation. Michael tried to get a look at the Widow. How was she coping? Hopefully she'd be pleased to see him when he called. Not today, obviously. Tomorrow. Through the crowd there was just a glimpse of the back of her head bent forward, an arm on her shoulder, her son's, presumably. Michael had a sudden shuddering memory of his sister's arm curled around his shoulder at Matthew's mother's funeral. How he'd hated it and wanted to shake it off, but hadn't because he knew it would only bring more clucking attention on himself. Michael was taken completely by surprise at this unwanted memory of that chilly day. After all, he had not mourned her and rarely thought about her. Dom's funeral wasn't happening in the same church and this great event didn't resemble, in any way, that strained, cold ceremony. Maybe it was something to do with bringing the boy to a funeral for the first time, or returning to this wretched city after nearly two years out of it. Whatever it was, it really shocked him that he had to quell this urgent impulse to tell him all about his mother. Lay it out there; how she'd died giving birth to him; how everything would have been so much simpler and better if they'd both died. Michael knew he hadn't the slightest intention of saying any of this. It was astonishing that it had even flitted across his mind.

The Bishop emerged with his entourage of concelebrants and, beneath the soothing hum of requiem Mass, Michael thought about the real purpose of this pilgrimage, his plan to visit Dom's home tomorrow. How important it would be to play it as a relaxed and friendly gesture of condolence, nothing more; a personal call out of respect and affection for a long-time colleague, bringing along his sad-eyed son, who used to call him Uncle Dom. When the time came to broach his other business, there shouldn't be any difficulty or awkwardness. Michael hoped everyone would recognise it simply as a task that had to be done. He was fairly sure it wouldn't take him long to go through Dom's papers. After all, he knew the kind of thing he was looking out for. It was just to be sure, to be sure, in case there was anything at all that might prove embarrassing or compromising in the future. That was important. Everyone might be feeling loyal and sentimental now, but who knew how things would change with time?

*

Francis loitered at the bedroom window watching other children playing on the green. He felt despondent – rather like Frank and Joe, whenever their investigations hit a dead end. His dilemma was this day off school, Because of it, Francis' plan to buy his next Hardy Boys book tomorrow was stymied. Thwarted.

Ever since finishing *The Hooded Hawk Mystery*, Francis promised himself he would read all Frank and Joe's other adventures. He investigated the library first, but they only had two. *The Melted Coins*, number 43, and *The Haunted Fort*, number 29. But it only took a week to read them and, like the Hardy Boys themselves, Francis no sooner concluded one mystery than he wanted to start into the next. Visiting O'Mahony's Bookshop every day after school only increased his anticipation. There was the row of Hardy Boys books, blue down the side, with the name of the book printed in black, along with the number in the series and the writer's name, Franklin W. Dixon. Sometimes Francis took one down just to stare at the cover. It was always a picture of dark-haired Frank and fair-haired Joe doing something dangerous or scary. When none of the staff was looking, he would sneak the book open to read the description of the story on the inside cover. If he ever managed to get enough money then definitely he'd buy *The Wailing Siren Mystery* first. Number 37. But where would he get seven and six?

Then one morning, waiting for the bus to school, he had a brainwave. If he got up early enough and walked to school, he'd save the bus fare. And what if he walked home at dinner-time and back to school again after dinner? His mam gave him sixpence a day for the bus. Francis quickly added up that walking all the time would mean saving two and six a week. Multiplied by three was seven and six, which meant he could buy a new Hardy Boys book after only three weeks. As long as his mam and dad didn't find out what he was doing.

Three weeks later Francis brought seven and six in sixpenny bits into O'Mahony's and bought number 37, *The Wailing Siren Mystery*. Three weeks after that he bought *The Mystery of the Desert Giant*. Number 25. Next he got *The Clue of the Screeching Owl*. Number 26. He didn't mind all the walking, even in the rain. It was worth it for that moment when he held his brand-new Hardy Boys story. On the way home from O'Mahony's, each time he bought one, he examined it front and back and inside. He read the description on the inside cover, then he looked at the page with the list of Hardy Boys adventures to remind himself of the ones he hadn't bought yet. Then he always read the page that said things like 'This edition pursuant to agreement with Grosset and Dunlop Inc. New York NY USA'. No matter how many times he read these words he still couldn't work out what 'pursuant' or 'Inc.' meant. Then he read the list of chapters. Contents they were called. He loved trying to detect from the names of the chapters what might be happening. Sometimes it was easy – 'Snake Trouble', 'Attack in the Night', 'Dangerous Waters' – but sometimes the titles were mysterious and intriguing: 'Scarlet Clues', 'An About-Face', 'A Ruse'. Finally he would, with great care, open the last page, covering it with his hand so he wouldn't see how the story ended, and check the page number in the top corner. He liked knowing how long each new book was. By now his anticipation would be at fever-pitch, but still, he never started to read the actual story until he got home and sat in a corner of the front room or lay on his top bunk.

Next on his list was number 38, *The Secret of Wildcat Swamp*. But, because of the day off school, his mam hadn't given him any bus fare today. So now he was sixpence short. He would have to wait a whole extra day. Francis didn't think that was fair. He felt trapped in a hopeless quandary, but he could think of no way out. He just wished the Minister hadn't died.

*

Éamon could hear in Bishop Murphy's voice an undercurrent of genuine grief. He had already noted, amidst the coughs and throat-clearing in the packed cathedral, an occasional echoing sob. He was aware that thousands waited in the square outside, all along Cathedral Place and up Mulgrave Street almost as far as the entrance to the cemetery. For once it might be accurate to say a city was in mourning.

It was tempting to envy men like Dom who detonated in mid-flight, whose spirits soared and burst and rained down particles of inspiration and comfort on those below. Michael Collins, John F. Kennedy… Éamon knew only too well the staying power of their legend. Perhaps that was why, throughout the ceremony, he prayed silently, not for Dom, but for himself. He accepted God's will, of course, that he had not been chosen for such a death, but still he wondered, not for the first time, was it a penance? What sin had he committed that seemingly doomed him to this endless slow dissolve, departing this world particle by particle as it were, drifting to some inconsequential end, out of place and time?

Éamon's mind might be tired and troubled but, as yet, it was never cluttered or confused. He understood very well that while his death, when it eventually came, might be a notable event, it would not have anything like the impact of Dom's tragic passing, which had already served to embalm his greatest achievement. Free Education could never, in the future, be spoken of merely as a clever scheme or a populist policy. It had become a cornerstone with his name etched on it. Éamon knew his own obsequies would be carried out with all the reverence and dignity the State could muster, but it would be a cold occasion marked by academic discussion and re-evaluation. Someone would undoubtedly pronounce it the end of an era, but Éamon's precise mind recognised how erroneous that phrase already was. His era had ended long ago. It was years since he had seen the sights and, these days, could scarcely understand the sounds of his country any more. Nor was his country hearing him. He couldn't even call himself a ghost, for he no longer had the capacity to inspire awe or dread. Éamon wondered if he was, in the most correct sense, a relic, an object of reverence certainly, but only as a necessary ceremonial prop, an old man with a wreath who would not even know where to lay it without the quiet guiding hand of his aide-de-camp.

Colonel Seán whispered in his ear the names of six cabinet ministers who were now stepping forward to shoulder the coffin to the hearse. Éamon recognised in their gesture a genuine desire to express collegiate grief, but he also perceived the politician's animal impulse to cleave to the latest source of enchantment. In the past, ambitious men had clung to him, hovered at his shoulder, content merely to gulp in the precious air around him. Now, as these ministers marched slowly past, cradling their precious burden, Éamon guessed they no more saw him than he could see them.

Outside the cathedral Colonel Seán's hand politely signalled him to wait. Another discreet whisper told him that An Taoiseach and the ex-Taoiseach were now beside him. The coffin was being placed in the hearse. Éamon heard a ferocious clicking of cameras and then, quite suddenly, a kind of silence. Not the silence of a vast, spreading valley, empty of humanity, but of a great crowd in an urban soundscape; a feeling of breath held, of words unspoken.

The ordeal was nearly over. Éamon was familiar enough with the city to know that the journey to the cemetery would not take long. At the graveside, he would stand, erect as always, listening to a familiar threnody composed of prayers for the dead, Amhrán na bhFiann, and a twenty-one-gun salute. After that, he could shuffle back to his prison cell.

Gussie Strong could just about make out the familiar figure of Dev in his viewfinder. He had managed to climb a wall and sit himself on a pillar at the far side of the square so he could see clearly over the heads of the crowd. But now there was another problem. At this distance, his lens was so wide it showed the entire front of the cathedral so, when the coffin and all the mourners came out, everyone looked so small it was impossible to tell who they were. Dev was the only one he could identify because, even so far away, the old bastard had a shape to him that was different from everyone else. Gussie was raging. Until now he had only ever shot stuff for the family or some local event like the St Patrick's Day parade. He'd brought his camera to work a few times because he hoped to sneak out and grab footage of some of the famous people who were always arriving at Shannon Airport, but on the day Jayne Mansfield visited he was caught and told he'd be fired if he ever brought the camera into work again. This funeral was his first real chance to shoot an event with famous people at it, even if they were only politicians. Gussie knew the funeral would be the main headline on the television news tonight and wanted to compare his shots with the ones the professionals got, and secretly thought he could do better. It was too late now. Even if he tried to push his way through to the front of the crowd the hearse would probably have left by the time he got near enough, and anyway, with such a crush, there wasn't a hope in hell of getting a clear view. So he stayed where he was and just kept shooting at all the tiny people getting into tiny cars and slowly driving away from the church.

*

Baz Malloy had left Rossaveel early and arrived in good time. The nearest parking place he could find was on Sexton Street. As he walked back towards the cathedral he thought about what exactly he wanted to shoot. He had already satisfied himself that he was not here to atone, in some obscure way, for thinking ill of a man who had subsequently, tragically and prematurely, passed on. Nor had he any interest in recording the formal ceremony, the slowly passing hearse, the tricolour-draped coffin, the weeping widow, the mound of floral tributes, the mournful faces of cabinet colleagues. Let the official news cameramen do that. Baz wanted to shoot faces in the crowd; reveal how ordinary people behaved at such an extraordinary event. Could the lens discover their true thoughts?

It was easy to get through the crowd-control barriers at Mulgrave Street because he had an impressive-looking camera on his shoulder and he flashed his old RTE staff card. Baz was surprised at how many people had gathered. Crowds were lined on both sides of Cathedral Place down to where he could see the funeral cortege begin its journey. Ahead of him, Mulgrave Street was packed as far as it was possible to see. He realised immediately that, with the cortege moving slowly, it would be easy to keep ahead of it, finding faces, capturing reactions as they watched Dom's remains pass by. He chose a first position on the corner of Mulgrave Street and Cathedral Place and scanned the crowd on a tight lens. People were chatting amongst themselves, some jigging a little because they had been waiting so long in the cold.

He panned and stopped, arrested by the face of a man in his late twenties with longish fair hair. The man appeared to be alone – at least he was not talking or listening to anyone. There was something deeply sad about his face in repose. And photogenic too – although of course it was faces of character that Baz was after, not beauty. Still, there was something oddly compelling about this delicate face. Why did he look so sad? It felt like an odd question to ask about someone at a funeral but, after all, the fellow was not a participant, just a face in a crowd of onlookers. The cortege had not even approached yet. Had this striking young man been so deeply affected by Dom's death, or was he preoccupied with some other melancholic thought? Perhaps his face always had this quality. Baz was strongly tempted to stay focused on him until the hearse passed, but reminded himself that he was not in search of the unusual, the extraordinary, *l'étranger* in the crowd. So he panned away from the young man, looking for more typical subjects.

Brendan Barry, entirely unaware that he had been under the scrutiny of a camera lens, was actually thinking about Gavin Bloom. He had, quite suddenly and inexplicably, felt lonely. Everyone around him seemed to be chatting, exchanging easy clichés about Dom, what a character he was, what a loss he would be to the city and the nation, how sad for his wife and children. Brendan had wanted his own wife and child to come with him today but Elizabeth would not hear of Ian going. It wasn't good for him, apparently. What wasn't? Reality? He was sick of this bullshit and pretence. When Gavin Bloom came into his head he wondered, at first, why him, out of all the men who passed his way? Though he had been with him more often than anyone else in the last two years, he had never thought of this as meaning anything. Maybe Brendan thought of him now because he knew Gavin would be a good laugh at an occasion like this, although of course such a thing could never happen. It was unimaginable, the notion of the pair of them standing together, part of a crowd in his own town, chatting away, like they'd done in Bartley Dunne's or as they rolled back to Gavin's flat, holding each other upright, laughing like lunatics.

Along with everyone around him Brendan automatically blessed himself as the coffin passed and remembered how, years before, as a young, inexperienced and rather fragile night manager, he had to help haul a crazily drunk and belligerent Dom away from poor old Mattie, the night porter. It took three of them, himself and two Party associates, to subdue him. Brendan remembered hanging on his back, simultaneously terrified and excited. Dom had been like a bucking bronco. Later, when he got home, he woke Elizabeth, partly to tell her the story, partly because of an urgent desire to make love. That definitely dated it. If they were still having sex, then Ian would have been only an infant. So long ago. The hearse had disappeared. Dom had passed on. Only then did Brendan recall that on the night he first met Gavin, Dom had been there too. Strange. He made up his mind to find an excuse to go to Dublin as soon as he could.

*

There was no one else in the house now. All was silent. Francis was in his mam and dad's bedroom staring at a mound of loose change on the windowsill. Pennies, threepences and even the odd sixpenny piece – chickens and rabbits and greyhounds. Every night when his dad came home from work he always emptied his pockets and threw the coins onto the sill. He might do this for a few nights before sorting and counting them. Francis, still brooding about his Hardy Boys book, had remembered this money and gone in to see what was there. It was quite a big pile. If he took sixpence his dad wouldn't even notice, and sixpence was all he needed. After all, if the Minister hadn't died he would have been at school today and his mam would have given him sixpence for bus fare. So it wasn't really stealing. But was it so hard to wait one more day? He could buy *The Secret of Wildcat Swamp* on Thursday instead. But he had been counting the days and saving for the last three weeks. All he had thought about was going to O'Mahony's straight after school tomorrow. He was only sixpence short. He looked at the mound of coins. There were loads of pennies and plenty of threepences but not many sixpenny pieces. If he took three pennies and a threepenny piece and, if he removed them very carefully without disturbing the pile, then no one would know. But Francis couldn't stop a question coming into his head. Would Frank and Joe steal money from their father, Fenton Hardy, the renowned private investigator? He knew the answer was no. But it wasn't the same thing at all because Frank and Joe never seemed to need money. They drove a car and had their own motorboat and a phone in the house as well as a shortwave radio. He couldn't imagine the Hardy Boys ever being short of sixpence for anything.

Francis thought of the cover picture of *The Secret of Wildcat Swamp*, with the wildcat on the rock above Frank and Joe, waiting to pounce. He thought of having the book in his hands and couldn't stop himself reaching out to lift three heavy brown pennies from different parts of the pile. He saw a little silver threepence that looked easy to dislodge. He plucked it out, stuffed the coins in his pocket and ran out of the bedroom.

*

The official funeral disappeared into the cemetery. Baz did not attempt to follow. It was over now, as far as he was concerned. He slumped on the edge of the O'Grady monument at Munster Fair Tavern. He placed the Éclair carefully on the ground between his legs and rubbed his aching right shoulder. The experience of the last twenty minutes had been a strange one, woven from a complex mosaic of faces. He had moved along Mulgrave Street just ahead of the hearse, his eye pressed to the viewfinder most of the time, scanning the crowd in search of interesting subjects. It was on-the-fly, seat-of-his-pants, *cinéma verité*, but he had managed to grab a truly fascinating random sample of the inhabitants of this tough old city. Certain faces and reactions lingered in his mind. The old fellow, with a shock of white hair, and ears that were almost the length of his head, who didn't seem to be aware of the tears spilling down his broken-veined cheeks. A trendy young one with a brand-new short-cropped hairdo and dangly earrings got so lost in her sorrow that she forgot about the cigarette burning away in her hand. A little kid with a mournful face, perfect for the day that was in it, kept nervously biting his lip and looking up at the adults around him as if needing to be reassured that the whole thing was not his fault. And Baz had filmed so many more, two rolls of faces etched with genuine grief and sense of loss. It was, looking at it in one way, quite mad. None of these onlookers knew who this dead man really was. It was quite probable that most of them had never met or spoken to him. Of course, in truth, they were not mourning the death of an actual man at all, but of a persona they really did know, a persona called Dom. He was what Yeats had described: 'Character, isolated by a deed, to engross the present and dominate memory.' Baz knew now he had been obtuse ever to ask himself who the man really was. It was entirely the wrong question. The crowds that gathered in sorrow had got it right. They understood that it wasn't just the man who had passed on, the flawed, complex human that almost no one could claim honestly to know, but that their favourite character, Dom, had died too. He was gone and something had gone with him. Perhaps all those faces Baz caught on camera looked bereft because they sensed that it was Hope lying in that hearse, under that tricolour.

Twenty-seven: June 6th

The plan had been to take off somewhere for the day. Wicklow. Brittas Bay, if it was warm enough for swimming. Gavin would organise a picnic. There were lots of secluded dunes if the notion took them. Brendan said he expected to reach Dublin around midday. When he arrived at the flat, Gavin was ready with food and swimming gear but had just one request. The radio news had said the American embassy was opening a book of condolences for Robert Kennedy. Ballsbridge wasn't really out of their way. They should go and sign it. Brendan shrugged and said, 'Why not?'

Both men were surprised at the length of the queue that snaked round from the embassy building up Clyde road, almost as far as St Bartholomew's church. Brendan's immediate reaction was that they should forget about it and go, but Gavin felt they might as well wait, now that they were here. People continued to arrive and soon at least another hundred were behind them. All along the line there was this mood for talking. Everyone saying the same things over and over: another Kennedy dead, so soon after Martin Luther King, something dangerous in the air. The chat rippled freely through the crowd. Gavin, used to engaging with strangers, was enjoying himself hugely amongst all these like-minded people so, when he first noticed Brendan's unease, he assumed it was only because the line was not moving. After fifteen minutes, word trickled back that the embassy wouldn't be letting anyone in until two o'clock. Brendan immediately said they should go. Now.

It was only thinking about it afterwards that Gavin understood more fully why Brendan had not liked being in that queue of people, out in the June sunshine, yapping on about Kennedy and King, the May riots and Vietnam. It was because it had dawned on him that all the people around them had recognised and taken for granted what he and Gavin were – a couple. And whereas Gavin was beginning to sense how much he liked this situation, Brendan already knew he did not.

The line finally began to move, but still far too slowly. When, after another half an hour, it was clear that it would be at least as long again before they got to sign the book, Brendan muttered that, at this stage, they could forget about Brittas because by the time they got there it would be more or less time to turn around and go home. Gavin, feeling the need to adopt a similar whispered tone, said no big deal, they could do something else. Brendan said what? Gavin said whatever, relax, they could decide. Brendan said, fine, he'd go and relax over a pint in Paddy Cullen's and wait for Gavin there. Gavin said, surely, having stayed this long he might as well hang on. Brendan said he'd prefer to hang on in the comfort of Paddy Cullen's. Gavin wanted to shout after him as he walked away, but couldn't bring himself to do it. He also wanted to scamper after him, but wouldn't let himself do that. Alone now in the queue, he stopped chatting with those around him. Had they noticed this humiliating incident. Were they sniggering quietly?

After signing the book, Gavin left the embassy and began walking towards Paddy Cullen's, but at the bridge he stopped, bewildered, angry, the truth of the situation becoming clear. Brendan Barry had been uneasy for exactly the same reason Gavin had been content. There was no point in pretending otherwise. So what was he to do about that? He didn't know why an approaching number 8 bus, heading towards the city centre, prompted an immediate decision, but as he ran across the road waving it down, all Gavin was sure of was that he didn't feel like seeing Brendan at that moment. Possibly ever again.

*

If she lived to be a hundred Ann would never understand why Mary Storan got most of her groceries in Curtin's. The prices they charged! Worse, she kept a book, so it cost her even more. It wasn't as if she couldn't afford to pay cash – Mikey earned more than Fonsie. Why not do a weekly shop at Winston and Besco's, pay cash and get everything cheaper? If she only bothered to organise herself, she could be like Ann and go on Tuesdays for the double Green Shield stamps. But there was no talking to her. Ann, waiting just inside the door, watched the eldest daughter of the Curtins unhook the old copybook with Mary's name on it. It drove Ann mad to look at Dympna Curtin, with her scraggy orange hair and a nose on her like a bird's beak, calling out every last item, for the whole shop to hear, as she wrote it into the copybook: 'Two packs Craven "A", cottage loaf, half-pound of cooked ham, one tin of Batchelors…'

Mary said, 'Thanks Dympna,' and picked up her shopping bag. 'Thanks indeed,' Ann thought, 'thanks for robbing her.' Of course she bought the odd thing in Curtin's herself when she was stuck and she knew the children bought penny sweets and ice-pops, but that was it. Glad to be getting out, she turned and saw, through the glass panel of the shop door, Francis walking up the road towards her.

'Look at him.'

Francis was now very near the shop. Ann put her hand on Mary's arm to stop her leaving.

'What? What's up?'

'He's coming home from school. Why isn't he on the bus? Why is he walking home?'

Mary was surprised at how agitated Ann seemed to be getting. As Francis passed by, she pulled back to make sure he didn't see her, then she opened Curtin's door and peeped out after him.

'Sure, Ann, I often see him walking home. He passes the flat.'

'What?'

'I see him walking in to school as well, the odd time.'

'What!'

Mary wondered if she'd opened her big mouth a bit too wide, but honestly, what harm was there in the child walking home from school? Sure he'd be nine next week. Was Ann afraid he'd get knocked down or what?

'I thought you were getting him to do it to make sure he got a bit of exercise.'

Ann had now left the shop and was watching her youngest disappear up the road.

'But I give him his bus money every day, every single day. And you see him walking in to school as well as walking home?'

'Well, a few times. But I mean, it's not doing him any harm is it? Here, come on and we go back for a cuppa.'

By the time Mary got her to the flat and made the tea, Ann had revealed the whole story. On the previous Wednesday night, while Fonsie and the boys were glued to the telly watching Manchester United in the European Cup final, Ann had decided this was a good time to do a proper clean-up of the boys' room. All these Hardy Boys books that Francis was obsessed with were thrown everywhere, of course, and she was stacking them neatly when, whatever way she looked, she noticed the price on the inside cover of one of them: seven and six.

'Jesus, Mary and Joseph! I never knew they were that dear, Mary. And he has seven of them. Now, one he got from Marg Strong for Christmas but he bought the rest himself. Six Hardy Boys books? At seven and six each? Where did he get the money? Of course, I said nothing about it to Fonsie, but God forgive me, Mary, I started thinking, what if he was stealing them out of the shop?'

'Ah, Ann. Francis? No.'

'I know, but still, stranger things have happened.'

'And now you're wondering if he paid for them out of his bus money?'

'What do you think?'

'I'd say you might be right. And sure, if you are, isn't that grand?'

'How is it grand?'

'Well now, Ann, it's a lot better than stealing.'

Mary Storan had a point, and her casual good humour about the situation helped calm Ann.

'I mean, wouldn't it be worse if he was spending it on fags like some youngfellahs? And isn't reading supposed to be a good thing?'

Ann had had far more worrying thoughts about how Francis was getting his hands on these books, so this solution to the mystery didn't seem so bad at all. In a way she had to hand it to the child for being clever enough to think of it. Of course Fonsie would never see it that way. Dishonesty was one of those things that really made him angry. He'd say that, by taking money for bus fare and spending it on himself, Francis was as good as stealing.

When Ann got home there wasn't a sound in the house. Marian had started her Inter Cert yesterday so she wouldn't be home yet. Ann automatically said a quick prayer that things had gone well for her today. Martin was probably above in Baker's field with his pals. She tiptoed upstairs. Francis was in the boys' bedroom, lying on the top bunk, utterly unaware of her presence, his face hidden behind his latest Hardy Boys book. She could see the title: *The Sinister Signpost.* He was never happier or quieter than when he was reading. She'd love to find out for certain how he was paying for those books. Then she thought of something. The school holidays were starting in a couple of weeks and, when they did, Francis wouldn't be getting his daily bus money. So, if she was right, that would put a halt to his little gallop for the summer at least. Ann decided there was no point in telling Fonsie about this. Better to wait, say nothing and watch what happened when the holidays started. She'd enjoy solving this little mystery all on her own.

*

After three pints, it dawned on Brendan Barry that something was up. Gavin was not coming. He rang the flat from the coinbox in Cullen's. After another pint he rang again. And a third time. Then he drove to the flat and buzzed and buzzed. Brendan went off for a few more pints and brooded. Around midnight he came back to the flat and buzzed and buzzed and buzzed. This time he could see a light on in what he knew was one of Gavin's windows. Part of him felt like kicking the door down, but instead he thought fuck him and decided, on the spot, to drive home. Thirty miles out of Dublin, tired and blinded by stupid bastards who wouldn't dim their lights, Brendan began to regret his choice. He could have done something else, he could have gone to Bartley's and picked someone up, got himself a free bed and a warm body. Too late to turn back now, there'd be nothing doing at this hour. Ninety miles to go.

By the time he finally sat in his own driveway, still a bit drunk, Brendan's only desire was to be left alone in the world. No hassle, no aggro of any kind. Just slip into the house and tiptoe to the spare room. Escape into sleep for a few hours.

Even closing the car door as quietly as possible, it still sounded like a pistol shot. The front door was easier to manage. He was in. Now the stairs. He eased himself down to the second-from-bottom step and started to slip off his shoes.

Click! His own bent-out-of-shape shadow appeared on the floor in front of him as the landing light fell on him. It was a couple of seconds before he could bear to look up at Elizabeth. If she was surprised at his return, there was no sign of it on her face. She'd probably seen his car from the bedroom window. Even in this situation, there were no questions. Husband and wife just stared at each other silently for a couple of seconds and, before Brendan could think of anything to say she, very quietly, spoke: 'Don't wake Ian.' And went back to bed.

Twenty-eight: October 5th

Gussie had been thinking about going to America long before Mike Dwane sent the photo of himself with a gang at some beach party. He was stripped to the waist, with his hair gone long and stringy, looking completely off his face. On the back of the photo he'd scribbled, 'Where it's at man!' and underneath he wrote in brackets, 'I rode the bird on the left!!' She had gleaming teeth and luscious tanned skin. Had he really? Mike was a bit of a hammer man, all right. He'd qualified as a waiter in May and was off like a greyhound out of the traps. The thing was, for Gussie, going to America actually had nothing to do with beach parties or getting high or riding women, although he wouldn't say no to any of that. It was about something else entirely, something he didn't even dare put a name on, something that went back to the time he talked to Richard Harris. Even before that, maybe, only he never knew it. So far he hadn't told anyone what he was thinking. When he heard some of the other lads in the catering school talking about emigrating, he kept his trap shut. He had been saving, though, and surprised himself by putting away enough to get as far as California. Once he got there, any old job would do at first and then he'd see if there was a chance at all. Some kind of a start.

In films. That's what he wanted.

Gussie knew all the terms: Clapper Loader, Focus Puller, Operator, Gaffer, Best Boy. He'd love any job like that. Surely it was possible. In California it was probably just a trade like any other. He knew a lot about camerawork already. His head was so full of it, it was bursting to get out. At least in California he could say it out loud. Tell other people. They wouldn't laugh at him. So now the only question was when to go. The start of next year was sort of in his head, but that was coming very soon and he hadn't really made his mind up. It was his brother Ritchie helped him decide – though he didn't know it.

Lately, Gussie had been getting really sick and tired of Ritchie this and Ritchie that at home. It would give an aspro a headache. All coming from his mam, of course. Ritchie had qualified in August and Krups had asked him to stay on full time. Got down on their knees and begged, judging by the way his mam told the story. Gave him a huge rise. Ritchie had a lovely girlfriend from a respectable family. Doing a strong line for nearly a year now, wasn't that great? His mam wondered why Gussie never brought a girlfriend home. Gussie would have loved to tell her that, even if he went out with someone long enough – which he hadn't – the last thing he'd ever think of doing would be to go through all the shite of bringing a girl home for tea. But he never said that, of course. This week, though, he'd had enough, mainly because of all the *Oklahoma* stuff, which had given him a massive pain in the hole.

What happened was Áine, the girlfriend his mam was mad about, had persuaded Ritchie to join this musical society. His mam was thrilled skinny; oh, much nicer than those old pop bands Ritchie used to be involved in and didn't herself and Fonsie love going to the musicals anyway. The big show of the year was on this week: *Oklahoma*. Ritchie and Áine were both in the chorus and Áine's mother and father were in the show as well, playing big parts. His mam nearly had a conniption when she realised that Áine's father and mother were Cormac and Louise Kiely. She kept saying wasn't that amazing now, because she and Fonsie had seen them lots of times over the years in *The Merry Widow* and *The Desert Song* and *South Pacific*. They were both great performers. His mam couldn't wait to see the show and everyone who crossed her path in the last week got a dose of *Oklahoma* and Ritchie and the Kielys. Gussie had been in a foul mood at work all day yesterday because he was so sick of listening to her.

'Final call for Aer Lingus flight EI 105 to New York, JFK.'

Gussie heard this announcement every working day. Normally it was just a routine crackle of words. This time it made something go off in his head. Final call. It made up his mind for him.

This morning he'd gone to a travel agency and found out exactly how much a flight to New York or LA in early January would be. He hadn't made his mind up whether he would go and check out the Big Apple for a few days first and then hire a car and mosey across America or just get an immediate connection to LA. Gussie really liked the driving idea but if he was on his own mightn't it be a bit lonely and dangerous? And California would be warm at that time of year, so maybe it made more sense to fly there straight off. Anyway, the important thing was that he had made up his mind he was going. Once he told his mam and dad, then he really would be breaking free.

On the way back from the travel agent Gussie dropped into the Spotted Dog for a small one just to get himself in the right frame of mind for talking to his mam. Then he walked home quickly before the effect wore off. At first he had the impression that his mam didn't understand what he was telling her; next thing he couldn't get a word in edgeways.

'What? What are you talking about? – Is this the latest? Another of your notions? – Are you out of your mind? Will you go 'way and cop yourself on, you're not even qualified – oh sure, I know you know it all, you didn't even need training – well you're not going, it's as simple as that. You can put that right out of your head – 'twould be more in your line to start looking for jobs for when you qualify. Look at the big raise Ritchie is after getting – You're not and that's that! – Don't you dare raise your voice to me! Jesus, Mary and Joseph! If my blood pressure goes up because of you!'

The mistake had been to talk to his mam first instead of his dad, but the damage was done now. Every time he'd opened his mouth she'd just screamed back at him. She went right off the deep end. Lucky she hadn't got the smell of drink off him as well. In the boys' bedroom, Gussie, sullen, raging, but a bit frightened at how demented his mam had got, waited for his dad to come home. It was really quiet downstairs now, although he did hear her snapping at Martin and Francis a couple of times. Well, he was sure about one thing. She wasn't going to treat him like Martin or Francis. He was nearly twenty and well able to look after himself. She could lose her head and scream and roar and go into convulsions if she wanted. He was going to America, simple as that. What was the big deal, anyway? Mike Dwane was younger than he was and his parents had had no problem with him going.

He heard his dad come in and then her squawking away. Not a word out of poor Dad, of course. Gussie felt a bit sorry for him. Just what he needed on his day off. Well, he'd have to sort it out with her because Gussie had made his mind up and that was that. Footsteps on the stairs. The door opened quietly. Gussie sat up in the bed. His dad looked at him, searching for something to say.

'Mam's very upset… What did you have to go and upset her for?'

'I just told her I'm going to America. What's the big deal?'

'And you didn't think that would upset her?'

'Why should it?'

'You know how much she worries about all of you. Of course she was going to get upset.'

'I don't see why.'

'Because you're walking away from your apprenticeship. But apart from that, you should have been thinking more about not upsetting your mother. You remember what happened last year the way she ended up in hospital –?'

'That was completely different. Francis was after getting a belt of a hurley.'

'It doesn't matter what causes the upset. It just shouldn't happen at all. When I left the house today she was in great form, looking forward to seeing Ritchie tonight in *Oklahoma* –'

How Gussie didn't swear out loud when his dad mentioned Ritchie and fucking *Oklahoma* he would never know.

'– next thing I come home and you've caused holy war. Now I don't want you upsetting her again, do you hear me now?'

'I wasn't trying to.'

'Well don't, then. Have a bit of consideration.'

Gussie wondered if that was that. His dad seemed to have finished giving out, but still stood there. Was it over or not? It wasn't.

'The best thing is if we hear no more about this… this idea of yours for a while, all right.'

'Dad, I've made up my mind. I'm going to America –'

'I'm not saying you're not. All I'm saying is, don't upset your mother about it. Won't that make everything much easier in the long run?'

Gussie shrugged. It was impossible to argue with his dad's quiet tone.

'Just… give it a bit of time. How long more before you qualify?'

'Nearly a year, but I'm not waiting until then.'

'I'm not saying that. I'm just saying think about what you want to do but think about your mother as well, and don't be going out of your way to upset her.'

'I'm not going to say I'm not going.'

'You don't have to say anything. The best thing now is for no one to say anything, all right?'

Gussie, for peace's sake, nodded.

*

For however long it lasted, Baz Malloy forgot he was physically present in the middle of this mayhem on a street in Derry. There was only the reality of the shot. He rolled camera and framed two uniformed RUC men. The older one was barking into a megaphone, the other whispering into a small transmitter clipped to his lapel. Baz panned to a line of uniformed backs pushing forward against a crowd of protestors. He followed the line, which broke and shifted. A baton suddenly appeared in the centre of his frame, as one of the RUC men lifted it shoulder-high in readiness. Baz managed to hold it in shot for a few seconds before it disappeared into a convulsion of bodies. In the corner of the frame he glimpsed two officers drag someone away. He was about to pan with them when a banner appeared in shot: CIVIL RIGHTS MARCH. The protesters carrying it were attempting to push past the police line. The banner twisted and fell. A few of the protestors stumbled through and, as bodies surged forward, Baz was knocked back, but something prevented him falling, a car he guessed, but there was no time to look. He framed again as some of the policemen grabbed the banner from the protesters and re-formed their line. Baz tracked in closer and closer. Despite being surrounded by dozens of police and protestors, no one looked down his lens. It was as if he wasn't really there. On the left of his frame the police line was now holding firm, on the right there were hands raised in Nazi salute and Baz could hear clearly what the protestors were shouting: '*Sieg heil! Sieg heil!*' When the RUC pushed forward, Baz lost his position and, for a moment, all he could see in the frame was the back of a police cap in massive close-up, then he bumped against another parked car.

By the time he twisted his body round to the other side, the march had become a running battle. Now he could forget any notions he might have had of lens-changing and refocusing. He'd have to keep it wide and loose if he was to have any chance of shooting something decent. As he ran with the crowd, Baz roamed left and right, searching for meaningful action. For several long seconds the shot was nothing more than a confusion of bodies retreating down the street. For no reason, other than that he suddenly appeared cleanly in the middle of frame, Baz targeted a young officer who casually pushed protestors back as he moved across the road. When the young officer raised his baton, utterly without warning, and whipped it across the ear of a man who was walking away from him, not even looking in his direction, Baz was perfectly positioned and caught the moment clearly, in all its terrifying nonchalance. He was no more than two feet away as the man roared and dropped. If Baz had been standing there as a normal observer instead of behind a lens he would have instantly backed away in shock and horror, but because the film was now the reality, he held the young policeman in frame and pursued him without wavering. Sure enough, it wasn't long before he found another head to crack. As this victim fell, an older RUC officer ran into shot and grabbed his young colleague as if trying to calm him. Then a woman, hardly more than a girl, appeared and stood protectively in front of the injured protestor, who was still on the ground. Baz liked the way his framing emphasised the incongruity of a handbag hooked safely on her arm even in the midst of crisis. The tableau was erased as RUC men spilled into the foreground, all with batons raised. Baz briefly discovered one of the injured protestors being helped to his feet, but a moment later the frame was invaded by a running maul. Panning, he spotted an older officer chasing a protestor, who tripped and fell. Baz surged closer and, in contrast to the casual assault he had caught on camera earlier, this time he bore witness to an angry beating. The officer wielded a long black stick with both hands and with such force that his own hat fell off to reveal a surprisingly distinguished head of white hair. He stopped the beating to pick up his hat and, as he put it on, seemed to glance directly into camera. Baz realised that, for the only time since he had started shooting, someone was looking him in the eye. Then the white-haired officer ducked away into a muddle of uniforms. Baz did not try to pursue him, but stayed focused on the victim, a young man wearing, of all things, a three-piece suit. Two friends dragged him to his feet. Everywhere Baz now pointed his camera he found RUC men roaming, batons ready. He saw one officer raise his toward a protestor who just managed to leap across a car before the blow fell. Baz followed this policeman, keeping him cleanly in frame, but the RUC man had found no other victims when, less than a minute later, the roll of film ran out.

Baz finally plucked his eye from the viewfinder and let the Éclair sink down by his side. The noise of the street seemed much greater and, for the first time, he felt unsafe. He retreated to the nearest shop entrance and looked for the quickest, safest route back to where Miriam would be waiting, near the Guildhall. Hopefully she had managed to stay out of danger.

Baz experienced a moment of sentimental melodrama when he saw Miriam waiting at their car, anxiously scanning the landscape. She didn't quite come running towards him in slo-mo, but her embrace when he got to her was intense, even though she managed to make her voice sound relaxed.

'So, you weren't sure if you'd get any interesting material at this peaceful civil rights march?'

Baz smiled and described what his lens had witnessed as best he could. In retelling the story he experienced a growing elation. Miriam said this footage should be broadcast somewhere straight away, it sounded remarkable. Baz said perhaps, but there were other cameramen there too. On the long drive back to Rossaveel they talked and talked, trying to make some sense of what had occurred today. Neither of them had ever been to Derry before. Baz had never even crossed the border. Miriam had once visited the Giant's Causeway in 1960 when she was still in art college. She wondered was this eruption just part of the student unrest that was sweeping across the US and Europe or was it a purely Irish row, some kind of reawakening of old sectarian hatreds? Unfinished business. Baz admitted he had never had the slightest interest in the North until a couple of hours ago. Even the instinct that brought him here today had been casual, just another small element in the project he had been slowly developing since March. But now? Well. For the length of a roll of film today, a street in Derry had become his only reality. He had engaged with an intensity that he had never experienced in his whole career. He remembered how, when shooting *Insurrection* in studio a few years back, he had rehearsed and rehearsed every nuance of a complicated crane shot that snaked through the burning GPO to find Pearse standing alone facing the flames. Making art out of history. But today's urgent, spontaneous, unrehearsed, jagged encounter felt much more like true art. Wasn't this what Capa had done at Normandy? Baz told Miriam how, in the moment, he had experienced the thrill of being the one allowed to choose – admittedly without any time to think about it – which fragments of a historic moment to record and which to exclude. He was also conscious of uglier instincts it brought to the surface. Already he understood that his motive for tracking after that RUC man at the end was in the hope that the guy would assault someone else, and that his instinctive disappointment when the film ran out was because he hadn't managed to complete his shot on a suitably operatic moment of violence.

*

Ritchie threw a punch and the farmer tumbled over. For a second Ann thought he really had hit him. It was so well done. Then farmers and cowmen rushed at each other and a big fight started. The audience laughed. Áine's father, Cormac Kiely, who was playing Zeke, separated them and started singing about how the farmer and the cowman should be friends. Fonsie always liked Cormac Kiely in these shows. He mightn't be the world's best baritone, but he had great stage presence and really knew how to perform a song. He was always a big favourite with the audience. Ann kept watching Ritchie to see if he was doing all his actions right. She thought he looked lovely in his check shirt and cowboy hat with the yellow handkerchief around his neck. And his dancing was much better than she'd expected. He was as good as any of them. Of course, the chorus had been rehearsing every night for weeks. The Cecilians had a very high standard. It took her ages to spot Áine, on account of her wig. If it hadn't been for that big smile she wouldn't have recognised her at all. Ann thought it was lovely that Ritchie and her had been put together for the barndance. They both looked like they were having a great time.

When another fight broke out, with the women joining in this time, Louise Kiely, who was playing Aunt Eller, came forward and fired a gun in the air. It was so loud even the audience got a fright. The music stopped and so did the fighting. All the farmers and cowmen looked really scared as Aunt Eller walked up to Zeke and pointed her gun at him. When she told him to sing, and he started off in a frightened, quavery voice, Ann heard Francis laugh out loud. Then the orchestra joined in, really fast this time, and everyone started singing and dancing and all the territory folk were pals again. Ann thought it was just lovely. She had completely forgotten the bad mood she had been in since her row with Gussie. She glanced over at Fonsie, who was tapping his knee along with the music. He looked and whispered, 'The orchestra is very good, isn't it?' She smiled back and nodded. Everyone was very good. It was all beautiful and bright, the music, the singing, the acting, the dancing, the colour and light. She was so happy that Ritchie was part of this and meeting lots of nice people. She looked over at Marian and Francis and could see that both of them were enjoying the show too. Francis, especially, was glued to it. Marian really was getting more confident about herself since she got such good results in her Inter Cert. Maybe she might think of joining the musical society? She wasn't much for singing but she'd be great backstage. The other fellah, of course, would love to be up there showing off.

When the show finished with a 'Yeow!' from everyone onstage, the packed audience in the Crescent Hall clapped and cheered and whistled. Because it was the last night they did a little encore of 'The Farmer and the Cowman' and the audience clapped along and sang. Ann noticed that Francis was singing all the words. How in God's name was he able to do that after only hearing it once? She nudged Fonsie, 'Do you hear this?' He listened for a couple of seconds and said in his dry way, 'Well, he might be a play-actor but we can forget about him being a singer.'

There was a party afterwards. Ann and Fonsie were invited. Áine had told them there was no problem with Marian and Francis going along, but Fonsie said that as it was already eleven o'clock he'd drop Francis home to bed and come back. Ann asked did he really think there was any hope of getting that child to go home without an argument and pussing? Anyway look, she pointed out, Áine's youngest sister – what was her name? – she was only around nine, too, and she was still here. Fonsie gave up.

As the performers came back out in their party clothes and the room filled up, Francis enjoyed wandering around, looking, listening and trying to recognise people from the show. Everyone was happy and excited and there was lots of squealing and squawking and shrieking. He spotted the man who played Curly. He looked older in real life. It was easy to recognise the woman who played Ado Annie because of her nose. Francis started singing her song, 'I'm Just a Girl Who Can't Say No', to himself. It was his second favourite song in the show after 'The Farmer and the Cowman'. He could remember all the words of the first part and most of the second part. He saw Mr and Mrs Kiely talking to his mam and dad. Mam had her biggest smile on. Francis was glad. She'd been in such a rotten temper all day after that row with Gussie, he'd been afraid they wouldn't go to the show at all, but now she seemed really happy. Music and singing always made her feel better.

Francis looked hungrily at the long table full of sandwiches and buns. He wished somebody would start eating so he could, too. Everyone was so busy drinking they weren't bothered about the food. He saw a man giving Marian a glass of something. She looked around and then shook her head but he smiled and tried to put it in her hand. She said no again but she was smiling, too. Francis recognised him now as the fellow who played Will Parker.

There was a strange-looking man at the far end of the table. He stood dead straight with one hand resting on his hip and a drink in the other hand, which he held close to his mouth as he looked around. He had a particular look on his face. Francis tried to think of a good word to describe it. A glare? No. A grimace? No. A scowl? Sort of. Then he remembered a word from the Just William books. It described the look on Violet Elizabeth's face: a pout. There was something else strange about the man. Francis studied him, trying to figure out the mystery. Then he realised. The man with the pout was wearing make-up. There were dark lines and some blue around his eyes. His lips looked pink and shiny. He must have forgotten to take it off. Francis tried to remember him from the show. Was he in the chorus? He was about the same age as Ritchie and he definitely hadn't played Curly or Will or Judd or… Just then, because of the way the man with the pout stretched his neck as he looked around, Francis remembered him. He was the Dream Curly in the ballet part of the show, the part that Francis thought had gone on too long and didn't seem to fit with the rest. And now the dancer himself didn't seem to fit in at the party either. Francis couldn't stop staring at him, though he wasn't sure why. As if there was a mystery to solve. Some secret. Ritchie and Áine appeared in front of him, holding hands.

'Hey, Fran, did you like the show?' Francis said it was brilliant.

'Oooh, I'm delighted you enjoyed yourself!' said Áine and when Francis told her he thought Mrs Kiely was very funny, Áine shrieked with laughter. 'Oooh, God now! Don't say that to my father. He thinks he's the funny one in the family. Oh, Ritchie, look! Peter's chatting up your Marian. You never know! Franny, don't move now for a sec. There's someone I want you to meet.' Áine ran off. Francis started asking Ritchie questions about the show. How often did they have to practice the dances? Who told them when to go onstage? Why did they all have orange faces? He had heaps more questions but Áine came back, dragging a little girl with her. She was nearly the same height as Francis with coloured ribbons in her hair.

'Now Gráinne honey, this is Francis. He's Ritchie's little brother, remember I told you about him? And Francis, this is my baby sister Gráinne.'

Francis didn't know what he was supposed to say and the girl looked on the ground and didn't say anything either. Áine thought this was very funny. 'Ah, they're shy. Well, maybe you won't be so shy one of these days. Now, come on and we'll get you something nice.' She was already holding her sister's hand and now she grabbed Francis. He didn't like this but, as she was pulling them to the food table, he went along with it. Áine kept laughing and talking as she filled up plates for them. Then she told Ritchie to get serviettes and brought them over to two empty chairs. 'Sit down there and have a nice chat, the pair of you.' Ritchie gave them serviettes and Áine put the plates on their laps. 'Ah, don't they look sweet! Enjoy yourselves now.'

She put her arm around Ritchie's waist and they tripped off. Francis started eating one of his sandwiches. He was afraid even to look at Áine's sister because he couldn't think of anything to say to her. Now Áine was talking to his mam and dad, and her mother and father, pointing over at them. They were all smiling. Francis tried to think of things to say, but everything he thought of was stupid. Anyway, he didn't really want to talk to Áine's sister. He wanted to sit on his own looking at the grown-ups drinking and laughing. Where was the man with the pout? Francis looked all around, but there was no sign of him. If he'd left the party with his makeup still on, people in the street would be laughing at him. Francis hoped someone warned him. Out of the corner of his eye, he noticed the girl's small hand pick up a bun. At least she was eating. If she talked to him he'd talk back. But she didn't. So the two nine-year-olds sat side by side, eating. Silent.

1969

Twenty-nine: January 10th

'Most of you made a great effort. Some of you just didn't bother and that gets on my wick. I get very annoyed when I see fellahs who are well capable of doing something not even trying. But most of you tried very hard, I have to say. I know it wasn't an easy composition to do.'

The boys of 4A murmured in agreement with that. Mr Wade smiled.

'But that's why you're in the "A" class. It's not supposed to be easy. Think of it this way: if I gave you a composition called "A report on last week's episode of… say… *Daniel Boone*" you'd have written pages and pages. This composition isn't really any different.'

Mr Wade turned and looked at the blackboard. On it was written 'A report from Northern Ireland'.

'Imagine there was a big row on your street and all your neighbours were fighting and setting fire to things and the police had to be called in –'

4A laughed.

'I know, it's funny to think of it, but if it happened it wouldn't be so funny. So. Imagine you arrive into class the next day and I ask you to give me a report on the big row that happened on your street the night before. You'd all be full of it, every single one of you would be able to stand up and tell me all about it. Isn't that right?'

Most of 4A mumbled 'Yes sir' reluctantly. Mr Wade picked up a copybook and opened it as he spoke. 'Now, like I said, a lot of you made a good fist of it. But there was one composition that, to my mind, really stood out. It was so good I'm going to ask the boy who wrote it to read it out for the class.'

This was something new. Mr Wade never asked boys to read out ecker. Francis looked at the copybook in Mr Wade's hand. He wished it was him. More than anything he wanted it to be him, even though he knew it would be John Hennessy, who always came first in exams, or maybe Anthony Doyle, who was the fastest at working out sums and brilliant at spelling, or even his best pal Ian, who always came in the top four. Francis had never been higher than fourteenth. He looked around, feeling really jealous.

'Francis Strong, *tar anseo*.'

It wasn't until he felt Tommy Quinn, who sat next to him, pushing him in the back and he saw Ian grinning over at him and nodding to him to stand up and he looked again at Mr Wade smiling at him, holding out the copybook, that Francis was sure his name really had been called. He got up and walked to Mr Wade's desk.

'*Anois! Bígí ciúin a bhuachaillí!* Francis is going to read out his report from Northern Ireland.'

Francis opened the copybook and looked down at the handwriting that Mr Wade was always telling him was grubby and careless and had to improve. The class was silent. Now he didn't dare look up because he knew that some of them would be making faces and messing and trying to put him off. He was nearly afraid to open his mouth in case his heart would jump out of it. This was the best thing that ever happened to him in his whole life. When he read out the name of the composition, he could barely hear his own voice. He tried to make it sound stronger.

> 'We left Belfast on Wednesday evening. I was very excited. There were thousands of us. We were all marching to Derry for Civil Rights…'

When Mr Wade first started to teach 4A about Northern Ireland, he told them that this was something they wouldn't find out about in their schoolbooks. They would have to watch the news on telly or read the papers that their fathers brought home. Francis' dad never bought a paper except on Sunday, so he started watching the news at six o'clock and nine o'clock every night. The very first thing he saw about Northern Ireland gave him a big shock. It was a march in Derry. People wanted Civil Rights but the police started battering them with batons for no reason. The people marching had no weapons. One poor man got bashed on the ear. It reminded Francis of the time Bernard McMahon hit him with a hurley. That was ages ago, but he hadn't forgotten the awful pain. Why did the police do that? Didn't they want people to have Civil Rights? Mr Wade said that everyone should have Civil Rights, but, in Northern Ireland, Catholics didn't. Francis wondered was that why the Protestants he saw on the telly all had fancy names, like Major Bunting, Captain O'Neill and Reverend Ian Paisley but the Catholic names were normal like John and Gerry and Bernadette.

Every night there was something on the news about Northern Ireland: crowds on the street and people making speeches and police waving batons and cars and shops being set on fire. Francis heard so many new words and phrases he started writing them all down in his copybook so he wouldn't forget them.

Loyalists, Nationalists, Paisleyites, Republicans, Extremists, Revolutionary Socialists, Anarchists, orgy of violence, baton charge, water cannon, maintenance of peace, harassment, indiscriminate.

It was exciting but very confusing.

> 'On the first night the Extremists stopped us marching through Antrim Town. My friends and me didn't want to start a fight. The RUC brought us to a hostel where we could sleep without harassment. My friend said to me, 'Don't worry, when we get to Derry we will get our Civil Rights...'

Then the Christmas holidays came and Francis completely forgot about Northern Ireland. He loved Christmas and this year there were three things that made it brilliant. Going into town to see the lights and visit Santa, getting presents of more Hardy Boys books, and the ceremony of a thousand candles at the Redemptorists on Christmas Day. The lights on O'Connell Street and William Street were the best ever. His dad said the Corporation got them from Blackpool in England. Francis visited Santa three times. His mam brought him to Santa at Todds, his Godmother Mary brought him to Santa at Cannocks and his brother Gussie gave him the money to go to Santa at Roches Stores but he had to queue up himself.

The first time Francis ever saw the ceremony of a thousand candles he was only five and, since then, he looked forward to it every year. It was always on at six o'clock on Christmas night. The Redemptorist church was huge; it was more like a cathedral. There were candles everywhere on the altar, high up and low down, in front and to the side. Once the church was full, the choir began 'O Holy Night' and then all the Redemptorists came out with long flaming sticks and started lighting up each candle. It took at least ten minutes just to get them all lit. Then the electric lights in the church were turned off so that it was dark everywhere apart from the altar, which looked like it was on fire. One of the Redemptorists began Benediction and everyone replied:

'Blessed be God
Blessed be his Holy name
Blessed be Jesus Christ true God and true Man
Blessed be the name of Jesus
Blessed be his most Sacred Heart
Blessed be his most precious blood.'

As he prayed, Francis' eyes were glued to the flaming altar. The only words he could think of to describe his feeling, were what his mam said every year after the ceremony: 'Well, wasn't that just beautiful, now. That was the real Christmas.' He couldn't help thinking about all the money he had stolen from the window sill. After the first time, he'd kept taking sixpence every week so he could buy Hardy Boys books even faster. But his mam and dad had bought him two more for Christmas, *The Secret of Skull Mountain* and *The Mystery of the Spiral Bridge.* His Aunt Marg had bought him *The Secret Warning* and Aunt Mona had bought him *The Crisscross Shadow.* It was brilliant that they all got him ones he hadn't read yet. Francis didn't have to be as good a sleuth as the Hardy Boys to deduce that his mam and dad must have organised it. That made him feel even more guilty, and he promised God he wouldn't steal any more money for Hardy Boys books ever again. He knew he should do more than that to make up for it, but he didn't know what.

> 'The next day we marched to a town called Maghera. There was more trouble there. In the town Protestants and Catholics were fighting each other. The RUC could not maintain the peace. We tried to tell people that we were against violence and we wanted Civil Rights for everyone…'

When school started again after the Christmas holidays, Mr Wade told 4A that for their ecker he wanted them to write a report from Northern Ireland, so Francis started watching the news again. He also asked his mam and dad if he could stay up and watch *7 Days* as well. His dad asked what did he want to do that for and his mam said, oh, any excuse not to go to bed and Francis said Mr Wade had told them they had to learn about Northern Ireland. His mam said that was a queer thing for nine-year-olds to be learning about, but his dad said Mr Wade was his teacher and he must have his reasons, so they let him stay up and watch *7 Days.*

That week all the news was about a big march from Belfast to Derry. It would take four days. One of the things that Francis noticed when he saw the marchers on the telly was how young so many of them were. There was no one his age, but most of them looked like Ritchie and Gussie or even younger. They were all holding banners and shouting into megaphones and telling reporters what they thought. One girl called Bernadette Devlin was on the news every night giving out. His mam thought she was great. 'Oh, that Bernadette Devlin, she's well able to speak up for herself, she's afraid of no one.' Francis was surprised at his mam saying that, because Bernadette Devlin didn't look much older than Marian and he was sure that if Marian was out protesting and giving out on the telly, his mam would kill her and say she was making a show of the family. Francis thought about all the people he knew who were that age; his brothers and their pals, his cousins, other boys and girls on the street. He couldn't imagine any of them out marching with banners singing 'We Shall Overcome' and 'We Shall Not Be Moved'. But maybe no one had ever asked them? He liked the idea of marching and talking on the telly about Civil Rights. It would be a fab thing to do. That was what gave him the idea for his composition. He would pretend that he was one of the young people on the march from Belfast to Derry.

> 'The RUC told us to keep walking to the bridge at Burntollet. They would make sure we were safe. But there were Paisleyites and Extremists hiding in the hills above. Suddenly! they appeared and started throwing stones down on us indiscriminately. No one from the RUC helped us. Some of my friends said it was a trap. The RUC wanted us to get injured. I do not know it if was true or not.'

On the telly Francis had seen two young girls in tears. These girls looked even younger than Marian but they weren't a bit shy. They said that the RUC had promised to protect them but when the stones rained down there were no police to be seen. They were very angry and upset. Francis thought that was really unfair. Why were these Extremists throwing stones at girls? All the students were doing was marching.

> 'They called us Revolutionary Socialists and some of my friends were battered so much they had to go to hospital. The man in charge talked to us on his megaphone. "Do you want to keep marching?" he asked. We said "Yes!" So we kept going all the way to Derry. We all held hands and sang "We shall overcome some day". I felt very happy.'

The last news report Francis had seen before he wrote his composition had been the most violent. It was at night, which made the pictures look even more frightening.

> 'The shops on the street were on fire. The police turned their water cannon on us. I tried to escape but a policeman came running at me. He had a big baton in his hand. He hit me on the head. There was a sound in my ear like a bee buzzing. My head went round and round. I fell over, unconscious. When I woke up I was in hospital with a huge bandage on my head. We only wanted Civil Rights but, instead, we got an orgy of violence.'

When Francis finished reading, he looked up straight away to where Ian was sitting. His best friend was staring at him with his mouth open. Francis could tell that he was really impressed. Then he heard Mr Wade.

'*Maith an buachaill. Bula bos gach éinne.*'

The class started to clap loudly. Some of them cheered too but that was only for a mess. Francis looked at Mr Wade who was clapping as well. As he went back to his desk he heard his teacher say that doing the report as if he was on the march was a very imaginative way for Francis to show how well he understood the situation, but Francis didn't think he understood the goings-on in the North at all. And, secretly, he knew he didn't care about that. What he liked were all the new words and phrases he had discovered. And he liked Mr Wade telling him that his ecker was good. And, most of all, he loved being asked to stand up in front of the teacher and the whole class and read it out loud.

*

Gussie was passing the grotto in his 1961 Black Zephyr when he saw Francis on his way home for dinner. Perfect timing. He pulled in and rolled down the window. 'Do you want a lift?' He was delighted to see Francis' eyes nearly pop out of his head.

'Where did you get that?'

'What do you mean where did I get it? I bought it. Are you getting in or not?'

If he'd been fired out of a cannon his baby brother couldn't have jumped into the car faster.

'A Zephyr. Is it really yours?'

'Yeah. Got it this morning.'

'Wow!'

Gussie enjoyed seeing Francis goggle-eyed, lost for words for once. It didn't take very long to travel the remaining hundred yards. He parked in front of the green but didn't get out. He wanted his mam to see him sitting in his new car.

'I was asked to read out my composition in front of class this morning.'

'Good for you. Go in and tell mam to come out and see the car.'

Gussie watched him haring to the house. He knew Francis would love being the first one with the news. A few kids playing on the green came over to stare. It was only a few seconds before Marian and Martin came flying out. Then Ritchie and Francis. Then his mam. Gussie leaned his elbow out the open window, dead casual.

'What do you think?'

Marian said it was gorgeous, could she sit in the front? Martin, without asking, opened the back door and hopped in. Francis followed. Ritchie looked in the window at the dashboard and asked what year was it? What was the mileage? Was the engine OK? Gussie wondered if he was a bit jealous.

'How much was it?'

'How fast does it go?'

'Remember Mr Mac used to have one like this?'

What was his mam going to say? It wouldn't be anything complimentary anyway, that was for sure.

'It's very big isn't it? Wouldn't you have been better off with something smaller?'

Was that the worst she could think of? Gussie didn't let himself get annoyed.

'Here, sit in, Mam. Marian, get out for a sec.'

His mam came round and sat in next to him.

'Very comfortable.'

'A bit better than the lorry all right.'

'That lorry brings us wherever we want to go. Many a time we were glad of that lorry. What about the insurance?'

'It's insured, don't worry.' Gussie didn't tell her that the insurance cost more than the car. 'Do you want to go for a spin?'

'Now? No, sure we're just having our dinner.'

Wails from Francis and Martin to go for a spin, but his mam sent them all back into the house. As she got out she said. 'It's very nice. If you have time you could give me a lift into town after dinner. I've a few bits and pieces to get in Moran's.' Gussie said, 'OK.' His mam said, 'Come on so, your dinner's ready.' He watched her go back into the house. The money for the car and the insurance was the money he'd saved for America, so she couldn't give out about how he spent it. He got out, locked his new car, warned the staring kids not to go near it and went in for his dinner.

That afternoon he drove his mam into town, waited outside Moran's, then brought her home again. He could tell by the way she sat back that she was enjoying the luxury of it, even though she didn't pass any remarks. After he dropped her off he went for a pint in the Spotted Dog, then drove to the Wire factory. He waited outside and blew the horn as soon as he spotted his cousin, Tony Crowley, leaving work.

'Jaysus, where did you get that crate?'

'Bought it this morning. Want to go for a spin?'

'Ten gallons to the mile is it?'

Gussie drove Tony home to wash and change out of his work clothes. His Aunt Marg and cousin Mary came out to admire the Zephyr. Then he and Tony went to Punch's for a few. After that they drove to South's for a few more. Finally they ended up in Geary's Hotel. Around midnight they fell out and drove round the corner to the Franciscan Hall where Reform were playing. It was packed, there was loads of talent and, thanks to Tony mentioning the car, they got off with two birds from Kildimo, who didn't mind a bit of kissing and a feel as long as they got a lift home. After that, Gussie dropped Tony back to his house. It was gone two when he arrived home. He parked right up against his dad's lorry, got out, and stood brooding over the old jalopy and the car that was going to change his life. He'd be qualified in a few months and he could take off, anywhere he liked. In the summer there was always plenty of bar jobs in Killarney or Galway. He'd move there. Yeah, get digs or share a flat. It sounded great in his head, so Gussie wasn't sure why it didn't make him feel more elated. He lurched across the green to the house, not realising he had forgotten to lock his car. Luckily there were no thieves around Rowan Avenue.

Thirty: June 19th

Francis woke in a state of apprehension after a restless night's sleep, convinced that something would go wrong and he wouldn't be able to go to Dublin today with Ian and Mr Barry. Nevertheless, he washed carefully and put on the clothes his mam had told him he had to wear and checked, again and again, the bag he had packed. It was now almost nine. So far there had been no sign of a mishap, but that did not ease his anxiety even the teeniest bit. Sure enough, as his dad poured him a cup of tea in the kitchen, disaster struck. They both heard the horrible gruesome sound from upstairs: his mam vomiting. What had made her so sick? Surely not the cake? Yesterday, for his tenth birthday, his mam had brought home a stupendous cake from The Dane. It had real cream in the middle with chocolate icing on top. His mam had cut it into eight slices, one for everyone else and two for Francis because it was his birthday. But she had cut only a teeny slice for herself. No, it couldn't be the cake.

His mam was coughing and choking now. His dad said nothing, but put down the teapot and went upstairs. Francis knew for sure that he was doomed. His mam was supposed to bring him in to Tait's Clock in Baker Place, where Ian and his father would be waiting to collect him. Francis had said loads of times that there was no need for his mam to bring him, he knew where Tait's clock was and he went in and out to town on his own all the time. The real truth was he didn't want his mam to bring him. He preferred to meet Ian and Mr Barry on his own. His mam said it would only be polite to say hello to Mr Barry and thank him for being so kind and, anyway, she didn't want the man thinking that they just let Francis wander around the town all by himself like a tinker. But of course his mam had to go and get sick at just the wrong time and he knew his dad would say that if his mam couldn't bring him in then he couldn't go at all. Fate had decreed that he would not spend tonight in Dublin. It was unbelievably unfair.

These depressing thoughts did not prevent Francis from eating his fried bread and drinking his tea and remaining alert for any noises that might give him a clue about what was happening upstairs. It had all gone quiet. Maybe… Was it possible his mam was feeling better? Then he heard his dad coming back down and he could tell, even from the way he was walking, that the news was not going to be good. Doom-laden thoughts assailed Francis, but still he fought against them. There must be a way out. He had to think fast! As his dad turned at the bottom of the stairs, a troubled look on his face, inspiration struck. If his dad said he couldn't go to Dublin because his mam was too sick to bring him in to Tait's clock, then Francis could say that was unfair to Mr Barry and Ian because they wouldn't know what was going on and they'd be left waiting around like fools, so his dad would have to let Francis go on his own. Yes!

His dad came into the kitchen and remained standing up as he poured himself a hot cup of tea. Francis knew that he was preparing to deliver the ill-fated news and, at exactly the same moment, he also realised that his clever idea wouldn't work because his dad would just say he'd go to the public phone box near the grotto and call Mr Barry to explain the situation.

'Mam is feeling a bit sick so she won't be able to bring you in this morning.'

Francis' heart sank. His worst fears realised. The words were a crushing blow.

'So if you're ready to go straight away, I'll drop you in on the way to work.'

Ready? Francis had been ready for at least two hours. His bag was packed since last night. Ready? He nearly knocked over his teacup as he leapt from the chair. He wanted to go pronto, get into the lorry before his dad changed his mind.

He was going to Dublin after all!

As he thumped up the stairs to collect his bag, his father hissed at him, 'Shh. Go quietly. Didn't you hear me saying that mam isn't feeling well? Do you think of no one but yourself?'

Francis tiptoed the rest of the way. He recognised that look in his dad's eye, the one that said he was really annoyed. Disrespect or dishonesty were the things that always made that look appear. Did he think that Francis was being disrespectful to his mam by making noise when she was sick? Francis didn't mean it that way, he was just in a hurry to get his bag because his dad said they had to leave straight away. He crept past his parents' bedroom. The last thing he wanted now was his mam shouting at him and giving out. The sooner he got his bag and escaped from the house, the better all round. His mam would be glad to get him out from under her feet, too.

Of course, having been told to be ready straight away, he ended up waiting in the lorry for ages before his dad finally appeared. They were going to be late now. Would Mr Barry wait for them? It wasn't until the lorry pulled away that Francis allowed his anxiety to ease and excitement to grow, but, once it did, it soon ballooned into expectancy and exhilaration and the certainty that this was going to be the best day ever. As they rattled along Hogan Road Francis saw lots of boys and girls around his age out playing and thought gleefully that none of them was going to Dublin to be shown around the television studios and spend the night in a big hotel with his best pal. How lucky was he?

When Fonsie Strong got out of his lorry and greeted Brendan Barry, who was lounging against his Cortina, neither of them had the slightest awareness that they had met once before, exactly ten years ago. Today's meeting was even more brief than the previous encounter and, like before, not much was said.

'Mr Strong. Brendan Barry.'

'I'm Fonsie. Sorry to keep you waiting.'

'You're grand, we're only just ahead of you. All set, Francis?'

'Yes, Mr Barry.'

Francis ran over to the Cortina as Ian got out. Francis was

surprised to see that he was wearing long pants for the first time. Was that because he was ten?

'Listen, I'd better go or I'll be late for work. And thanks very much for inviting him. It'll be a great birthday treat.'

'I hope so. Ian asked for Francis especially. They get on like a house on fire.'

Neither father realised that the other was referring to his own son's birthday. Like ten years before, both men had other worries, mostly related to their wives, and so neither was really thinking about the other man. It briefly crossed Barry's mind that Fonsie Strong was older than he expected. Late forties, he guessed. His lorry looked about late forties too. To Fonsie, Brendan Barry seemed a friendly sort of young fellow with a nice easy way about him. His main hope was that he was a safe driver. At least the Cortina looked almost new and in good nick. Apart from these fleeting observations about each other, the minds of both men were elsewhere. Fonsie was concerned about how frantic Ann had got when Dr Greaney told her yesterday she was expecting again. It was a shock all right at forty-four, but it was God's will and, if she didn't worry herself too much, Fonsie was sure it would work out all right. He certainly didn't think it was going to kill her and he wished Ann would get ideas like that out of her head. Brendan was thinking about how he had watched Elizabeth as she got Ian ready this morning and imagined her reaction if he tried to tell her all the things she never asked about, forced her to listen to the dirty details. Knowing Elizabeth, she would probably block her ears and start moaning. She didn't want to know what he was or who he went with, and the truth was that Brendan didn't want to tell her. He was glad that, on this occasion at least, his wife genuinely seemed to think that this trip to Dublin was purely a birthday treat for Ian.

The two fathers smiled and parted. The fact that they didn't shake hands was not a sign of unfriendliness or even unease. It was just the way it went.

Francis thought the drive to Dublin was brilliant fun. Mr Barry knew lots of silly riddles, and the boys raced each other to be the first with the right answer. Sometimes Ian said, 'I know that one, you asked me that before.' Mr Barry said, 'Well, don't say the answer then, let Francis have a go.' While Francis was thinking, Ian jigged up and down, keeping his lips shut tight and made a noise 'mmmmmmm' as if he was going to burst if he didn't tell. Then Mr Barry started playing I-Spy and when, after a few rounds, he said, 'Something beginning with P,' it was Francis who got the answer first. 'Posters.' Because of the election the previous day, there were posters everywhere, big billboards with slogans: 'Fianna Fáil: Let's back Jack', 'Fine Gael Will Win', 'Labour: The Seventies will be Socialist'. On lamp-posts and telegraph poles along the road there were small posters with the names of each candidate.

'Well done, Francis.' said Mr Barry. 'OK, let's play a new game, let's play Cheer and Boo.' The boys looked at each other, puzzled.

'Daddy, we never heard of a game called Cheer and Boo.'

'Well, that only goes to show that you don't know everything after all. Are you like Ian, Francis? Do you think you know everything too?'

'He does know everything. I know nearly everything and Francis knows everything.'

Francis had never heard Ian say anything like that before. Did he really think that or was he only messing?

'Is that true Francis, do you know everything?'

Mr Barry's eyes were smiling at him in the rear-view mirror. Francis blushed.

'No, Mr Barry.'

'Well, there's one thing I know for sure. I know that there's no chance in the whole world that either of you could ever have heard how to play Cheer and Boo. Not a chance. You know why?'

'Why?'

'Because I just made it up.'

The boys groaned.

'OK, here's what you do. You know the names on the posters

are the names of the candidates, So the game is you each pick a Party to cheer for and everytime you see a poster you have to shout out the name on it and then either cheer if it's your Party or boo the other Party, OK? The first one to shout the name and cheer or boo gets a point. I'll keep score and whoever wins will be in charge of the government. You got that?

'Is this a stupid game, Daddy?'

'Of course it is. All the best games are stupid. Now, first you have to pick your Party. OK, who wants to cheer for Fianna Fáil?'

Francis had no idea why he didn't shout 'Me, me, me!' like Ian did. He just didn't.

'Maybe you weren't ready that time, Francis. Will we do it again?'

'Daddy, that's not fair, I was first.'

'No, it's all right Mr Barry.'

'Are you sure you're not just being polite?'

'No. Let Ian be Fianna Fáil.'

'Yeah!'

'Ah, you must be from a Blueshirt house. Are you?'

Francis didn't know what he meant.

'So, do you want to cheer for Fine Gael?'

Francis remembered that after the Minister died last year there was a by-election and the Fianna Fáil candidate was a relative of the dead minister and his Granny said, 'Typical, who does that crowd think they are – the aristocracy?' So Francis didn't like him. All the Fine Gael posters had a picture of a teacher in his school called Mr Kennedy and everyone said what a nice smile he had, so Francis decided he liked Mr Kennedy. Did that mean he wanted to cheer for Fine Gael? He could see Mr Barry's smiling eyes waiting for an answer. Ian nudged him.

'Go on, pick.'

'What'll it be Francis, Fine Gael or would you prefer Labour, maybe? Are you a bit of a Socialist? Well, tell you what, why don't you cheer for both, they're all against Fianna Fáil anyway. OK, so are you ready? See that poster coming up? Who is it, Ian?

'It's Tom O'Donnell.'

'And cheer or boo.'

'Boooo!'

'Very good. Now Francis, can you see any posters?'

'Yes. Stephen Coughlan.'

'That's Labour. Cheer or boo?'

'I cheer.'

'Well, go on so.'

'Oh… Yeah.'

'Ah, Francis, come on! Louder.'

'Yeaaaahhh!'

'Much better. OK are you ready? Starting – now!'

Even though it was really silly, once they got into it the boys loved the game. It was boisterous and uproarious but they also had to be eagle-eyed and quick to read from far away. As they travelled from county to county the names of the candidates kept changing. On small country roads there weren't so many posters. The boys would spot one from far away and watch it coming closer and closer until it was near enough for one of them to read and shout.

'Michael Smith, yeahhh!'

'Richard Deasy, yeahhh!'

'Thomas Dunne, booo!'

Sometimes three or four posters would be bunched together almost completely covering a telegraph pole. The boys soon learned to say names very fast to collect more points.

'Paddy Lawlorboo! Tom Enrightyeahh!'

In the big towns there were so many posters they couldn't shout out fast enough. By the time they went through Portlaoise the boys had got faster and more excited and the shouting got louder and louder.

'oliveryeah!!flanaganboo!!berboo!!cowan!!geryeah!!connolly boo!jameskellyyeah!!Jameshoulihancharboo!!lesmacdonaldyeah!! johngalvinboo!!'

Mr Barry, laughing, said, 'Stop, stop!' He couldn't keep

score because he couldn't hear any names any more, only meaningless noise. 'It's a cacophony,' he said, which Francis thought was a brilliant word. The boys answered him by chanting yeah!boo!yeah!boo! until finally he managed to shut them up by promising to stop for ice-cream, but only if they would calm themselves. He said that was enough cheering and booing for a while. They stopped in Monasterevin and Mr Barry said he was going to have a good old-fashioned sixpenny wafer, with ripple ice-cream. Ian asked for an Iceberger. Francis wanted a Brunch, but a Brunch was sixpence, so he thought he should ask for an ice-pop instead, which was only threepence. Mr Barry looked at him.

'An ice-pop? A plain old ice-pop. Is that all? Really?'

Francis went red. He looked at Ian who shrugged.

'Francis, just have whatever you want.'

He remembered his Uncle Seán in the Irish American bar in Ballybunion promising to buy him an ice-cream if he sang a song. Francis sang '*Trasna na dTonnta*' for him, and Uncle Seán said, '*Go hanna mhaith.*' It was hours afterwards when they left the bar, but all Francis could think about was the ice-cream Uncle Seán was going to buy him. He walked along Main Street with his mam and dad and Uncle Seán and Auntie Mona and Martin and his cousin Eva and they kept stopping at shops that sold ice-cream but they only looked at the souvenirs and the picture postcards and then walked on, nattering about all sorts of things. Then they went into the casino and his mam and dad played Wheel 'Em In with pennies and Martin and Mary went on the Bumpers and Francis saw Uncle Seán put sixpences into the horse-racing game, Derby Day, and he won once. Francis, though he was only six, could tell that no one was thinking about his ice-cream. But Uncle Seán had promised him. Then Auntie Mona and his mam said they'd wander back to Mrs Brosnahan's with the children and his dad and Uncle Seán said they'd pop in to Harty Costelloes for a quick one. As they separated, Francis knew if he didn't say something he'd never get his ice-cream. So he spoke up: 'You promised me ice-cream.' Even though Uncle Seán said straight away, 'Oh, I'm sorry. I did, didn't I?' his mam grabbed him and slapped the back of his legs. 'How dare you, the cheek of you!' Uncle Seán looked really sorry that he had forgotten. 'Ah no, Ann, in fairness now, I promised the poor child.' But his mam took no notice. 'You're not buying him ice-cream under any circumstances, not after that. The cheek of him, too much auld talk, that's what's wrong with him.'

But now, looking at Mr Barry's face, Francis could see that it was all right to ask for any ice-cream. And anyway, his mam wasn't here to tell him not to be cheeky.

'Can I have a Brunch?'

'A Brunch. That's more like it. A man of sophisticated taste.'

The three of them sat in the car, silent for a couple of minutes, enjoying their ice-creams. Francis and Ian ate theirs in funny ways, trying to make the other laugh. Ian squeezed his Iceberger so that the ice cream came out the sides, then, showing his teeth, he chomped like a beaver. Francis nibbled the red and white biscuit crumbs off the top in a very dainty way without taking any ice cream. Then he did the same down either side. Then, without warning, he took a huge bite. That made Ian laugh.

As they drove out of Monasterevin, Mr Barry turned on the radio to listen to the sponsored programmes. When the music for the Jacobs programme started he was delighted and sang along with it, 'Wah wa-wa waaaaaahh, wah wa-wa waah wa-waaaaahhhhhh,' and when the presenter, Frankie Byrne, spoke, he imitated her perfectly. Listening to him, Francis remembered that, for a long time, he thought Frankie Byrne was a man, partly because Frankie was a version of his own name and partly because she sounded like a man. But then he found out it was a woman with a deep voice.

'Now, the problems I talk about today may not be yours, but they could be – someday.'

Mr Barry laughed. 'Good woman, Frankie, there's no one like you. I tell you, lads, a truckload of cigarettes and whiskey went into making that voice.'

All the way to Dublin they listened to Frankie reading out the letters that listeners sent, looking for answers to their problems. Helen said her new boyfriend expected her to pay for herself when they went to the pictures or a dance. He claimed it was because women should be treated equally, but Helen wondered was he just mean? What did Frankie think? Frankie thought that if this fellah wasn't treating her to the price of a cinema ticket now, in the first flush of romance, it didn't bode well for the future. 'On the money, Frankie – literally.' Mr Barry said. Catríona was doing a line with a very nice lad for over a year and recently he had invited her to go away with him for the weekend to a music festival in the west of Ireland. She was sure that all the arrangements would be perfectly proper, but she was worried about what people would say. Frankie said she understood her concerns, but a person who spent her life worrying about what others thought sometimes ended up never doing anything – and regretting it. 'She tells it like it is, lads,' said Mr Barry. Noreen was going out with a man for fifteen years and now they were both over forty and she was afraid he was never going to propose. Frankie said she didn't want to dash Noreen's hopes, but she wondered if perhaps this man just wasn't the marrying kind. Mr Barry laughed loudly at this. Francis didn't know why it was so funny. All the letters were from girls. Did Frankie ever get letters from boys with problems?

As they started passing factories and housing estates it seemed like they must be arriving in Dublin, but fifteen minutes later there were even more factories and the housing estates were getting bigger. Francis began to notice the TV aerials and wondered why they went so high. They looked at least three times higher than at home. They passed a housing estate that seemed to go on and on for miles and the aerials were like a neverending steel forest in the sky. He asked Mr Barry why.

'That's so they can receive the British channels.'

'Can people in Dublin watch BBC?'

'BBC One, BBC Two and ITV. If they have the right aerial.'

'And can they still watch RTE as well?'

'They sure can. It's only us poor fools down in the sticks who're stuck with one channel. Discrimination, boys, that's what it is. You know the way in America they go on about racial discrimination? Well, here in Ireland we have telly discrimination.'

They asked Mr Barry how long more before they were really in Dublin. He said, 'This is Dublin. It's all Dublin. The Big Smoke.'

Francis said, 'No, the middle, where the GPO is.'

'Oh, you want to see the GPO? I wouldn't normally pass it on the way to the hotel but if you want me to go that way it's no problem.'

Nothing was a problem for Mr Barry. He drove along by the river and turned up O'Connell Street. They were able to pass the GPO slowly because the traffic was so heavy. The boys wondered what it must have been like when it was set on fire in 1916. They asked was the whole street in flames, were there British soldiers everywhere with Gatling guns and cannon? How had the Volunteers escaped and into which street? As they talked, Brendan suddenly remembered that day when Gavin showed him around the set of the GPO in Studio One. Jesus. Over three years ago. He recalled the particular moment so clearly. Standing high above the set, even above the lighting grid, in the darkness of the metal gantry, his hands had gripped the safety railing as he'd leaned over to get a bird's-eye view of the impressive replica below. Then he'd felt a hand placed gently, nervously, on his. A few seconds passed and then, without speaking, and, without thinking much about it, he had turned his palm upward and clasped the hand. The kiss seemed to follow quite naturally. How it all began. And continued so long – on and off. How had that happened?

Mr Barry didn't seem to hear Ian's question and then suddenly he said, 'What? Oh that. That's the Gresham Hotel, very swish, one of the country's top hotels. Along with the Inter-Continental, of course.' Mr Barry then kept talking as they turned back down O'Connell Street and crossed the river. He pointed at what he said were famous places and statues of famous people. He told the boys lots of things about them. He talked so much they didn't get a chance to ask him anything and suddenly they arrived at the Inter-Continental Hotel. It was even bigger than Francis expected, much bigger than the Inter-Continental where Mr Barry was manager or other hotels back home like the Royal George. The huge lobby was full of people all dressed up, sitting around on couches, smoking and drinking. While Mr Barry talked to a girl at the desk, Francis nudged Ian and pointed to a group of men in suits, laughing and drinking over by the wall. 'Gangsters, planning a robbery?' he said. Ian nodded and looked around too. He nodded towards a baldy man, sitting all alone reading a paper – or was he just pretending to read it? Ian said, 'Private eye? International spy?' Mr Barry was joking with the girl at the desk. He seemed to know her very well.

'Doreen, I know you have my usual suite ready for me but I was wondering have you anything at all for these two itinerants? An auld broom cupboard now would be fine.'

The girl looked at the reservations book with a very serious expression on her face. 'Mmm, I'm not sure if there's anything available, boys. Oh wait, we have a special room put aside. It says here, for a handsome, well-mannered boy who's just turned ten years of age. That's not one of you by any chance is it?' For a second Francis was amazed that the girl knew about his birthday but when Ian said, 'Me, that's me. I was ten yesterday,' he realised his mistake. Francis didn't know why he had never told Ian that they had the same birthday – that to him they were sort of twins. Because he had said nothing that first time, years ago, when Ian invited him to his house for his party, it seemed to become harder after that to find a way to tell his friend. Each year, as the day approached, Francis thought about revealing this amazing little secret and then each year he stayed silent. Why? To him it was magical and significant and fateful that he and his best friend had been born on the same day in the same town, maybe even the same hospital, so why not say it? Francis had thought about this so much that he sort of knew why he didn't. He was afraid, and what he was afraid of was, what if he told Ian and Ian didn't think it was important at all? Or, worse, if he wouldn't be his friend any more? But why should that be? That was stupid, wasn't it?

'Looks like you're in luck, lads.'

Mr Barry threw open the door of room 516 and waved a hand. 'There you go.'

Francis knew that Ian wasn't as excited as he was because he had already stayed in this hotel with his mother and father and probably stayed in lots of hotels before. Francis had never stayed in one in his whole life. The room had two huge beds, each of them bigger than the double bed Gussie and Ritchie slept in. They had four pillows each. The curtains were thick and went all the way to the ground just like curtains on a stage. There was a writing table with a telephone, and a big television.

Mr Barry said, 'OK boys, you have five minutes exactly to wash yourselves and get ready before we go to RTE, all right?'

Brendan closed the door of 516 and went to 518, conscious of a feeling quite unusual for him. Could it really be guilt? After all, he was able to tell himself quite honestly that both boys were having a whale of a time and he had pulled out all the stops on the journey to keep them amused and he was quite certain that Gavin would entertain them mightily showing them around the studios. If Brendan was using them a little for his own ends was that so bad? He thought about this as he undressed and had a quick shower. Did he want a room all to himself tonight or not? He did. So, rather than dump Ian in a room on his own, wasn't letting him bring a pal along the best arrangement? It was. So end of story, no harm done. A bit sly, maybe a bit mean, but as he had no intention of changing his plan for tonight, Brendan accepted that he'd just have to cope with this little spasm of conscience as best he could.

*

Francis was a bit surprised when Mr Barry turned round with a really big smile as he drove into RTE and asked if he was enjoying his day out so far. When Francis said, 'Yes.' Mr Barry said, 'You're sure?' and Francis nodded and said it was brilliant, the best time ever. Mr Barry, still smiling, said, 'Good.' Then they went into the studio building.

A man standing near the reception desk waved at them as they came in.

'Mr Barry and entourage, right on time. Now, let me see, at a guess I'd say this is your young swain and you are the best pal, is that right?'

'Got it in one. This is Ian, the birthday boy.'

'Ten, I hear. Have I been briefed correctly?'

'Yes.'

'A fine age, an impressive age.'

Because of the way he smiled at Ian, Francis was sorry the man didn't know it was his birthday too.

'And his *compañero*, Francis. Boys this is – do you want them to call you Gavin or Mr Bloom?

'No formality around here, I'm Gavin lads.'

'Now, you should know that Gavin is one of the most important people in RTE. He's a senior floor manager, which is very close to being God. Nothing moves in the studio without Gavin's say-so.'

'Actually, I'm just the carpet that everyone sweeps their dirt under.'

Francis didn't know what that meant, but it sounded funny the way Gavin said it as he turned and walked away. He walked fast, talking all the time.

'Why don't we dip our lips in cuisine de canteen before starting the tour. The place is in a lather of excitement today on account of the election. The rumour mill grinding away even more mercilessly than usual.'

Francis began to think that Gavin had a way of making everything he said sound funny. It was partly the words he used, and partly the way he made a face or a gesture as he spoke. And he said things that meant one thing but seemed to mean something else as well. Francis thought he was like an actor. He said funny things about the food in the canteen and when the boys spotted people they recognised from television – Brendan O'Reilly, the sports presenter and Brian Farrell, who was on *7 Days* and Thelma Mansfield, who introduced all the programmes – Gavin had something funny to say about them all. Soon, the boys were giggling every time he even raised an eyebrow. When they finished eating their sausages and chips he said, 'Let the grand tour commence, gentlemen.'

First, they went to the news studio, or the broom cupboard as Gavin told them everyone called it. He allowed them to sit where Charles Mitchell sat every night. He told them to look straight at the camera, counted them down from five and gave them a cue. Giggling, they said. 'Good evening, here is the news read by Ian Barry and Francis Strong.'

Then they went to Studio Three which was a bit bigger, but they were only allowed take a quick peek in because *Buntús Cainte* was being recorded. Gavin asked them if they spoke any Irish and they told him that in school they did every subject through Irish. Gavin gave Mr Barry a look and said, 'Oh, we're not dealing with muck here are we? So you don't need a programme like *Buntús Cainte* to teach you, then. It's probably a bit low-grade for geniuses like you.' 'Yeah, a bit,' said Ian cheekily. 'Oh, I'm getting the lash already. His father's son, I see.' said Gavin, winking at Mr Barry. 'So tell me this, what are your favourite television programmes?'

'*Mission Impossible,*' Francis said, straight away.

'Yeah, I like that too,' said Ian, 'And *Ironside.*'

'And *The Avengers.*'

'And *The Saint.*'

'And *Mannix.*'

'And *Marty Feldman.*'

'And *I Dream of Jeannie.*'

'And *Green Acres.*'

'And *Get Smart.*'

Gavin, laughing, said, 'All British and American programmes. RTE not up to your high standards, is that it?'

Francis said, 'Well, my mam and dad always watch *The Riordans.* I like it too.'

'Oh, don't feel you have to reassure me, especially as I'm off to America myself very soon.'

'Gavin is going to live in New York,' Mr Barry said. 'He's got a TV job there. How about that?'

The boys looked at each other, very impressed. Francis said, 'My brother Gussie wanted to go to America but my mam wouldn't let him.'

Gavin winked. 'Ah, that's mothers for you, Francis. I'm hoping to get away before mine finds out about me.'

'And what about your wife?' said Ian.

Mr Barry said quickly, 'Ian, that's none of your business.'

'Sorry,' said Ian.

Gavin just laughed. 'Well, the way it is with me – how can I put it? – I'm a free agent. The world is my oyster.' Francis liked the sound of that.

They were now outside another studio. 'OK, my fine feathered friends, this is Studio Two. There was a programme on here last night and the set is still there. What I want to know is, can you tell me the name of the programme?' They went in and even though the set wasn't lit up properly both Francis and Ian knew straight away what show it was. '*Like Now!*' they both shouted. It looked weird without the flashing lights and the dancers and the bands.

'So, what do you think of *Like Now!*?' Gavin asked.

'Yeah, it's kinda good.' Francis could tell Ian was making that up. So could Mr Barry, because he was smiling when he said, 'Ian isn't really into rock music, hasn't hit that age yet.'

Francis was thinking that Martin was going to be so jealous. He never missed *Like Now!* Francis had only ever watched bits of it. Some of the bands on it were really freaky – 'Far out,' Martin would say, which meant he thought they were fab.

'My brother loves it, and my sister watches it too. My brother likes Deep Purple and my sister likes the Mamas and the Papas.'

'Well, everyone to their own taste, no matter how zany or peculiar. Isn't that the way it should be, Brendan?' said Gavin, and whatever way he said it, and the way Mr Barry grinned, Francis thought he must mean something else as well.

Finally Gavin showed them the biggest studio. Studio One. It was ginormous, bigger than the green in front of Francis' house. Because there were loads of people buzzing about, getting ready for the election programme, they had to stay out of everyone's way, so Gavin led them behind the set, along the studio wall, to a narrow steel stairs and pointed up. He started to climb the stairs and the others followed. It was dark and steep so Mr Barry stayed behind the boys in case one of them slipped or stumbled. The stairs went up, way up, until they were above the lights, and the ceiling was just over their heads. There was a steel walkway along the wall on two sides. They could lean against the railing and look down on the whole studio floor. Everything seemed small now, even the huge sign on the set.

GENERAL ELECTION '69

Gavin whispered, 'Studio One is where we do all the big shows like the *Late Late*, which of course you won't have seen but you probably –'

'Sometimes I'm let stay up to see the first few minutes.'

'I'm never allowed see it. It's not fair.'

'Don't look at me, Ian. Talk to your mummy about that.'

Gavin said, 'Well, if you ask me, no child should ever be let anywhere near the *Late Late Show*. There's terrible things happen on that show. Oh yes! Sinful things. Not fit for the eyes of a good Catholic boy. I'd keep well away if I were you.'

Francis knew he was being funny again. Listening to him made him wish even more that he was old enough to see a whole *Late Late Show*.

'Do you ever work on it?'

'Now and then. But most of the time I work on dramas. It's what I suppose you'd call my area of expertise. I've done dozens and dozens of dramas. In fact, I have a particularly happy memory of one we made right here in this studio –'

Francis noticed a change in Gavin's voice. He wished he had the right word to describe it exactly. Definitely, he sounded more serious.

'– It's still the biggest and most expensive drama we've ever done. It was called *Insurrection*. Brendan, do you remember *Insurrection*?'

Francis was so excited he couldn't stop himself speaking.

'I remember it! I saw it!'

Gavin had been smiling at Mr Barry, but now he looked at Francis, genuinely surprised.

'Really? No you couldn't have. It was three years ago. You're probably thinking of something else.'

'No, I remember it. It was about the 1916 Rising. I watched it every night for a whole week.'

'That's right, it was on every night. You really saw it?'

'Yeah, it was brilliant. And were you the floor manager?'

'For my sins. We nearly set this studio on fire making it.'

'Was that the part when the GPO burned down?'

'That's right.'

Francis was amazed. He could tell Gavin was amazed too.

'That was here? You did that here?'

'The magic of television, Francis. We turned the whole studio into the GPO and set it on fire.'

'Wow!'

'Yeah, I remember standing right here on the last day of the production, looking down on the set with a friend of mine... It was a very special moment.'

*

When the tour finished, Brendan gave Ian the car keys and told him not to drive away without him. He and Gavin watched the boys race each other to the car, all excited, already involved in some imaginary adventure.

'Thanks a million for doing that. They'll be talking about it for ever.'

'Not at all. Sure, you know me, any excuse for a performance. They're really nice kids.'

'I enjoyed it too.'

'Of course. You love the bit of glam.'

'So, listen. I'm bringing the lads to the Coffee Dock for a bite of dinner later. Why don't you come along? They'd love it if you did.'

'No, I don't think so.'

'Enough of children for one day?'

'No, not at all, they're bright kids and I love an adoring audience. But ah… no, it's probably best not to –'

'Come on, Gav. It'd be a laugh.'

'No… No, Brendan.'

'I think you want to. And I mean… It could be the last time I'll ever see you.'

'Oh don't be such a drama queen, dearheart. There's fellahs off to the moon in a few weeks' time. A bit of transatlantic travel is nothing these days.'

'But you know what I mean?'

'Of course I know what you mean. I always know exactly what you mean.'

'So… how about it?'

'I might… I'll see how I feel.'

'Do.'

'I might.'

*

Francis was delighted when he saw Gavin arrive into the Coffee Dock and look around. He tapped Ian's foot and nodded towards him. Mr Barry said, 'What's up?'

'There's Gavin, Daddy.'

'Hm? Oh yeah, he said he might drop by if he had a chance.'

Mr Barry waved. Gavin waved back and came over. Francis watched him as he – what was the best word? Not swaggered, or swept – as he *paraded* over. Along the way he recognised someone and gave them a big smile and salute. His long hair danced as he moved and the way he dressed, with his flowery shirt open at the neck and his bell-bottom jeans, it was like he owned the world. A free agent. That was what he said.

'Not too late, I hope?'

'No, we've just ordered. Burgers and chips and French-fried onions and mushrooms and all the trimmings.

Gavin ordered the same. Mr Barry asked what was the latest word on the election.

'Well, you'll be happy. It's looking like Fianna Fáil again. Same old, same old.'

'Oh well. Does that mean the seventies won't be Socialist?'

'Ha ha. Definitely time for me to spread my wings and fly.'

Even with their mouths full of burger Francis and Ian still managed to bombard Gavin with questions about television. He had amusing answers for everything and told lots of stories about mistakes that happened while they were making programmes. 'Cock-ups' he called them. Francis had heard loads of new words today. He hoped he would remember them all. As Gavin was telling a story about a bull running loose in the farmyard where they were shooting a scene for *The Riordans*, Francis remembered something his mam had told him to find out.

'Gavin, you know the way in *The Riordans*, Tom Riordan is married to Mary Riordan and Batty Brennan is married to Minnie Brennan.'

'Yes.'

'Well my mam said that she was told that, in real life, Tom Riordan is married to Minnie Brennan and Mary Riordan is married to Batty Brennan.'

'Well, you can tell your mam that she's absolutely right.'

'Really?'

'Absolutely. I know, it's all upside down, isn't it? You see, that's the weird and wonderful thing about real life, Francis. It's never the way you expect it to be. That's the big secret they never tell you.'

Francis wasn't sure exactly what Gavin meant, but he believed him. He knew there were things adults knew that they didn't want children to know. Sometimes his mam would be talking to his dad, or his godmother Mary Storan or his Auntie Mona and suddenly their voices would go into a whisper and then get louder again, 'Ah but you see what happened there was… whishwhish-whishwhishwhish… you see now? Anyway, say nothing for the moment, there's big ears in the room…' and he knew the whispered bit was some secret thing he wasn't supposed to know. Was that what Gavin was talking about?

'Will you stop messing with the kid's head!' said Mr Barry. But he was smiling and Francis could tell that he really liked Gavin. He wondered how long had they been pals and for a second he thought it would be brilliant if Gavin was his dad, like Mr Barry was Ian's dad. But then wouldn't he miss his own mam and dad? What if Gavin was his big brother and Mr Barry was his best pal and they took him and Ian everywhere? That would be just stupendous.

Mr Barry ordered more wine, and told the boys they had to have a Knickerbocker Glory. No meal in the Coffee Dock was complete without the Knickerbocker Glory experience. It was scrumptious, with ice cream and fruit cocktail and cream and raspberry sauce and chocolate on top, all in a tall glass. It was so huge that Ian couldn't finish his and Francis had to force himself. He thought he was going to burst. While they were struggling with their desserts, Mr Barry and Gavin had two more bottles of wine. Mr Barry looked at his watch and said, 'Look at the time. Ten o'clock. Come on, bedtime.'

He told Gavin to order more wine and he'd be back in a few minutes. In the lift he was smiling and he asked the boys if they had enjoyed their day out, as if he didn't know that already.

While they were getting into their pyjamas Mr Barry gave them their orders, 'Now you can watch a bit of telly. You can have a laugh, I'm no fool, I know you won't go to sleep straight away, but don't wreck the place and when I come to bed in half an hour – see the clock? Quarter to eleven, all right? – if there's a peep out of you at that stage then we won't have a very happy end to the day. Now, you won't let me down, will you?'

The boys, sitting on their beds, promised solemnly. Mr Barry left and they looked at each other. Francis knew that Ian wouldn't have ordinary striped pyjamas, the kind that everyone had, the kind they sold in Moran's. He was wearing Martin's old pyjamas, and he knew Martin was in bed now wearing Gussie's and Gussie and Ritchie had the same kind, too. Francis could tell that Ian's mother had made his. They were only one colour, dark red, and made out of a shiny cloth. On the pocket 'IAN' was stitched in blue thread.

'What's up?'

Francis realised that he was staring and Ian had noticed. A few times in class Mr Wade had said, 'There's Francis Strong staring off into space again,' when he had been staring over at Ian. Now he turned away quickly, jumped off the bed and switched on the television.

'Let's see if they have more than one channel.'

He twisted the round switch on the side. Each time he did it a different programme came on. The first thing they saw was a shot of New York from way above. A man with a very hoity-toity English accent was speaking. He said New York was made by men. Then Francis twisted again and the next channel was definitely RTE because it was the election programme. The boys recognised the set even though it looked completely different on the telly. The next channel had an ad for Cadbury's Flake with a girl looking like she was in heaven as she slowly put the Flake into her mouth. The boys stared. Francis waited until the ad was over before changing channel. The next one had an American programme. It was funny. There were men and women all wearing judges' wigs and dancing. They were all chanting, 'Here come de news, here come de news.' When Francis twisted again there was only hissy snow on the screen.

'Four channels,' said Ian 'Go back to the funny one.'

Now there was a girl with blonde hair and she was trying to say something but she kept giggling and mixing up her words and then a man came up to her and said, 'That's easy for you to say.' Then other funny-looking people popped up and said things really fast that made the boys laugh. Francis thought they were a bit like Gavin. Sometimes he didn't know what they were saying but it sounded funny. Francis liked this show but he couldn't help wondering what was happening on the other channels, so he suddenly jumped up and twisted. The hoity-toity Englishman was still talking, saying that cathedrals were built for the glory of God but New York was built to the glory of Mammon, Money, Greed. Then Ian twisted and it was the election programme again and a politician was saying that the voters had obviously decided they did not want change, then Francis twisted and the English news was on. Then Ian twisted and it was the funny programme again, with a really small man holding a big flower who said his name was Henry Gibson. He said a funny little poem about a fly, which made the boys laugh again. Then Ian jumped up to twist again but this time Francis pulled him back. Ian escaped and a chase around the room started. Francis couldn't catch him and then they stopped suddenly because they both noticed the freakiest-looking man on the funny programme. He had very long hair and a very white face. He was playing a tiny guitar, the tiniest guitar anyone could imagine, and singing in a high voice, sort of like a girl, except no girl would really sing like that. The words sounded like 'Tiptoe through the tulips with me'. A normal-looking man with a jacket and tie was standing next to him, listening. He kept looking at the camera as if he was puzzled. The two boys started laughing. It was the funniest thing, but at the same time Francis wished he knew what was really going on. Who was this freaky man? Why was he singing like that?

Then the boys started a pillow fight. They turned it into a game where they had to protect their own bed and at the same time invade the other's bed. The winner had to get onto the other bed fully and jump on his opponent to stop him from escaping. The funny programme was still on and now there was fast music. They were all dancing and every few seconds the music stopped and someone would say something funny, but the boys weren't really listening any more. They were too wrapped up in their battle. Francis was better at attack, but even when he got onto Ian's bed, Ian always wriggled away and invaded Francis' unprotected bed. Because of all the food he had eaten and because he was laughing so much, Francis thought he was going to get sick. The boys didn't notice how loud the game had got until they heard the phone ringing. Ian, looking guilty, picked it up.

'Hello… Daddy… yeah we're OK… just watching telly… No, no noise… well maybe just a tiny bit… OK, bye Daddy.'

Ian put down the phone and went to turn down the volume. The funny programme was just ending: 'He said was I sure we weren't making any noise, because someone complained. He'll be up in five more minutes. We'd better go to bed I suppose.'

Ian got into bed but Francis stood for a while in front of the telly, switching from one channel to another, trying to imagine what it would be like if they had this at home instead of just one channel. Every evening his mam switched on the telly at six o'clock and it stayed on until she or Dad switched it off before they went to bed. If they had all these channels it would be brilliant in one way but, definitely, the family would end up fighting about what to watch and his mam's blood pressure would go through the roof.

He stopped switching when he saw young people who looked like the college students who marched for Civil Rights. But these young people were in a library, taking books from the shelves and sitting quietly at tables, reading. It was the programme with the hoity-toity Englishman talking, but this time Francis was surprised to hear him say that people in the past were not as well-read, bright-minded, curious and critical as young people are today. He said history is ourselves. There were more shots of students walking around the grounds of the university and sitting on steps talking. Francis thought it looked like a nice life. He turned to ask Ian did he ever think about going to university, but Ian was fast asleep.

Francis got back into bed and lay looking at his friend. He seemed to sleep so calmly. He was always calm. Francis wondered if that was the thing he liked about him more than anything else, more than that he was clever and funny and different? Ian was always at ease, bouncing around, happy in himself. It never bothered him what anyone else thought about him or what some boys said about him behind his back. Ian was just who he was. Francis wished he could be more like that.

Today had been a stupendous day. So much had happened. His mind was so full of things that sleep was impossible. He just lay here, looking at his friend sleeping. Ian's face was turned towards him, his arm hanging out of the bed. It would be so easy to reach out and catch his hand if he wanted to.

The cry – a kind of a howl – sounded like it came from the other side of the wall near him, but he knew that couldn't be, because that was Mr Barry's room and there wasn't anyone in there. Had it come from the telly? There was a picture on the screen of a huge sculpture. It looked like a naked man struggling to escape from a block of stone and the hoity-toity Englishman was saying that, above all, he believed in the God-given genius of certain individuals. Francis got out of bed, turned down the sound and listened. Was that someone laughing in Mr Barry's room? It was so low it was hard to tell if he was imagining it. He got back into bed. The blue glow from the telly lit up Ian's face. Where was Mr Barry? He phoned ages ago. Maybe he only said he was coming in five minutes to give them a fright and he was still down in the restaurant drinking with Gavin.

Right then, the room door opened and the light from the corridor came in. Straight away Francis closed his eyes and started breathing as if he was asleep, just like he did whenever his dad came to check if he was reading under the blanket with his flash-light. He heard quiet footsteps on the carpet. Even though he knew it had to be Mr Barry, he felt nervous for some reason. After a few seconds of silence he heard his voice.

'Fast asleep.'

From further away someone else whispered. Francis knew it was Gavin.

'Can I have a peek?'

'Sure'

His footsteps hardly made a sound.

'Ah, don't they look sweet.'

'Exhausted, I'd say.'

'They've had quite a day.'

'They sure have.'

'You like being a dad, don't you, Brendan?'

'Well, I suppose I am one.'

'Imagine if…'

The silence seemed very long before Mr Barry asked the question Francis was dying to ask.

'Imagine if what?'

'Oh – oh nothing. Just a mad notion. So ridiculous it's not even worth saying out loud.'

Francis heard the click as the television was turned off and sensed the room get darker. The door closed and after a few seconds he dared open his eyes. He could see nothing.

Thirty-one: November 15th

Baz Malloy's eyes were hanging from his head. What time was it? Just after five in the morning. That meant seventeen straight hours crouched at a Steenbeck with nothing but a flask of coffee and a few sandwiches, but he'd done it; viewed every single roll. Eighteen months' work. Was there a story worth telling in there? There were several probably.

It could be a tale of protest. There was plenty of that from his six trips to the North and the footage he had shot of the march on the British embassy in Dublin and the student occupation in Earlsfort terrace. There was a political yarn of a different kind from the recent general election. Baz had captured some great unrehearsed moments with candidates on the campaign trail. There was a much bleaker story of rooted poverty and desperation – something that the much-vaunted economic recovery had failed to dislodge. It was drearily present in images, not just of homeless shelters and itinerant camps, but of life on small farms and council estates he had visited.

However, perhaps because this viewing was such a concentrated experience, the material revealed something else quite unexpected. It was a story harder to pin down but, as roll followed roll, its significance grew in Baz's mind. It was less a narrative than an atmosphere, an experience, something that was still emerging, that hadn't quite gestated yet. At its simplest, Baz saw it as a matter of contrasts. He had shot many faces. Some were downcast or bent in prayer and, viewing them now, it seemed like they were hiding from him. But then there were other faces that confidently looked his camera in the eye. There were people who, when he asked them a question, fell nervously silent as if wary of being caught out. These were people who seemed to prefer a more comforting world of wink and nod. But then there were others who were happy to say what they thought, put it on record.

There was another kind of contrast too, one that Baz found most exciting. From the beginning he had decided to use colour stock but, as he viewed hour after hour of the material, it seemed to him that many of his images might as well have been shot in monochrome. It wasn't just that the light was dull and the backgrounds were grey, the people also seemed persistently and complacently drab. Did they feel some need to creep about the world unnoticed? At first, the look of it depressed the cinematographer in Baz, but then he began to realise how this dreariness might serve to highlight the contrast when something or, perhaps more significantly, someone different appeared: the shock of colour, wild hair or the miniest of mini-skirts. These images would then announce themselves even more brazenly from the screen.

It was all there, somewhere in these rolls of film, the story he wanted to tell – no, not tell. To reveal. As yet he had no idea how he might shape it and, at this hour of the morning, was in no state to start thinking about that. All Baz Malloy knew was that it wouldn't be straightforward because the narrative was itself unfinished. Right now he was exhausted. He would have been happy to lie down and sleep until 1970.

*

For the entire cab journey from his little place in Brooklyn to midtown Manhattan, Gavin chattered so incessantly that he didn't let the driver get a word in. He gabbed about how, even though he had visited New York several times over the years and loved it every time, it was sooo different living here, and oh man was he enjoying every minute of it: about how endlessly fascinating it was just ogling people on the street doing their thing; about how he was still being a bit of big girl's blouse when it came to using the subways and were they really as dangerous as people said? Although of course a cab driver was hardly the right man to ask, was he, dearheart, it being in his interest that people never ventured down below, so to speak, when they could could ride a yellow cab – which he loved by the way; about the nightlife which Gavin said was so much more fabulosa than even he had expected, and look, no sooner had they turned onto Broadway then the rain had cleared up. No need for his umbrella after all. Still, better safe than sorry, not kosher to arrive for his first day on the job looking like a wet rag.

A tiny part of his brain kept telling him to cool it, bring it down a notch, Gavin, take a breather now and then and let the other guy get a word in, but it never happened. Was it a kind of pleasurable hysteria at his new life or just first-night nerves that was making him more outrageously gabby than normal? Jesus, it was Ed Loebwitz after all, the first director to encourage Gavin's talent and the man who had offered him this opportunity. What was there to be nervous about? And today was only a rehearsal day, so no pressure. Still, it was the beginning of a whole new thing, so it was hardly surprising that he might spin ever so slightly out of control.

When the cab pulled up outside the rehearsal rooms on West 47th Street, Gavin paid the driver and sprang out like a kid anxious to get inside the fairground. It was the loud aggression in the driver's voice that shocked him, even more than the words.

'Hey, fairy! You forgot your wand!'

For a moment Gavin didn't even know what the guy was talking about. Then he understood, but his first instinct remained: ignore the voice and walk on. Forget the umbrella. Just. Get. Away. In Ireland he had never experienced this, never ever had that name shouted at him in the street. Fairy? Was this how it was here? It was horrible.

But then, whether through some sense of being reborn out of the noise and chaos of the people and traffic all round him in this towering city, or because of what he had heard about recent events in the Village, or whether it was that, no matter what the circumstances of place or time, when push came to shove, Gavin Bloom wasn't the kind of man to be threatened – whatever it was, he changed his mind about what his reaction should be. After all, to be fair to the driver, at least he hadn't muttered it under his breath, or made a face behind his back, or kept his sneering thoughts to himself. His was not the Irish way, but the New York way. He had spoken out loud and clear and so, surely, could be replied to in kind? Gavin turned and saw, from the smirk on the driver's face, how delighted he was at his own wit, and with what pleasure he would later repeat the story to his colleagues: 'So I says to him, I says, hey, fairy, you forgot your wand!' Gavin suddenly understood that the remark was not so much intended to be threatening as jocose, although that was not a word the taxi driver would have employed. 'Just breaking your balls' – was that what he would say? Well, fair enough.

Gavin walked back without a word, opened the passenger door and picked up his umbrella. Then, with the aplomb of Mary Poppins, the fairy turned and tapped his wand on the smirking driver's shoulder.

'You. Turn to shite.'

As he sashayed off, Gavin was pleased to hear that the taxi driver's laughter sounded genuinely appreciative.

*

The band was playing 'Ob-La-Di, Ob-La-Da' and the dance-floor was crowded. Ann Strong was thrilled that everyone was enjoying themselves. She had made a decision to forget all her worries and fears on this special occasion and, sure enough, it had been a great day so far. After all, it was now her seventh month and nothing bad had happened yet. Surely it was God's will that she and the baby would be healthy? Take her medication and avoid stress, Dr Greaney had said. Easier said than done, but so far so good. Dr Greaney said lots of women her age had babies. Ann had made her own outfit for today and tailored it very carefully so that she just looked fuller but there was no big awful bump.

This wedding was just the tonic she needed. The ceremony had been absolutely beautiful. Áine's parish priest, Father Moriarty, was a lovely man and great fun. He had made everyone feel so relaxed and welcome. In the church, after the ceremony, he had come down to say hello to Ann and give her a special blessing. 'He's going to be a happy healthy baby,' he said. She could see him now, up on the dance-floor with the rest of them, joining in the fun. Why couldn't her parish priest, Father Mullaly, be like that? He had to be invited as well, of course, but he'd sat there with a puss on him the whole time and left straight after the meal. He barely said hello to Ann and Fonsie, although she heard him chatting away to Áine's father, Cormac. Ann would never dream of saying it out loud, not even to Fonsie, but she really did not like the man and hardly ever went to her own parish church any more. It seemed to her he was looking down on the people. Not like the Redemptorists, who treated everyone respectfully.

Ritchie was dancing with Áine's mother, Louise. Fonsie was up on the floor as well, having a laugh with Áine. Ann thought it was great the way the Strongs and the Kielys got on so well. She was going to miss Ritchie so much. He had never been a day's trouble and, well, sign's on, there he was, settled with a lovely girl, a beautiful new house, semi-detached, and permanent now in Krups. She just had to pray that things would work out so well for the rest of them. To her surprise Marian had invited some boy to the after-party. Tim. It was the first Ann had heard anything about Marian having a boyfriend. She looked at them on the dance-floor. The youngfellah hadn't a clue how to dance, sure none of them did any more, but he seemed decent enough. Anyway, Marian was too sensible to let that kind of thing interfere with her studies. She knew well that getting her Leaving Cert meant that she'd never have to work in a factory or a shop. She could be a secretary in an office with nice people, which would do her grand until she got married.

Ann spotted Gussie holding up the bar with his two cousins. Could he not have a dance and enjoy himself like everyone else? Did it have to be drink all the time? And that car of his of course, all show. Trying to be the big fellow, throwing his money away. He needed to cop himself on fast. At least he behaved himself today with his best man's speech. Ann was glad she got Fonsie to warn him about dirty jokes.

Everyone on the dance floor waved their hands in the air and shouted the chorus of 'Ob-La-Di, Ob-La-Da'. Ann saw Mary Storan and Mikey trying to get Francis to jive properly with Áine's little sister Gráinne, but of course he wouldn't behave himself, jumping around, acting the eejit. If she lived another hundred years she'd never make that child out. Either he had his head stuck in a book and there wouldn't be a word out of him for hours, or he'd be doing the giddy-gooley around the house, trying to be funny, starting arguments, giving smart answers, driving everyone mad. Mary and Mikey had minded him at their table for the meal. She came over to Ann afterwards to tell her the goings-on.

'Well Ann, the laughing we had. That child's appetite. He ate two portions of turkey and ham and four trifles.'

'Four?'

'Yes. His own first, then mine – 'cause you know I never bother with desserts – then Mikey asked this lovely old waitress if there was any more trifle, meaning for Francis, but didn't she bring two, one for Mikey as well. Of course he didn't want it, so Francis gobbled number four, no bother.'

Ann looked at her youngest jigging around the dance-floor like a mad thing and thought, well, if he gets sick now, he'll only have himself to blame.

Where was Martin? She couldn't see him on the dance-floor and, looking around, there wasn't a sign of him anywhere in the function room. Ann immediately wondered had he sneaked off somewhere for a smoke? She had been trying to catch him out now for a while, ever since she got the smell of tobacco off his clothes a few months ago. Lately she didn't know what he was getting up to when her back was turned. Mona had told her he was spotted a couple of weeks ago, strolling through the park, with his arm around some girl, brazen as you like. And him only barely fourteen? Brother Murray told her that no matter how often he was slapped, it didn't do any good. He seemed determined not to pass his Inter Cert. What then? If he couldn't get an apprenticeship what was he to do with his life? Ann told herself to calm down and not be getting upset, today of all days.

'Madam Strong, will you join me? Shall we take a twirl? Show these young ones how it's done?'

Cormac Kiely was smiling down at her. Ann had been up for one waltz with Ritchie earlier but hadn't done any fast dancing so far because she was worried that, in her present state, she'd only look ridiculous. But Cormac was such a nice man and such good fun. And really, when she thought about it, on a happy day like this so why not just let go and enjoy herself? Ann took Cormac's hand and, shoulders swinging, they capered onto the packed dance-floor.

*

Áine's brother Bill was driving the couple to Dublin Airport for their honeymoon flight, so they had to leave early. Everyone came out to the front entrance of the Shannon Arms Hotel to see them off. Gussie and a few others had hung cans and put a JUST MARRIED sign on the back of Bill's car, like in the films. Looking at Ritchie and Áine in their going-away outfits, arm in arm, laughing and posing for the last few pictures, Francis tried to imagine himself in his big brother's place. He often did this. Whenever he watched Ritchie play football, he could see himself making the same tackles and passing the ball even more cleverly. When he rode with Ritchie on the back of his motorbike it was easy to imagine himself zooming along a big empty road. But some things didn't fit. A few weeks before, Ritchie brought Francis out to the new house he and Áine had bought. The big sign at the entrance said:

KERRY VIEW
GUINEY DEVELOPMENTS

Ritchie and Áine's house was finished, but further along more were being built. Ritchie told Francis they had been very lucky.

Their house cost three thousand seven hundred but the next ones would be four thousand two hundred for the exact same semi-detached house. Francis didn't understand why. Ritchie said that was just the way it was, the luck of the draw. He helped his brother clear the mess in front of the house so they could start to dig and prepare what would become their lawn. As they worked, Francis noticed how cheerful Ritchie was. He tried to imagine himself like him, grown-up, happy, living on this road. But he couldn't. Trying to work out why that was so, he remembered the thing Mr Barry's friend Gavin said, and wondered was that it? Maybe Francis was a free agent? Maybe the world was his oyster too?

As the smiling, waving couple finally got into the car, Gussie and his cousins were roaring out the chorus of 'Where Do You Go To, My Lovely?' Francis realised that Gussie didn't have his 8mm camera with him. He'd miss them taking off. Francis ran back into the function room and found the camera on the bar counter. He grabbed it and brought it back to his brother.

'Can I film them driving off?'

'No. You don't know how to use it. Give it to me.'

Francis knew from the way Gussie was swaying that he'd make a mess of it. He had watched him enough to know what to do. The car engine started.

'Please let me.'

'OK, but if you break it, you pay for it.'

Francis put his eye to the viewfinder, turned the clockwork dial and released it. Just in time. The clicking sound began and he saw the flickering image of the car pulling away, the cans dancing on the road. Then waving guests came running into the shot and the JUST MARRIED sign was blacked out by all the bodies.

Ann didn't cry, but watching Ritchie drive off with his new wife, naturally she recalled her own honeymoon. London, just after the war. They'd stayed with Fonsie's brother Peter and, even though the city was practically in ruins, Ann remembered how everyone was so full of fun, making the best of it. Laughs and songs. She and Fonsie had talked seriously about emigrating that time. Peter said he could fix him up with some job in the Royal Mail. Imagine if they had. All the children would be English. She was glad they'd stuck it out here, hard as it was. Hadn't things turned out fine so far?

Ann thought about the night seven months ago when Cormac and Louise had so kindly invited Ann and Fonsie to their lovely home for dinner to celebrate their children's engagement. It turned out to be a right good session with many laughs and Noble Calls. Cormac Kiely knew all the old songs. Afterwards, in bed, she and Fonsie had started talking about Ritchie and all their memories of him since he was baby. Ann didn't mention it when she thought of the rattly old bed in the tiny spare room in Peter Strong's house in Croydon. Of course, she couldn't be sure which night exactly Ritchie was conceived, but it was definitely some time that first week after they married. The strange thing was, just as all that was going through her head, Fonsie started to kiss her and next thing he was pressing her back on the bed. She wrapped her arms around him and squeezed to let him know he could keep going and, next moment, she felt the excitement of his cracked palms scratch along her thighs as he nudged her nightdress up and then, in no time at all, they were crushed together. In all their years married it had never been their habit to speak during such moments, but this time, in the cascade of excited breaths and moans, Ann was sure she heard Fonsie whisper, 'I love you.'

ACKNOWLEDGEMENTS

Thanks to Donal Beecher, Ann Richardson, Tony O'Dalaigh, Harry McGee, Neal Shanahan, Louis Lenten, John McGuigan, John Allen, Phillip McMahon, Sheila Phelan. To Ben and Sophie for taking it on and making so many intelligent suggestions and, most of all, to my agent Gráinne Fox, without whose advice and support this book might not exist.

ABOUT THE AUTHOR

Gerard Stembridge is the author of two novels, *Counting Down* and *According to Luke.* He has also written and directed film and television. Credits include *About Adam* with Kate Hudson, the screenplay for *Ordinary Decent Criminal* (starring Kevin Spacey, Colin Farrell and Linda Fiorentino), and he co-wrote *Nora* (a film about James Joyce and Nora Barnacle, starring Ewan McGregor and Susan Lynch). He is the co-creator, with Dermot Morgan, of *Scrap Saturday.*